The Riddle

of

The

Reluctant Rake

PATRICIA VERYAN

The Riddle

of

THE

RELUCTANT RAKE

ST. MARTIN'S PRESS
NEW YORK

Library of Congress Cataloging-in-Publication Data

Veryan, Patricia.
    The riddle of the reluctant rake / Patricia Veryan. — 1st ed.
        p.   cm.
    ISBN 0-312-20474-4
    I. Title.
PS3572.E766R536   1999
813'.54—dc21   99-36352
                                                                    CIP

First Edition: November 1999

10 9 8 7 6 5 4 3 2 1

The Riddle
of
The
Reluctant Rake

1

London
February 1814

It had rained again yesterday, but despite the cold and wet, the Horse Guards on Whitehall had been a noisy place, thronged with military gentlemen, the scarlet coats of guardsmen predominating, but augmented by the green jackets of riflemen and the occasional blue coat of an artillery officer. Voices had been brisk, boots had stamped firmly, spurs had jingled and optimism had been an almost tangible entity, for it was rumoured that Field Marshal Lord Wellington had received the funds he so desperately needed, and that his army was on the move again, preparing to "make a run" at the forces of the French Marshal Soult.

Today, the rain had stopped and a weak sun shone upon Whitehall's wet pavements. Yet inside the imposing building that housed the Horse Guards there was an unnatural quiet. Voices were kept low, men trod softly, spurs seemed not to dare jingle, and there was everywhere a sense of gravity and depression. One of their own faced a court-martial verdict today; a young and popular officer against whom the charges were so serious, the evidence so hard to believe yet so incontrovertible that a finding of guilty seemed inevitable, and such a verdict must result in the death sentence.

At the end of a certain narrow corridor the hush was even more marked. Little clusters of officers stood about conversing murmurously, their troubled eyes turning often to a closed door outside which a sentry stood as if carven from stone. Not a sound penetrated the door; partly because it was of heavy oak, and partly because the inside room was, for the moment, deathly still.

Six army officers sat at a long table in that room. They were all past forty; the eldest among them, and President of the Court-Martial Board, was a colonel whose iron-grey hair and lined countenance placed him in the sixties. He was conferring with his board members, the other men leaning forward in their chairs to participate in the low-voiced discussion. From time to time they paused and glanced curiously at the tall young lieutenant-colonel who stood alone and at attention before them. A very solitary individual this, his head well up and his shoulders back, but his face strained and deathly pale. It was a striking face, framed by thick dark hair, the cheek-bones high and finely cut, the thin nose slightly Roman, the chin a firm jut. Today there were black shadows under the intensely blue eyes, but even so he looked younger than his nine and twenty years; young to have achieved his high rank.

Behind him, spectators and those who had been summoned as witnesses occupied four rows of chairs. Most were army officers, but there was a naval captain, a scattering of distinguished-looking civilians, three non-commissioned officers, and a very tall and imposing white-haired gentleman wearing the uniform and medals of a retired General Officer.

The President of the Court-Martial Board shook his head and looked grim. His companions leaned back in their chairs and every eye turned to the accused.

"Colonel Hastings Chatteris Adair," said the President, "throughout your trial your counsel has striven to prove you innocent of the charges against you. You have been given every opportunity to call witnesses, to establish your character, to chal-

2

lenge those who testified against you. For the past three days this Court-Martial Board has considered your case in the greatest detail. You stand accused of gross dereliction of duty. You were sent to England with vital despatches from Field Marshal Lord Wellington. Having completed your mission, you failed to return at once to France, as you had been ordered. Nor did you report to your superiors as to why you disobeyed your orders, choosing instead to drop out of sight. A very young unmarried lady of Quality also disappeared, and when her distraught family appealed to Bow Street to find her, she was discovered in a hotel room with *you*, sir! And both of you in an intoxicated and extremely, ah, compromising condition. Not to wrap it in clean linen, Colonel Hastings, you were unclad and—and in bed together!"

Despite the fact that they had heard all this before, a murmur of disgust arose from the spectators. The President of the Board raised one hand and the room quieted again.

"To all intents and purposes," he went on, "you deserted. In time of war. Nor have you been able to offer any cogent explanation for conduct that is *beyond doubt* unbecoming an officer and a gentleman. Quite apart from your own crime, the reputation and the life of a young girl has been ruined. However"—he glanced at the white-haired General Officer among the spectators—"out of respect for your distinguished family, your impeccable military record, and the apparent lack of any former—er, libertine tendencies, this Court has given you every opportunity to prove your innocence. Your defending counsel has failed utterly to do so. Yet, before judgment is passed, we will offer you one more chance. If you yourself have *anything* to say in your defence, sir, you had best say it now."

The sword, noted Hastings Adair, lay on the table. If the point was turned towards him—as it almost certainly would be—he would be shot. Provided he was spared the ultimate horror of a public hanging. God . . . ! They'd given him a last chance. Think! Dammit! Think! What could he say that he had not already said? Grandfather was somewhere behind him. The old gentleman must be heartsick . . . Papa hadn't come. Of course. Wellington would be infuriated: one of his officers disgraced, and so terribly disgraced. And that poor girl . . . She'd seemed such an angelic little creature . . . And, above all—*why*? Why had it all happened? He gritted his teeth. He was wasting time. Must say something . . .

"I can add nothing to what I have already said, sir." His voice was hoarse but steady, thank heaven. "I had never met the lady prior to the Farringdon ball. I thought she was unhappy, and when I asked her to dance she desired instead to sit and talk. Later in the evening I took her down to supper, and at about half past one o'clock she sent me a note asking that I escort her home. I gathered there had been some sort of disagreement between her and her brother—"

"Untrue!" A tall red-headed young man in the front row sprang to his feet and shouted ragefully, "You lie in your teeth, Adair! If you escape the hangman—" At a gesture from the President, two burly troopers ran to seize him and attempted to drag him to the door, but he fought them, his voice rising "—you will answer to me, damn you!" Struggling, still hurling threats, he was bustled into the outer passage and the door closed.

The buzz of comment ceased when the President took up some papers and leafed through them. "You have testified that you met the lady at her carriage, where you fell asleep, awakening two days later to find yourself under arrest, with no knowledge of having deserted your regiment or seduced the lady. A pathetic tale! Do you still hold to it, Colonel?"

"Yes, sir. If you will just speak with Miss Prior—"

"Your victim," interposed the President icily, "collapsed and has been taken to her family's country seat, where she now lies in a state of shock, and unable to speak with anyone. Nor is it necessary that she testify. The evidence of the Bow Street officers who found you says all, alas, that need be said. And since you have nothing to add . . ." He glanced at his fellow officers. "I believe we are in agreement, gentlemen?"

With grave reluctance, five distinguished heads nodded.

The Counsel for the Defence came forward and stood beside the accused. The room was so hushed that had the proverbial pin been dropped it would have sounded like a clap of thunder.

The President said, "Colonel Hastings Chatteris Adair, you have been tried in a fair and impartial procedure of court-martial. It is the finding of this court that you are—guilty, as charged."

Adair closed his eyes briefly, and his fists clenched very hard at his sides. When he looked up, the sword on the table had been moved. The point was now levelled at him.

He felt sick; there was a buzzing in his ears, and the room seemed to waver. As from a great distance he heard the cold, merciless words that sealed his doom.

". . . and hanged by the neck, until you are dead . . ."

Sitting on the edge of his cot, hands loosely clasped between his knees, Adair did not move when the door to his cell was opened. For hours he had sat thus, alternating between rage and despair, re-living it all over and over again, and finding never the least crumb of hope or explanation.

A pair of highly polished boots stamped into his field of vision. They had come for him, then. Was it morning already? Was he to die today?

"Repenting, are you?"

The cold voice brought him to his feet. "Grandfather! I didn't think—I mean, I thought you wouldn't—"

"I am here," said General Sir Gower Chatteris, "to have it from your own lips."

Adair was tall, but the old gentleman was an inch taller. His keen blue eyes, so like those of his grandson, hurled lances of ice, his hands were locked behind him, and his demeanour was so fierce that the hand Adair had tentatively stretched out was lowered.

"Tell me," barked the General, "that you were entrapped. That the gel drugged you. That you were struck down and held prisoner. Tell me it was some vicious blackmailing scheme. So

5

far as I know, Hastings, you never have lied to me. Look me in the eye now, and say you are innocent, and—" His whiskers vibrated, he blinked, and for just an instant anguish was in his eyes. "And—by God!" he went on harshly, "I'll fight the lot of 'em to the far side of hell!"

Adair's eyes misted, and his throat was so choked up that for a moment he could say nothing. "I—don't know," he managed helplessly. "I swear, sir. It's just as my counsel—"

"Confounded mealy-mouthed ineptitude that he was!"

"It's just as he said. I never met the lady before that night. She was charming, but—to say truth, sir, not—not the type I—and much too young to even think of—"

"I take it that you're saying they all lied. That you did *not* meet her on the sly several times prior to that miserable ball? That you did *not* share a night with the wretched wanton? That you weren't found in her bed?"

"Yes. I mean—no. I don't deny what—I mean, *where* we were found, but, why, or how—I swear, I cannot understand—"

"Poppycock, sir! Claptrap! Do you suggest a plot? Why would anyone go to such lengths to ruin you? Tell me that! You were discovered by witnesses of sterling character. The Priors' coachman, the maid, and the hotel manager each testified—well, dammitall, *you* know what they testified! And now all you can do is mumble and stammer nonsensicalities. You condemn yourself out of your own mouth, by God, but you do! Well, I hope you're proud of yourself, sir! Your unrestrained lust has destroyed a lovely young girl, thrown mud all over our family name, fouled the proud heritage of your regiment! Your father and your brothers are held up to shame and disgust and can scarce venture out in public, and much chance poor Hudson has for that cabinet post he has worked so hard to snabble! Your mother is half-crazed with mortification and I think would strangle you herself had she the chance. I can well imagine what Wellington must think of all this! You are a disgrace to yourself and to your family, sir! I have only one hope left to me—that you—" the old gentleman's voice broke, and he finished threadily, "that you may face your death with some faint semblance of courage!"

On those bitter words he turned and marched out of the door the gaoler held open for him.

He left behind a man who still stood staring blankly at the door and on whose ashen face shone the bright traces of tears.

"Better wake up now, old fellow."

Adair started. He'd thought he wouldn't sleep before they came for him, but at some time during these nightmare hours of darkness he must have dozed off. A dark grey sky was visible through the high barred window. He sat up hurriedly. This was the day, then. The priest must have come . . . His stomach gave a painful lurch. Mustn't look scared. And—Lord, but he was scared!

He blinked up at the man who stood by the cot. "Yes, Father. I'm—ready if you . . ."

"Deuce take you, Hasty! I'm not your father! Don't be such a lunkhead!"

"Broderick!" Adair's shoulders slumped, and he put a shaking hand over his eyes. 'Another reprieve,' he thought numbly. 'For how long this time?'

A mug of hot coffee was pushed into his hand, and Lieutenant Tobias Broderick sat beside him. He was a sturdily built young man, with Saxon fair hair and blue eyes that just now were full of compassion. Wounded during the Battle of Vitoria, he had been sent home and had met Adair while staying at the home of a friend. Later, they had been ordered to help resolve a critical situation that had taken them across the Channel into Brittany, and by the time it was resolved a mutual liking and respect had sprung up between them.

Adair drank the coffee gratefully, and summoned a smile. "Not a social call, I fancy, Lieutenant? So I won't embarrass you by saying how good it is to—to see a friend."

The drawn white face and that twitching apology for a grin appalled Broderick. "The trouble with you, Adair," he scolded, "is that you're too high in the instep. If you didn't outrank me, I'd punch your head for that remark."

Adair searched the cherubic young face with a painful desperation. "Toby—*are* you here as—as a friend?"

Taking a long pull at his own mug, Broderick then said gruffly, "Course I am, chawbacon. Partly, anyway." Before Adair could pounce on that qualification, he went on, "You don't think we believe it? I mean, old Jack Vespa, and Consuela, and Paige and me, we all know it's a—a damned tapestry of lies. We don't know how—or why. But we believe you, old fellow, never doubt it!"

Adair bowed his head, overcome, but his hand went out gropingly. Broderick took and gripped it strongly, and after a brief emotional silence he said, "Now, Colonel, sir, as Counsel for the Rebuttal I need some answers. If you don't object."

Adair smiled wearily. "Why? I can't add anything to what has been said in Court, and—"

"But I wasn't in the Court, old lad. None of your friends were allowed to darken the curst doors, in fact."

The truth was that Jack Vespa had been deeply involved in hearings on another matter, and Paige Manderville had been recalled and was even now with Wellington's army in France.

Adair said, "You're very kind, Toby, and I'll answer any question you put to me, but—what good will it do? I've an—an imminent date with the hangman, and there's nothing to be done at—"

"That's been ruled out." Broderick caught the mug that tumbled from Adair's hand, and said contritely, "Sorry, old fellow. Didn't want to break it to you right away, y'know. *Hasty?*" He sprang up, seized his friend by the shoulders and forced his head down between his knees. "Dammitall," he grumbled, "if you're going to pop off in a faint I'll have to call the guard and I won't get my answers!"

Adair waved him away feebly, and sat straight again. "Tell me—for the love of God . . . ! You mean—you *can't* mean—I've been cleared?"

"Er—well, no. Not cleared, exactly."

"What then? A re-trial?"

"Not—ah, not that, either." Adair stared at him, and Broderick said unhappily, "From what I can make out, Lord Wellington wrote to his brother. Lord Richard Wellesley, I mean. And Lord Richard took the matter to Prinny."

"The *Regent* intervened?"

"I don't know about that, but the upshot is that—er, that they've decided not to hang you after all. Jolly good, what?"

Suddenly very cold, Adair stood and faced him. "Dishonourable discharge?"

Standing also and looking utterly miserable, Broderick said, "More or—er, less."

Adair wrenched away, stumbled to the window and gazed out at the grey sheeting rain. "My God," he whispered. "I'm to be—cashiered, is that what you're trying to say?"

Broderick cleared his throat and mumbled something about no prison sentence.

"A public—ceremony?" persisted Adair. "Drummed out? The whole hideous rigmarole?" His voice rose. Agonized, he cried, "D'you think I want *that*? Doesn't Wellington *know* I don't want it? Lord above, I'd sooner be hanged!"

"I collect Old Nosy thought—er, where there's life there's—"

"*Hope*? Hope for what? To be kicked out a marked man? I'll be despised wherever I go! My family . . . my friends . . ." Adair turned and seized Broderick's arm. "Toby—*please*! Get me a pistol. You can smuggle one in somehow, and I'd sooner—"

"Give up?" Aching for him, Broderick brushed the clutching hand from his sleeve. "Play the craven? 'Fore heaven, I expected better of you! It's a beast of a coil, but if you're innocent, at least you'll have a chance now to prove it."

Adair's ashen face burned to a slow flush. His eyes were so

tormented that Broderick could not meet them and had to look away. "Blast you," whispered Adair brokenly. "Blast you! If you were in my shoes . . ."

The door was swung open. The guard called a curt, "Time's up, Lieutenant."

Not trusting himself to speak, Broderick left without a word. He was sweating, and he wiped his face and felt drained as he strode along the narrow passage.

Adair's words echoed and re-echoed in his ears. "If you were in my shoes . . ."

With a murmur of thanks he took the cloak and hat a sergeant handed him and a moment later was outside and in the cold rain.

"If you were in my shoes . . ."

"I'd choose the pistol," he muttered. "Poor fellow. Most decidedly, I'd choose the pistol!"

Two days later a pale winter sun broke through the early-morning clouds to gleam upon steel breastplates, shining helmets, and fixed bayonets. A light but very cold breeze stirred the horses' manes and tails and ruffled the plumes on the helmets of the men of the Household Cavalry. Row upon row, those military units still in or near London were drawn up on the parade ground. Silent and stern and unmoving.

To one side, a group of officers and high-ranking government officials waited almost as silently, but there was a slight stir among them when the prisoner was escorted out.

The steady beat of the drum began, and Hastings Adair clenched his fists until the nails bit into his palms.

For as long as he lived, every detail of that scene would haunt his dreams. He tried not to see faces as he was marched in front of the assembled officers and men, some of whom he had fought beside. Their scorn was an almost palpable thing. Among the spectators he caught a glimpse of red hair that glowed like a flame in the sun. Rufus Prior. So poor little Alice's brother was here. He could only pray that no member of his own family would witness his disgrace.

The interminable march ended at last.

The beat of the drum was loud in the hushed silence.

Now came the ultimate degradation.

Despite the cold, he was sweating. Who would have dreamed when Grandfather bought him a pair of colours that his military career would end like this? He'd always wanted to be a soldier. Always hoped to distinguish himself; to serve his country and bring pride to the old gentleman. He'd risen rapidly until he attained the regimental rank of major with a battlefield rank of lieutenant-colonel, and Grandfather had been proud. Now . . . Lord above!

A colonel was standing before him. He couldn't see the man's features clearly, but he knew he was what they'd unkindly referred to in Spain as a "Hyde Park soldier"—one of the Whitehall crowd.

He fought against shrinking back as the colonel reached out and grasped the epaulette on his left shoulder. It refused to tear. The drumbeat kept on . . . rhythmical . . . remorseless . . . The colonel tugged again. It would be nice, thought Adair, to faint. Mustn't faint. He'd brought enough shame on his family . . . The colonel had a little knife now; the left epaulette was wrenched away, and then the right. The buttons on his tunic were next. One at a time, while he kept his head high somehow, and the drumbeat never faltered, and the sun shone, and the breeze blew . . . and it was such a ghastly nightmare.

And they were wrong, damn them! He had done none of it! Not knowingly, at all events. Did his record count for nothing? Didn't they know he was an honourable man . . . ? 'Lord God, why are you letting this happen?'

The last button fell. His sabre was removed from its scabbard and snapped across the colonel's knee. He was turned and marched in front of the rows of scornful faces again, with his jacket hanging open, the shoulders torn, the buttons gone, his knees threatening to buckle under him, and that demoniacal drumbeat following his every step.

An eternity later he was being escorted from the parade ground, the drummer following.

The ordeal was over.

He was a ruined and disgraced man.

He would never be able to serve in the military again; never be allowed to hold any kind of governmental post; never be able to run for public office. He'd be lucky to find work as a ditch digger. His only logical course was to get out of the country, and as fast as possible, before Miss Prior's family, or an outraged citizenry, visited their own brand of justice on him.

Suddenly, a searing rage burned through him. Leave England? Leave this cold and damp and proud little island that he so loved? Never!

Toby was right. He had a chance now to find out who had done this, and for what possible reason. If it took the rest of his days, he'd track down the damnable blackguard who'd destroyed him, ruined a gentle and innocent girl, and broken an old man's heart.

'Before God,' he vowed savagely, 'I swear it!'

2

Toby Broderick had been kind enough to bring Adair a coat
to replace his shredded jacket and drive him to Adair Hall
off Grosvenor Street. There had been little talk between the two
young men during the journey, Adair feeling too wrung out to
make conversation, and Broderick guessing at and respecting
his state of mind. As the jarvey pulled up his hack, the front door
of the mansion was opened.

Adair said, "I am more than grateful to you, Toby. So I won't
ask you to come in."

"No, by Jove!" said Broderick vehemently. "Thank you. Er,
what I mean is, er—quite."

The jarvey cracked his whip and the coach scurried around
the corner before Adair reached the top of the steps.

The butler admitted him with polite dignity but without the
smile he had always received in the past. He had given up his
London flat when he joined Lord Wellington's Peninsular Campaign, and he went straight up to the second-floor suite he occupied on the rare occasions when he was in England. A maid
who was dusting industriously on the first-floor landing bent
lower at her task and gave him not a glance, but he knew she

had seen him, and a muffled giggle from somewhere close by strengthened his conviction that every servant in the house was aware he had come home.

He rang for a footman and requested hot water and a light luncheon. The man's eyes were hostile, and he said with wooden impudence that the family was taking their lunch in the breakfast parlour. Adair turned from his wardrobe and stared at him. "Perhaps," he said icily, "I did not make myself clear."

The footman fled and returned in a very few minutes with a ewer of steaming water, and a maid who carried a tray of cold sliced chicken and ham, a wedge of cheese, warm bread, a mince tart and a tankard of ale.

Adair washed, and ate while he changed clothes. He would have to move his belongings; his parents wouldn't want him here. No doubt of that. Nor would he be welcome at his club. He scanned himself in the cheval-glass. A pale and haggard face stared back at him; a stranger with sunken and shadowed eyes who looked ill at ease in the civilian garments, although they had been tailored by a master and were a perfect fit.

The passage was empty when he left his suite, but as he went down the stairs he heard a rustling that spoke of a feminine gown. With remarkable boldness a woman said, "Shameful, I calls it!" Adair's hand tightened on the banister rail, but he knew that if he turned there would be no sign of whichever maid had dared make the insolent remark.

Other ears had heard, however. On the landing below him a lady said sharply, "Whoever just spoke so rudely had best leave this house before I discover her identity—as you may be sure I shall do!"

Adair heard a dismayed gasp, then he was on the landing and the eldest of his female cousins was hurling her plump self into his arms. He was mildly surprised. Firstly, because of this demonstration of affection, and secondly because the rather shy girl had made such a martial declaration. He was fond of most of his cousins, but there had never been a particularly strong bond between him and Minerva Chatteris. The daughter of his

14

mother's brother Jerome, a Major of Artillery who had fallen at the Battle of Corunna, Minerva's best feature was a pair of deep-set grey eyes. Her many friends were wont to describe her as having a "kind" face. This, she certainly had, but one of her brothers had remarked that the trouble with Minna was that everything about her was "too" for her to be judged pretty. She was a touch too plump; her nose was too snub, her mouth too wide, her hair, which was luxuriant, was too mousy, and she was far and away too tender-hearted, the slightest set-back for anyone she knew turning her into "a watering pot!" Obsessively fond of dogs, she had established quite a name for herself by breeding beautiful King Charles spaniels. She had appeared quite contented to make this her life's work, and nobody judged it remarkable when she remained "on the shelf" long after two younger sisters had made gratifying alliances. Nor could anyone have been more surprised than her mama when the daughter she had come to think of as being doomed to spinsterhood had attracted the interest of so fine a prize as Julius Harrington, M.P.

Adair put his cousin from him and looked down at her wonderingly. "It is very good of you to have come, Minna. Did my Aunt Hilda bring you up from Woking?"

"Julius—Mr. Harrington—did. Oh, but you look *dreadful*, Hastings! Poor dear! What a ghastly time you have had."

His eyes became veiled. "Were you at the Horse Guards today, then?"

"Goodness, no!" She shuddered. "I could not have borne it. Especially since we *know* you are not guilty! As if you could ever do such—frightful things!"

He hugged her and managed to mumble his gratitude, and true to form, she wept copiously all over his cravat.

His nerves were already taut and this kind demonstration quite unmanned him. It was all he could do to take out his handkerchief and dab at her tears, and he was dismayed to see how his hand shook. Minerva smiled up at him mistily, then glanced down to the first floor landing where her fiancé waited, his round face troubled.

Adair ushered his cousin to the lower hall and put out his hand uncertainly. Julius Harrington seized and wrung it hard. He was some seven years Adair's senior, and although they were not close friends they knew and liked one another. The scion of a family that had become wealthy in shipbuilding, then gone on to greater successes in maritime trading ventures, Harrington had shown an interest in politics and had mounted a brisk campaign to become Member of Parliament for his small north-country district. Having won the election with a comfortable majority, he had at once removed to London, and returned to his district as seldom as possible. Of barely average height, inclining to portliness, his curling brown hair beginning to thin on top, he was no more handsome than Minerva was beautiful. But he had a fine pair of green eyes, a ready smile, and a cheerful and amiable disposition that had soon made him popular in both social circles and the House of Commons. He never embarked on long and boring speeches, he was a sympathetic listener, and always ready to work on a committee or lend a hand in time of trouble. Some unkind colleagues had been heard to remark that Harrington could rise to the highest office simply by having lacked the gumption to offend anyone or take a stand on any controversial issue.

He now said huskily, "My poor fellow! They have treated you vilely."

"Thank you," said Adair, amazed that this man should risk public censure by associating with him. "You are very good to have come, but you should not have brought her, you know."

"If Julius had been unwilling, I would have come alone," declared Minerva stoutly. "*Someone* in the family must stand by you, Hasty!"

"We want you to know that we're with you," said Harrington as they walked slowly along the wide corridor. "Both of us. Even if the others—"

"Others?" The muscles under Adair's ribs tightened painfully. "Who else is here, Minna?"

She hesitated, and Harrington said, "The whole lot, I'm

16

afraid, my dear fellow. Your parents, of course; the General; both your brothers—"

"Nigel came down?" interrupted Adair sharply.

"He said it was too—ah, uncomfortable at Oxford," said Harrington.

The door to the drawing room opened and the butler hurried to them. "His lordship requests that you join the family, sir."

Adair nodded. "Take her away, Harrington. No, Minna! I am more grateful than I can say that you and Julius have faith in me, but there's no need for you to be exposed to—to any more of this nasty business."

She hugged him and said anxiously, "You won't go away or—or do anything silly, will you, my dear?"

"At the moment, I have no plans beyond the next hour." Adair smiled, dropped a kiss on her brow and shook hands again with her devoted suitor. Then he took a deep breath and followed the butler to the drawing room.

It was a large and luxurious room, the décor reflecting his mother's excellent taste, although he always found it rather oppressively formal. The murmur of conversation ceased as he entered. It seemed to him that the air vibrated with hostility, and Harrington had been right—or almost right. A quick scan of the company revealed that two of his uncles on his father's side were present—both scowling at him; Captain Sir Joseph Adair, who commanded an East Indiaman, was absent, although his ship had returned to Bristol a week ago. Three of Mama's brothers had come, and also scowled at him. His elder brother, the Honourable Hudson Adair, a handsome and usually elegant man who now looked rumpled and distracted, darted a rageful glance at him. He suffered a shock when his younger brother, Nigel, met his eyes with a glare that could only be judged hate-filled. The boy had always put him on a pedestal; the idol had fallen, understandably. Lady Caroline Shand, every bit as proud as her parents, was the only one of his three sisters to have come, and looked ready to strangle him.

Joshua Adair, Viscount Esterwood, had taken up a position

by the fireplace. A tall man who had kept himself trim, his thinning brown hair only slightly touched with grey, he was as distinguished as ever, but he had been wounded in his most vulnerable area—his pride, and there was rage in every line of him.

Hastings gathered his courage, walked forward, and bowed. "I have brought you grief, Father. I am sorry for it."

"By God, but you have," snapped his lordship.

Samuel Chatteris, his puffy features an even brighter red than usual, roared, "I wonder you dared show your face, Hastings! I won't name you 'nephew,' since I refuse to acknowledge you!"

"As do we all!" Major Roger Adair had served for many years in India and thoroughly enjoyed recounting one or another of his hair-raising experiences to long-suffering friends. "Buried us in shame, be damned if you ain't!" he shouted. "Not worthy of our fine old name! Ain't that the case, Will? I haven't dared set foot in my club, by Gad, have I, Will?"

Thus appealed to, Willoughby Chatteris, the youngest of the General's surviving sons, murmured, "Right-o, old fellow." He glanced in embarrassment at Hastings, and added apologetically, "He hasn't, y'know, Hasty. Sorry."

Samuel Chatteris rolled his eyes at the ceiling and muttered something about "sapskulls."

Willoughby reddened and retreated to a far corner of the room. A diffident, withdrawn individual, who lacked both the physique and the good looks of most Chatteris men, he seemed, rather, a washed-out copy of them, for he was thin and stoop-shouldered, his colouring pale, his rather protuberant eyes a watery blue, and the straight hair that sprang from his low forehead a light nondescript brown. He had never married and was generally believed to be "a little strange." His mission in life appeared to be to make "lists," though of what and for what conceivable purpose no one had ever been able to determine. He had inherited a sizeable fortune and a large country estate from a maternal aunt who believed that Fate had dealt harshly with "poor Willoughby." When his brother had been slain at Corunna, Willoughby had opened his lonely house to his bereaved sister-in-law and her brood. His friends had been sceptical, but it had proven to be a success. Mrs. Hilda Chatteris ran the house and held the accounts nicely in balance. Willoughby was fond of his nephews and nieces, and enjoyed having a family around him. His niece, Minerva, had beguiled him into sharing her canine interests, so that when he was not busied over his Lists, he could usually be found at the kennels. His was not a gregarious nature, and that he and the volatile Major Roger Adair should have struck up a friendship baffled the rest of the family, but friends they were and whenever the Major desired support, he called on Willoughby.

The Reverend Mr. Taylor Chatteris, learned, handsome and soft-hearted, now fixed his gentle blue gaze on his nephew and said sadly, "Whatever were you thinking of, Hasty?"

Several of the assembled gentlemen immediately informed the clergyman exactly what Hastings had been "thinking of"; Mr. Fergus Adair, a very stout man of small means, questionable ethics, and a large thirst became so ribald, in fact, that the Viscount was obliged to remind him there were ladies present.

"Have you come here to confess your guilt?"

The querulous voice was that of his mother, and Hastings turned to her at once. In his youth Lady Esterwood had seemed an omnipotent being; seldom seen, but always gracious and awesomely beautiful. Vanity decreed that she eat sparingly, which the General often declared had caused her to be "scratchy," and her perpetually haughty expression had given her mouth a permanent disdainful droop. But at five and fifty she was one of the foremost *ton* hostesses, and still a remarkably handsome woman, blessed with a pair of dark blue eyes, beautiful white hands, and a fine soprano voice. She had been proud of her soldier son's rapid rise to the rank of lieutenant-colonel, and overjoyed when he'd been "mentioned in despatches." He had been her "darling boy" then. Today, striking in a gown of powder blue velvet, with a blue and white shawl draped across her shoul-

19

ders, she leaned back in her chair and regarded him as she might have viewed a slug that had crawled across her slipper.

Adair said, "I came only to remove my things, Mama, and to make my apologies to you all for—"

"For making me the target of every gossip-monger in Town?" she interposed shrilly. "I dare not venture out on the streets! Do you realize I had planned a ball in honour of your brother's Cabinet appointment? Even had I the courage to hold it, no one would come!"

"You couldn't hold it now at all events, ma'am," drawled Hudson Adair, his bitter gaze on his brother. "Any hopes I entertained along those lines were dashed, thanks to our gallant Colonel! Ten years of work! Ten years of guarding my tongue and catering to the powerful ministers whose backing I needed! And they were *ready* to back me! I *had* the appointment! Or as good as. But you bowled me out, didn't you, Hastings? I hope—"

"You, you, you!" interposed Lady Caroline fiercely. "All you ever think of is your precious career, Hudson! What of Shand, I ask you? What of *me*? The Dowager had at long last agreed to remove to the dower house and give us the mansion on Grosvenor Street. Now, she won't even let us in the front door for fear we should be recognized by some of her cronies! You're not the only one to be hurt, brother dear!"

And so it went, one family member after another, all voicing their fury and frustration, while Adair stood pale and silent, letting the storm break over him until a new voice rang out:

"If you are all done with bemoaning your fates, perhaps we may hear what Hastings has to say."

Through the immediate silence every eye turned to the white-haired old gentleman who stood tall and proud in the open doorway, the epitome of a British General of the Army. The men who were seated rose at once, and the Viscount hurried to welcome his father-in-law.

General Chatteris gripped his hand, then turned to Hastings. "Well?"

"I'd not intended to intrude on my father, but he summoned me. I am sorrier than I can say to have caused you all such distress and humiliation, but I had hoped—" Hastings paused, then said rather wistfully, "I had hoped someone might have asked me—whether I was guilty, and—"

Lady Esterwood leaned forward. "Do you deny it, then?"

"I believe I am innocent, Mama. I cannot prove it. At the moment. But . . . it would have been nice if one or two of you could have stood by me. It seems that only my cousin Minerva—"

"Minerva!" exclaimed the Viscount with contempt. "The girl has not two brains to rub together, and as for that nincompoop she means to wed, she'll be fortunate if even a merchant's son don't draw back now!"

"If you are all finished then," said the General, "I—as head of the family—will close this unfortunate chapter in our history." He turned to his daughter as a murmur of discontent reached his ears. "What was that, Andrea?"

Lady Esterwood flushed but said boldly, "I think you heard me, Papa, but I'll not retract. From the time Hastings was a small boy you were determined to control his life. You took him out of Eton and had him tutored. If he had been allowed to go to Oxford as I wished, instead of being packed off to the Royal Military Academy, we might not now be facing utter social ruin and humiliation!"

"Is that a fact, my lady?" said her sire awfully. "I interfered with your plans for the boy because it was plain you were going to turn him into a stuffy pedantical snob—as you did with his brother! I'm sorry, Hudson, you're a good fellow, but there it is. Hastings had the makings of a fighting man, and all the qualities of a fine officer. And as for Oxford . . . if only half the tales I've heard about that milquetoast factory are truth—!" He broke off, glared at young Nigel, who was staring at him in open-mouthed astonishment, then went on quickly, "Furthermore, madam, I'll remind you that Hastings Chatteris Adair was not conceived by you alone, but that your husband had a hand—er, a role to play!"

"Papa!" exclaimed my lady, red-faced and scandalized and all too aware of the grins on several faces.

"That's who I am," agreed the General. "And it's *my* hand holds the purse-strings! Your mighty husband the Viscount has the sense to know which side his bread is buttered on—which is more than you do, Andrea, so hold your tongue!" He turned his fierce gaze from his fuming daughter to his quiet grandson. "As for you, Hastings, you must be aware that from the start of this shameful business we have all met regularly and discussed in great depth what steps might become necessary. Frankly, we did not expect things to turn out in this particular way. It now is of the first importance to try and restore the family honour which you have so sadly tarnished. To that end, it is desirable that you leave the country as soon as may be. And change your name. We will make arrangements for you to take ship to the Americas as soon as a berth is available." He drew a paper from his pocket. "I have here a bank draft that you can draw on in the interim. A generous sum will be left with the ship's purser in your name. The same amount will be sent to you quarterly for as long as you need funds."

"Provided," put in the Viscount with glacial emphasis, "that you never again use your real name or make any attempt to contact us or return to England."

"Do you understand?" snapped the General.

Hastings had stared blankly at the old gentleman throughout this terrible verdict. Now he turned and looked slowly around at these people he had thought he knew, but who might have been so many strangers, glaring at him with such merciless condemnation and contempt. Nigel looked positively murderous, and only in the eyes of his clerical Uncle Taylor, and Uncle Fergus, who was probably half lushy, did he think to find a glimmer of compassion.

"Answer me," demanded his grandfather harshly.

Hastings knew how much he had shamed them; he'd known they would be furious, and he had been prepared for scorn and recriminations. He had not expected this. Stunned, he had to struggle to keep his voice steady. "I understand that—that I am being disowned, sir. That I am to become a—a 'remittance man.' Isn't that the term for banished and pensioned off family pariahs?"

"What would you?" asked the General, his own eyes briefly pleading.

Suddenly, Hastings' chin tossed upward. It was a gesture that would have drawn a grin from Field Marshal Lord Wellington. It was familiar to Lord Esterwood also, who said hurriedly, "He has no right to—"

He was too late.

Hastings' voice rang out sharp and clear. "I would know whether the collective rage of my family has been visited on me because I violated an innocent young girl and disobeyed orders—or because my disgrace was made public before it could be swept under the rug, and may therefore interfere with your social prestige and—"

The rest of his remark was drowned in an explosion of wrath. White with rage, the Viscount snarled, "That will *do*, sir! How *dare* you take such a tone with me?" The puffy red face of Samuel Chatteris became a puffy purple face as he roared that Hastings Adair was "a conscienceless young roué and a libertine!" Fergus Adair sprang to unsteady feet and almost fell down as he staggered about and howled incoherencies; and Major Roger Adair had to be restrained by his nephew Hudson and his clerical brother-in-law from making good his threat to knock down "the young rogue."

"Enough!" thundered the General. "Do you want the servants to hear us washing our dirty linen?" It was a reminder to daunt them all, and when quiet was restored, he added grittily, "I could respect you more, Hastings, was that proud head of yours lowered, and your disgraceful conduct repented, which I see no sign of! I warn you that you have gone your length with this family."

"I understand, sir." Hastings bowed. "Good day, ladies . . .

23

gentlemen." His back very straight, and his hands tight-clenched to hide their trembling, he walked to the door.

Hudson Adair called, "Hey! You forgot the bank draft."

Hastings said, "Oh, no. But I thank you all for the offer."

Nigel ran to lean back against the door and demand wildly, "What have you done with her, you damned villain? Where—"

"That's enough out of you, boy!" snapped the General. "If you cannot conduct yourself like a gentleman in front of ladies, then hold your tongue!"

Appalled, Hastings reached out to grasp the arm of this brother who had always been closest to his heart. "Nigel—for God's sake, try to believe—"

Nigel beat Hastings' hand away as if it burned him. "Like hell I will!" he said, a sob in his voice.

"Go!" roared the General.

Nigel wrenched the door open and ran out.

Taylor Chatteris said sadly, "Poor lad. He's taking it hard. But Hudson is right, Hastings. You must have funds."

Adair tried not to recall the anguish in Nigel's eyes. "You are very good, Uncle," he said. "But I have funds of my own. And I cannot take the General's money under false pretences."

This sinister remark caused them to come crowding around him.

"What d'ye mean—'false pretences'?"

"You want more lettuce, is that it?"

"We've told you our terms!"

He nodded. "You have." His voice hardened. "Now, I'll tell you mine." He ignored the Major's sputtered "The confounded *insolence* of it!" and went on: "I intend no disrespect. The General, my parents—all of you have my sincere gratitude for making my life—up to now—pleasant and rewarding. However, whatever you believe, I love my country and I have not the least intent to leave it. Never fear, as far as possible I'll keep out of the public eye."

Hudson said uneasily, "But—deuce take it, you'll be a marked man wherever you go! What will you do?"

"God willing, prove my innocence!"

Hastings left them as they all began to shout at once.

Back in his suite, he poured himself a glass of Madeira and then sat on the bed staring at it. He shouldn't have spoken to his elders with such disrespect . . . especially with Mama and Caroline in the room . . . If only they'd not all railed at him so. But how could he blame them? He'd brought disgrace down on them, and they were such a deuced proud lot. He smiled mirthlessly. As he was himself. Well, he'd just have to make things right. Somehow. Lord only knew how. And at this moment he could scarcely think, he was so desperately tired. The bed was inviting. Perhaps he could have a brief rest before he left. But that was out of the question. If he delayed, his outraged family might detain him and have him packed off to the Americas by force.

He finished the Madeira and was reaching for his riding crop when someone scratched on the door. His nerves jerked tight. He couldn't take much more bitterness and anger. Sighing, he stood and swung his cloak about his shoulders. "Yes?"

The door opened and Mrs. Redditch's angular face came into view. The housekeeper's stern exterior hid a very fond heart, but perhaps she condemned him too. He said with a rueful smile, "Hello, Reddy."

"Oh—Colonel," she gulped, and pressed a handkerchief to her lips.

"My 'colonel' days are past, I'm afraid. What can I do for you?"

She dried her eyes ferociously. "It's about Burslem," she managed. "Miss Minerva says I must let her go, because she made a rude remark about you. But—but she has no family, sir, and she's honest and a hard worker. Without a good character, I don't know what would become of her. It was indeed unforgivable for her to say such a thing, but I thought—if she were to come and apologize . . . ?" Her dark eyes searched his face.

"Burslem" must be the maid who had voiced her opinion of him on the stairs. He thought of the apologies he himself had tendered today, and of how they'd been received. "All right. Bring her in."

Burslem's square face was white where it was not reddened from weeping. She looked to be nearing forty; a big-boned, coarse-featured woman, who tore at her very creased apron and kept her gaze on Adair's boots. The housekeeper nudged her and told her to "speak up," and she said hoarsely, "Oh, sir, I'm very *very* sorry, sir, that I said that there rudeness. I got no right ter say a thing like that, I know. Nor I don't 'spect you'll forgive, but—but I do begs you, Colonel, ter give me another chance. I won't never do such a thing 'gain. I promises faithful."

Mrs. Redditch watched Adair anxiously.

He asked, "Do you believe I am guilty, Burslem?"

"Oh, no, sir! Cross me heart and hopes ter die, I never—"

"Because," he interrupted, "if you really believed me guilty of those crimes—especially concerning the young lady—you would be quite justified in such an opinion. Indeed, if I thought anyone had behaved in such a disgraceful fashion, I'd not hesitate to condemn them."

She looked at him uncertainly. "Is you saying, sir, as you done it, and I were right ter say what I did?"

He smiled. "No. I'm saying that if you *believed* I had done it, then you would be wrong to condone such behaviour. Though, it isn't always wise, you know, to be quite so—er, outspoken."

She looked from him to the housekeeper. "Is I forgiven then, Mrs. Redditch?"

The housekeeper said. "I think you may stay, Burslem. Is that all right, sir?"

He nodded. "But don't start crying again, please."

Burslem's already tearful eyes had brimmed over. She bobbed a curtsy, mumbled, "Thank ye, sir. Oh—*thank* yer! An'—an'—Gawd bless yer, sir."

He called to her when she reached the door, and she swung around, watching him fearfully. "Will you try to believe I *didn't* do it?" he asked.

She nodded, beaming through her tears, then, dashing them away with her apron, was gone.

Adair turned to the housekeeper. "Will you try to believe it also, Reddy?"

"Certainly not, Master Hastings! Since I never believed any of it in the first place! In fact—" Mrs. Redditch's words ended in a faint scream as she was swept up and whirled around and a smacking kiss was pressed on her blushing cheek.

3

"he thing is," said Toby Broderick, handing Adair a glass of Cognac and peering at him uneasily, "how could anyone have known you were coming here?"

It had been late afternoon by the time Adair's immediate necessities were packed and loaded into a hackney coach. He'd said his farewells to the tearful housekeeper and those members of the staff who had gathered to wish him well, and he'd started down the front steps, determined not to slink away via the back door. A last look at the great house that had been "home" all his life had revealed his brother Hudson watching from a drawing-room window. There had been a frown on the handsome features, but to his astonishment this man who had probably suffered the most because of his notoriety and disgrace, had raised a hand—not quite in a wave perhaps, but more than he'd hoped for. He'd gone then to the livery stables to retrieve his horse. Despite his name, Toreador was too gentle a creature to be exposed to the battlefield, so he'd been left in England to be exercised by Nigel during his owner's military absences. The big dapple-grey greeted Adair with affection and after a mutually fond reunion Adair had ridden him beside the coach. There had been no trouble until they'd approached Vespa House, where Broderick was staying. As they'd turned the corner onto the quiet London square, Toreador had given a snort of fright and danced sideways, and in that same instant a brick had come flying at Adair's head. He'd managed to keep his seat when the brick had struck him a glancing blow, and luckily, he had sustained nothing worse than a painful lump, but, as the outraged jarvey had said, if it had landed squarely he'd never have met up with his friend—not in this world, anyway!

Pondering, he answered slowly, "Nobody knew I was coming here. I hadn't really decided to take advantage of your kind offer until I left my father's house."

"Then you must have been followed." Broderick settled himself into one of the fireside chairs in the luxurious drawing room and leaned back comfortably. "London's a mad place, but people don't trot about heaving bricks at all and sundry on the spur of the moment. Did you see the lout?"

Adair shook his head, then regretted it. "I caught a glimpse of a shabby fellow running like the wind. Only saw his back. But I'll go bail I wasn't followed. I was prepared for a possible display of public anger against me, and kept my eyes open. There was no one within fifty yards of me when I turned the corner."

Broderick eyed him sceptically and thought he looked too exhausted to have been able to see for five yards, much less fifty. He said, "In that case, you were recognized hereabouts by some nasty tempered rabble-rouser who hid in the trees or down some area steps. Only answer, dear boy."

"I was recognized by some rabble-rouser who didn't expect to see me," said Adair ironically, "but who chanced to have a brick tucked into his pocket, just in case."

"All right, then. What *do* you think?"

Adair's head was throbbing and he was finding it hard to think at all. He said wearily, "Those who know me well would also know that if I was no longer welcome at my parents' house I'd be less welcome at my club. A logical guess would be that I'd turn to a friend. You and Jack Vespa are friends who'd likely stand by me, and Vespa's not using his Town house just now."

"*Ergo*—a lucky guess," muttered Broderick. "But—you've other friends who'd help out, my dear fellow."

"Perhaps"—Adair stifled a yawn—"perhaps there were brick-carrying louts watching their houses as well. It's jolly good of you to let me camp here for a spell, Toby. You're sure Vespa won't mind?"

"Lord, no. Jack won't live here, y'know. He keeps the house open for his mama, but she's down at Richmond for the month. Jack told Manderville and me that we could stay here whenever we pleased, so long as it didn't inconvenience Lady Vespa."

"It's a jolly fine house. I only hope my occupancy doesn't bring a brick or two through the windows."

"Deuce take it, I hadn't thought of that! I simply must break myself of this foolish habit of collecting notorious friends! No, I mean after all, Manderville's known to be a rascal; Vespa's father damn near swindled the government and went about murdering anyone who got in his way; and now look—a Lieutenant Colonel who's *persona non grata* from the Hebrides to Guernsey! Dreadful!"

Adair smiled wryly. "I suppose I must get used to it. Being ambushed, I mean. The devil's in it that I can't blame people."

"The trouble is that ambushes are so blasted hard to guard against," said Broderick, looking grave. "Well, you've only to glance at history, haven't you? Of all people, one would think Julius Caesar would have had the sense to protect himself—fella was a genius, no doubt of that. But having irritated people by wanting to be declared a god, what must he do but go swaggering back to the Senate and then wonder why he was done away with! And look at poor Königsmark—dallied with a prince's wife, and—"

"*Poor* Königsmark? From all I've read of him, the man was a murderous adventurer who'd slit your throat as soon as look at you!"

"Oh, very likely, but he must have been short of a sheet to jaunter about when he knew the prince was out for his blood.

30

Nobody knows for certain what happened, of course, but there's a widely accepted theory that hired assassins surrounded his carriage and put a period to him. Only think how foolish he must have felt to have failed to take precautions. Now Marat, you'll agree, *il est toujours premier en classe!* No, really. I mean what idiot with half a brain-box wouldn't think it a trifle unusual if a strange young woman popped in to interview him in his bathtub? If he'd had the commonsense of a mangel-wurzel he'd have kept an eye on the wench and she'd not have had a chance to finish him off with her handy little knife. You have to admit . . ."

Broderick, a brilliant scholar, was known for his tendency to launch into learned discourses. His voice was soothing, the leaping flames on the hearth were mesmerizing, the room was warm, and Adair was very tired. His head started to nod, but he roused when Broderick said, ". . . if you don't object, that is."

"Eh? Object to—what? Oh, Gad! I'm dashed sorry, Toby. Didn't mean to drop off like that. You were talking about ambushes, I believe?"

Too good-natured to take offence when his friends failed to benefit from his little lectures, Broderick grinned. "Some time ago. And you were about to tell me what did happen the night of the Farringdon ball. You don't have to, of course, but the more I know of it, the better my chance of helping—somehow, sometime."

"You'd be wise to stay clear of it. Not that I'm not grateful, but—"

"But keep my long nose out of your private affairs, is that it?" Broderick stood, and suddenly very much the aristocrat, said, "Time you was in bed, at all events. You're properly against the ropes. Forgive my gauche curios——"

"Oh, for Lord's sake, do stop! Of course I want your long nose in this ugly business—provided you don't complain if it gets snipped off." Smiling, Adair held out his glass, and Broderick gave a relieved grin and hurried to refill and return it.

"Actually, I know quite a lot already," he said, sitting down again. "You had one evening free in London before trotting back to France, so you accepted the Farringdon invitation. What I hadn't known was that you were acquainted with this Miss Prior. You being such a dashing, heroic sort of"—he laughed and warded off the cushion that was hurled at him—"sort of fellow, and a lieutenant-colonel to boot. I'm told Miss Prior's a timid mouse, the kind hostesses have to browbeat their male guests into asking for a dance."

Adair sobered. "It's her first Season, I gather. The prosecuting counsel said that we'd been meeting on the sly, but there's not a vestige of truth in it. I'd never met the lady before that night. The fact is that I was en route to beg Dorothy Haines-Curtis to dance with me, but I chanced to hear that wart Talbot Droitwich sniggering about "the Prior wallflower" that no sane fellow would dance with. Miss Prior was sitting at the side, and she looked—oh, you know how it is for girls who don't 'take.' "

Broderick nodded. "A sort of helpless desperation. Poor little things. Is that why you asked her to dance?"

"Yes. Only she wanted to sit and talk instead. I expected to be bored to tears. But I wasn't, Toby. It took a few minutes to put her at ease, but I managed to make her laugh, and in no time we were chattering like old friends. She has a delightful sense of humour and quite a charming way of teasing. In fact, I enjoyed being with her, and later I asked to be allowed to take her in to supper."

"Did you dance with her afterwards?"

"No. I liked the girl, but I—well, I didn't want to seem too particular in my attentions. I went into the card-room and threw some dice with Aubrey Suffield, who had the unmitigated gall to try and buy Toreador. I've told him repeatedly he's my favourite saddle-horse and I'll never sell him, but Suffield said if I cared for the animal I'd sell him now, because when I go back into action I'll likely get killed and then what will become of him. Damned gloom merchant!"

Broderick laughed. "You know Suffield. He'll stop at nothing to get any hack he takes a fancy to, and that dapple-grey of yours is splendid and a strengthy beast besides. Suffield likely wants to enter him in one of the cross-country races he's always organizing."

"Very likely, but he'll never get the chance, and so I told him. If I should turn up my toes, Toreador will go to my brother Hudson, and if Hudson dares sell him to Suffield, I'll—I'll come back and haunt him!"

"Hudson? I thought you once told me you'd bequeathe him to young Nigel?"

"That was my intent, though I never told Nigel." Adair stared rather fixedly at the glass in his hand. "When all this—ghastly business came up, my man of affairs said I must make a will. And—well, poor old Hudson has really worked terribly hard for that Cabinet appointment, and now, thanks to me, he's lost it. I know he's always coveted Toreador, so . . ." He shrugged.

"A sort of consolation prize, eh? A jolly nice one, if you was to ask me. So what did you do? Abandon Suffield to his dice?"

"I was putting a flea in his ear for refusing to take no for an answer when a page brought a note from Miss Prior, begging that I escort her home."

"Hadn't she been brought by her family?"

"By her brother, Rufus. A lad with a red poll that looks likely to ignite when the sun hits it, and a disposition to match. Miss Prior wrote that they'd quarrelled and she didn't want Rufus to take her home. Naturally, I assumed she'd have her maid or some other lady with her as chaperon. But when I climbed into her carriage she was alone." He paused, then said, "And that's the sum and substance of it, Toby."

Broderick stared at him. "What d'ye mean, the 'sum and substance'? Ain't none of either that I can see. Don't be shy, Hasty. What happened then?"

Adair said stonily, "Nothing. I saw her sitting there, and woke up two days later in a cell with one of Ed Whinyates' rockets ricochetting around inside my skull."

"Poor Whinyates. He never really knows where those blasted

rockets are going but he still believes they'll help us win the war. Do you say you don't remember the drive? Taking her to the hotel? Frisking about? *Nothing?*"

"No. And furthermore, I know damned well I wouldn't have 'frisked about' with that angelic little soul. Lord, Toby, she's scarce out of the schoolroom! Acquit me of interfering with innocence!"

"Oh, of course, dear boy. No question. None. Er—whew!" Broderick leaned back and shook his head. "You don't recall feeling ill? Or hurt?"

"Not until I woke up. If you're thinking I was struck down, that was my first hope, but there wasn't a mark on me. If I was drugged, I'd be deuced glad to know how, or when. I had supper, as I said, with Miss Prior. In the card-room I took a glass of Cognac, but at least half an hour elapsed before I received her note and went out to the coach. If the cognac was drugged, I'd think it would have started to affect me long before that. And furthermore, that the onset of symptoms would have been more gradual; not that I'd be fully conscious one minute and then— nothing for the following thirty-six hours."

Broderick nodded glumly. "What about Miss Prior? Surely she could shed some light on the matter?"

"Oh, surely. Unhappily, the poor lady is said to be very ill, and has been whisked off to her father's country seat. It's out near Tenterden, I believe." Adair yawned, and apologized. "Enough of my troubles. What of you, Toby? I'd thought you were called back to duty?"

"Was. I'm on detached service, actually. I've had to testify in Jack Vespa's murky mess down at Alabaster Royal, and now I'm cooling my heels here, waiting to be interrogated about his antics in Brittany. Be dashed if ever I knew such a fellow for getting himself into trouble—though you bid fair to catch up with him! And never mind trying to turn the subject, Hasty. What d'you mean to do now?"

Adair stood, and stretched. "Go to bed. Sorry, old lad, but—"

"No, no. After the day you've had . . ." It was very clear that

34

Adair was quite done up and could scarcely keep his eyes open. "I'll light you up the stairs," Broderick offered. "And on the way you can tell me where you mean to start. The lady and the coachman, I fancy?"

"Just so."

"If you like, I'll go down to Tenterden and sniff about the neighbourhood, while you have a chat with the coachman." He held open the drawing-room door and barely prevented his friend from stumbling into the wall. "What did he have to say at your trial?"

"Enough to help win me the death sentence! And then he seems to have—taken French leave."

Incredulous, Broderick pulled him to a halt. "You don't mean it! Didn't they try to find him?"

"Said they did. Couldn't. Perhaps . . ." Adair blinked drowsily at the end-post of the stair railing before realizing it wasn't Broderick. "Perhaps you'll have better luck."

"Devil I will! No, get up, do! You can't go to sleep on the stairs. And don't be ridiculous. *I'll* go to Tenterden. If you dared show your nose anywhere near Miss Prior's family, you'd likely get a hot reception!"

"Very likely," agreed Adair, sitting on the next stair. "Be dashed lucky if . . . if they don't shoot me out of hand."

"Quite. That's why—Hasty? Wake up! Oh, egad! *Hey*! You, there! Never mind about snuffing the candles. Come and help me haul the Colonel upstairs!"

———

Despite his exhaustion, Adair's habit of rising early prevailed and before Broderick was awake he had already eaten a quick breakfast, ordered up a post-chaise, packed a valise with sufficient clothing and toilet articles for a journey of several days and was en route to his bank. This was a task he dreaded, for he was well known in London, but he must have funds.

The morning was dull and very cold, with leaden skies and the smell of snow on the air. He found himself thinking hopefully that most of his acquaintances were unlikely to be abroad at this hour of a wintry morning. Sooner or later he would face someone he knew, but a craven voice whispered that it would be so much easier if he could avoid recognition until the public outrage had cooled a little.

The chaise drew to a halt. There were many people hurrying about. No one he knew, thank heaven. He had a few words with Toreador, who was tied on behind, and told the post-boy to drive around for ten minutes and then return.

Even at this hour the bank was a busy place. The clerk who usually handled his account was waiting on another man. Adair walked towards his table. A prosperous-looking merchant was making his way in the same direction. He glanced at Adair, paused, frowning, then turned aside. The muscles under Adair's ribs contracted painfully, which was stupid. It was probably a simple case of the fellow deciding to go to another table. He wouldn't let himself glance after the man, but moved up swiftly when his clerk was free. The clerk looked at him steadily. Disgust came into his eyes, and he did not offer the usual smiling "Good morning, Colonel." Adair withdrew a large amount. The money was counted out in silence but with studied insolence. Adair put the cash in a leather bag he'd brought for the purpose and left, his ears burning to the contemptuous snort that followed him.

Outside, he thought with enormous relief, 'That's done!' and walked towards the kennel.

"Well, well! You don't want for gall, Adair! I give you that."

The sardonic voice was all too familiar. Thorne Webber. The last person he would have wished to encounter at any time, least of all today. The post-chaise rattled around the corner and pulled up. He could jump in and retreat at the gallop. A fine spectacle that would make, he thought cynically. He tossed his leather bag inside and turned to face the man who, until this wretched fiasco, had been one of his few enemies.

"You cannot know how your opinion weighs with me," he said coldly.

Five years Adair's senior, Thorne Webber was tall and well built, the many capes of his driving coat accentuating the breadth of powerful shoulders. His grandfather, a successful mill-owner, had founded the family fortune, his father had added to it the manufacture of umbrellas—a modest venture that had shown a surprising profit, and Thorne Webber was today a very rich man. His wealth had brought him power and many friends, but he was shrewd enough to know that their "friendship" was extended to his money and that without it they would desert him en masse; more galling, the awareness that behind their smiles and fawning servility was a disdain for his humble origins. He had a deep loathing for Hastings Adair, and his heavy features reflected his triumph as he responded, "It ain't just my opinion. Every gentleman in London holds you in abhorrence! When I think how you *dared* to victimize my brother over a trifle, while you—"

"Your brother had a fine young soldier damn near flogged to death for refusing to shoot an old Spanish woman who couldn't understand what she was being told to do. Had I not ridden up, the trooper *would* have died! If you call that a 'trifle'—"

"I call it *discipline*! And thanks to your molly-coddling interference my brother was demoted to lieutenant for—"

"If I'd had my way he'd have been demoted to private! Any God-fearing man seeing that boy's back would have intervened."

"Aye, well, you won't be 'intervening' in any more military decisions, will you, *Mr.* Adair?"

Adair gave him a contemptuous glance and turned to the post-chaise.

"What a damned shame no God-fearing man was able to protect the poor girl you assaulted and ruined!" Webber grabbed Adair's shoulder, wrenching him around as he trod onto the step. Adair staggered and Webber's riding crop flailed across his face.

"There's for you, libertine!" howled Webber. "In behalf of the gentlemen of London!"

Reeling and dazed, Adair half-fell against the side of the coach. Through a red haze of pain he could hear Webber shouting, egging on the men who were gathering around.

37

Webber trumpeted, "Here's a merciless villain wants thrashing, chaps!" His riding-crop arced upward once more.

"No, he don't! Let be, Webber!" A fine amber cane blocked the whizzing riding crop but was beaten from its owner's hand. It spun at Adair. Half-blinded, he managed to catch the cane and he peered at it stupidly, wondering who had dared come to his aid. The handle was gold, and a small crest containing an anchor was intricately wrought in gold. Minna's betrothal gift to Julius Harrington, he thought dully.

"Stand clear, Harrington," bellowed Webber. "We know how to deal with womanizing deserters!"

"Then you should know he ain't neither," cried Harrington staunchly. "If you'd just use your brains for once—"

"Move out of the way, you stupid block!" Webber's roar was echoed by angry shouts and a suggestion of tar and feathers won instant approval.

Harrington tore the chaise door open and pushed the swaying Adair inside. "Too many," he panted. "Go, Hasty! Go!"

"No. Wait!" Adair struggled to his feet.

The frightened post-boy cried, "Lorramighty!" cracked his whip and set the coach in motion.

Leaning from the window, Adair tossed Harrington his cane and called, "Thanks . . . Julius!"

The horses thundered around the corner, and Harrington, the bank, the angry crowd and the roaring Thorne Webber were lost to sight.

Adair held a handkerchief to his throbbing cheek. It felt as though Webber's riding crop had cut to the bone, and he was relieved when he found no bloodstains. The whip had marked him, though; small doubt of that, nor of the interpretation that would be put on the welt by anyone he met. It had been a cowardly blow and would do nothing to diminish Webber's reputation as an arrogant bully. Nor would it be of any help to Colonel Hastings Adair. Settling back onto the seat, he muttered a correction: "*Mr.* Hastings Adair."

The tale of his latest disgrace would sweep London in an

hour, and Thorne Webber would gleefully spread it about that he had run away like a whipped dog. He thought grimly, 'Grandfather will love that!' He'd have to return to Town directly after he'd found and talked with Miss Prior. His only hope of retrieving a shred of his honour would be to call out Thorne Webber. He considered duelling to be a ridiculous and outmoded solution to quarrels, although it was still widely practised in France. Still, he was a fine shot, and under the present circumstances, he had no choice. He wondered if Toby and Jack Vespa would be willing to act as his seconds.

Singletree was undoubtedly a charming estate when viewed in summertime. The gentle valley would be lush and green then, and its pastures dotted with the sheep that had brought prosperity to this part of The Weald. Even blanketed in snow, as it was on this cold February afternoon, the manor-house presented a pretty sight, smoke spiralling from several chimneys and lamplight already glowing in some of the latticed ground-floor windows. Adair had dismissed the post-chaise when he'd secured a room at the White Ram, a tiny and remote wayside inn. Now, guiding Toreador along Singletree's winding drivepath, he thought inconsequently that the name of the estate was ill-chosen since there were trees everywhere. Of more concern was the sort of reception he could expect from the Prior family. Hostility, certainly; perhaps violence. The pistol in his pocket was a reassuring weight. If necessary, he was resolved to hold Miss Prior's menfolk at bay until they agreed to let him see her.

Occasional snowflakes drifted down as he dismounted and secured Toreador's reins to a post at the foot of the entrance steps. A wide terrace ran along the front of the two-storey stone house and he was crossing it when the front door flew open. A young man wearing riding dress rushed out and ran at him.

"Filthy swine!" he howled, his clenched fist flying at Adair's jaw. "How *dare* you show your wicked face here, when—"

The flaming red hair had warned Adair, and he dodged the

blow deftly, caught the enraged man's wrist and with a supple twist sent him sprawling.

"Rufus? Who is it?" A tall young woman hurried from the house. Adair had a fleeting impression of fair windblown curls, a superbly cut riding habit that enclosed a superbly shaped female, and eyes somewhere between blue and grey that widened as they rested on Prior. "What . . . on earth . . . ?" She crossed quickly to help him up. "Did you fall?"

"Aye. With the aid of his fist," snapped Prior, his face almost as red as his hair. "Keep clear, Cecily. This is the slimy varmint who assaulted poor Alice!"

The girl gave a sort of leap and turned on Adair, her eyes narrowed with rage. "And you let him knock you down? Have you no pistol about you? Shoot the monster!"

Prior's hand darted to his coat pocket, but Adair's pistol was levelled before he could withdraw the weapon.

"Easy," cautioned Adair. The girl, who was quite remarkably attractive, started to back away. He added, "And if you've any affection for this fire-eater, ma'am, I'd suggest you stand still. I'd not wish to feel obliged to put a ball through his foot."

She glared at him, but halted. "You *wretched* creature," she said, her voice low but ringing with fury. "You must be stark raving mad to come here. My uncle will return at any moment and he'll know how to deal with you!"

"Somebody already has," jeered Prior. "Look at his face. A horsewhip, applied by some public-spirited citizen, unless I mistake it."

"Then it was well done, but a small payment. Hanging is what the revolting libertine needs!"

"A kindly lass, aren't you," said Adair. "I did not come here to listen to your nonsense. All I want, Prior, is a few words with your sister. I mean no harm, but—"

"Oh, do you not?" The girl's lip curled contemptuously. "Did you mean poor Alice 'no harm' when you—"

Prior had climbed to his feet and now interrupted sharply, "What makes you think my sister is here?"

"He thinks no such thing," said the girl. "He knows perfectly well she is not!"

The snow was getting heavier, great flakes floating down to cling to their hair and garments, and it was very cold, but the chill Adair felt now had nothing to do with the weather. He said desperately, "Don't fence with me. Everyone knows she's here." He paused, for it seemed to him that they exchanged a tense look, but neither spoke, and he went on: "If she had been well enough to testify at my trial she could have cleared me. I demand to see her, and I warn you I'll not be fobbed off with a lot of fustian!"

"Rubbish!" the girl exclaimed. "If I scream our servants will come, and—"

"And find Prior with a smashed foot," said Adair. The fact that the door was still wide open and no servants or other family members had appeared was odd, and he'd begun to suspect that the house was empty. "All I ask is five minutes with the lady. Five minutes only. You can stay with her. She must have told you by now what really happened, and—"

Made reckless by anger, Prior sprang at him. Adair had no wish to shoot the boy. He leapt aside and flailed his pistol in a hard swipe which landed just below Prior's ear. The redhead went down and stayed down.

"Stand clear, Cecily!"

A new arrival entered the scene: a frail-appearing lady of advanced years, whose elaborate gown had the tiny waist and full panniered skirts fashionable thirty years earlier. Adair stared in astonishment as she tottered onto the terrace. Snowflakes fell on her powdered hair but she advanced with erratic determination, the heavy blunderbuss she held in both thin hands pointing more or less at him.

He lowered his own weapon. One did not, after all, threaten an old lady. "Have a care with that, ma'am," he warned, stepping back a pace.

"Don't tell me what to do, you black-hearted toad! Not content with ruining my beloved granddaughter, you dare to come

41

here and render my grandson sense——Lud!" She gave a little yelp as her high-heeled and buckled slipper slid on the thickening carpet of snow.

The girl, who had started forward, uttered a shriek and sat down abruptly as Adair shoved her aside.

The blunderbuss exploded with a deafening roar.

Adair had ducked just in time to hear the familiar and wicked whine of shot flying over his head. Straightening, he returned the pistol to his pocket. The old lady had fallen. "Oh, Jupiter!" he groaned, hurrying to lift her.

Confused, she gasped, "Thank you, dear boy," and clung to him gratefully.

"Are you all right?" he asked, steadying her.

"Quite all right, but—but I'll confess I had never—never realized how those horrid guns work in both—directions at once! There. You are most kind, sir, and—Oh! Oh, my goodness! No, you're not! You're the rogue who has ruined my darling Alice! Where is my naughty horse-pistol? Why they call them that I cannot fathom, for if anyone fired it, one would bring down a whole herd of horses!"

"Just so, ma'am," he said, a twinkle creeping into his eyes. "But actually, it is a blunderbuss."

"Is that the case? Oh. Well, give it me at once! At once, I say!"

"It's empty now, ma'am," he pointed out, handing it over obediently. "Please believe that I did not harm your granddaughter. And you should not be out in the snow. If I were—" He broke off as the blunderbuss whizzed at his head.

"*Roué!*" shrilled the old lady. And wielding the weapon ferociously, sliding on the snow with each word, went on, "Evil . . . viperous . . . murdering . . . libertine!"

Adair drew back. Outraged gentlemen he could face. Angry termagants he could deal with—to a point. Hysterically vengeful old ladies reduced him to a craven.

The girl was tugging at Rufus Prior's pockets, searching for his pistol, no doubt.

A fine pickle he would be in, thought Adair, to have to wrestle with two women.

He bowed and retreated, their enraged cries gradually muffled by the snow and a rising wind.

4

Although it was not yet four o'clock, the light was failing as Adair turned Toreador back down the drivepath. The snow was becoming ever more dense, the flakes so large as to limit visibility, and he had to strain his eyes to distinguish the gates. He held Toreador to a walk on the rutted drive, but when they reached the improved paving of the lane, urged him to a trot. The White Ram Inn was no more than three miles to the east, but in this snowstorm he'd have his work cut out to find it once darkness fell.

His thoughts lingered on his encounter at Singletree. During the course of his Army career he'd had to deal with some decidedly odd people, but deuce take him if he'd ever laid eyes on a more peculiar group than the one he'd just left! Young Rufus Prior was so hot-at-hand, it was a wonder that red thatch of his did not ignite all by itself; the old lady was a spirited creature also. She had probably been a beauty in her day, but clearly some of her wits were wilted. As for that lanky shrew named "Cecily Somebody," she had a pretty face, but her temper was uncontrolled; if she'd found Prior's pistol he had no doubt that only the thick screen of snow had prevented her from putting a bullet in his back as he'd ridden out.

They'd all lied like troopers, confound them! Pretending poor Miss Alice wasn't in the house. She was there, all right! The tense glance that had passed between Prior and the Cecily chit had convinced him they meant to try and gull him. It was downright evil that although Miss Alice must have told them long since what had really happened on that fateful night, they'd been willing to let him be executed rather than make the true facts known and risk sullying their family name. Never mind the tragedy to his own family! Never mind that his career was wrecked and his honour in shreds! He scowled at the snow-flakes. They'd won this round, he acknowledged grimly, but, by God, they wouldn't defeat him! He'd get into Singletree and search the place from cellars to attics even if he had to hire a pack of vagrants to help him! And once he found Miss Alice Prior, Lord help the man—or woman—who tried to keep him from questioning her and—

At this point a dark shape loomed up directly ahead. His heart leapt and his hand darted for his pistol but he gave a faintly embarrassed grin when he realized that he was confronted by nothing more menacing than a tall holly bush. "I yield the right-of-way, Sir Holly," he muttered, reining Toreador aside. The big grey snorted at the sound of his voice and Adair nodded. "You're right, my dappled friend. What the deuce is a holly bush doing in the middle of the road?"

The answer was all too obvious. Dismounting, chilled by the icy breath of the wind, he drew his warm scarf higher. The light was almost gone now but it was sufficient to show him that he was off the road and in lightly wooded country. He swore softly. This was no night to be lost in the open. If he didn't find the White Ram or an obliging farmer soon, he must contrive some sort of shelter or both he and Toreador could be frozen stiff by daylight.

He caressed the grey's neck and promised that they'd search

for a few more minutes and then he'd find a likely tree and start collecting branches. Toreador nuzzled at his neck and blew small clouds of steam to mingle with the snowflakes. "Never doubt my ability," said Adair. "I've built a shelter often enough in Spain. We'll have a roof over our heads one way or—"

"You will need no roof, Colonel!" The feminine voice came clear and contemptuous through the gloom. "A shroud, more like!"

Adair whipped around.

Miss Cecily stepped closer, the reins of a fine chestnut mare in one gloved hand, a long-barrelled duelling pistol in the other, and snowflakes on the hood of her pelisse and collecting on her brows.

"Well, well," said Adair mockingly. "Come to play executioner, have you? I wonder you found me in this blizzard."

"Your tracks were easy enough to follow."

"They'll be gone when you turn back. I wish you joy of finding your way home after you've murdered me."

"I don't have to murder you now, Adair. A ball through one of your knees and the storm will do the rest."

He stared at her. "Lord, but you're a cold-blooded chit!"

"I've no doubt you are an expert on cold-bloodedness, whereas Alice Prior is the most gentle, kind-hearted, truly good person I have ever known. She was—" Her voice shredded slightly and Adair stepped back a pace as she waved the pistol to emphasize her remarks. "She was my dearest friend from our childhood days. The one person I could always turn to when—" The sentence went unfinished, then she said harshly, "And you—*you*, a man trained to kill, and with a reputation as—as, what do they call creatures like you? a Bond Street Beau?"

"The devil! That's not so! I'm seldom in England and—"

"You dared—you *dared* to lure away and—and violate that pure angel, and—"

"Again—untrue! I never even met the girl until that night!"

"Liar!" she hissed. "Did you think she would confide in no one? She told me she was deep in love with you!"

Adair gasped, "She *named* me?"

"She loved and trusted you. And you destroyed her—just as I shall now avenge her!"

Watching her narrowly, he asked, "Am I your first victim?"

"My last, I pray." She aimed the pistol carefully. "I might grant you a quicker death if you tell me what you have done with Alice."

"If I am to die, madam, I've a right to be told the truth first. No need for you to persist in this rubbishing stuff about Miss Prior being lost. At least allow me to know what this is all about, and why you are preparing to kill a man who you must be aware is innocent of any wrongdoing."

There came the sound of the hammer being drawn back. Adair tensed. This crazy woman really meant to shoot him!

"I will count to three," she said, her voice steady and merciless. "One . . . Where is Alice?"

"Do you really think I would come here seeking her if I knew?"

"Two . . . She's dead, isn't she? You evil, *evil* man—you killed her so that she could not speak against you!"

"But of course. And then I came here, risking your righteous indignation—"

"Indignation!"

"—to enquire after the poor lady I had already buried."

"Three . . . God forgive me, but—"

Adair flung himself to the side but there was no pistol shot. Instead the girl stood there, fumbling with the trigger and half-weeping with frustration.

He sprang to seize the pistol. "Couldn't bring yourself to shoot an unarmed man, eh? Give it here!"

"How may I give it to you," she demanded furiously, "when the wretched thing is caught on my glove?"

He peered at the trigger. "So it is," he said, standing well clear of the wavering muzzle. "Now if you will just keep still, my foiled assassin—"

Instead, she jerked free, then jumped back.

"For heaven's sake, have a care!" exclaimed Adair. "That Manton likely has a hair-trigger, and—"

"I should have known it would fail me," she cried bitterly. "I hate guns!"

"Yet were prepared to fire one."

She gave him a contemptuous glance. "Oh, I would not have, of course. Even for my dearest friend. You counted on that weakness, didn't you?"

"I'd count on it with less apprehension if you would stop waving the pistol about."

For a moment she stood watching him, irresolute, then she said, "I suppose I had as well. My dear little Alice—I have failed you abominably!" She flung the weapon away from her with loathing.

"Hey!" shouted Adair, ducking.

The pistol vanished into the swirling snow, but through that white curtain came a flash and a sharp retort.

"Of all the shatter-brained things to do," said Adair angrily. "Did no one ever tell you—" He stopped abruptly. Miss Cecily Somebody looked odd. In fact, she looked very odd indeed. She appeared to be shrinking even as she stared at him, her eyes huge in a suddenly dead-white face.

He leapt forward and caught her as she crumpled.

"Oh, dear," she whispered, and fainted.

———✦———

"If you dare lay one finger on me," panted Miss Cecily, her right hand holding the collar of her blouse tightly closed, "I pr-promise you will . . . regret it!"

Adair set down the pan of melted snow he had managed to heat on the fire. When he'd attempted to carry the girl into the bedchamber of this isolated two-room cottage she had set up a screech that would have wakened the dead and had insisted on being laid on the sofa.

"You will be more like to regret it if I do not," he answered coolly.

48

"That is the—the thanks I get for g-guiding you to this cottage."

"Which will protect us from freezing, I hope. But I've done no more than wind my handkerchief about your arm. The wound must be cleansed and properly bandaged." He stepped purposefully towards the shabby sofa.

"Stay back!" She shrank away, her eyes—a blue-grey which he thought quite beautiful when they were not hurling hatred—were very wide and betraying fear as well as pain. "Much you care for my needs! You left me to bleed to death for—for hours, and now pretend to—"

"It was a few minutes only. I had to get the horses into the lean-to. Thank the Lord there is one! I value my grey."

"Whereas my life counts for nought! Charming! And it did not take that long to tend the horses!"

"No, but we needed firewood. Whoever lives here has not kept up the woodpile."

"It was a gardener's cottage. But—but my cousin stays here some—often."

"Does he. Well, I am here at your disposal now, if you will stop wasting more time with this nonsense."

She muttered something fretfully, and he felt a pang of sympathy. It must have been a strain for her to decide to murder him, and now she had been painfully injured. He took off his cloak and flung it over a straight-backed chair. "Be sensible, Miss Cecily, or whatever your name is, and let me—"

"I am Miss Hall. And—and I have brothers. Five. And all—very fine sh-shots."

"I wonder they did not teach you more about duelling pistols and hair-triggers." He smiled and said gently, "Yes, I understand that I am a monster and naturally you do not want a monster to tend you. To say truth, this monster would be very glad to let someone else do the business. But there is no one else at hand, and we must count our blessings, Miss Hall. Another half-hour out in that blizzard, and neither of us would have seen tomorrow. Providentially, here we are, with a roof over our heads and a fire on the hearth. And your cousin was so good as to leave these few sticks of furniture, which are better than nought, eh?" While talking easily, he had put aside her pelisse and started to unbutton her blouse. "You have managed to take a pistol ball across your arm, and unless you wish to bleed to death I must—"

"Let be," she half-sobbed. "Just—just cut the sleeve off. Please."

"I wish I might. But I need the blouse for bandages, since I fancy you do not wear petticoats under that very fine riding habit."

"Of course I don't!" she said impatiently, "How on earth could—Oh, I collect you are trying to reassure me, but—Now what are you doing? Ow!"

He had bent closer to slide an arm under her. "You see? You're hurting yourself." She was warm and fragrant against him as he raised her, and fumbling at her back, his cheek came into contact with soft, satiny skin. He muttered, "Now—if I can just—"

"Oh, heavens above! Close your eyes! Don't *look*!"

Furiously embarrassed, he snapped, "For heaven's sake, don't be so missish! I have no designs upon your virtue, I promise you!"

She said faintly, "You likely said the same to . . . to poor Alice!"

Despite the brave words there were tears on her long lashes. She was certainly in pain, and she really was a courageous chit. He reached for his cloak and handed it to her, closing his eyes obediently. "Here. Cover yourself, Lady Modesty, but I must be free to come at your arm." He waited while she strove and muttered to herself, then asked, "Are you respectable at last?"

"As far as—as possible."

Those great scared eyes were fixed on him. He said, "Be easy, ma'am," but he could imagine her state of mind, if she really believed he had done away with her cousin. He slid the blouse down over the handkerchief he had wrapped around her upper left arm, tore the blouse into strips and fashioned a pad, but when he began to ease his clumsy bandage away, he found that his hands were trembling. He had seen hideous wounds on the battlefield, and several times had acted as a makeshift surgeon to aid a stricken comrade. This was only a flesh wound, but to see a woman's white flesh so cruelly torn horrified him. Miss Hall flinched and drew in her breath. "I wish I had some brandy," he muttered.

"For—for you, sir? Or—for me?"

He glanced at her, and saw a faint twinkle in her eyes.

"Both," he said with a grin.

After he had sweated his way through some long minutes of bathing the wound, she asked, "Have you ever done—this sort of thing—before?"

"Are you questioning my credentials? I wish I could say I had not, but war being what it—"

She gave a little whimper, and he recoiled. "Oh, God! I am so sorry to have to hurt you. But—at least it is a shallow wound. You've no bones broken."

She said threadily, "You look worse than . . . than I feel."

"You are very brave," he said, wishing he had some basilicum powder or anything that would serve as an antiseptic. The wound was clean now, at least, and the bleeding much lessened. He told her he would bind it up tightly, and that at first light she would be taken to a doctor.

She did not answer. Her eyes were closed. He thought she had swooned again, and he put the pad in place, then proceeded to bandage the injury as tightly as he dared.

Miss Hall opened her eyes abruptly. She appeared to be momentarily confused, and uttered incoherent cries as she struggled to sit up. Adair's cloak slid to the floor, revealing the dainty and very well-filled bodice of a camisole.

"Ooh!" shrilled Miss Hall, lifting her right hand concealingly. "You're *looking*!"

Adair wrenched his fascinated gaze away. Reddening, he protested, "For heaven's sake, woman! I've seen more revealed in—or out of—an evening gown! Do try not to—"

51

The outer door crashed open.

An enraged masculine voice roared, "Be damned if he ain't at it again!"

Springing up, Adair turned quickly, but he had not the slightest chance to avoid Rufus Prior's flying fist.

～∞～

"I may have been mistook, this time," growled Prior, "but he warrants a deal more than a bloody nose."

"If this is your cottage," said Adair stuffily, "dare one hope you've some blankets?"

"For goodness' sake, take him out and put some snow down his back," said Lady Abigail Prior, turning from a soft-voiced exchange with her granddaughter to cast a shuddering glance at Adair.

"I've blankets for the ladies, not you," said Prior, opening a cupboard that appeared to be stocked with bottles, a large bowl of apples, some candles and several untidily folded blankets.

Adair held Prior's handkerchief to his streaming nose and observed that the ladies were indoors with a fire to warm them. "My horse is not. I'll take one of those, if you please."

Prior did not please, and when Adair ignored his belligerence and commandeered a blanket, he grabbed for his coat pocket, only to pause and look chagrined.

"Miss Hall took your pistol, alas," said Adair mockingly.

"And we want no more bloodshed tonight," said Lady Abigail. "Do as the Colonel says, Rufus. We're properly marooned and the beasts have little protection out there. Oh, and you'll find a fruitcake in my coach. I've been meaning to take it down to Mrs. Flynn in the village."

"For how long?" Prior tossed three more blankets at Adair and unearthed a lantern.

Her ladyship frowned thoughtfully. "Long enough for it to be nicely aged, but if you don't care for it, there will be that much more for the rest of us."

Swinging the door open and admitting an icy blast, Prior said softly, "You're my prisoner, Adair. Keep it in mind."

"At least I have a mind." Adair slammed the door shut, and bowing to the teeth of the wind shouted, "You've evidently lost yours! Why bring the old lady out on such a night?"

"You don't know my grandmama! You may thank your stars you were flat on your back when she saw Cecily and thought you'd shot her! She was ready to claw your eyes out!"

This, Adair did not doubt, and he said nothing while they unsaddled Toreador and Miss Hall's mount and led Prior's pair from between the shafts of his light travelling-coach. Fortunately, there was a bin of oats in the lean-to, and Adair was less anxious when Toreador had been rubbed down and was munching contentedly, with a blanket tied over him.

Prior's remark turned his thoughts back to Lady Abigail's arrival. He had been somewhat confused at that moment, but he'd heard her screech of fury, followed—mercifully—by Miss Hall's admission that she had "accidentally dropped" the pistol and that he had brought her to the cottage. Prior had been disgusted by his cousin's blunder, but the old lady had expressed her gratitude for Adair's efforts and pointed out that he could very well have ridden off and left Cecily in the snow. Shocked, he'd protested, "As if I would have done such a thing!" Prior had laughed scornfully, but both ladies had watched Adair in such a considering way that he'd begun to hope—

He howled as Prior rammed a large snowball down the back of his neck so forcefully that he was driven to his knees.

"Just trying to help your bloody nose," chortled Prior.

Adair said wrathfully, "Since you feel so obliging, you can let me have the lantern for a minute."

"Why? So you can smash it on my head and ride off free as air?"

"Idiot. Who could ride off in this air? Give it to me."

Instinctively obeying that note of command, Prior surrendered the lantern and watched curiously as Adair searched about on hands and knees. "What the deuce are you looking for? My unhappy sister ain't down there, I promise you."

"Good of you to tell me. Perhaps you'll be so generous as to also advise me where you've tucked her away!" Adair rolled swiftly to the side as Prior uttered a bellow of rage and plunged at him. He was ready this time. A bewildered Prior found himself seized in an iron grip, flung to the side, and, before he could make a recover, rendered helpless by the arm twisted up behind him.

Adair said harshly, "Don't much like it when *you're* the accused, do you?"

"Damn you! Let be! You—you're breaking my arm!"

"It would be so easy," muttered Adair, but he released his grip, shoved Prior away and resumed his search of the ground.

Massaging his arm, Prior said sullenly, "I'm freezing! Whatever you're looking for, look in the morning."

"I'm looking for my emerald pin. It was in my cravat when I left the inn where I'm racking up." The pin, a family heirloom, had been his twenty-first birthday present from the General. He had always prized it, less for the size and beauty of the stone than for its sentimental value. He wouldn't normally have worn it on a brief visit to the country, and the knowledge that he'd done so because it seemed to provide a link to his family made him curse such folly.

Prior was putting up the poles of the carriage. "If you mean to crawl around till you freeze, you have my blessing," he grunted. "We'll haul you away in the morning."

Adair's hands were so cold he could scarcely feel them. He'd been able to detect no gleam of gold, and he cursed bitterly as he gave up the search and climbed to his feet.

Prior took a box from the boot of the coach and peered at it dubiously. "This is the fruitcake, I hope." He bent to hold it closer to the beam of the lantern, disclosing a small label neatly inscribed: "Nun's Fruitcake."

"I'll read it for you," offered Adair sardonically.

Prior swore at him.

Adair grinned and continued to direct the lantern's beam at

the ground as they went out into the full force of the storm once more.

"Your pin must be of great value," shouted Prior.

Adair said brusquely, "It is beyond price."

Shortly after three o'clock in the morning Adair threw another log on the fire. When he woke again at six the flames were sputtering but gave off enough light to enable him to move about noiselessly. Accustomed to harsh campaign conditions, he had slept in comparative comfort on the hearthrug. Prior was still snoring on the sofa. The ladies had retired to the small bedroom and there was no sound from beyond that door. The wind had died down during the night, and when Adair eased the front door open there was no inrush of frigid air to betray him.

Outside, it was still dark and very cold, but it had stopped snowing. Toreador greeted him affectionately and he spoke softly to the grey as he saddled up, then turned to the other three animals. The sky was lightening, the brighter eastern glow giving him his direction. He'd scribbled a brief note to Prior, but riding out, leading Miss Hall's hack and her grandmother's coach-horses, he felt the ultimate villain.

Toreador snorted and tossed his head.

Adair said, "I know, I know. I'm not behaving like a gentleman. But I mean to search that confounded house, and it won't hurt—well, it won't endanger the lady to wait just a little while longer to see a doctor."

He turned northward for a mile before releasing his appropriated horses in a patch of woodland. Cecily Hall's lovely eyes haunted him, but the tracks of four horses were clear in the snow; Prior should have no difficulty following them. The redhead's opinion of him at about this time was easy to imagine, but he told himself that they had the fire and there was still some of that very good fruitcake for a makeshift breakfast.

He kept to the trees for some distance, emerging eventually

at the foot of a hill, and then guiding Toreador to the west. It was daylight now, but there were few people abroad on this cold early morning and he stayed well clear of occasional travellers in case they might later be questioned by Prior. He was soon cantering towards Singletree. The lodge gates came into view and he began to rehearse what he would say to Mr. Prior. It would be a tricky situation, he thought grimly, but by heaven, if it was humanly possible—

His reflections were interrupted by the pounding of rapidly approaching hooves. A large group, by the sound of it; too many for him to deal with. He sent Toreador plunging behind some tall shrubs and swung from the saddle to hold the grey's nostrils.

Scant seconds later a dozen or more mounted men rode through the gates. The husky individual in the lead drew rein, and as they gathered around him proceeded to bark out commands. A young man, a groom by the look of him, appeared to venture a suggestion. The leader's voice rose to an irritated roar, cutting off the youth's remarks. He waved his arms imperatively and there were no more comments.

Between the low-crowned hat and the muffling scarf Adair glimpsed bushy red eyebrows. This harsh-voiced gentleman must be the father of Rufus and Alice Prior. He was clearly leading a search party. The stern-faced men separated into small groups and rode off in varying directions, the youth who had spoken trailing along dejectedly.

There could be no doubting whence had come young Prior's hot temper, yet Alice was such a gentle, shy little creature. Miss Cecily Hall seemed cast in the same mold as her uncle. To think of her made Adair squirm. He could have saved the search party considerable time by directing them to the cottage. On the other hand, Mr. Prior was more likely to shoot him than to listen. Besides, this was an undreamt-of opportunity and he dared not waste it. He watched until the searchers were out of sight, then turned Toreador onto the Singletree drivepath.

The maid who answered the prolonged clamour of the doorbell was very young and pale, and clearly frightened. Pushing past her, Adair demanded authoritatively to see Mr. Alfred Prior.

"Master be—be out, sir," she faltered.

"What—at this hour?" He turned on her and warned, "See here, my girl, I am Major Newton. Lord Holland has sent me down from London on a most urgent errand. Do not dare tell me untruths, or you are like to end in prison!"

She half-sobbed an insistence that she was telling the purest truth and went on to explain that there was some of the family lost in last night's storm, and all the men out seeking them. Tears came into her eyes and she looked so pathetic it was all Adair could do to preserve his fierce pose. He next demanded the housekeeper, but (much to his relief) that lady had gone to visit her ailing mother the previous day and was likely not able to get back "on account of all the snow, sir."

In apparent exasperation, he snapped, "Then summon whoever *is* in charge here! I'm commanded to search this house from attic to cellars, and I must have help!"

Her jaw dropped. "Search . . . the house, sir? Whatever for?"

"Whitehall has reason to suspect that a foreign spy has abducted Miss Prior. I am ordered to make sure she is not hidden somewhere on these premises." Ignoring the maid's screech of fright, he went on, "If you're the only person here, then you must assist me. If there are secret passages or priest's holes, you had best tell me if you wish to avoid prosecution for aiding a traitor."

The poor girl looked ready to faint. She gulped that she'd never heard of any secret rooms in the house. There was the fire-boy she could call though he wasn't of much account; still, she'd be only too glad to do anything that would help the Major.

"You can tell him to first take my horse to the stables," said Adair. "But I don't want him unsaddled. I cannot waste too much time here."

He was obeyed; the fire-boy soon joined them in the attic and twenty minutes later Adair had rushed them through most of the upstairs rooms. Unpleasantly aware of the need for urgency, he had no need to feign impatience.

The fire-boy cooperated enthusiastically. He was a stocky

lad not yet in his teens, with untidy black hair and a perpetual sniff. He was far more quick-witted than the maid and clearly regarded this opportunity to search the attics and bedchambers of his employer as a fine lark. He corroborated the maid's statement that Miss Alice was nowhere in the house, and that she had vanished in the middle of a rainy night soon after she was brought home from London Town.

"I suppose you saw the lady slip out, eh?" jeered Adair.

The boy flushed. "I never did," he said pugnaciously. "But I got ears, ain't I?"

"Which will be boxed if you take that tone with me!" Adair thumped the wall experimentally. "Do you say you heard the lady leave?"

"Ar, sir," said the boy, backing away from this fierce soldier and keeping a watchful eye on him. "I heered a coach, I did. And a gent talking soft. And it weren't none of our lot. If y'please, sir."

"Oh, you *wicked* boy," exclaimed the maid, opening the door to a small dressing room. "You never told the master that! How could you have heard a coach when you sleep down in the cellar?"

"P'raps I weren't in the cellar," he said with defiance. "P'raps I'd crep' into the pantry and found a left-over chicken wing an' a jam tart goin' to waste. An' p'raps that there coach come to the tradesmen's entrance, *not* the front door. Wot then, Millie Bell? Think you knows so much! Hah!"

"I knows enough to know what the master will say when he finds out you didn't say nought about that there coach!"

The fire-boy looked scared momentarily, then retaliated that if Millie Bell "bubbled" on him, he'd say she was in the kitchen stealing food with him.

This terrible threat drew a squeal from the maid and a command from Adair that they stop arguing and search the last bedchamber. It was a fruitless effort, but Adair was cheered by the conviction that this disappointing search was not a complete loss.

En route to the stairs, he asked, "And did you recognize this gentleman's voice, lad?"

The boy shook his head. "But I know who it was."

Adair jerked him to a halt. "Devil you do! Who, then?"

"Why, that there Colonel they was goin' to hang, a' course."

"Like what they should've," said the maid.

Adair frowned. "And you've not seen Miss Alice since that night?"

"No more has no one else." The maid sighed. "Such a sweet-natured young lady, she were. Her poor brother is quite aside of hisself. How could any man be so wicked?"

Downstairs, Adair rushed them through the servants' quarters, kitchen, pantry, breakfast and dining rooms, a small study, a morning room and a large drawing room, none of which gave up any hint of the missing girl, a secret room, or a priest's hole. They were emerging from the drawing room and turning towards the cellar steps when an irked female voice demanded, "And what may you be about, dare I ask?"

The newcomer was a large woman with the unmistakable air of a long-time retainer. Her neat but plainly cut garments and the black bonnet with the severely curtailed poke told Adair that she was Mr. Prior's housekeeper. He introduced himself as Major Newton, and added with smooth courtesy, "Are you by chance Mrs. Prior, ma'am?"

The maid giggled and put a quickly concealing hand over her mouth. The fire-boy grinned broadly, but the housekeeper, clearly flattered, introduced herself as Mrs. Heath, and accepted Adair's brief explanation of his activities without question. It was, she declared, a terrible tragedy that had come down upon the Prior family. She shook her head solemnly. "A judgment, to my mind."

Adair told her he must now search the cellars and asked about possible secret rooms or such contrivances. Mrs. Heath said she had been with the family in one capacity or another since her twelfth year. "If there was any such things in this house, Major, you may rest assured I would know of 'em. The master trusts me implicitly—and with good reason. And the butler, who retired just two years since, was a very talkative old gentleman and told me plenty." She tucked in her chin and nodded portentously. "I asked him once if we had a priest's hole or secret entrances, and he said the only secret things here was to do with the family, not the house!"

Opening the cellar door, Adair asked, "Is that what you meant by 'judgments,' ma'am?"

She glanced behind her, walked with him to the top of the downward flight of steps, and half-whispered, "There's *things* goes on in this house, sir, what is—not *respectable*! If it weren't that I'm so fond of poor little Miss Alice—may she rest in peace, and her brother, Mr. Rufus—who is proper heart-broke, I'd have packed my bags long since, that I would! There is *strong spirits* served here, and too often, I say! And the *gambling* when there's guests come! Even the ladies wagering, sir! Dreadful!"

Adair had encountered her type before: people so devout that they saw "sin" everywhere. He thanked the pious lady for her confidences, assured her they would not be repeated, and said that he would have to question the Priors' coachman, although he believed the people from Bow Street had already done so. "A James—um—be dashed if I can recall! James . . . Grove—is it?"

Mrs. Heath shook her head. The Major, she said, must be thinking of another person. "Our coachman was Walter Davis, sir."

"Was?"

"Then, he was. And what with all the upset and uproar, Mr. Prior has not got round to taking on a new man. Not but what I expect the head groom will get the position. Undeserving as *that* one may be!"

So it was true that the coachman had left the Singletree estate. Adair persisted sharply, "I refer to the man who drove Miss Alice Prior home from the ball. Is he no longer employed here?"

"No, sir. Proper uppity he became after the sad doings. He

was called to testify at that wicked Colonel Adair's trial, and the day after he came back he ups and says as he don't care to work in a house where such things go on, and he packs up his carpet-bag and off he goes without giving one day's notice! The impudence of it I can scarce believe, and where he expects to find another situation, with the master roaring that he won't give him a good character, I cannot imagine."

"Impudence, indeed," agreed Adair. "It is imperative that I question him. Where may he be found, Mrs. Heath?"

"Now that I could not say, Major, no more I could when the Runners come from Bow Street. If he had family, he never spoke of them. Could have sailed off to the Americas, for all we know!"

Chilled by that possibility, Adair persisted, "He must have come from somewhere. What was his previous situation?"

"He was a groom at the estate of a very wealthy gentleman— a Mr. Rickett. I don't know whereabouts, but when his old gentleman went to his reward, Davis came to Singletree. That were nigh ten years since."

"You have a most remarkable memory, ma'am. I don't suppose you know if this Mr. Rickett left an heir?"

"I know as he didn't, Major. He had never married."

Frustrated though he was, Adair smiled at her so admiringly that the good housekeeper blushed and admitted with a girlish giggle that she wouldn't have known all this save that she was present when the men from Bow Street had questioned Mr. Prior.

A bell rang somewhere.

Adair tensed, and Mrs. Heath moaned that she did pray it was not more of "those horrid busybodies from the newspapers!" Murmuring excuses, she hurried away.

Adair prepared to make a dash for freedom. He heard no loud voices or hurrying footsteps, however, and disregarding the fact that he was cutting things very fine, he cut them finer and ran down the cellar stairs. Just this one last area, and he could be sure that Alice Prior was not being hidden here from a censorious world.

The cellars ran the length of the house and were more cluttered than any he'd ever encountered. He rummaged about amongst old trunks, discarded pieces of furniture, handle-less saucepans, dressmakers' figures, boxes of outmoded shoes and the like, with no success. There were several half-windows so that the area was not completely dark, but if there was a concealed room or a trapdoor, he was unable to detect either. His spirits lifted when he saw a tall screen blocking off a far corner of the room. Starting towards it eagerly, he heard a sound behind him, and whirled around.

A tall shape hove up against the light and a male voice demanded irately, "What the devil are you doing down here?"

5

onfound you, Toby!" gasped Adair. "You near gave me a heart seizure! What would you think I'm doing, but searching this house? And how the deuce do you come to be here?"

Broderick replied airily, "Thought you might need a helping hand. I knew you'd be reckless enough to prance down here in spite of all my good advice. And what have you to show for it—beside that nasty welt on your face?"

Adair flushed. "Thorne Webber decided to play the defender of virtue, but this was before I left Town."

"Much Webber knows of virtue! So what must you do next but rush in where angels fear to tread, and clump about like a bull in a china shop!" He kicked a lampshade from his path, then swore as his boot went through the rotted silk and he was obliged to tear the offending article away. "Gad! What a collection of rubbish!"

Adair grinned. "Speaking of bulls in china shops . . ."

"If that's all the thanks I get . . . !"

"No, it isn't, of course. I'm truly grateful for your help, Toby. Especially that you would be so noble as to arrive at this hour of the morning. You surely didn't drive straight from Town?"

"I reached Tenterden late yesterday in the middle of that miserable blizzard. I was dashed sure you were lurking about the vicinity, but there was no searching for you then, so I rented a room at the Woolpack and—"

"At the—what?" asked Adair, edging behind the screen.

"The Woolpack. An inn. Splendid old hostelry. It's fifteenth century. I'd think you would have heard of it. The whole town is full of history. Legend has it that the tower of Saint Mildred's Church is so high it broke the Goodwin Sands." Broderick took up a small box and examined it curiously.

Adair called, "How on earth could a church steeple cause the break in the Sands?"

"Eh? Oh, well, some abbott or other commandeered the stones that were supposed to be used to repair the sea-wall, and used them to build the church tower." He shook the box in his hand. "This is an interesting little piece, Hasty, and full of— something, if I could just get the lid off . . . which I curst well cannot seem—by Jove! That's a jolly fine screen you found. I wonder if the old boy would let me buy it."

Adair emerged from behind the screen and said sharply, "You've met Mr. Prior?"

Still admiring the screen, Broderick replied, "From a distance, perhaps. I saw some men rushing about hither and yon, and a big fellow took off his hat and waved it at me. Demanded to know if I'd seen two ladies and a young fellow, who seem to have got themselves lost. I shouted that I hadn't and before I could finish, off they went. Rather rude old duck, but one glance at his fiery nob and I guessed who he must be. So I thought I'd best nip along here in case you'd—er, *carpe diemed* as it were, whilst they were absent."

Adair sighed. "That's all I seized, unfortunately. And now my 'moment' is gone and it's past time for us to leave."

They started towards the steps, picking their way over the debris.

"No sign of your quarry, I take it?" asked Broderick sympathetically.

"None. Miss Prior's not in this house. Not at present, anyway. I'm sure of it."

"Hmm. Mrs. Heath was right then."

"I wonder she let you in. You didn't enquire for me by my real name, surely?"

"D'you take me for a flat? Told her I was to meet a military friend here. Fast thinking, what? She piped up with "You must mean Major Newton?" So I agreed, just in case you were using an alias, and she said you were down here. Wish I could open this little box. No telling what might be inside. . . . Nice woman, Mrs. Heath. And brews a rather good cup of coffee. In fact—"

Starting up the steps, Adair said, "Coffee?"

"Yes. The lady asked if I'd breakfasted, which of course I hadn't. So she kindly brought me coffee and a muffin, and showed me around a bit. There's a portrait of your friend Miss Alice in the drawing room, did you notice?" He halted, saying dreamily, "I vow I never saw a sweeter face. Does she really look like—"

Exasperated, Adair seized him by the arm and dragged him up the stairs at speed. "Chawbacon! Prior and his crew may stroll in here at any minute! Come *on!*"

Fortunately, there was no sign of Mr. Alfred Prior or his party when the two men reached the upper corridor, but Mrs. Heath came bustling to offer refreshments, saying she was sure the master would wish them to await his return. Adair managed to refuse her offer without offending the kindly woman, claiming he must report at once to Lord Holland. He risked taking the time to ask if she had any idea of the location of the vanished coachman's previous employment, but she could not recall and again suggested he wait and talk to Mr. Alfred Prior, who might be able to help. Having a very fair idea of the help that would come to him from Mr. Prior, Adair said it was not of great importance and they went in search of Broderick, who had wandered off. He was discovered in the drawing room, gazing raptly at Alice Prior's portrait. Adair apologized to the amused housekeeper and dragged him away.

65

Outside, the sun was pale but bright and the temperature had risen markedly. Large patches of green were breaking through the white blanket on the lawns, and clumps of snow dropped with soft squelching sounds from the trees. They waited on the terrace for their horses to be brought round and Adair muttered, "If ever I saw a man so captivated!"

Broderick reddened. "Miss Prior has a dashed sweet face."

"Oh, I agree. But if you must fall in love with a portrait, friend, I'd advise that you choose another! We don't even know if the poor lady yet lives!"

The stable-boy came running with their mounts. There was still no sign of the search party and as they rode out, Broderick said a relieved "I think we squeaked through that action fairly. What next? Back to Town?"

"No." Adair turned aside into the concealment offered by a dense grove of sycamores. "You can do me a great service, if you will, Toby. I seem to have lost my emerald pin."

"Oh, bad luck! Not that beauty your sire gave you?"

"My Grandfather, actually. I'm fairly sure it fell while I was at Rufus Prior's cottage, and—"

"Hold up! You were—*where*? What's all this?"

Adair offered a considerably edited version of his encounter with Miss Cecily Hall and company. He knew Broderick was staring at him, and finished hurriedly, "I tried to search about, but it was dark and if my pin was there, it was probably covered by the snow. I can't venture back there, but you might be able to. I'd be everlastingly grateful."

"So I should think! Cavorting about all night in lonely cottages with young spinsters—"

"And her cousin and grandmama!"

"—And trying to slither by with not a word to me! If ever I heard of such naughty conduct—if I've heard the whole, which I doubt!"

"You know very well I'm a black-hearted villain. What would you expect?"

"I'd expect you to have realized you've now added two more

ladies to your Victim List, and that you'd have run like hell back to Town."

"In which case I'd never have been able to search Singletree, would I? Still, you're perfectly right. I mustn't involve you in my troubles, so—"

"No you don't! You promised me your gratitude, which I will hold over you forever, you realize. While I'm earning it, what shall you be doing, dare I ask?"

Adair replied that he must go into Tenterden at once, and cut off Broderick's further questions by giving him directions to the cottage. Not waiting for a response, he sent Toreador cantering off.

"Hey!" howled Broderick.

Adair waved, called his thanks and urged Toreador to a gallop, too ashamed to admit to his friend that he had deserted a damaged young lady shamefully, and must now find a doctor to attend her.

* * *

Tenterden was a pretty sight on this brilliant winter morning, the roofs of its tile-hung Tudor cottages and red brick Georgian houses still wearing snow's white mantle. The High Street of the old market town was bustling. It was unlikely that he would be recognized here, but Adair reined Toreador to a sedate walk to avoid drawing attention to himself.

A chimney-sweep, already covered with the fruits of his labours, hurried from an alley and his long brushes missed Adair by a whisper. Toreador shied, Adair swore, and the sweep jumped back, causing a well-dressed matron to emit a piercing shriek and warn her two children against touching "the dirty man."

The sweep grinned cheerfully and apologized "to all concerned."

The matron sniffed and turned her ire on Adair, exclaiming indignantly on the evils of sullying the ears of innocence with strong language.

Several passers-by halted and watched in amusement.

'So much,' thought Adair, 'for not attracting attention!' He bowed and tendered his own humble apology, and with a fierce "Hah!" the lady led her small innocents away.

The two criminals exchanged wry grins. Leaning from the saddle, Adair reached down. "I stand in need of some luck," he said, as they shook hands. "And information."

The sweep was only too willing to oblige. He was not a local resident, he admitted, but often plied his trade here, and thus was able to direct Adair to the house of the apothecary. His reward caused him to declare that he could "allus tell a true blue gent" and they parted, each well satisfied with the other.

The apothecary dwelt in a sizeable house located at the north edge of the town. A gig was drawn up outside, a liveried coachman waiting beside it. Adair tied Toreador's reins to the picket fence and walked up the path. As he approached, the front door opened and a short grey-haired man ushered a very large lady onto the steps.

Adair stood aside politely.

The lady's voice was far from feeble, and she apparently felt that her complaints should be communicated to everyone within earshot. She was evidently of some consequence, for her maid clung to one arm and murmured comfortingly, while the apothecary supported her other arm and agreed with her every wail. Despite the litany of ills she recited, her eyes flickered over Adair with appreciation and she slowed her steps, gazing at him pleadingly. He bowed, but it was very clear that one word of sympathy would draw him into a discussion of her woes, and he did not speak. She sighed, but went on her way in full cry and at a pace that caused Adair to grit his teeth. To ease his frustration he turned away from the noisy trio and went into the house. He entered a large and immaculate waiting room. None of the chairs ranged around the walls was occupied, which was a relief, but as the minutes passed, his impatience mounted. He stalked over to the window and was glancing out when the apothecary hurried inside, closing the front door behind him.

"Well now, sir," he said, rubbing his hands briskly. "I regret having delayed you, but—"

"I can delay no longer," said Adair. "A lady has been hurt, and you must go to her at once."

"Go—where?" said the apothecary, his smile fading. "What lady?"

"I believe her name is Miss Hall, and—"

"By Jupiter, sir! Miss Cecily hurt, is she? Well, I don't wonder, the way she rides! If I've told her once, I've told her a hundred times—"

"You may tell her again. The sooner the better," urged Adair.

"Yes, yes. Well, don't fly into a pucker. Not a case of life and death, I trust?"

"Probably not, but I'm not familiar with the neighbourhood and it took time for me to find you. The lady suffered a nasty cut and has had a long wait."

"Well, I shall go with you, but first I must get my bag, and my hat and coat." He rummaged about in a cupboard, moving aside various coats and searching among a collection of hats and umbrellas. "Dreadful cold snap we've had, eh?" He wound a thick scarf about his throat and put on a hat which he promptly tossed aside. "Now instead of scowling at me, young man, tell me where we are to go. Is Miss Hall at Singletree?" Another hat was tried on and discarded. "This won't do. I must not take cold, else—"

"*Will* you hasten?" growled Adair. "The lady is at a cottage, I believe owned by Mr. Rufus Prior. You know the way, I expect? I must be off."

The apothecary leapt back from the cupboard. "What d'ye mean, you must be off? You brought your coach for me, I presume?"

"No, I did not bring my coach! I am a passer-by merely, and promised to send help. Heavens above, man! That hat looks very well."

"The brim is bent," argued the apothecary, peering at himself in a small wall mirror.

Seething, Adair snarled, "You're not going to a Carlton House ball! *Hurry up!*"

"You are rude, sir." The apothecary put his hands on his hips and said with an injured air, "I do not scruple to tell you so! If you expect me to walk to Rufus Prior's cottage, sir, you had best—"

"Good Lord above! Find yourself a hat, and I'll go and pole up your hack to your gig, or cart, or whatever you jaunter about in!" Striding to the door, Adair wrenched it open.

Two shrieks and an oath rent the air.

Rufus Prior, one arm about Miss Hall, had taken hold of the door handle and was jerked inside, Miss Hall being pulled in willy-nilly.

"You!" Abandoning his charge, Prior jumped at Adair, his fists flying.

From the corner of his eye, Adair saw the girl more or less flung into the nearest chair. He also saw that she looked pale, which troubled him. This was no time to reason with young Prior. He sidestepped the hothead's whizzing fist, decked him neatly, and turned to bend over Miss Hall.

"I am most dreadfully sorry," he began, scanning her anxiously.

"Monster!" shrieked Lady Abigail, coming up to flail her reticule at his back. "You stole our horses! You are a very bad man!"

"No, but I left you a note and they were where your grandson could find them easily enough," said Adair, fending her off as best he might. "I'd not have done it save that I simply had to have an uninterrupted hour or so in which to—"

"To do—what? Knock my cousin down again?" said Cecily Hall with disgust.

"Brute!" screamed Lady Abigail. "Bullying ruffian!"

"Ow!" said Adair as her small fist connected squarely with his ear. "If you will have done, ma'am, I'll—"

She kicked him hard, and losing patience, he picked her up and tucked her under his arm.

"Don't hurt her! Oh, don't hurt her!" cried Miss Hall, coming to her feet.

"He's not hurting me, dear," said Lady Abigail, suspended, but ceasing to make swimming movements.

"You're the one who is hurt, Miss Cecily," said Adair, thinking that she was even more beautiful than he remembered. "I've been trying to get this idiot to come and help you, but—"

"But this 'idjut' is just about to blow your head off!" The apothecary, who had left the scene, now returned aiming a bell-mouthed blunderbuss at Adair. "Coming into my surgery with your hoity-toity airs! Throwing my clients about! Unhand Lady Abigail this minute! If ever I heard of such a thing!"

Her ladyship said shrilly, "Put that hideous weapon down at once, Jedidiah Bright! Miss Cecily and I are in the line of fire, you fool!"

"Gad!" muttered Adair, setting her down hurriedly and stepping aside.

"Now I gotcha!" said Apothecary Bright with a triumphant grin.

"Nonsense," said Lady Abigail, her cheeks rather pink as she straightened her garments. "There is no need for gunfire."

"You never wants me to let him go, marm?" asked the apothecary, bewildered. "He's liable to do for the lot of us!"

"Stop being so ridiculous and tend to Miss Hall." Ignoring the wavering blunderbuss, Adair crossed to bend over Rufus Prior, who was beginning to sit up, holding his jaw and muttering to himself.

"If someone will help Miss Hall into my surgery, I'll be only too glad to tend to her." The apothecary marched into an adjoining room, calling over his shoulder, "Nor I don't need to be ordered about by ill-tempered strangers what has no appreciation of the importance of a gentleman's hat!"

Adair reached down a hand. "Come on, Prior. Your cousin needs your help."

Miss Hall gave him a caustic look. "You are all consideration, Colonel."

Prior blinked at him stupidly.

Her ladyship said, "You're to blame for all this, Adair. You carry her."

"I would sooner *crawl* than have him touch me," declared Miss Hall with loathing.

"Well, I cannot carry you, child," pointed out Lady Abigail reasonably. "And Rufus is—indisposed. Come along, Colonel." She looked at him with an unexpected gleam in her eyes. "You've mauled two of us today, might as well try for a *trois*."

"*No*, I tell you," cried Miss Hall, coming shakily to her feet.

"Oh, be still," said Adair, and with a deft and sudden movement had her in his arms. He caught a breath of a fresh sweet scent, then saw her boot fly out. Tightening his grip on her distinctly feminine form, he said sternly, "One kick, madam, and I might very well drop you, which would do that arm no good!"

The neat boot hesitated, then was lowered.

"That's a good girl," said her grandmother. "He is very strong, as you see."

Adair followed Apothecary Bright into the surgery and lowered his burden very gently onto an examination table. Miss Hall lay and glared at him. The apothecary went off muttering about getting some hot water. Adair said, "You'll want your grandmama here, Miss Hall. I'll leave you now."

"No, you don't," said Lady Abigail, taking hold of his cloak. "I had thought you would have left at dawn, sir. You must know our menfolk are searching for us. Why did you stay in the area?"

"So as to search your house, ma'am."

"Search Singletree?" exclaimed Miss Hall, taken aback. "Of all the brazen effrontery! I'll wager you got short shrift from my uncle!"

Lady Abigail said in an odd voice, "I cannot think you will still claim you were seeking poor Alice."

"Believe it, ma'am. I was sure you had her hidden there."

"Rubbish," said Cecily. "Of all people, *you* know Alice is not at her home."

"I know it now." Adair detached her ladyship's clutch from

his cloak, and on an impulse pressed a kiss on her small gloved hand. "But I'll find her and clear my name however you may try to stop me."

He was gone, the swirl of his cloak and the jingle of spurs followed by a shout of protest from Rufus, and the rapid pound of hooves on the lane.

Lady Abigail looked after him thoughtfully. "Now, I wonder why he would take so desperate a risk as to show his face at Singletree if he really has my sweet little Alice hidden away somewhere." She turned to the apothecary, who came back into the room carrying a steaming bowl. "Why was he here, Bright?"

"He said as how Miss Cecily had been hurt, marm, and sorry I was to hear it. But there was no cause for him to order me about the way he did." The apothecary opened several drawers and investigated the contents apparently without success. "Now I've mislaid my scissors, drat it!" he muttered, and went out again.

Lady Abigail said musingly, "So Adair took another risk—and for your sake, child."

"Better late than never!"

"True. But it was chancy. He must know that if your uncle had confronted him, he'd very likely have been shot."

"What a very great pity Uncle Alfred missed his chance," said Cecily in a fretful voice.

"But you will admit, my love, that it is strange."

"I think it a deal more strange that you would give such a rogue the benefit of the doubt, Grandmama!"

Lady Abigail hurried to bend and kiss her. "That arm is paining you, and you are worn out, my poor lamb. But—I know men, Cecily. The Colonel may be a rascal, but he is a charming rascal, and—"

"And you rather enjoyed being swept up and held so ruthlessly, did you not, ma'am?"

"Now you are being saucy." Lady Abigail added rather wistfully, "He was really very gentle with me."

"And kissed your hand with such an air, no?"

"Don't sneer, my pet. It may be that he is indeed a calculating and conscienceless libertine. But—how dreadful it would be if he really is not the villain who has taken our dear Alice. He is quite ruined, you know, and I think—"

Apothecary Bright returned at that point, followed by Rufus Prior, who looked sheepish and untidy.

Cecily whispered, "And *I* think you are a naughty flirt, Grandmama!"

The snow was almost gone now, but Broderick's search around the cottage had yielded no sign of Adair's emerald pin. "Well, I tried, old boy," he murmured, poking about the roots of a rose-bush.

A hard jab in his back told him he had been overheard. He turned quickly and came nose-to-muzzle with a hunting rifle aimed by a ferocious-looking gentleman with bristling red eyebrows. "I say now," protested Broderick. "No need for hostilities, sir! I'm only looking—"

"What you are is trespassing," growled the ferocious gentleman. "Who in the devil are you? And what are you looking at on my son's property?"

There were six of them. Not fighting men, but well able to make things uncomfortable for him; noting which, Broderick said with his engaging smile, "Ah, then you will be Mr. Alfred Prior. I've heard of you, sir, and—"

"All England has heard of me since my child was stolen," snapped Prior. "Why are you lurking about? If I thought you were involved in the business—"

"Not lurking, sir," said Broderick earnestly. "Looking. At the birds, sir."

Grins were exchanged by the members of the search party.

Prior said incredulously, "Looking—at the birds? Are you daft, man?"

"I am a Professor of Ornithology," lied Broderick. "I am birdwatching, Mr. Prior. I'm dashed certain that is a fieldfare. Do you see the little chap in that tree?"

"He were lookin' down—not up, sir," offered one of the men, with what Broderick judged a vindictive smirk.

"Just so. Thought I saw an egg. I know that sounds unlikely, at this time of the year, but the entire business is unlikely. That a pair of fieldfares should be here all alone, I mean. They usually travel in flocks, you see. Large flocks, which are very talkative. Shy little brutes around people, though, and why—"

"Why should I believe one word of that gibberish?" demanded Mr. Prior. "What's more, you don't look like a professor to me. Where are your notebooks, or your glass?"

"At my home. In Oxford. I did not come here to look for fieldfares, I do assure you, but when I spotted the little fellow, I was bound to—"

Prior's expression was extremely ominous and Broderick said hurriedly, "Actually, I had a theory about—about your daughter, sir. It occurred to me, you see, that if Colonel Adair spoke the truth and he did not abduct the lady, she might be still in the . . ." He began to back away uneasily. ". . . in the vicinity, or—or there might be some—er, sign . . . as it were."

"What it is—you're one of those triple-curst busybody newspaper writers," roared Mr. Prior, swinging up the rifle, which had sagged during this exchange. "Get him, men!"

Relying heavily on the unlikelihood that even so belligerent an individual would actually shoot a newspaper writer, Tobias Broderick took to his heels and ran like a deer. Coming in sight of his big bay horse, he could hear hoofbeats close behind him and he vaulted into the saddle. Quadrille had been named for what Broderick termed "his many fancy steps," but his caperings were the product of temper rather than grace. To be sprung upon irked him so that he went into a spin, a buck, and several savage kicks. Luckily, his antics alarmed the mounts of Mr. Prior's retainers, and once he started to run, there was no coming up with him.

As the uproar faded behind him, Broderick bowed low in the saddle, muttering bitterly about heartless rascals who sent their friends into harm's way while they themselves lounged about Tenterden probably enjoying a satisfying breakfast.

When he reached the White Ram Inn, he lost no time in conveying these sentiments to Adair, whom he found at the desk, settling his account. "Since you almost caused me to be murdered," he declared, "you owe me at the very least a hearty breakfast."

The prospect appealed to Adair, but he proposed that they put some distance between themselves and Mr. Alfred Prior before satisfying their hunger.

They delayed only to collect Broderick's valise from the Woolpack before heading back towards London. Their progress was annoyingly slow, for snow still lingered on some of the country lanes, and to Broderick's chagrin they did not come upon another inn and were frequently obliged to detour, being halted at length by a large beech tree that had fallen across the road. A countryman with a cart drawn up and two small boys helping him was sawing branches for firewood. He was a cheerful individual and gladly imparted the information that there was a fine inn not more than a mile to the west. "Best cook in these parts, gents," he said, "even if the owner be a foreign lady."

"I don't care if she can only speak Chinese," said Broderick, reining Quadrille around the obstruction. "Just so as she knows what to do with an egg!"

They had no trouble locating the Castle and Keg, and found it to be a charming old whitewashed structure that sparkled with cleanliness. An ostler hurried to take their horses, and they were welcomed into the inn by the proprietor, a plump little lady with keen black eyes and a Welsh accent. Mrs. Rhys showed them into a cozy coffee room and a table set before the hearth where a fire blazed fragrantly. They were soon enjoying a breakfast that Broderick declared gratefully was "fit for a King!" While they ate he gave Adair an account of his introduction to Mr. Prior, and expressed his regret that he'd been unable to find the emerald pin. "This whole journey has been a lost cause for you, Hasty. Better luck next time, eh?"

"I don't count it a complete loss," said Adair. "The fire-boy at Singletree claimed that in the middle of the night that Miss Prior disappeared, he heard a coach pull up to the side door, and a gentleman speaking softly."

"Did he, by Jove! Don't recall hearing of that before, but I don't see how it can help you—unless the boy recognized the fellow's voice."

"It wasn't brought out at the trial, but it could certainly help if it could be proven that the coach carried Miss Prior off, and that it happened whilst I was in a cell in Whitehall."

"By Jupiter, but that's truth! We must get word to the Horse Guards at once! Is that where we're bound?"

"It's where I'm hoping you'll go for me. I want to see if I can find out where Mr. Prior's coachman has got to. Evidently he used to work for a gentleman—now dead—named Rickett."

"If the old boy's stuck his spoon in the wall, you're not likely to learn anything from him. Unless there's family living there."

"According to your friend, Mrs. Heath, Rickett had no family. Still, there may be friends or long-time servants still in the area who could give me some information on the vanishing coachman. Worth a try, Toby."

"Might be, at that. Where did this Rickett fellow live?"

"That's the first thing I have to find out. Shouldn't be too difficult, though."

Broderick agreed blithely that it should be a simple task, and kept to himself the reflection that the late Mr. Rickett might have lived anywhere from Land's End to John o'Groats.

6

Before leaving the Castle and Keg, Adair asked Mrs. Rhys if she knew of a deceased gentleman named Rickett, or his erstwhile coachman, Walter Davis. The little widow eyed him curiously. "I do not know a Rickett. There was a fellow named Davis who worked at a nearby estate called Singletree, but I cannot think he would be a friend of yours, sir."

"The thing is," he evaded, "I was sent down from London to tell him he has come into a small inheritance, but he appears to have left Singletree without giving notice and told no one where he was bound. So far, I've been quite unable to trace him."

"Ah. Well, I cannot say I am surprised." She pursed her lips. "Cantankerous, I always thought he were. Used to come into my tap sometimes on his day off and often as not would end up quarrelling with my regulars. You'll be one of them solicitors, eh, sir? Which puts me in the wrong, for I'd have taken yourself for a military gentleman."

"Actually, my brother is in the legal profession," said Adair, not altogether untruthfully. "Since I was coming this way, he charged me to find Davis for him."

"And ye don't want to disappoint him, naturally, being family.

Surely, I wish as I could help ye, sir. But . . . Wait a bit! Here's my head ostler. He used to throw darts with Davis. Frank! Come and see if you can help this gentleman!"

The ostler was a slow-talking, amiable sort of man who had expressed a great admiration for Toreador. He allowed that he knew Walter Davis, adding a qualifying, "Not well, mind." And in response to Adair's questions said that from something Davis had once told him, he'd supposed the man had previously worked near a big school. "I asked him, joking-like, if he put his money down to go to any of they lecturings, and he laughed fit to bust and said when he put his money down it were at the races."

Adair's heart gave a leap. A "big school" and "the races" could mean Cambridge and Newmarket. "Jove, but that's a great help," he said, and having rewarded Frank generously, was soon in the saddle again, and riding to the northeast with hope as his companion.

Three days later, hope had almost died. He had not dared pursue his enquiries with the Watch or the local Constable, and the several vicars and curates he'd approached had been willing but unable to provide the information he sought. For a whole day he haunted the area around the Jockey Club; there were no meetings at this time of year, of course, but the various "coffee rooms" were almost always patronized by a few sportsmen, owners, professional jockeys, or stewards. Mingling with these devotees of the sport proved unproductive, although Toreador attracted much interest and Adair received and rejected three offers to buy the animal. He turned his attention to the patrons of taverns and alehouses, but although his generosity in replenishing tankards won him popularity and offers of assistance, he learned no more of the whereabouts of the Rickett estate, or Walter Davis.

Disheartened, he was preparing to return to London one chilly morning when a maid brought word that he was wanted downstairs. He had registered at this small inn as Mr. Chatteris and spread his enquiries under that name. Twice in these few days he'd had the sense that he was being watched. On neither occasion had he seen anyone following, but if he had been recognized there could be trouble. Therefore, he went down by the back stairs, alert and poised for action.

The proprietor was alone at the desk. A gaunt and taciturn man, he said, "Outside, sir. Waiting in the stables."

Adair eyed him keenly. He was no more truculent than usual, nor was the contempt evident that might be expected if he knew his guest was "a notorious libertine."

"Who is?" he asked. "And what does he want of me?"

"Old Bill Oxshott. And whatever he wants will lighten your purse if you don't take care, sir. He's likely heard about the questions you been asking and the tankards you've kept filled. Slippery as a snake is Old Bill and nowhere near as honest. I don't usually allow him on my property, but he were insistent as he knowed something you'd want to hear."

Adair thanked him for this less than glowing recommendation and made his way to the stables.

A small, wizened individual, well past middle age, was talking to Toreador, who watched him warily over the rail of his stall. As Adair approached, the man gave a sudden shrill cackle of laughter, and the big grey tossed his head and drew back.

Adair drew back also. That this person seldom if ever bathed was very evident. He said coolly, "I believe you wished to see me."

The little man spun around, disclosing a sunken and weathered face sadly in need of a shave. Narrowed dark eyes scanned Adair in a brief appraisal. Snatching off a greasy cap, he smoothed back long wisps of grey hair and said in a shrill whine, "By grab, but you give me a fright, guv'nor. And me, with a poor old heart as don't need no frights. Crep' up on me unawares, you done, sir. Not as I mean ter say you *meant* to fright poor Bill Oxshott into his grave." He cackled again and bent his head a little, leering up at the younger man's enigmatic face ingratiatingly. "Ye'll be the gent as is asking everywhere fer me good friend—Wally Davis. That right, sir? Or has poor old Bill got it wrong agin?"

"I have business with a man who was coachman for Mr. Rickett a decade or so ago."

Adair's tone was chill but the sly leer did not waver. "Ar, well that'll be me friend Wally, right enough." He sniffed noisily and wiped his nose on the back of his hand. "If ye'll tell me what it is you wants to know, sir, I'll search me memory. Though poor old Bill's brain-box finds it hard these days—downright painful at times, sir—to rec'lect things. Likely from not never having the rhino to buy proper nourishin' food, sir. Like—say, a chop now and then."

"If you can recollect the directions to Mr. Rickett's estate, perhaps you'll be able to buy a beefsteak or two, but don't be looking for the whole cow, Oxshott. I'm not a rich man."

"Old Bill" howled with mirth. "Not many soldiers is rich men, eh, sir?"

Adair looked into those cunning eyes steadily, and Oxshott gabbled, "S'prised ye, did I, guv'nor? Old Bill can allus tell a soldier-man by the set o' the shoulders and the way their heads is carried. High, sir. High and proud. Like yourn. Now take me, on the other hand. Just a humble and simple cove is Oxshott, as ain't too proud to ask if ye could just stretch to—say, a 'leg o' lamb,' Mr.—er, Chatteris . . . ?"

He was a crafty old rogue, right enough, but Adair found himself wondering what chances fate had offered. Few enough, probably. He said in a kinder tone, "I think you're a great rascal, Mr. Bill Oxshott." And above the resultant cackle, he added, "But, depending upon what you have to tell me, a 'leg of lamb' it shall be."

Old Bill rubbed his grubby hands and became a regular mine of information. Adair was given precise directions to the hamlet near the Rickett estate, which was now the Haley estate. As for his dear friend, Wally Davis had never spoken of his family background. "But he had parents, sir! Oh, yus! He had parents.

And still living, for I see Wally not more'n a year back and he tells me he'd like to go down and see his old mum. Surprise her like, he says."

"Do you know where Mrs. Davis lives?"

"No, sir. Wish I did. Might've earned meself some sassengers, eh, sir?" This winning no offer of a "sausage bonus," Oxshott sighed and continued, "Still, if ye goes up round what used to be Mr. Rickett's house, there might be others knows more'n old Bill. Blest if ever I met a more contrary cove. Argify a donkey's hind leg orf will Wally, but one thing no one can't deny—he knows his cattle, and he brung old Rickett's hacks into the smithy often enough. The blacksmith will likely remember him."

A short while later, trotting alongside as Adair rode out, Oxshott called a friendly "Jest foller the Bedford Road to the blue barn like I said, sir, then turn onto the bridge. There's a tolerable good inn on the far side as sets a nice table if ye're so minded. The Pilgrim Arms, it's called, after some cove name of Bunyan, though what he done there I dunno."

Adair waved, and letting Toreador have his head, soon disappeared from sight.

Oxshott's smile also disappeared. For a moment something almost like regret came into his eyes. Then he shrugged. "A cove got to live," he advised a passing crow, and began to count out the sizeable tip he'd just earned.

A sharp wind came up while Adair was riding to the southwest, but he was too encouraged now to feel the chill on the air. He knew where to find the elusive Rickett estate at last. With luck, a little searching about would unearth someone who would remember Walter Davis. The blacksmith Oxshott had spoken of sounded a likely source. Things were looking decidedly brighter.

As they had a way of doing lately, his thoughts drifted to Miss Cecily Hall. No shrinking violet, that lady, but one couldn't deny she was a lovely creature. Recalling the fierce way she had levelled that pistol at him brought a grin. She'd courage enough, certainly, and deep loyalties. He wondered where she was at that moment, and whether her indomitable Grandmama was caring for her.

A gust of wind set the trees swaying as he passed the blue barn and turned onto the bridge. An inn nestled under a huge oak at the far side of the bridge, as Oxshott had said. Smoke drifted from the chimneys, to be whisked away by the wind, and a tantalizing smell of cooking wafted on the air. Adair glanced at his timepiece. It was nearing one o'clock, a good time for luncheon at the "tolerable good" Pilgrim Arms and a rest for Toreador.

When he rode into the yard an ostler ran to take charge of the dapple-grey, and the host, a small man with a large smile, greeted Adair at the door. He was conducted across a neat parlour to the adjoining coffee room and a table remarkable for its cleanliness. This being a week-day, he was mildly surprised to find the room well patronized and ringing with talk. The noise level diminished while he was seated and several heads turned his way. He ran his eyes over the gathering just in case, but saw no familiar faces. A serving maid gave him a dimpling smile and took his order and he was soon enjoying some excellent cold roast beef, thick bread still warm from the oven, and a tankard of ale.

He was finishing his meal when an all-too-familiar voice rang out loud and clear. "As I live and breathe! If it ain't the infamous Colonel!"

The buzz of talk in the room trailed into silence.

Adair took a deep breath, lowered his tankard deliberately, and stood.

Thorne Webber's swarthy countenance was slightly flushed, the hard brown eyes glinting triumph. As before, he held a heavy riding crop and was raising it threateningly. "Still carry the mark I put on you," he blustered. "If I give you another, you'll likely run away as you did last time, but—"

Adair crouched, his hand flashed out and caught Webber's up-flung arm. With a quick shift of weight he continued the motion. Instinctively resisting that relentless upward pressure, Webber uttered a howl and the riding crop fell from his numbed hand. "Damn you!" he snarled, clutching his arm painfully.

"Now, now, gents!" The little proprietor rushed to dance about between the two men. "Now, now! Outside, if ye must, but—"

"You've broke my arm, you worthless carrion!" bellowed Webber.

"Dislocated, more like," drawled Adair. "The penalty for missed opportunity. You should have hit me when I wasn't looking, as you did in Town."

"I'll hit you, all right! By God, but I will! Host! Get me a doctor! You'll meet me for this, Adair!"

"Gladly. But the challenge is mine. You struck first, and—"

"Did the gent say *Adair*?" A beefy individual wearing a lurid purple neckerchief shoved back his chair so that it fell with a crash. "Hi, mates! This here must be that wicked devil of a left'nant-colonel what's gorn and ruined poor Miss Prior! And very likely murdered the little lady!"

"And what oughta bin put a end to afore this!" cried a very dark youth with a narrow pallid face.

Three other rough-looking men who were seated at the same table sprang to their feet, shouting their approval of these sentiments.

"Now—now!" wailed the proprietor desperately. "Not in the house, mates! Outside, if—"

"Outside it is!" roared the owner of the neckerchief. "We don't want no dirty woman-killers comin' here. They might buy their way free in Lun'on Town—but not in these parts! Ho, no! Come on, lads! Let's show this here nob what good country folks do with kidnapping rapists!"

More men were on their feet now, glaring at the "wicked colonel" and voicing their enthusiasm for justice so heartily that the windows rattled. Adair looked around that ring of hostile faces. Clearly, they were about to rush him. He stepped back, drew his duelling pistol, and aimed it steadily at the purple neckerchief.

The lusting charge halted.

"See that?" snarled his target. "A murdering varmint, right enough!"

"Go and fetch a doctor, damn your eyes," howled Webber.

Ignoring him, the dark youth snatched up a chair. "He can only get one on us, mates."

Adair smiled grimly. "Do you volunteer?"

He saw the youth's eyes shift. From behind him came a whisper of sound. He flung himself aside. A long cudgel whistled past his ear. He seized the arm that had wielded the weapon and tugged, and a tall ruffian was wrenched into the path of those who had again plunged to the attack.

All then was noise and confusion. A woman's voice called urgently, "This way, sir! Be quick now, do! Your horse is ready and waiting."

It was no time for heroics. Adair ran through the door that the host's lady held open and then slammed behind him. He tugged out his purse and tossed some coins onto the counter. "My thanks, ma'am," he called, and sprinted to where a scared-looking stable-boy held Toreador. The boy's eyes widened as Adair snatched the reins, mounted up even as the big grey was running, and was away at the gallop.

From the inn came shouts and wrathful curses. A small bloodthirsty crowd erupted through the front door. Someone fired a shot, but by then Adair was out of range. He had little fear of any other horse coming up with his superb dapple-grey, but even so, he knew his wisest course would be to leave the area and go back to Town. He swore softly. He had come so close to learning something of the elusive Walter Davis. Be damned if he'd give up so easily! If he were trapped again, he'd have no choice but to head for London; meanwhile, it was unlikely that the bullies behind him had the remotest idea of his next destination.

Having made up his mind, he continued to ride to the southwest, while trying to make sense of this latest imbroglio. He heard again the beefy fellow's roared threat to show what "country folks" do with kidnapping rapists. The lout had certainly not been describing himself, for both he and the dark youth had accents straight from the slums of the City. If they were Londoners they were probably Thorne Webber's hirelings, for it was stretching the bounds of credibility to suppose that Webber should have come into the Pilgrim Arms by chance. Besides, the leader of those bullies must have had prior knowledge of him, for he'd referred to him as a Lieutenant-Colonel, whereas most people simply addressed him as Colonel. On the other hand, for an instant it had seemed as if Webber had been surprised by the sudden and enthusiastic support he'd received.

More puzzling was how Webber had known he would be at the Pilgrim Arms on this particular day. He'd not known it himself until this morning, when Bill Oxshott had—Oxshott! A slippery rogue if ever there was one. Could Oxshott have been paid to send him to the Pilgrim Arms? Such a scheme must have required advance planning. Much as Webber loathed him, would he really have had him followed all this way and gone to such pains to set a potentially murderous trap? It did not seem very likely. Unless the man had some deeper motive for wanting him dead. Was it possible that Thorne Webber admired poor little Alice Prior, and had spirited her away to some secret love nest?

Adair smiled ruefully. "Toreador," he said, "I think your master is grasping at straws and conjuring up some very melodramatic nonsense!"

But before he had gone another mile there came again his ominous warning voice and the strong sense that he was being watched.

He detoured, riding in a wide loop, but when he returned to the road he encountered only an exasperated riding master attempting to instruct a dozen or so young boys on the fine points of equestrianship. The master, a rather prim and dandy-ish type, rolled his eyes heavenward in long-suffering fashion as they passed. Adair grinned, then enchanted the bored youngsters by allowing Toreador to show off his imitation of a whirligig and render an equine bow before cantering on, followed by a chorus of whoops.

A quarter of an hour passed, and he still could not dismiss the sensation of eyes boring into his back. This time he rode in amongst some trees and stayed hidden for several minutes. Two farm waggons, a lumbering coach drawn by four fat horses, a donkey cart top-heavy with hay and sacks of grain, and a clergyman riding a sway-backed cart-horse passed by, none seemingly interested in those who had preceded them.

Adair rode on, prepared for trouble.

He came to the hamlet at last, just as Oxshott had described it, lying on the west side of a fast-flowing river. Toreador trod daintily through the thick mud and debris that had accumulated on the approach to a narrow and obviously ancient walled bridge. Beyond was a quaint collection of thatched cottages grouped about a green with snow still visible under clumps of gorse. The ring of hammer-blows guided Adair to the smithy. The blacksmith was massively built, smoke-blackened and good-natured. He apologized for not stopping work, and Adair's questions had to be sandwiched between the strokes of the hammer meeting red-hot iron. The smith remembered Walter Davis well. "A quarrelsome sort of cove," he shouted. "But he knows hosses, does Wally. What's he bin and gone and done?"

Adair assured him that he knew of nothing to Davis's discredit save that he seemed to have disappeared. He repeated his untruth about the 'small inheritance' and the smith was so impressed that, briefly, he abandoned his task. Saying he would "rack his brain-box," he proceeded to seize his thick hair and jerk his head so violently from side to side that his eyes began to water. This startling performance ended in an admission of failure. He had been unable to shake loose any knowledge of where Wally Davis had lived prior to working for the late Mr. Rickett, and Davis had seldom spoken of his family. "I do know as he had a mum what took in washing from some castle," he offered. "Wally said she were a fine hand with a iron and starch."

"Can you recall the name or location of this castle?" Adair took out his purse. "I'd be most grateful."

"Lor' bless yer, sir, ye don't need to pay me. I'd tell yer soon enough, if I knowed. Don't. You can go up to the great house yonder." He gestured towards a nearby hill. "It belongs to a gent name of Haley now. But I reckon they won't know any more'n what I do. Most of 'em be Londoners. The only one as useter work fer Mr. Rickett, Gawd rest his clutch-fisted soul, would be Sammy Henshaw, and Sammy were just the bootblack in them days. Doubt if he ever spoke to Wally."

Adair thanked him and turned Toreador back onto the lane.

There was some difficulty ahead. A very large Berliner coach had come to grief and leaned sideways, blocking the bridge. The red-faced coachman was striving—with the assistance of a scared footman and several amused onlookers—to back his team.

"Lord, what a silly block," muttered Adair as he rode up.

A villager grinned at him. "It do be stuck fast, sir. A wheel went into a rut and the whole lot tilted over. Hi! Coachman! Do 'ee want a bootjack?"

Another wag yelled, "Some bacon grease, more like!"

There were hoots and laughter, and from inside the coach a feminine voice was raised in anger:

"Let me out at once, Peters! Did you not hear what I said, man?"

It was a familiar voice, and Adair realized suddenly that this was the same coach that had passed by while he'd waited in the trees to see who was following him.

The coachman moaned unhappily, "I heard you, milady. But open the door I cannot."

"The coach is wedged 'gainst the wall, ma'am," wailed the footman.

"Of all the ridiculous . . ." A younger female voice this, and a face appeared at the coach window. "Peters! Whatever were you thinking? We'll never come up with him at this—" Miss Cecily Hall cut off that annoyed and pointless remark and said, "You'd best send someone to fetch the blacksmith. He'll likely know what . . ."

Here, her glance falling upon Adair, she left a second sentence unfinished.

She seemed lovelier each time he saw her and was charmingly clad in a dove-grey cloak and hood that accentuated the clear blue-grey of her eyes. He was relieved to note that she looked well and showed no sign of having suffered an injury a few days ago.

Raising his hat, he said, "Come up with—whom, Miss Hall?"

Her colour was heightened. She stared at him speechlessly.

"Who is it? Who is it?" Lady Abigail Prior's angular countenance, framed by an enormous bonnet with three lofty black feathers, thrust its way to the window.

"Good day to you, ma'am," said Adair, taking off his high-crowned hat once more.

"Oh, dear," said her ladyship and vanished as the feathers caught against the top of the window, tilting the bonnet over her face. Fighting her way out of this embarrassment, she said rather breathlessly, "I think we're dished, Cecily."

Amused, Adair said wickedly, "In more ways than one. Do you think it proper, Lady Prior, to allow your granddaughter to pursue me in this, er—rather brazen fashion?"

There were some stifled guffaws from the onlookers.

Miss Hall, her cheeks now scarlet, gasped, "*Braz-en*? Ooh! I would not pursue *you* to—to the river bank yonder!"

"Then how remarkable it is, ma'am, that I could have sworn your coach followed me from Newmarket to—"

"And we will keep on following you," she said, recovering her breath but contradicting herself, "until you lead us to—" She glanced at the gawking and titillated spectators, and hesitated.

"Nor are we the only ones following you," put in her ladyship.

"He knows that, Grandmama," said Miss Hall. "Why else does he keep dodging about so?"

"Which being the case," said Adair, replacing his hat at its customarily jaunty angle, "I must abandon you, dear ladies, and get on with my—er, dodging."

Miss Hall nodded and said with a curl of her vivid lips, "Quite in character."

The smile died from his eyes. He said in a lower voice, "You have, between you, contrived to destroy my character, ma'am."

Not waiting for a response, he reined Toreador round and walked him away.

A farm-hand in smock and gaiters directed him to a spot where the river was shallow enough to be forded safely. Starting off, Adair was quite unable to resist a backward glance.

The pale winter sun had broken through the clouds. An artist, he thought, would have been delighted to paint the fiasco at the bridge. The coachman was attempting to respond to Lady Abigail, who was offering him a stream of shrill and conflicting instructions, which he relayed to the scared footman. The footman ran about looking ready to burst into tears, and the enormous coach was still hopelessly stuck, the four fat horses stamping about uneasily. Miss Hall's hood had fallen back and the sunlight awoke a bright sheen on her fair curls. It occurred to Adair that she was much more than pretty; she was, in fact, quite enchantingly beautiful. Watching her, he was startled to realize that he was staring like a besotted idiot.

He leaned forward and scanned the bridge, then called to the distraught footman.

In response to that authoritative hail, the footman ran to his side and gazed up at him as though he were in a tempestuous sea and had been thrown a lifeline.

"I gather that your ladies have been travelling for several days," said Adair. "If they are like most females, you probably carry a considerable amount of luggage in the boot."

"Nigh a ton, sir," quavered the footman with a nervous glance to the Berliner. "And what to do now, I don't know for the life of me. Mr. Prior will be fit to be tied, sir! And Peters and me will be lucky if we're not turned off! But with the carriage leaning like it is and the wheel-hubs tight 'gainst the wall, it's just too heavy for the team to pull free."

"I believe you. But this is a very old bridge. If you'll notice, the lower sides of the walls tend to slope inward. A very small lift of your wheels would bring them above the narrower space so that the hubs would clear the wall."

The footman blinked. "Aye. But—but *we* cannot lift the coach, sir."

"If you lighten it, the body will lift itself."

"*Lighten* it? How, sir? We cannot get the ladies out, nor us get inside to—"

"Then climb over the roof, you silly block, and haul some of those portmanteaux from the boot!"

The footman's jaw dropped. "*Me*, sir?" He looked down in horror at his fine coat and satin knee-breeches. Cl-climb over . . . ?"

"Well, be damned if I'm going to do it for you, and I'd not be in your shoes if Lady Prior takes a notion to try it herself!"

The image of his haughty mistress crawling over the roof of the Berliner brought a sudden grin to the footman's face. "Aye, sir," he said. "Right you are, sir. And—and—thank ye, sir!"

Adair nodded to him, and rode away.

When he glanced back while fording the river downstream, he saw the footman on his hands and knees atop the coach, while what appeared to be the entire population of the village cheered him on.

7

*A*dair's enquiries at the estate of the late Mr. Rickett won him nothing but blank stares and a clear mistrust of anyone trying to locate a long-forgotten groom. The only positive reaction came from the former boot black, now head groom, Sam Henshaw, who remembered only that Walter Davis had been a surly man they'd all been glad to see the back of.

Disheartened, Adair gave up and turned for home.

The afternoon was unseasonably bright when he reached London. To avoid neighbourhoods in which he was more likely to be recognized, he followed a circuitous route but he did not begrudge the time required. The great City had cast its spell over him long ago and it was no less fascinating today, showing a gentler face when bathed in sunshine. His gaze drifted fondly to the distant dome of St. Paul's, the splendour of Westminster Abbey and St. Margaret's Church, the numerous masts that moved busily along the glittering waters of the Thames, the sparrows that hopped their impudent way along railings and gossiped in the trees. Traffic was heavy, voices were loud but generally cheerful, and an alert ear could detect accents ranging from cockney to cultured, from the Home Counties to Scots. So many lives touching briefly, and each individual busied about his or her own concerns. He loved this dear, wicked old City, but for the moment, at least, it did not love him. Not a man of these hurrying costers or vendors or apprentices but would turn on him in disgust if he was recognized. His battle to clear his name was "making haste slowly," and if he lost that battle, if he was forced to leave England . . . Well, he would *not* lose, and he would *not* be driven from his homeland!

Escaping a woman who was determined to sell him a multi-coloured knitted scarf, and a vendor convinced that he could not live happily without a pint of cockles and mussels, he eventually approached Vespa House along the side alley. The groom who came to meet him looked shocked, and disapproval was written in every line of his stiff back as he led Toreador off to the stables. Adair entered the rear door of the great house feeling like an interloper.

Since Jack Vespa was not in residence, the mansion was sparsely staffed, and he encountered only a shy housemaid who took his saddle-bags and informed him that "the gentlemen" were in the large drawing room. Adair refused her offer to announce him, and entered that impressive chamber wondering if Vespa had returned to his house after all.

Toby Broderick was standing by the window talking earnestly. Adair paused in the doorway, seeing no one else in the room save for the marble statue of Venus that stood near the gilded harpsichord. At first he thought Toby must be rehearsing a speech before the "lady," but then he glimpsed a pair of gleaming Hessians sticking out from one end of a sofa.

". . . and you know dashed well there are all too many powerful men who dislike the war," said Broderick. "Some of the Whigs have never forgiven poor Sir John Moore for the retreat from Corunna, though Lord knows, without his splendid efforts it would have been a sight more of a tragedy. They tried their damnedest to back away from Boney then, and they're still at their tricks."

Adair's rap on the door went unheard as the man on the sofa

yawned and remarked that it was one thing not to like the war but quite another to conspire to put an end to it. "We know more about Bonaparte now. And anyone but a henwit must be aware that if we don't stop him he'll be across the Channel in jig time. I think you're making mountains out of molehills, as usual. It will all quiet down, just wait and see."

The deep drawl was easily identifiable. So Lieutenant Paige Manderville, whose dark good looks caused him to be dubbed "Beau" Manderville, was back in England. He and Broderick were friends of long standing who had met Captain Jack Vespa last year during the Battle of Vitoria. Wounds had sent all three home, and when Vespa had become the target of an ugly plot, Broderick and Manderville had stood by him. Adair himself had been involved and during some rather desperate encounters deep loyalties had formed between them.

Accustomed to the good-natured bickering that was customary for these two men, Adair wasn't surprised when Broderick argued:

"It won't quiet down unless we kick some of these dashed malcontents out of Whitehall! If you look back through history, there's an alarming trail of damage wrought by ruthless schemers whose mission in life has been to usurp authority and install their own brand of rule—usually despotic. Take our conniving Prince John, for example, or Mordred, or—"

Adair paused in amused anticipation.

"Who?" Paige Manderville's handsome head lifted above the sofa-back and he eyed Broderick incredulously. "Haven't heard of that one. A Whig, is he?"

"Block," snorted Broderick. "Mordred was King Arthur's evil bastard and mortal enemy, and—"

"What the deuce has he got to do with Napoleon Bonaparte? If you're going to trot out mythical plotters—"

"What makes you think he was only mythical? Did you know the Arthurian legends are firmly entrenched in Brittany as well as—"

Manderville groaned and flopped back down again. "Cease

and desist! I am newly home from the wars and in no condition to endure your latest lecture!"

"A few lectures would do that soggy brain-box of yours no harm, my poor pseudo-invalid."

At this Manderville sprang to his feet, his face almost as red as his military coat. "And just what might you mean by that snide remark? There's nothing pseudo about this blasted shoulder of mine, and if you—"

Adair said heartily, "Manderville! How good to see you. Are we—" He put out his hand, but recalling his disgrace hesitated and withdrew it. "Oh—egad! Perhaps you'd as soon I left."

"Another word out of you, Colonel, sir," said Manderville, marching over to seize and wring his hand strongly, "and I'll deck you instead of our almost-don here!"

It occurred to Adair that his nerves were not what they'd once been. During the thick of the fighting in some very savage battles, confronted by scenes to send a man's sanity reeling, he had managed, outwardly at least, to keep his emotions in hand. Even the mighty Wellington had once laughingly described him as "my unshakeable hussar," a rare accolade which had astonished almost as much as it had pleased him. Now, he was dismayed to find that this demonstration of loyalty and the warm light in Manderville's famous green eyes conspired to make his throat close up and his vision blur. He was obliged to turn away while he fought for the self-control that had so bewilderingly deserted him.

Quick to comprehend Adair's state of mind and come to the rescue, Broderick exclaimed, "Hey! A colonel has come among us, and just in time for tea! Let us all partake while we gossip."

The tea was carried in by a maid and footman. Gathered informally around the fire, the three young men compared notes while they ate heartily of buttered scones with jam, cheese and watercress sandwiches, lemon sponge cake, and biscuits.

Manderville, who had come from the front with despatches, and also to have his old shoulder wound examined, demanded to hear everything that had happened. Broderick did most of the explaining, his account leaving Manderville alternately aghast and hilarious.

Adair asked at length, "What luck at the Horse Guards, Toby?"

Broderick reported that as promised he had relayed the fire-boy's tale of the coach that had arrived at Singletree in the middle of the night when Miss Alice Prior had vanished.

"Now, that's promising, surely," said Manderville, pouring himself another cup of tea.

"It might be, were Whitehall not staffed by intransigent worm-wits!" Broderick said, exasperated. "Not only did they imply I had made up the whole tale, but they demanded to know where they could find Hasty." He glanced at Adair and added with reluctance, "I sent them off on a wild-goose chase, but you'd as well know they seem half-way convinced that Miss Prior has been done away with, and—er, well, the truth is—"

"That I'm the prime suspect, is that it?" Adair said bitterly, "Regardless of the fact that I was imprisoned at the time."

"The argument appears to be that you were allowed visitors and could have sent word to an accomplice to arrange the—er, business."

"What damnable nonsense!" Flushed with anger, Adair exclaimed, "Much chance I have of proving my innocence to such closed minds! Have I actually been named, Toby? Is there a warrant out against me?"

"Not so far as I'm aware. But . . ." Broderick looked unhappy. "There have been Runners from Bow Street and some dashed impertinent newspaper fellows swarming about your father's house."

Adair could well imagine Lord Joshua's reaction, and as for his mother . . . "Damn and blast them!" he groaned, running a hand through his hair distractedly.

"Quite," said Broderick. "Rather a sticky wicket, old boy."

Manderville, busied with the sponge cake, prompted, "Don't forget the letter."

"Jove, but I had!" Broderick jumped up and retrieved a letter

96

that was stuck irreverently in a fold of the draperies of Venus. "Came yesterday." He handed it to Adair. "Looks to be the General's writing."

Manderville demanded, "How d'you know it's the General's writing? Had several letters from him, have you?"

"I've taken a moderate interest in chirography, if that's what you mean."

"Well, it ain't what I mean since it's another of your jawbreakers that I never before heard uttered by man nor beast, so—"

"Then by all means permit me to explain," said Broderick grandly. "For your benefit, I'll use very small words. Chirography, or writing with the hand rather than printing, is a most interesting study, and has proven that no two people write in exactly the same way. Which makes forgery, for example, a tricky task."

"What stuff! I'll wager I could forge your scrawl so no one would know the difference!"

"If you had nothing better to do than to attempt such silliness you might hoodwink some dimwit, I grant you, but it is very difficult to disguise one's hand to the point that an expert would be deceived. The study of handwriting is not a new science. Leonardo da Vinci is said to have used mirror writing to preserve his secrets. The Chinese noted the connection between handwriting and personality in the eleventh century, and in 1622 Camillo—awwwk!"

Broderick's "explanation" had been lost on Adair as he read his letter, but the final word, being more of a strangled howl, broke through his concentration.

Manderville had come up behind Broderick's chair and was holding a cushion over the "almost-don's" face.

"Only way," he panted, glancing up, his eyes alight with laughter. "Have to put a stop to the flow of his blasted erudition, or—"

With a writhe and a twist, Broderick escaped. Flushed and breathless, his hair on end, and the lust for revenge written on his usually mild countenance, he sprang onto the sofa as Manderville darted behind it. "I'll put a stop to you!" he roared, and launched himself at his tormentor.

Briefly, Adair watched their struggle for possession of the cushion, then he left them. He was in the entrance hall, instructing a footman to send for his horse, when Broderick joined him and ordered the footman to wait for a minute. "Summoned, are you, Hasty?" he murmured, plucking a feather from his ear and leading Adair aside.

"Yes. You were right about the handwriting. The General and my father want to see me. I must get over there, Toby."

"Not on Toreador. He's too well known. Take Trouble. Paige won't mind."

"How generous you are with my peerless charger." Manderville came up wearing a crown of feathers. "Adair knows very well that Trouble savages any stranger who tries to ride him."

Broderick nodded, "Might have known you'd be mean-spirited about it. I'll be glad to let you take my Quadrille, Hasty."

This remark drew a hoot of derision from Manderville, Broderick's tall bay being every bit as unpredictable as his own prized Trouble. Adair left them arguing, and went to the stables to borrow one of Jack Vespa's mounts.

The afternoon was fading to dusk when he rode out, but mindful of Broderick's warning, he pulled his hat low and the cape of his cloak high. He reached his parents' house without incident and left his borrowed horse with a stable-boy who stared at him solemnly.

How grand it would be, thought Adair, to inspire once again the friendly smiles he'd formerly received from the servants; or at least not to meet with obvious condemnation from those who might have been expected to give him the benefit of the doubt. He clenched his hands hard, and went into the mansion prepared for another ordeal.

In the main hall a footman ran to take his cloak, gloves and hat. Loud voices could be heard emanating from the first floor. Adair climbed the stairs with reluctance. He paused as the drawing-room door burst open and his younger brother shouted rebelliously, "Well, I shall not!"

So Nigel had not returned to Oxford. Probably ashamed to show his face, poor lad.

Hurried footsteps and the youth was before him, looking haggard and distraught, eyes glittering ragefully in the pale face.

Hastings reached out. "Nigel, if you would just—"

"Do what?" Nigel drew away from his hand as though it were leprous. "Forgive you? Pretend I believe you innocent? Harrington, poor good-natured dupe, will likely forgive you. But I *never* shall, Colonel—or—or whatever in blazes you are now! *Never* as long as I live!"

He pushed past so violently that Hastings was staggered and had to make a grab for the stair railing.

For a moment he leaned there watching that headlong flight. Of all his family, he would have counted on Nigel to stand by him, but it was clear that the boy believed the whole ugly story. That awareness brought an aching sense of grief and loss and a reinforcement of his determination to vindicate himself.

"Took your time! Been in a brawl, I see. Not surprising." The words were barked out as though Major Roger Adair still stood on the parade ground under a hot Indian sun.

Hastings steeled himself to meet his uncle's contemptuous gaze. "My regrets, sir. I have but now—"

"Save your apologies for the General. Step lively. He ain't pleased."

That fact was all too apparent when Hastings entered the big room. He was relieved to find only four other members of the family present: his father; his elder brother, Hudson; his clerical uncle, Taylor Chatteris; and his grandfather, who stood before the hearth looking fierce.

Hastings bowed and greeted them with cool courtesy.

Lord Esterwood, elegant as ever, rose from an armchair. "I sent for you two days ago."

"I'm sorry, Father. I was from Town."

"Cannot blame you for that," barked Major Adair drily.

"Sometimes retreat is sound strategy. Though you wasn't quick enough to avoid Thorne Webber's riding crop, eh?"

Hastings flushed. "I have been in—"

"Tenterden," murmured Hudson. "And points east."

Hastings stared at him.

Interpreting his astonishment more or less correctly, the General said gruffly, "No, your brother did not have you followed. Between us, we have sources. Well?"

So at least they cared enough to be interested. Pulling his wits back together, he said, "I learned some details that were not brought out at my trial, sir. I hoped to trace the coachman who testified against me, but he left the Priors' service and appears to have vanished."

"Convenient," snorted Major Adair.

"That is not charitable in you, Roger," murmured the Reverend Mr. Taylor Chatteris in his gentle way.

"I ain't here to be charitable," bellowed the Major, irritated. "I've only to show my nose outside my door and I'm damned well besieged by the scandalmongers and—"

"As are we all," interrupted Lord Esterwood.

"May I know why I am here?" asked Hastings. "And why Nigel implied that Julius Harrington has cause to 'forgive' me?"

"Harrington was struck down on our doorstep two days ago," answered Lord Esterwood.

"Having risked coming here so as to declare his faith in you," added General Chatteris.

Dismayed, Hastings exclaimed, "Oh, egad! He's not badly hurt, I trust?"

"Your trust is misplaced," growled the Major sourly.

Hudson elaborated, "A fellow don't benefit from a rock aimed at his head."

"A fine state of affairs when our friends must take their lives in their hands if they dare to approach our door," said Lord Esterwood. "Need I add, Hastings, that your mother is outraged?"

"No, you do not need to add that scintillating observation," interposed the General tartly. "Hastings must certainly be fa-

100

miliar with his mama's silly starts! Yes, I said 'silly starts,' Taylor! Lady Andrea is my daughter and I shall not keep my tongue between my teeth only to win your saintly approval!"

Hudson put a hand across his mouth to hide a grin, and Major Adair guffawed while the unfortunate clergyman turned red to the roots of his hair.

"Harrington was not seriously damaged, and that is not why you have been summoned." The General marched closer to Hastings and said deliberately, "Rumour has it that you are a womanizing rascal, Colonel Hastings Chatteris Adair. So you may be, although I never saw evidence of it. But you were born and bred up a gentleman. I'll not believe you could ever harm a lady—much less murder one!"

His breath snatched away, Hastings stammered, "Then—then you believe I am innocent?"

"Innocent of murder, at least," qualified the Major.

"And on that charge we will fight them to a standstill," declared Lord Esterwood.

"Just so," said the General, his eyebrows bristling. "Well? What have you to say, boy?"

"I am—most grateful to you all. But—" Hastings paused. "*Are* you all agreed on this point?"

Hudson and his father exchanged a swift glance. Lord Esterwood said, "Not—er, exactly."

"Your Uncle Fergus ain't convinced," said the Major. "But I doubt he's been sober long enough to think on it."

Hastings said slowly, "And—Nigel?"

"This wretched affair has been a great shock to the boy," said Lord Esterwood, his face very grave. "To us all."

"Nonsense!" said the General explosively. "You'd have to have been blind as a bat, Joshua, not to see that two of your sons fell victim to the gel's charms!"

Hudson flushed darkly and exclaimed, "If you refer to me, sir, you have been misinformed! I don't even know Miss Alice Prior!"

"Nigel knows her," declared the General.

"Nigel?" Indignant, the Viscount protested, "He's just a boy!"

"I doubt he's as old as Miss Prior," said Hudson, reinforcingly.

"Who is frequently described as a child," argued the General, "although she is eighteen. By which age my own mother was wed and I was in the nursery!"

"Besides," put in the clergyman, looking shocked, "Nigel is away at Oxford for most of the year. You surely do not imply, sir, that he—"

"Of course I don't! Nor do I walk around with my head in a sand bucket! The boy danced with her at the Harvest Festival Ball last year. I saw his face. He's too young to do more than dream, but I'd wager he's been dreaming of her ever since. Which should tell you why this has been more than a shock to him."

Major Adair said grimly, "It would explain his disgust of Hastings, certainly."

———

Walking slowly down the stairs, Hastings was still astonished by his grandfather's revelation. That he himself should have failed to realize that Nigel was in love was understandable, since he was so often out of the country. But with Nigel up at Oxford, and Alice Prior closely chaperoned, it was remarkable that such a deep attachment could have developed. More remarkable that only the General appeared to have been aware of it. They must have been very careful. A sly inner voice whispered, 'What if Nigel is the one who spirited Miss Prior away? What if he—'

"Colonel!"

The low-voiced call broke into his introspection, and dismissing such disloyal thoughts, he hurried to join Mrs. Redditch, who awaited him at the foot of the stairs. The devoted housekeeper begged that he accompany her to what she called her "business room," to which few visitors were admitted.

Adair teased her as usual, calling her a "wild woman," which always gave her an attack of the giggles. As they passed the kitchen, delicious smells heralded preparations for dinner.

Mrs. Redditch closed the door to her little office and hurried to pour her guest a glass of Madeira, and with a guilty grin poured a small portion for herself.

Adair raised his glass. "To you, my dearest Reddy, with my thanks for permitting my notorious self to enter your 'sanctum sanctorum.' "

She smiled, and occupying the chair he pulled out for her, said, "As though you'd not been in here time and time again, Master Hastings!"

"True." He moved another chair from her small desk, and sitting beside her said wryly, "You were always kind to me, even when I was a scruffy schoolboy and lusted after your lemon-curd tarts. But I was not notorious then."

"No more are you now—in my eyes at least, sir. And—I think there are others in this house . . ." She hesitated.

"D'you mean my family? Yes, I suspect they're starting to believe me." Nigel's glowering countenance flashed before his mind's eye, and he muttered, "Some of 'em, at all events."

Watching his face, she said gently, "Don't take it so hard, sir. He'll come round. First love is often intense, you know, and Mr. Nigel such a sensitive boy. Fairly daft for the lady, he is."

He looked at her sharply. "I should have guessed that of all people, he would have come to you with his troubles."

"He did not give himself away for a long time, but I knew he'd fallen in love. When he came home at Christmas-time he was walking about as if he were six inches off the ground, and smiling at nothing, if you know what I mean. I didn't say anything, and I don't think anyone else noticed. It's just that—I know him so well, you see."

His father and mama knew their son, also, or should do. He thought with a sudden pang of resentment, 'Damnation! Why was he so secretive? Skulking about as though he were ashamed?' But Nigel was a younger son and had not yet found a promising career. He'd probably judged that a man of Mr. Alfred Prior's stamp would find him rankly ineligible as a suitor

103

for his daughter's hand. He said slowly, "What I cannot fathom is how they were able to meet."

"I have sometimes suspected that Mr. Nigel was in London more often than the family knew. When the word came about—about that dreadful ball and—and that you were accused of— Well, he was quite beside himself. No, don't look so distressed, Master Hastings. He did talk to me about it then. He wouldn't believe it at first. He kept saying you'd never do so wicked a thing. But then—the trial . . ." She shrugged helplessly. "He'll sort things out, you'll see, and he'll be so ashamed that he didn't stand by you as Mr. Harrington has."

"Poor fellow. He paid a high price for his loyalty. Was he badly injured?"

"He took a nasty bump, but declared he was not about to be scared off by a lot of rabble-rousing hooligans."

"He's a friend worth the having. I'd call and tell him so, but I suppose I'd best send a note round rather than tarnish his reputation by appearing on his doorstep."

"The General and his lordship thanked him profusely, I promise you."

"So I should think," said Adair, and wondered if his grandfather would now feel obliged to admit that Julius Harrington was an acceptable *parti* for Minerva. The old gentleman would probably be grinding his teeth and claiming his hand had been forced.

The housekeeper said thoughtfully, "You know, Master Hastings, I always believed you were very well liked. Who in the world would have gone to such lengths to disgrace you? It must have been so, do not you think?"

"I do. And bless you for your faith in me. I mean to get to the root of it, Reddy, and as soon as may be!"

"So you will, sir, I know it. But to think that those dense officers at the Horse Guards came so near to—" The threat of this fine young man ending his life on the gallows still made her blood run cold. She took a deep breath, cast a quick glance at Adair's expressionless face, and said quickly, "But—never mind that, eh, sir? We've turned the corner! Very soon now we'll know what wicked villain was really responsible for—"

She was interrupted by a scratch at the door. A rosy-cheeked housemaid came in, bobbed a curtsy, and enquired if Mrs. Redditch desired that tea be served.

"Goodness, is it that time already?" The housekeeper stood. "Yes. Her ladyship likes a tray taken up at five. Hurry and get started."

The maid said a meek "Yes, ma'am," slanted a coquettish glance at Adair, and whisked herself away.

"Saucy baggage," muttered the housekeeper.

"A new girl, isn't she?"

"We hired her after Burslem left, and—Oh, my! I all but forgot!" She opened a drawer in the desk, and started to search about in it. "The very reason I asked you to come here! I vow I must be getting old and my wits are to let! You'll remember Burslem, Master Hastings? The maid you allowed to stay on after she was so rude. Just before you left Town, it was."

"Ah, yes. Did you have to turn her off after all?"

"Not that, sir." The housekeeper took up a rather rumpled letter and clasped it to her bosom. "It's such a nice story! It seems Burslem has been walking out for over a year with one of the grooms on the estate of Mr. Willoughby Chatteris.

Adair said with a smile, "Reddy, I think you have a romantical heart. But your lovers must not have walked out very often, since my Uncle Willoughby's home is near Woking."

"True. And it was a sadness for them, until the young man was able to save one of Miss Minerva's dogs when it got itself caught in a poacher's trap."

"The plot thickens!" Walking to the door beside her, Adair said, "If I know my cousin, that lucky fellow was able to name his own reward."

"That's exactly what he did, sir. And Burslem was offered a very nice position down there. She was so excited there was no living with her, so I let her go right away. An upstairs maid she is. And I'd not be surprised to hear wedding bells in the future!"

105

"A nice story, indeed. Is that what your letter is about?"

"Eh? Oh, no, sir! Here, it's for you. Burslem was very grateful, and I expect she wanted to thank you. I only hope you are able to read it. Her writing is very poor."

Adair excused himself and deciphered the painfully printed message with little difficulty:

"Yu wuz kind to me sir, thank yu sir I told my Yung Man and he noze the koachman what workt fer Mister Pryor and he sez its Funny and yu mite want to no, respekful yors, Burslem."

Adair gave a whoop, seized the housekeeper and whirled her around in triumph.

Restored to her feet, Mrs. Redditch gasped, "Oh, mercy! Whatever did she say, sir?"

"Something terribly important! And if that isn't typical! Here am I searching high and low, and all the time the answer is here, under my nose!"

He gave the beaming housekeeper a strong hug. "Once again, you come to my rescue. Thank you! And forgive me, but I must leave you."

"Oh, no, sir! Why such urgency? Can you not stay for dinner? Where are you rushing off to this time?"

"Woking," he answered gaily. "To see a maid about a groom!"

8

"Y̶ou may have trotted in here without being stopped, *mon colonel,*" said Lieutenant Paige Manderville, strolling into the drawing room with a tankard of ale in one hand, "But you'll have the devil of a time trotting out again."

Adair had returned to Vespa House to reclaim Toreador and to let his friends know of his progress. He was standing by the glowing hearth listening to Broderick discourse on blackbirds while waiting for his horse to be brought round, but he now turned to look at Manderville questioningly.

"Two of 'em," drawled Manderville, sinking gracefully into a deep fireside chair.

"Bow Street?"

Manderville hesitated. "I'm not sure. They don't quite look constable-ish."

"But you're sure they're watching for Hasty?" asked Broderick, nobly overlooking the grammatical lapse.

"I suppose they could be students of architecture, but . . . No, they don't look the student type, either. You won't be able to leave tonight, my pippin."

"Devil I won't," argued Adair. "The skies are clear, and there's a fine full moon—"

Broderick said, "Which will make it all the easier for 'em to spot you."

"If I wait for the moon to set, it'll be too dark for me to find my way, and I want to reach my uncle's house tonight."

"Why the hurry?" asked Manderville curiously. "You can as well leave at first light."

It was not an easy thing to explain, this sensation that he occasionally experienced. A sort of tightening of the nerves; an increasing anxiety; an almost tangible warning of impending disaster. A gift, perhaps, but a gift he would gladly have rejected, although it had probably saved his life once in Spain when a group of Polish lancers had come up behind him while he'd been reconnoitering an enemy position. He answered rather lamely, "I just have the feeling I mustn't let any grass grow under my feet."

"Is that so?" said Broderick, at once interested. "Premonition, I'll be bound! Now there's a most interesting field of—"

Manderville put a hand over his eyes. "Don't start," he groaned. "If our intrepid colonel insists on this very unwise course, we must find a way to confuse the opposition."

"Jolly good notion," agreed Broderick. "Let us devise a plan of action, gentlemen!"

As a result of their "devising," some half-hour later a man who leaned in a shadowed nearby doorway jerked himself upright and hissed, "There he goes, mate!"

His companion, who'd been gainfully employed in trimming his fingernails with his teeth, looked after the departing solitary horseman and pointed out, "That ain't Adair's hack. He rides a big dapple-grey."

"Ar, and *he* knows as *we* knows it, so he ain't likely to ride it now, is he. Use yer wits fer once! He's headin' east. Means to make fer the docks and take ship, I shouldn't wonder. Come *on!*"

They sprinted to the corner, where a street urchin was walking their horses, but the doubter entered another caveat: "What if we both goes and it ain't him? What then, Charlie boy? We'll lose our pay, is what!"

"All right, all right! Gawd, what a blockhead! You stay and keep watch. I'll go arter the slippery cove!" So saying, "Charlie boy" was off at the gallop, leaving his partner to chew at his nails worriedly and return to his surveillance of the Vespa mansion.

Five minutes later, his caution was justified. A second horseman, muffled to the eyes, emerged from the side alley, rode rapidly to the corner, then turned northward.

"Aha!" exclaimed the remaining watcher. "He were too slippery fer you, Charlie know-it-all!" He ran to toss a coin to the urchin, mount up and race after the "slippery cove," muttering a triumphant, "Din't I tell yer?"

Scarcely was he out of sight than a fine dapple-grey left the side alley, to be guided by his cloaked and well-muffled rider towards London Bridge, and thence to the southwest.

Unlike Singletree, Blackbird Terrace was true to its name. There was a terrace, and there were many blackbirds, though by the time Adair reached his Uncle Willoughby's estate, the former was barely visible through the thickening mists, and the latter were all presumably tucked into their nests for the night.

Adair's shouts were at first unavailing, but a window in the gatehouse at length glowed to candle-light, and the gatekeeper emerged, yawning and pulling a heavy coat closed over his night-shirt. He held up a lantern and observed sleepily, "Oh, it do be you, Colonel."

"Yes. My apologies for knocking you up at this hour, Bailey. Is my uncle in residence?"

"Aye. Jest like 'e allus is, sir." The gatekeeper opened one of the high wrought-iron gates and advised that they was "all likely fast asleep up at the great house."

He was mistaken, however, for when Adair had left his horse

in the care of a drowsy groom and been admitted to the mansion, the butler relieved him of his hat and cloak and said that the master had not yet retired.

There came a rush of flying feet on the stairs, and an anxious "Whoever has come calling at this hour?" Minerva Chatteris gave a squeak of joy, and heedless of papered curls and the fact that she wore her night-rail, flung herself into Adair's arms.

"How lovely that you have come to us! Did my grandfather throw you into the street, poor dear?"

Adair kissed her and slanted a glance at the butler's studiedly expressionless countenance, but before he could answer his cousin rushed on:

"How is it that your face is so bruised? You've never ridden straight from Town? My goodness—you must be starving! Randall, we must have a tray for the Colonel, and tell Mrs. Sylvan to see that a fire is lit in the best guest-room, and—Oh, never mind! I'll come. Mama is from home, Hasty dear, but go along to my uncle."

Warmed by such a greeting, he asked, "Are you sure, Minna? It's past eleven o'clock, and I come without invitation."

"Stuff! He's still in his study and will be eager to see you at once. You're probably tired, so don't let him keep you up much longer." She hurried off beside the butler, calling over her shoulder, "I'll talk with you in the morning, Hasty."

Adair nodded and walked down the corridor at the end of which was the large and cluttered chamber Willoughby Chatteris called his study. It was a long corridor, the floors of random-width oak covered by only a few nondescript rugs; the walls hung with rather faded prints and a scattering of oil paintings. Adair had not visited this house for over a year, during which time his entire way of life had been shattered. It was rather comforting to find that Blackbird Terrace had not changed. The furnishings still reflected the styles of the previous century, the walls and the low ceilings still bore mute evidences of smoking chimneys and the occasional intrusions of rain-water. On the air hung the faint mustiness of age and wood fires and pipe smoke.

Viscountess Andrea had little patience with her erratic brother, and declared that Willoughby should have moved into the fine old dower house while the mansion was redecorated and modernized, instead of which he was letting the unoccupied dower house crumble away from neglect, while making not the least push to bring the great house he had inherited up to style. When he'd opened his doors to his widowed sister-in-law and her brood, Lady Andrea had cherished some hopes that Hilda Chatteris might persuade him to refurbish the old place, but the widow had been too grateful to be provided with a comfortable home to request improvements. And Minerva, thought Adair with a faint smile, was not the type to crave an elegant residence, her interests being focused on her loved ones and her dogs.

He knocked on the door of the study and announced himself, but did not at once go inside. There came a muddled muttering, much rustling of papers and slamming of drawers, and then a somewhat breathless invitation to enter. 'He's at his Lists again,' thought Adair, swinging the door wide.

Mr. Willoughby Chatteris rose from behind the battered desk that was set before the now closed window curtains. His usually pale face was pink and wore a somewhat guilty expression, both of which might have been inspired by the brilliant scarlets and purples of the velvet dressing-gown he wore. "Hello, my boy," he said, putting out his hand in his uncertain fashion. "Nice to—er, to see you. Didn't know you would be—ah, down this way, but you mean to stay for a day or so at least, I—er, trust?"

"You are very good, sir. Thank you, and if it doesn't inconvenience Aunt Hilda, I'll stay overnight, but I'm afraid I must be off tomorrow."

Relief dawned in the protuberant blue eyes. Returning to the big chair behind the desk, Mr. Chatteris said in a heartier tone, "That is our—er, loss. It won't inconvenience my sister-in-law. Hilda is down at Brighton. Her young niece is—ah, lying in, you know. Have a seat, my boy, and tell me how you go on."

"I go on seeking to prove my innocence, sir." Adair sat in

the chair that faced the desk. "But I fear I've already inconvenienced you, and that you were peacefully at work on your—"

"No such thing," interrupted his uncle hurriedly.

Adair glanced at a sheet of paper that had evidently fallen under the desk and lay beside his boot. Bending to retrieve it, he said, "I think you've dropped one of your Lists, sir."

He had a brief impression of neatly written columns, then a rush of displaced air and the sheet was snatched from his grasp. Uncle Willoughby must have moved like lightning. He looked up and for an instant saw rage in the usually meek eyes. Startled by such an unprecedented display of emotion, he said, "I beg pardon, sir. I've no intent to pry—though I'll admit I've often wondered what your Lists—"

Willoughby's laugh, a shrill and forced cackle, cut off his nephew's remark. "Just my little—ah, hobby. You would think it foolish, I'm very sure." He went back to his chair and thrust the paper hurriedly into a drawer. His face was redder than Adair had ever seen it. He all but gabbled, "Now—now what have I missed? The General don't—ah, keep me informed, you know. And unless your Uncle Roger rides this way, I'm left—left in the dark. As it—er, were."

'Good Lord, I properly sent him into the boughs,' thought Adair. He was fond of Willoughby, and if he judged him a rather weak-kneed man, he also thought him very kind and good-hearted, and not for the world would he upset him. He launched into an account of his activities, therefore, and by the time the butler came to say that his room was ready and a tray had been carried up for him, Mr. Chatteris seemed quite at his ease.

Adair said his good-nights and climbed the stairs. He was afire with impatience to talk to the housemaid, Burslem, and learn what her young man knew about Coachman Davis that he thought "funny." But he could scarcely have rousted the woman from her bed at this hour. At least, he was here now, and could interview her first thing in the morning.

In the quiet study, Willoughby Chatteris put his Lists in order. He kept out the sheet his nephew had picked up, and scanned it with almost frenzied anxiety. "How much did he see?" he whispered to himself. "He's so damnably quick! How much did he see?" He restored the Lists to his drawer, and bowed his head into hands that shook.

Adair was standing at the library bow window, watching two puppies frisk about on the lawns when a gruff voice announced, " 'Mornin' Colonel, sir. Mrs. Sylvan says as I could come now."

He turned eagerly. "Good morning, Burslem. Sit down, please. How do you go on in my uncle's establishment?"

Square and plain and as uncompromisingly grim as ever, the maid perched on the edge of the chair he drew up for her. She said that she liked her new situation very well. And with an un-expected blush, added, " 'Sides, it's very agreeable fer my young man and me to be able to see each other more'n once a month."

"I'm glad it has worked out well for you." Adair leaned back against the arm of the sofa. "And I thank you for the letter you left me."

"Why, you was kind t'me, sir. Else I wouldn't never have been kept on at Adair Hall, an' then, no matter what my young man done for Miss Minerva, they'd not have let me come here. That's why I writ to you and hopes as I wasn't steppin' past me station."

"Certainly not. In point of fact, I've been most anxious to talk with you. You wrote that your young man knows Walter Davis, the Priors' coachman."

"Yessir. That is ter say as he knowed him—at one time. My Henery—" Her blush deepened and she said shyly, "That's his name, sir. Henery. He'll tell you hisself all as he knows when he comes back. You jest missed him by a day. He's drove Mrs. Chatteris down ter Brighton. I don't know how long the mistress means ter stay. Not long, likely. Could ye come back?"

'More time lost!' thought Adair impatiently. "I can, of course. Or I can ride down to Brighton and see him. But this is rather urgent, and you may be able to help me if you will. Henry saw Davis recently, did he?"

"Last week, sir, as ever was! All dressed up flash, he were, and with a nag as Henery says must've cost him a pretty penny, and trying to act the gent—which he ain't and never will be! And talking about how he'd got his 'just reward,' and about—well, he carried on about you, sir."

"Did he, by Jove! Nothing to my credit, I'll wager."

"Right you are, sir. Talking loud like he does when he's put down a few tankards, Henery said. And saying as how he'd knowed no good would come of Miss Alice slipping out on the sly to meet her beau—meaning you, Colonel. And how he was honour-bound to speak out at your trial the way any honest man oughter do. 'Honest' being just what Wally Davis ain't, says Henery."

"Is that what he meant when he said that something about Davis was 'funny'?"

Burslem's rather hard eyes became very round. She threw a nervous glance at the door, and leaning forward said in a dramatically lowered voice, "What it was, Davis kept on filling up of his tankard, sir, and bragging about how well he'd done fer hisself. And how a cove with a brain in his head could make proper use of his chances and come up in the world. And the more he drank, the louder and more cocksure he got, till everyone in the tap was tired of listening to him, and some of the other customers started poking fun about Davis being like one o' them Indian nobbys—or whatever they is."

"A nabob? It sounds as if he's come into money, certainly. It would be interesting to know how he earned this alleged 're- ward.' "

"He tells my Henery as he got it 'cause he done a real service for his master." Burslem tucked in her chin and nodded solemnly. "But Henery ain't one as is easy gulled. 'I don't believe a word of it, lass,' says he ter me. 'Bin up ter no good, more like.' The other gents in the tap, they felt the same, and they laughed. Davis started to get ugly, and they says as how he'd best hang on to his 'reward,' else sure as check it would all go 'fore he could wink a eye. On drink, they said, and fast women—if you'll excuse the expression—and the races. And Davis says not no one needn't worry about Wally Davis and his 'reward' 'cause there was plenty more where that come from. And he started mumbling about 'someone' who thought they'd seen the last of him, but they hadn't."

Adair asked tensely, "Did Henry find out who is this 'someone'?"

"He were curious, he said, sir, and asked Davis who he meant. But Davis seemed as if he'd got scared, and wouldn't say no more, and went off with a bottle, though he were already very well to live, as they say." She shrugged and said apologetically, "It's not much, sir, and it mayn't be of no use, t'you, but my Henery knowed Wally Davis when they was boys, and wouldn't trust him then as far as he could throw him. And he says as Wally ain't changed; not a bit."

In which case this unsavoury coachman could scarcely have been trusted to tell the truth in court. And if—as seemed probable—for some inexplicable reason he'd been paid to lie, his sudden affluence would be accounted for.

Encouraged, Adair said, "It is indeed of use. You've been a great help, Burslem, and I thank you. One last thing—will you tell me, please, where I can find the coachman's family? I was told he planned to visit his mother, so he's probably either with her or she can give me his direction."

Burslem said regretfully, "Now that's what I can't do, Colonel. When old Mr. Davis went to his reward, years ago, that were, the widow had to move out of their house. Henery said Wally only come this way again to crow over his old 'qaintances, but where his mum and kinfolks live now, Henery's got no notion."

"And that's dished me again, Minna." Adair threw a ball for the spaniel pup that had presented it hopefully. "Each time I think to find a promising clue, I run into a brick wall!"

Walking beside him through the windswept gardens, Minerva said with ready sympathy, "How frustrating it must be when you have tried so hard. Do you mean to ride down to Brighton and talk to our groom?"

"Perhaps. Though I think Burslem told me as much as her Henry knows. There's another avenue that might be worth exploring. I learned that Mrs. Davis is a fine laundress. And that she takes in work for a castle somewhere in the southland."

His cousin looked dismayed. "Good gracious, Hasty! There are castles everywhere! How would you know where to begin?"

"I don't know, of course. But I'd think the poor woman would have wanted to be somewhere near to where she'd lived for so long. Don't you agree?"

"I expect she would." Minerva looked dubious, however, and said hesitantly, "Farnham is nearby. And there is Herstmonceaux. And Parham, perhaps?"

"I think we can eliminate the great houses. The fellow distinctly said a castle."

"Oh. Well, let me see . . . There's Arundel, and Lewes, and Windsor, of course."

"True. And yet I cannot think washing would be sent out from such illustrious old piles. Surely they'd have laundry maids on their staff?"

"Do you know, Hasty," said Minerva gently, "I really think that would apply to any castle worthy of the name."

He nodded. "Well, then, I'll just have to seek out some shabby old places that are *un*worthy of the name."

"How dauntless you are!" With a responsive smile she said, "You won't fail. I know it!"

He took her hand and held it. "I wish I could tell you how much your loyalty means to me. And I am much in debt to Julius, you know."

"What, because he has faith in you? Why should he not? I

know some of the family don't exactly approve of him as my betrothed, or hold him in high regard, but he has very strong principles and he stands by his friends."

"He certainly stood by me when Thorne Webber gave me this." He touched his bruised cheek. "Despite the fact that it was in the middle of Town with many spectators. He didn't tell you?"

"Why—no. How very good of him. He said nothing of it."

"Nor of the fact that he was attacked on our doorstep? I see he did not, and I have frightened you."

She had turned pale and said falteringly, "He said he had slipped in the snow."

"If he did, it was with the aid of a rock thrown at him because he dared call upon the untouchable Adairs." Bitterness shadowed his eyes. "You'll have to keep him away from us, Minna. Or from me, at all events. I've no wish to bring disaster down upon you."

They had reached the fenced dog runs. Minerva opened the gate and the spaniels came rushing to them, barking and leaping about joyously. Surrounded, Adair bent to stroke silken coats and caress the heads that were eagerly presented.

Watching him, Minerva breathed a sigh of relief that the exuberant animals had banished the grim expression she had never seen before.

"You've some jolly fine pups," he said laughingly, and failing to dodge a long tongue, exclaimed, "But I've already washed my face, you rascals—down with you!"

Minerva was justly proud of her dogs and each one had to be presented to her cousin by name before she called to her kennelman to rescue Adair from his admirers.

"You've done very well with this hobby," he said, closing the gate behind them. "Or has it become a full-fledged business venture?"

"It really has, you know. We call it Blackbird Kennels, and Uncle has had cards printed that I can give out. We seem to be earning quite a reputation, and I actually had two gentlemen bidding against each other at Christmas-time."

"Splendid! You deserve it. One of these days, when I'm a staid married man with a home of my own, I'm going to ask you to save the pick of a litter for me."

"Nothing would please me more than to see you happily wed," she said fondly. "And you will be in deep disgrace if at least one of my dogs doesn't dwell under your roof."

"You have my word on it. But for the present, m'dear, I must be off on my castle-quest, so I'd best go and say my farewells to my uncle."

Her smile faded. "I doubt Uncle will see you, but don't worry. I'll say farewell for you."

"Thank you. But why won't he see me? Never say I really upset him last evening?"

They had started back to the house but at this she halted and turned to look up at him in a worried fashion. "His man sent down word that Uncle had passed a restless night and would sleep late this morning. Why should you fear that you have upset him?"

"I interrupted him while he was working on his Lists, I'm afraid. He whisked them all out of sight, but one fell, and when I took it up, the poor old fellow practically had an apoplexy."

"Oh dear! That silly hobby of his! I vow it is becoming an obsession, and he is more and more *secretive* about it! None of us even dares ask *what* he lists. Or why. Mama says it's his only toy."

Adair grinned, and as they walked on said, "Perhaps it is, poor old fellow."

"An engrossing one, certainly. But you know, Hasty, the more he keeps his precious Lists locked away, the more curious we all become. The boys think he is writing a book, and when they are here from school it's all Mama and I can do to keep them from invading his study and spying on him, the scamps!"

"Those wild brothers of yours! I can well imagine. Still, it's good that my uncle has such an interest, Minna. If it keeps him happy and occupied, where's the harm in it?"

118

The words were no sooner spoken than icy fingers seemed to slide down his back.

His slight shiver did not escape Minerva and she asked anxiously, "Are you cold? You should have brought a warmer cloak, dear."

He said that it was delightful to be mothered, which restored the smile to her pleasant face.

But he knew that the sudden chill he'd felt had nothing to do with the weather.

The trouble with searching out less illustrious castles was, Adair soon discovered, that all too often they were either in ruins or depressingly dreary. On the second day of his quest he had made his way to the fourth historical edifice on his list, only to find that it had been turned into a foundling home where such luxuries as fine laundry were not likely to be indulged in.

It had been a dull day of wind and fast-scurrying clouds, with not one glimpse of the sun. Adair was weary, and even Toreador was less spirited than usual. The next name on the "likely list" was Greyrock Castle. The pedlar who gave him directions was a frivolous sort with a pair of eyes that seemed to hold an amused twinkle. When Adair asked if anyone was in residence at the castle, he answered, "Oh, there's folks there. Off and on," then slapped the reins on his donkey's back and drove away chuckling to himself.

"Half-wit," muttered Adair irritably.

This lane certainly was well travelled if not well kept, and following it towards a wooded hill he was fully prepared to discover an abandoned stone shell at the summit.

Toreador broke from the belt of trees, and Adair swore furiously. The pedlar had the last laugh, all right!

Greyrock Castle was not a castle at all, but a large and apparently thriving inn. Two coaches stood in the yard, and ostlers were poling up the team of a third. A stable-boy ran to take Toreador's reins.

"No!" said Adair angrily. But the light was failing, the wind was ever more chill, and he was quite ready for dinner. Greyrock Castle looked to be a fine house; the exterior half-timbered, the latticed windows clean, some already bright with lamplight, and smoke curling from a cluster of chimneys. The stable-boy watched him uncertainly. He said, "Oh, very well," and swung from the saddle.

The boy grinned and with the air of an expert in such matters, said, "You got a very nice hack here, guv'nor."

"Yes, and he is accustomed to the best of care," warned Adair, a smile robbing the words of their severity.

"Then he come to the right house," said the boy pertly. "Everything's prime here, sir. Be you staying overnight?"

"Possibly. If the host has a room for me." And although he was in the wrong sort of castle, he said out of habit, "And if you've a fine laundress."

"That we do, sir." The boy checked as he started to lead Toreador off, then called, "Only I dunno if the Widder Davis be taking any work this week."

9

There were only three occupied tables when Adair went down to dinner early that evening. He was in high spirits and he nodded cordially to the elderly gentleman with his two elderly ladies, and to the young couple at the window table, and exchanged a cheerful "good even" with two merchants who haggled over business even as they ate.

The serving maid brought him the wine he ordered and he was pleased to find it a good claret. He had to wait for his beefsteak, and occupied his time by recalling his incredulity when the stable-boy had tossed off that remark about the Widow Davis. The host had shown him to a small but clean room, while informing him that the inn was built over the ruins of the original Greyrock Castle. He verified that they had a washerwoman on the staff, and yes, there was also a local woman who occasionally did *blanchisserie,* or fancy laundering, if some person of Quality desired it. Adair said that he carried "a message" for the lady, and in response to the immediate look of curiosity lied that Mrs. Davis had once worked for his mother. The host accepted this falsehood and was so accommodating as to write down the widow's direction and bring it to Adair's table with the wine.

The directions were involved, but Adair did not doubt he'd be able to follow them. Tonight, the world was a brighter place and nothing could dim his optimism. He knew at last where to find the widow, and hopefully he would soon confront her unpopular son. By heaven, but he'd have the truth from the fellow if he had to choke it out of him! The General and those dunderheads in Whitehall would have to pay heed when he produced a perjured witness—as he was sure Davis was.

His dinner was plain but good, and after he had done justice to it and to the baked apple with cheese, followed by a glass of port, he went up to bed.

He'd been in the saddle all day, and physically he was tired, but his mind was wide awake. Try as he would, his thoughts kept reverting to the question of whom he had so antagonized that the trap had been devised which had so nearly brought about his death. And as always he wound up with no answers but only the unchanging and infuriating—*why*? He was not without enemies—he'd yet to meet the man who could claim to be universally liked. But it was hard to imagine anyone—even so sour-natured an individual as Thorne Webber—going to the trouble of arranging such a devious and complicated revenge. Most fellows with a deep grudge would simply have called him out; though, of course, a duel would entail personal risk. But if some madman lacked the courage to face him, would not an ambush, or a hired assassin, have presented a swifter and less risky way to put a period to him?

Perplexing thoughts; more than enough to disturb a man's rest. Yet as Adair drifted off to sleep, his mind was occupied not with the machinations of his unknown enemy but with the memory of fair curls and eyes of a clear blue-grey that could light as quickly with laughter as with scorn. A truly rare beauty was Miss Cecily Hall . . .

An indeterminate time later a rough hand awakened him. The candle was lit. The host and a manservant bent over his bed and were shaking him.

He started up, at once wide awake. "What's wrong?"

"You is!" growled the host. "If I'd knowed who you was you'd not have set foot in my house, by grab but you wouldn't! A filthy woman killer under my roof! Lor'! My good wife is like to have a spasm!"

Angered, Adair snapped, "I have killed no woman! Whoever filled your ear with such stuff is a lying scandalmonger!"

"So you say! By my lights he done me a favour! This is a Christian house and from what I hears even if it ain't been proved as you done away with the lady, there's no denying you ruined the poor little thing. Burn me ears if we won't have to scrub this room from floor to ceiling! Out, Mr. Wicked Chatteris, or whatever you calls yourself! Not as I blame you for hiding yer own shameful name. Out o' my house! Now! Or I'll have you kicked out!"

His clothes were hurled at him; he had to dodge his boots. The door was wide and several interested faces peered inside. Somebody laughed and the kindly-appearing old gentleman who had sat with the two elderly ladies in the dining room declared indignantly that if he'd guessed Greyrock Castle catered to criminals he'd never have come here.

Adair swung the door shut. He was seething with rage and mortification as he pulled off his nightshirt. Someone had recognized him evidently, and had lost no time in spreading the word.

A glance at his timepiece told him that it was just past one o'clock. Most likely he'd have to sleep under a hedge for the rest of the night. He dressed rapidly, but in very few minutes a pounding on his door and a demand that he get out so that the room could be aired brought a dark flush to his face.

He stalked out grimly. The uproar had evidently roused several of the guests, and men in dressing-gowns or with cloaks thrown over their night-rail had gathered in the narrow passage. Ignoring their disgusted taunts, Adair was obliged to push his way through them. Someone stuck out a foot and he stumbled. A laugh went up. As he reached the top of the stairs a strong hand shoved at his back. He fell and it was all he could do to regain his feet half-way down the flight.

Somehow, he kept his head up and with their jeers and insults ringing in his ears made his way to the lower hall, bitterly conscious of how ghastly it was to be despised by one's own countrymen. The only good thing about this latest humiliation was that it had taken place so far from Town and his family would not hear of it.

He picked up the saddle-bags he'd dropped when he fell. Straightening, he found an emaciated young man smirking at him while manipulating a notepad and pencil. "Lieutenant Colonel Adair, I believe?" he said in a high falsetto. "Or at least— you was a colonel at one time. I'm sure the readers of the *Gazette* would be interested to know of your reception in this peaceful countryside. Are you here to—"

"Out of my way!" growled Adair, shoving him aside.

"—to visit friends, perhaps?" called the newspaper writer mockingly. "Or might one better say—to hide yourself?"

Adair, his mouth set in a thin line, acknowledged bitterly that his family would be shamed by yet another lurid newspaper account.

Outside, the wind had risen and carried on its icy breath a stinging sleet. He saddled up Toreador himself while a yawning ostler offered no assistance and when he rode out shouted insults and sent a hail of stones after him.

Adair fought down his fury and rode on. He must not become soured. These attacks weren't really directed at him, but at the cunning villain who had planned the whole ugly business. And that unknown enemy must be close by, still working his venom, for there was no doubt in Adair's mind but that the same person was responsible for the attack at the Pilgrim Arms as for his ouster from the Greyrock Castle Inn. A persistent antagonist, who must be dogging his footsteps and seizing every opportunity to throw a little more hellish notoriety his way. But—why? Why? Why?

He ducked his head to a booming gust and thought vengefully of the time when he would catch this scheming Unknown at his tricks, and what he'd do to the miserable bastard.

"Hello?" Clang! Clang! "Hello, there!"

Adair jerked his head up and realized he had heard the clamorous bell for a minute or two but had been too lost in anger to pay heed. He was passing a drive guarded by a pair of iron gates. A woman clad in a long cloak and hood was struggling to close the right-hand gate but it sagged crookedly, besides which it was clearly too heavy for her. Each time she had almost secured it, the wind tore it open again and it crashed against the centre post, this causing the bell-like tone. She had set a lantern in a sheltered spot and as Adair dismounted and made his way to her side she took it up and he saw that she was a nun.

"Good evening, Sister," he said above the bluster of the wind. "Might I be of help?"

"Well, I hoped you might," she shouted. "But I apologize if I interrupted your prayer. You were—praying, weren't you?"

He smiled cynically. The lady would not feel so guilty if she knew how far from holy had been his thoughts at that moment. "Not exactly, ma'am." He tethered Toreador to a shrub and reached for the gate. "Allow me to close this for you."

She scurried through to the inside. "You have to loop this chain over the centre post, else it won't stay shut. "Yes, that's right. I was afraid it would be too heavy for me, but I came down because the noise was disturbing everyone. Thank you so much, sir."

"I'm glad I was able to be of service." Touching his hat respectfully, Adair prepared to mount up.

The nun watched him, then called, "It is very late, sir, and such a dreadful night. Have you far to travel?"

"I hope not, if I can find a room somewhere."

"Dear me." She sounded dismayed. "I doubt you will, at this hour, you know. I hesitate to offer—it's not a very cozy place, but—well, we have a room above the barn where our gardener sleeps sometimes. Mother Superior is away, but I am sure she would say you are welcome to take shelter there."

He hesitated. "You're very kind. But—is it allowed? I mean, if this is a nunnery—"

"It is the Nunnery of the Blessed Spirit, but you will not be in it. I mean, not in the main building. The barn roof does not leak anymore, and you would be out of the rain at least, and you could stable your beautiful horse, if that would suit."

Adair lost not a moment in assuring her that it would suit splendidly.

The barn proved to be a sturdy structure, weather-tight and with an oil lamp which the nun lit from her lantern before she left him. A shabby coach, poles up, stood next to an old farm waggon. Four horses blinked at him from their stalls. He rubbed down Toreador, let him drink from the water trough, and settled him into an empty stall, then he climbed the ladder to the loft. To his right was a big pile of hay; to his left a trestle-bed and a large old seaman's chest. A rickety wash-stand against the wall boasted a tin pitcher and bowl, and a dusty mirror hung on a nail above it. It was a far cry from his suite at Adair Hall, but he'd slept in worse places, and compared to the stormy night he'd just escaped, was sheer luxury. He opened the chest and found two thick blankets. He spread one on the hay, wrapped the other around him, and stretching out on his fragrant couch, fell into a deep sleep.

He awoke with the dawn, but someone had already left a ewer of hot water at the foot of the ladder, with a note inviting him to breakfast in the kitchen.

The sun came up while he shaved, and a very deaf groom arrived to tend the horses and roar that he would bait the dapple-grey.

Adair thanked him and stepped into a brilliant morning. A few dark pink clouds drifted against a blue-green sky, the pale sunlight set every bush and tree sparkling with jewels and transformed the drops from the eaves into cascades of diamonds. The air was fresh and bracing. He banished the lingering hurt of last night's humiliation. This was going to be a better day. Today, he would find Walter Davis and discover the truth at last.

He was admitted to the side door of the nunnery by the plump little lady he had met in last night's storm. She introduced herself as Sister Ruth and took him into a stark but spotless kitchen where two other nuns were already busily at work. Willing hands spread a snowy cloth on a corner of the large central table, knives and forks were set out, and amid many shy glances and some muffled giggles Adair was served two soft-boiled eggs and thick slices of buttered bread and blackberry jam, all of which, he was informed in whispers, were products of the nunnery farm. While he ate, Sister Ruth spoke to him in sporadic bursts. He gained the impression that their Order was quite poor, but when he had finished the steaming mug of coffee that completed his breakfast, his attempts to pay for their hospitality were refused politely, but with such firmness that he dared not persist.

Nothing would do but that he must be shown their small flock of chickens. Speaking darkly of the wicked habits of foxes, Sister Ruth led the way, and the other kitchen workers drifted along in the rear. After he had admired the fowl, there were cows and goats to be proudly displayed. Adair glanced back and found the procession now numbered six ladies, coming along two by two. By the time they reached the vegetable gardens, ten nuns were in the train, and at the bakery where their breads and rolls and the famous Nuns' Fruit Cakes were created, the number had swelled to a round dozen.

Looking at their guileless, beaming faces, Adair said with a smile that he had never been so fortunate as to have so many charming ladies all to himself. There was laughter, shy questions were asked, and when he admitted he was from London Town, tongues were loosened and he was soon doing his best to respond to a battery of requests for the latest news of the City, fashions, and the progress of the war.

Conversation ceased abruptly when a tall middle-aged lady appeared. She said nothing, but shook her head reproachfully, and the nuns, looking guilt-stricken, fled. Adair bowed. This must be the Mother Superior, and she was obviously displeased to find her flock fluttering around a stranger—a male stranger, especially. Like most of Lord Wellington's officers, he was adept at soothing ruffled feelings. He thanked her profusely for the hospitality that had been extended to him, and expressed his sincere admiration of the neatness of the nunnery and the excellence of their farming endeavours. The Mother Superior watched him with her deep-set and beautiful grey eyes, and he was struck by the notion that they had met before, though he could not recall when or where.

As if coming to a decision, she said in a heavily accented voice, "You are charming, which you know, of course. My little ladies were naughty—but how shall I blame them? And it is *au fait accompli*. So you may as well come, *monsieur le colonel*, and let us make the show for you of our primary source of funds. Ah, but it is that I have startled you, no?"

She had, indeed. Word of his notoriety had reached even this peaceful oasis.

"You know who I am, Reverend Mother?"

"I know."

"Then—are you sure you—"

"Have the trust in you? But, yes. Your predicament it makes me desolate. We will hold you in our prayers. Now, please, you will come."

She led the way along a chilly corridor, her robes shushing over the flagged floors. Adair heard a soft tapping and murmurous voices and he was ushered into a long room that smelled of paint. The floor was littered with wood shavings. Several of the nuns bent over a table, scrubbing away with sandpaper at a large flat carving. To one side, three more were busied with paints and brushes. They all looked up when the door opened, and the youngest of them exclaimed, "Oh! He is allowed to see! I am so glad!"

"You have always too much of the talk, Sister Elizabeth," scolded the Mother Superior, but with a smile.

Waved forward, Adair looked down at a replica of the Crucifixion, wondrously depicted in wood. Awed, he said, "Jove! You are artists! Is this for your chapel, ma'am?"

"I wish it were. We have to sell it, alas. But the church that buys, they are most happy."

"I should rather think they might be! May I ask what these other ladies are about?"

The nuns at the side table were applying paint to a finished carving of a man and several women clad in biblical dress. The Mother Superior said, "The cross is to hang above the altar, and this group will be placed nearby. As you see, it depicts the faithful who waited on Golgotha that terrible day."

The detail of features, hands, even the sandals, astonished Adair. "Do you carve from life, ma'am? I'd swear—I mean, I think I've met that gentleman somewhere."

She said with a chuckle, "Then you have travelled in exalted company, Colonel. That is St. John. No, do not suffer the embarrassment. It is truth that we often take people we know for our models if they interest us. The next time you visit here, you may find that you too are destined to hang in some great church."

Which would be an improvement, he thought cynically, over his last brush with hanging.

Time was slipping away and he was eager to get to the Davis farm, but he could not leave without doing something to repay their hospitality. Recalling the noisy iron gate, he made that his contribution. The gate had come loose from the top hinges which were now sadly bent and rusted, and all three posts were sagging. As is the way of such undertakings, the repairs that he had thought would take an hour, took four. He was testing the closure of the mended gate when another procession approached. In the lead came the plump Sister Ruth, carrying a plate with a ham sandwich and pickles. Following her was the bearer of a dish containing an apple and a large pear. The next lady had a tray with a pot of tea, cup, saucer, and milk jug, then came the groom with a folding table, and bringing up the rear, the young Sister Elizabeth with a bowl in which was a slice of fruit cake.

Adair said laughingly that they would spoil him past permission, but the hard work and the cold air had whetted his appetite. He was quite willing to sit on a tree stump near the table and enjoy his lunch, while the nuns clustered around him, chattering like so many birds, as if he were the first male they'd met for years.

A coach came rattling along the lane and slowed. Adair's view was obscured by the *coiffes* and flowing robes of his companions, but he heard soft feminine laughter and realized he must present quite a picture, surrounded as he was by his pious friends.

It was now past one o'clock, and having finished his lunch and completed the repairs, he said his farewells. They all gathered to see him go. He offered a flourishing bow and received giggles, smiles and waves in return.

His directions to the Davis farm proved faulted. The host of the Greyrock Castle Inn had drawn a crude map, but the lane that should have led straight to the farmhouse wandered on for miles with no trace of any kind of habitation and only an occasional cow to munch placidly at him from beyond a hedge. He turned back, irritated, and at length was able to get clearer directions from a carter. "Ye'll be a friend o' Wally Davis, is that right, sir?" the man asked, eyeing Adair curiously.

"A matter of business, merely."

"Ar," said the carter with a sniff. "Nor *that* don't surprise me!"

It was one more indication, thought Adair as he rode on, that Walter Coachman did not go through life overburdened with admirers.

He reached the farm with no further delays and found it to consist of a run-down house with a few chickens scratching about the yard, and several goats in a small fenced pasture. There was no one about. He dismounted and looped Toreador's reins over a rail of the fence. The front porch sagged and was sadly in need of paint, but neat and tidy. His knock at the door won no answer, nor did his hail. He wandered around to the back. Some distance behind the house was a ramshackle barn and next to it a paddock where two horses grazed. He could hear a man's voice. If it was the disappearing coachman, he might very well resent having been rooted out. Adair checked the pistol in his cloak pocket and trod softly into the dimness of the barn.

A very aged man was tottering about wielding a hay-fork, though whether he was raking the hay or spreading it would have been hard to tell. And as he worked, he grumbled.

"... from the day as he was born. I told her, then. Years agone though it were. There was summat about them eyes of his. Shifty. I knew how it would be! But would she listen?" He shook the hay-fork at a rooster that had strutted into the barn and paused to tilt its head at him. "No, she would not," said the old man, staggering a little from this effort. "No more would she now! He's come home to give back what he owed, she said. *Owed!* Hah! Stole, more like! If she'd of listened to me—but who am I?" Here, becoming aware of Adair's presence, he shook the hay-fork again. "Who am I?" he demanded fiercely.

Adair drew a bow at random. "I fancy you must be Walter's grandfather, sir."

"And if you think as I be proud of that, ye're fair and far out! Which I'll speak me mind, no matter what she says. You're late. They've all gone."

He was panting and looked worn out. Adair went over to appropriate the fork and offered his arm.

"Do you expect your grandson to come back soon, Mr. Davis?"

"Well, of course I do," said the old man, clinging to his arm and scowling up at him irritably. "What you think? They was a-going to hang about for a sennight? Not even me daughter-in-law be that fulish, and a fulish woman she allus has been. Nor I don't want to sit on the hay bale, thankee, but ye can leave the fork there. I'd think ye'd know it be cold out here for old bones like mine." He fixed Adair with a reproachful look, and when a suitable apology had been tendered, said, "That's why I didn't go with 'em. Ye can give me a hand up to the house."

They emerged into the light, and the old man scanned Adair appraisingly. "You don't look like them as Wally useter choose for friends when he lived hereabouts. If ye could call 'em friends. You knowed him a long time?"

"Not—exactly, but—"

"Then why would ye bother to come?"

Adair boosted him up the step onto the porch. "I have a message for—"

"Ah. From they Bow Street folks, I shouldn't wonder. Wally were messing about with that lot a while since. I *told* her no good would come of it, though I'll own you could've knocked me down with a feather when t'other lot rid up!"

"Er—from Bow Street, sir?"

Mr. Davis gave a snort of impatience. "Bow Street me eye! Are ye quite daft? I mean the flash folks! The widder was fair bowled out, and so were I. Who'd a thought they'd come all this way? And him no more'n a coachman in spite of all his fancy talk."

Adair tensed. "Somebody else has come to see your grandson?"

"A course they has! Did ye think as you was the only one? And late, at that! I vow you young folk nowadays is . . ." Bristling, Mr. Davis listed the failings of today's youth while Adair watched and wondered if the poor old fellow was short of a sheet.

"Ah," Davis interrupted himself. "Here comes me grandson now, with his ma. And past time."

Adair's heart gave a jolt. He tightened his grip on the pistol in his pocket and turned to face the man whose lies had brought so much misery to him.

Several people were walking up the lane, following a woman of about sixty who appeared to be distressed and was supported

132

by a husky youth. His gaze fixed on the two of them, Adair said sharply, "I thought you expected your grandson, Walter, Mr. Davis?"

"By grab but you *are* looby," croaked the old gentleman, drawing back in alarm. "That there fine young chap with the Widder be me grandson Eddie. *Walter* died Monday. They just buried him!"

It was as if Adair had been struck with a hammer and he stood motionless, staring blankly at the funeral party. Only now did he notice that they all were sombrely clad, most wearing black.

Walter Davis was dead?

Surely, it wasn't possible. He must have come to the wrong place. Death couldn't have come so suddenly to a relatively young and healthy man? But—if it was truth . . .

In that event his desperate search had been for nought. The coachman had carried to his grave the truths that could have exonerated him and restored his good name.

In a voice that sounded very far away, he said, "My—my condolences, sir. I didn't know. The last time I saw Walter, he was in good health. I'd not have dreamt—"

"No more would any of us. Such a way as he had with cattle, who'd a thought he'd let any hack corner him like that?"

Adair said sharply, "Your grandson met with an accident?"

"Ar. That's what the constable called it. I say 'twere plain carelessness. A fine young thoroughbred it is, but more show than strength. You know how *they* saddle-hosses can be. Wally bought him with some o' that money he come by. Rid in here lording it over the rest of us, boasting about how he were the only one in the family as had done well for hisself. Much good it did him!"

"Did anyone see the accident, sir? Was he able to tell you—"

"Nobody saw it. We didn't even know what had happened till me granddarter Mary went to call him for supper. She set up such a screeching we all come running. There were nought could be done for poor Wally, and the hoss were so scared it was all we could do to get him out o' the stall. Ah, here they is now."

The mourners were entering the yard. There weren't many and, except for the widow, tears were noticeable by their absence. Three youngish women, five men, looking uncomfortable in their formal garb; a boy of about ten, who kept lagging back and appeared fascinated by someone behind him. Adair followed his glance and as they drew closer, saw a gentleman whose red hair shone like a flame in the winter sunlight, and a tall fair-haired young lady whose dark garments did nothing to diminish her vivid loveliness.

Adair gave himself a mental kick.

Miss Cecily Hall and her firebrand of a cousin must have known all along where Walter Davis had gone. They had followed his own search to make sure he did not get too close to the rogue. His sudden identification and ejection from the Greyrock Castle Inn was explained now. This fiendish chit and her fellow conspirators had arranged it. Very likely they were also the ones who had hired those bravos at the Pilgrim Arms in Bedfordshire, which piece of scheming he had mistakenly laid at Thorne Webber's door.

He stamped forward, saying between his teeth, "Damn them! Damn them!"

"Hey!" croaked Mr. Davis, grabbing his arm. "Wally might not have been a credit to us, but I won't have no cursing at his funeral!"

Breathing hard, Adair fought for control. The old man was right. Whatever Walter Davis had been, his family had enough trouble.

Miss Hall's eyes met his own. He saw them widen briefly. Rufus uttered a muffled snort, and she said something in an urgent under-voice.

"My condolences, Mrs. Davis," said Adair.

The widow said unsteadily, "I doesn't know ye, sir. Be ye a friend o' my Walter?"

134

With an ironic glance at Adair, Miss Hall interposed, "Major Newton is with us, ma'am. You arrive tardily, Major."

"So I see," said Adair, just as ironically.

They were invited to come inside and "have some vittles." Adair declined politely, but Rufus Prior, smiling down at a newly arrived village belle, accepted at once. Eddie Davis said that some neighbour ladies had been preparing food, and it would be a kindness to his mother to partake of the refreshments "and give Walter a proper send-off." Perforce, Adair followed as the mourners trooped into the house.

In the small parlour a table was set with plates of sandwiches, biscuits and little cakes, and there were jugs of lemonade and home-brewed wine.

Adair paid his respects to the other family members, and as more people arrived he was included in their discussions of the coachman's death. All he learned, however, was that it had been "a fair dreadful thing; a real shock; a example of how a man could be hale and hearty one minute, and gone to meet his Maker the next."

Throughout their talk the eyes of the men turned constantly in one direction. It had grown warm in the parlour and Miss Hall had removed her cloak. The black gown she wore was classically simple. 'She lights up this room,' thought Adair, and had to remind himself that she was his enemy and, having failed to bring about his execution, had meant to shoot him. And yet she haunted his dreams and just now his stupid heart had leapt at the sight of her. 'You're behaving like a lovesick boy,' he thought savagely as he gravitated to her side. "I congratulate you," he murmured. "You have outmanoeuvred me. Though I fail to understand why you felt it necessary to have me thrown out of the Greyrock Castle, since Davis was already dead."

"We did nothing of the sort." She spoke softly, but indignation flashed in her eyes. "I have never even heard of such a place. We came here because my grandmama wanted to talk with Walter Coachman. We were most shocked to learn of his death." She added with a curl of the lip, "And you must not feel obliged to thank me because I vouched for you just now."

"*Touché!* I wish I could understand why you did so."

"A whim," she said with a careless shrug.

He looked at her levelly, but she avoided his eyes. He asked, "Have you just arrived in the area?"

"We arrived in time to attend the service, as you might have done had you not dallied with all those nuns."

So hers was the laugh he'd heard when that coach passed by. The odd little nunnery came back into his mind's eye. He said, "They were kind enough to allow me to rack up in their barn." And he wondered why he thought of the little nunnery as having been "odd."

Before Miss Hall could comment, Eddie Davis brought the local curate over to meet her. It developed that the clerical gentleman was cousin to the vicar of her own parish. A garrulous individual, he was delighted to make her acquaintance and bombarded her with questions as to his cousin's health and family, the manner in which he conducted his duties and the size and prosperity of his congregation.

Adair slipped away. He went first to the barn and found four young boys peering with ghoulish awe into an empty stall. This, they informed him, was where Walter Davis "got his head bashed in."

Adair went inside and prowled about inspecting the walls and flooring while four pairs of eyes watched his every move with growing curiosity.

A lad whose face was liberally dusted with freckles was at last unable to contain himself, and asked, "Wotcher looking for, sir? Bones and brains?"

Adair stood straight. "No, you young ruffian. I'm looking for any damage the horse might have done."

A small boy asked anxiously if Mr. Walter's horse was to be shot.

"Oh, I doubt that," said Adair with a reassuring smile.

"I hope not, sir," the boy said. "He's a fine hack, and don't act mean, not like my pa's old nag."

A moment later they answered a summons to go home for supper, and forgot their interest in the tall stranger.

Adair wandered out to the paddock to take a closer look at Walter Davis' "fine hack." It was a sleek young chestnut thoroughbred given to sudden starts and caperings about. Adair called to him. The chestnut flung up his head, trotted over, then raced off again, mane and tail flying. Adair said, "Be calm, friend. I won't hurt you." The horse approached uneasily, but allowed his neck to be caressed. Adair told him that he was a fine fellow. Actually, he would not have chosen the animal for his own stable; it was too high-strung, besides which there was a tendency to throw out the right front leg when it ran. Still, it was a handsome creature, and would have allowed Walter Davis to cut a dash before his friends and family. Certainly, he must have parted with the equivalent of several years of a coachman's pay to buy such a mount.

The chestnut tossed his head suddenly, and went off at the gallop.

Adair became aware of the scent of violets. Without turning, he said, "What do you think of him, Miss Hall?"

Her musical voice answered, "He's a pretty sight. Rather too fidgety for my taste. Is he the animal who . . . ?"

"So I am told."

"You sound dubious."

"Not about the horse." He turned and said gravely, "I was wondering if your pistol was at my back."

"Not just at the moment." A dimple peeped beside her mouth. "I have to curb my murderous tendencies under the present circumstances. These people have sufficient grief. Though I think few of them cared very much for poor Walter."

Her hostility seemed lessened. He probed cautiously, "Are you getting tired of pursuing me, ma'am?"

She fired up at once. "We followed you *only* because we thought you would lead us to wherever you had hidden Alice."

"Whereas I was searching for your ex-coachman. I'm very sure he lied at my trial, and that he knew what really happened.

137

You said Lady Abigail wanted to talk to him. Will you tell me why?"

"She will tell you herself when she arrives. The apothecary was to drive her from the church. But I—well, I believe Grand-mama has come to think we may have judged you unfairly." Her beautifully shaped lips drooped. She said sadly, "If that is so, we are back to where we started in our search for my dear cousin. You were our best hope."

He bowed and said ironically, "And I, alas, am due to be arrested at any moment. My search for the real culprit may be cut short, because someone has now set it about that I've done away with the lady."

She gave him a quick glance. "It is a rumour we did not originate, I promise you. We have gone beyond vengeance or—or pride, and pray only to know that Alice is safe."

"If we were to pool our knowledge, ma'am, and work together, we might both achieve our gaol."

"Grandmama had the same thought. But—even were I to trust you—"

"Which you are not sure you do."

"Even then, there is nothing I could tell you."

"You could tell me what your cousin said after she was brought home."

"She spoke to no one. She was not conscious from the time you were—found, till the night she vanished."

"While I was in gaol."

"You could have arranged—"

"Oh, for heaven's sake! You cannot still believe that I would spend all this time in futile searching. If I were so enamoured of the lady as to have abducted her, is it not more likely that I'd wish to be with her?"

"How can I know what you might do? I scarcely know you."

He bowed and said formally, "Then allow me to introduce myself. You know of my family. My full name is Hastings Chatteris Adair. I am nine and twenty, and a younger son. I attended Eton briefly before entering the Royal Military Academy. My regimental rank is major, my army rank is lieutenant-colonel—or it was, I should say. At present I have no rank, and my best prospect is to escape the hangman's noose."

"Thank you for the summary. But as to your relationship with my cousin, who is lovely and sweetly natured and—"

"And little more than a child. I do not pursue children, ma'am."

She scanned him searchingly. The very blue eyes met hers without wavering, the lips were rather thin but well-shaped, the firm chin high-held. The wind had blown his dark hair into a charming untidiness about the bruised but finely cut features. She saw pride in that face, and determination, but not ruthlessness; indeed she had several times been struck by the lurking smile that could creep into his eyes. But she had learned early in life to mistrust good-looking men, and this young colonel was very good-looking indeed.

"There," he said. "I have told you of myself. Will you respond by telling me whatever you know of your ex-coachman? His friends, his acquaintances, his lady love, if there was one."

He was answered by a new voice.

"There was not—so far as we could tell." Impressive in a gown of stiff black bombazine, and with a black lace veil over her powdered hair, Lady Abigail Prior joined them and extended a hand regally. "You should be careful of nuns, Colonel. They can be as inflexible as they are pious."

"Good afternoon, my lady." He bowed over her thin-gloved fingers. "Will you give me your opinion of your late coachman?"

She considered for a moment, then said, "To utter pleasant platitudes because someone has gone to their reward is, to my mind, hypocritical nonsense. Walter Davis was an ill-natured man with a slippery eye. The other servants did not care for him. No more did I. My son valued him because he had a way with horses, and had driven, ridden, handled, and trained them for most of his life. Is that of any use to you, Adair?"

"Insofar as it reinforces my suspicions, ma'am."

They both stared at him.

139

He said with a shrug, "I cannot find it logical that such an expert would have allowed a half-trained animal to corner him and smash his skull."

Cecily Hall pointed out, "Davis was fond of the bottle, you know."

"And had likely been so for years. However foxed, he would have known better than to enter a stall with a nervous horse. Further, if the animal was so scared as to have trampled a man to death, wouldn't you expect that there would have been considerable damage to the stall while it plunged about?"

"There probably was," said her ladyship.

Adair shook his head. "I just inspected that stall, ma'am. There are one or two small gouges merely. Horses are big animals, shod with iron. One or two I've had to deal with have been nervous and have kicked holes in barn walls with little effort."

"Oh . . . good gracious," said Cecily in a half-whisper.

"Are you saying what I think you are saying?" asked Lady Abigail intently.

"I am saying that I believe Walter Davis was murdered," said Adair.

10

~~~

Briefly, Adair's dramatic announcement rendered both his hearers mute. Cecily's lower lip sagged in a way he found tantalizing, then she exclaimed in that same breathless fashion, "Heavens above! How dreadful!"

"You think he was killed deliberately, and it was made to seem an accident?" asked Lady Abigail. "Why? Only to keep him from talking to you?"

"To kidnap a lady is a hanging offence, ma'am, Quite apart from what he must guess I will do to the rogue who brought all this misery upon us—when I find him."

Cecily wrinkled her brow and murmured, "But why would anyone do such a wicked thing in the first place? Surely if the kidnapper is madly in love with Alice and knows himself ineligible, he could have lured her to a run-away marriage at Gretna Green. It would be shameful, I grant you, but without the need to implicate you, Colonel."

"Unless Adair has some extreme vindictive enemies, my love," argued Lady Abigail.

"Vindictive enough to want him dead, and to now do away with the only witness who might have cleared his name?" Cecily paled to an afterthought. "Such a villain would not hesitate to murder our dear Alice!"

Driven by a need to banish the fear from her eyes, Adair said, "If he meant only to murder her, there would have been no cause to lure her away,"

Lady Abigail nodded. "And, do you know, Cecily, I find it very hard to believe that any man would be so evil as to take the life of that sweet child."

'Except to protect himself,' thought Adair, but not voicing that qualification, he said, "I dare to hope that you both are beginning to change your minds about my part in this sad business. I can't tell you what that means to me."

"It means that you may add our names to the list of people who believe you," said Cecily, smiling at him.

"In addition to your family." Lady Prior added keenly, "They *do* support you, I trust?" Before he could respond she gave a snort and threw up her hands. "I might have known! A fine set of knock-in-the-cradles!"

Cecily looked appalled, but as usual, the old lady's use of cant terms amused Adair. He said, "No, but they will come around, ma'am, I promise you. It was a very great shock to them all." Lady Prior's lips parted and he went on quickly, "I have some loyal friends who are trying to help; my Uncle Willoughby Chatteris is on my side, and most of my family hold me innocent of harming Miss Prior at least—even if they're not convinced I didn't make off with the poor lady."

"Willoughby Chatteris . . ." said Lady Prior musingly. "Now why is that name so familiar to me, child?"

"I cannot think, Grandmama. A friend of Rufus, perhaps?"

"Hmm. I shall ask him, so I must go and wrench him away from the little village beauty who has enchanted the tiresome boy."

Cecily said, "Colonel Adair suggested that if we pool our knowledge, Grandmama, we will have a better chance for success."

"Just so. I had the very same thought, you will remember."

"In which case, ma'am," said Adair, "may I ask if you learned anything from the apothecary? You drove with him so as to ask questions, I presume."

"Correct. But the man had little to tell me that I did not already know. He confirmed the fact that our unfortunate coachman was slain by a blow to the back of the head."

"The *back* of the head?" said Cecily. "I was told he was trampled to death."

Adair said, "He could have been trying to escape the stall, I suppose. Forgive an unpleasant question, but—were there numerous wounds, my lady?"

"The one fatal blow," she answered. "And some bruises."

"No bones broken, for instance?"

"Apparently not. Is that something the constable should have noted, Adair?"

"I'd think he would find it odd that a horse's hooves flailed about in a frenzy inflicted only bruises—apart from the fatal blow."

"It certainly doesn't sound as if Davis was trampled," agreed Cecily. "What do you mean to do next?"

"Seek out your late coachman's grandpapa and try to discover if any strangers have been lurking about the farm of late."

"Very good. I shall do the same. I'll start with Walter's brother, poor man."

Adair said with a grin, "You are not likely to hear him complain, I think. He has scarce been able to take his eyes from you all afternoon."

"Which you would only know if you had been watching her also!" Lady Abigail frowned at Adair's red-faced confusion and turned to her granddaughter. "Never waste that demure look on me, miss. And take care not to bewitch young Davis. Meanwhile, I will weave my webs around that nice curate who is so eager to know everybody."

They parted then, Adair striding off to the stables and the two ladies returning to the house.

Cecily said, "Well, Grandmama, are you really convinced of his innocence?"

Lady Abigail paused to glance after Adair's tall figure. "So convinced that I could weep for my part in this. He is no Tragedy Jack, and keeps himself well in hand, but it is a tragedy for all that."

They walked on in silence for a moment, then Cecily said, "Did you see his eyes when you asked if his family supported him?"

"I did, and knowing that prideful cat of a mother of his, I am not surprised, but I'd have credited old Gower Chatteris with more kindness! Still, we were as gullible. We were all so sure."

"In the face of the evidence and our own coachman's sworn testimony—what were we to think?"

"I hold us excused to that extent. And we did not know him, after all. But for his own *family* to have turned their backs on him while he almost was hanged! Unforgivable! Well, child, perhaps we can help set things to rights." With an oblique glance at her granddaughter, she added: "You would like that—no?"

Cecily blushed but said firmly, "I cannot like *anyone* to be falsely accused and persecuted, ma'am, so do not be thinking of names for prospective great-grandchildren!"

———◦◦◦———

The light was fading when Lady Prior's coach rumbled away from the Davis farm with Adair riding inside and Toreador tied on behind. Rufus Prior was on the box, having growled that the colonel may have hornswoggled his female relations but he was not so easily gulled and would prefer the company of Coachman Peters.

"Rufus doesn't really believe you guilty," said Miss Hall, seated beside her grandmother.

Lady Prior agreed. "What it is, he's embarrassed because you will keep knocking him down."

Amused, Adair promised to mend his ways. "Now, may we compare notes? Did anyone uncover a significant clue?"

"Since I am the eldest, I will speak first," declared Lady Prior. "My curate—goodness, what a social climber!—said that Walter had boasted about 'his fine gentleman.' No name given, but the curate gathered this was a person of wealth and rank who had previously employed Walter in a matter of great delicacy."

"Did your coachman say what the 'delicate matter' was, ma'am?"

"Only that it was quite recent, and because he was such a clever fellow and kept his eyes open, he was now entrusted to find something."

"He said the same to his brother," put in Cecily eagerly. "And he said he would soon be a rich man whether his fine gentleman liked it or not."

"That sounds like prospective blackmail," said Adair. "When and where did this interesting conversation take place, do you know?"

"The afternoon of his death. Eddie Davis said that they were walking along the lane together but Walter suddenly stopped speaking and stared into the trees they were passing as if he'd seen someone there. Evidently he was very frightened and all but ran back to the house. Eddie put it down to strong spirits. He said Walter was out of sorts after that and decided to leave the farm next day. Had you any better luck, Colonel?"

It had been difficult to question Mr. Davis without seeming to do so, especially since the old gentleman tended to ramble off at a tangent each time he was almost brought to the point. "Not until I made a remark about tramps," Adair answered. "That properly sent him into the boughs. He was convinced some vagrant had been watching the farm and was after Walter's horse."

"More likely, he was after Walter," said Lady Abigail, looking grim.

Cecily said, "Especially if Walter's boasting was overheard."

"In which case," said Adair, "Davis sealed his own fate, for he would have been judged a potential danger to his 'fine gentleman.' I only wish I knew what he was hired to find."

"My little curate had the notion it was a legal document—perhaps a will," said Lady Prior.

Her eyes wide, Cecily exclaimed, "Only think, there might be some great fortune at the root of all this scheming. Perhaps we should try to discover who may be in the way of coming into an inheritance."

"An inheritance!" exclaimed Lady Prior. "*Now* I remember where I met Willoughby Chatteris! And you should too, Cecily. It was about two years ago, soon after the Warren-Wyants inherited the title and the fortune. They had been poor as church mice, if you recall, and to celebrate hosted that splendid Christmas party."

"Yes, of course!" said Cecily, laughing. "They were trying and trying to persuade a gentleman to dress up as Father Christmas for the children, and Mr. Chatteris and his niece arrived all unsuspecting with an adorable puppy the Warren-Wyants had ordered for their little son."

Lady Prior nodded. "Your uncle was pounced upon and bullied mercilessly, Adair. He had no least chance to escape!"

"Uncle Willoughby was their Father Christmas? Jove, but they must have had to use several pillows."

Cecily said, "And a false beard. He looked so funny, but the children adored him, and I do believe he . . ."

The rest of her remark was lost upon Adair.

'A beard . . .'

The Nunnery of the Blessed Spirit . . .

The Mother Superior with the French accent . . .

He knew now what had struck him as so odd about the nunnery.

And that he must return to Blackbird Terrace at once.

‹⸙›

The prospect of journeying after dark did not appeal to Lady Prior and she decided to overnight at the nearby home of a friend. The coach pulled up when they reached the Basingstoke

Road. It was agreed that if anything new was learned it would be shared immediately.

"If you should wish to reach me," said Adair, "Miss Minerva Chatteris at Blackbird Terrace will know where I may be found." His gaze slanted to Cecily. "I am very sure my cousin would welcome a visit from you both."

"She might be more pleased to receive Rufus," said Lady Prior tartly. "For some odd reason he is much admired by the ladies. Miss Chatteris is not engaged, as I recall?"

"My cousin is now betrothed, ma'am. To Mr. Julius Harrington."

My lady was tired and having snapped that she had "never heard of him," told Adair they must not delay since it was already dusk.

He climbed from the coach at once, conscious of a reluctance to say his farewells to these ladies who had joined the small band who believed in him. To Miss Cecily Hall, especially.

⁓

The lodge gates were wide and there was no sign of Gatekeeper Bailey when Adair reached Blackbird Terrace. Uncle Willoughby must be entertaining guests, or perhaps Aunt Hilda had returned. To judge from the uproar at the kennels, something had caused the dogs to be wild with excitement.

He rode towards the stables, but detoured abruptly when he saw that the front doors of the house stood open.

A shrill scream brought him from the saddle in a flash and he raced up the steps, tearing the pistol from his pocket.

The entrance hall was lit by a single candle. A lamp lay smashed on the floor and oil was spreading. He checked as he saw one of the footmen lying motionless, but there were sounds of desperate conflict from farther down the corridor and he dared not delay. Running, rage seared him as he heard Minna screaming and Uncle Willoughby shouting hysterically.

A rough male voice roared a demand to "hand 'em over! Quick-like!"

147

Adair burst into his uncle's study and a scene of chaos.

Minerva was struggling in the arms of a burly ruffian wearing a head mask. A second intruder, similarly masked, was wrenching out the drawers of the desk, while Willoughby tore at his back and alternately screeched curses and dire warnings of retribution.

Adair levelled his pistol and shouted, "In the King's name! Stop or I'll blow your head off!"

This grisly threat caused the two bullies to jerk around and stare at him.

He waved the pistol and demanded, "Take your paws off the lady. Now!"

Minerva was released. Weeping and panicked, she ran to Adair.

The rogue at the desk saw, as did Adair, that she would pass between them, and he sprang to grab her.

Adair leapt forward and whipped her clear, then fired, and with a scream the thief staggered back to lean against the bookcase and clutch his arm.

The ruffian who had held Minerva ran at Adair, a dagger upraised.

Adair tore off his cloak and sent it swirling out to envelop and blind his attacker, then flailed the butt of his pistol at the head of the floundering man, who melted to the floor without a sound.

Minerva screamed, "Hasty!"

The sound of the shot had alerted others. Adair heard someone behind him and dodged aside, barely avoiding the knife that would have plunged into his back. He drove his fist hard at a masked face and as the man reeled back the hooded mask came away in Adair's hand, revealing familiar brutish features. From behind came a powerful chopping blow to the base of the throat that staggered him. An iron hand seized his arm and wrenched away his pistol. He tore free, and from the corner of his eye saw that Uncle Willoughby had vanished; in his place were three more of the thieves, these rogues not wearing masks.

Something smashed against his back and he was sent hurtling across the room. He collided with a chair and crashed down, but managed to retain sufficient of his wits to roll away from the poker that whipped at his face. He clambered to his feet again. Once more the poker whizzed at him, a savage grin behind it. He ducked, then kicked out. A choking wail, the grin vanished and the poker fell. He snatched it up and whirled around; ready.

"Finish the bastard, you clods!" screamed a pain-filled voice.

The fellow he'd shot, thought Adair, crouching. The remaining three bullies spread out. They were uniformly big and muscular, and his back throbbed and his side was hurting like hell from his collision with the chair. It would be very agreeable, he thought grimly, if Uncle Willoughby or some of the servants came to help. Now.

Whatever else, these hirelings knew their trade; as one man, they charged.

Hopelessly outnumbered, Adair gritted his teeth and vowed to leave his mark on the ruffians. He beat a club away, then swung the poker in a deadly arc that sent his assailants into a hurried and profane retreat, but they pressed in again at once. A knife glittered from his left and the poker became a sabre that he rammed under the knife wielder's ribs, drawing a howl from the man. A fireplace log was hurled, and brushed Adair's ear as he ducked. A long club flailed out and his sway to the side wasn't quite quick enough; he felt the impact excruciatingly. Blows seemed to rain at him from all sides. The poker was beaten from his failing grasp, his bones turned to sand and his eyes grew dim.

As from a long way off, he heard two vaguely familiar howls:
"Tally ho!"
"Into the breach!"

Feet stumbled over him and he was dully surprised to find that he was on his hands and knees. Each time he attempted to climb up, he was trampled down again. In a remote and dispassionate way he thought that it was difficult to judge which was the most painful; his head or his side . . .

He'd never had much time for hunting, but he was at the hunt now and the hounds were quite out of control. They'd knocked him down and were jumping all over him, barking madly, licking his face. He opened his eyes and struggled to his knees through a sea of tails.

An ear-splitting gunshot sliced through the bedlam.

A feminine voice screeched, "Jolly good, Miss! Now I'll fire off this here blunderbuss!"

Horrified yells mingled with a frenzy of barking. Boots stamped in a mad rush to escape. Shouts, barks and scrabbling claws faded . . .

"After them, you men!" Uncle Willoughby's voice, unfaltering and shrill with excitement. "Smash the filthy murderers! Scrag the whole perishing lot!"

"I say, old top," panted Paige Manderville, hoisting Adair up by his right arm. "Your—your uncle's a—"

"A regular Tartar!" gasped Toby Broderick, gripping Adair's left arm.

Identifying the voices although he seemed unable to pull the features into focus, Adair said feebly, "Jolly nice . . .'f you to . . . drop in."

<hr/>

"If you hadn't come when you did . . ." Her touch very gentle, Minerva bathed the gash behind Adair's ear and shook her head. "Heaven only knows what might have happened."

Seated at the kitchen table, and all too aware of his various scrapes and bruises, Adair said faintly but doggedly, "What I want . . . to know—" He stopped with a gasp as she pressed a pad against the cut.

"Hold that," she commanded. "And don't talk."

"But—"

"Hush! Pray allow me to tend to poor Mr. Manderville. And

150

as soon as we have the house secure and all our wounded cared for . . ." Her voice trembled. "Then—you must all lie down upon your beds. Oh, my!" She pushed back the hair from Manderville's forehead. "What a nasty graze!" Hands busy again, she said, "I am so sorry that you were hurt when you and Mr. Broderick came so bravely to our rescue."

"Just a—a little bump, ma'am." Paige smiled up at her dazzlingly. "Nothing to make a fuss over. And it was a tidy brawl while it lasted. I'm only glad we were in time to help."

Adair managed, "What . . . brought you here, anyway?"

"Among other things"—Manderville slanted an oblique glance at him—"Toby has something to show you."

At this point, it occurred to Adair that neither Broderick nor his uncle was present. He frowned and tried to collect his muddled thoughts. "Where is everybody, Minna?"

"My uncle and Mrs. Sylvan—our housekeeper, Mr. Manderville—are helping the servants who were hurt. Our butler was knocked down; he is not a young man and is badly shaken. And our footman was quite brutally beaten. We have sent a groom for the apothecary, but I doubt he will come before morning."

"How fortunate we are to have your brave self to—to pamper us," said Adair.

Manderville agreed admiringly. "Yes, indeed, and with never a word of complaint when most ladies would be in high hysterics. Thank you so much, Miss Chatteris. You're a very brave girl."

Minerva blushed shyly, and in some confusion said that Mr. Broderick had gone with Burslem to check on Gatekeeper Bailey and to put the dogs away.

Manderville grinned. "I never saw so many tails wagging in one room. They accompanied us when we arrived. You've some jolly fine dogs, Miss Chatteris."

"And you are being gallant and stoical, when I'm sure your poor head must hurt dreadfully," she said. "Now I must put some basilicum powder on that nasty cut, Hasty, and then we'll get you to bed."

151

"But I want to know—"

"In the morning, dear." And with a courageous attempt at levity, she added, "Let us hope your quarrelsome friends don't come calling again. I'm only joking, Hasty. I know you don't really know such dreadful people."

Adair smiled but said nothing. He might not know the louts, but the one whose mask he had torn off had been with the group who attacked him in the Pilgrim Arms. His head was aching too fiercely to attempt intelligent reasoning. One word only came to mind. Coincidence . . . ?

———❧———

Adair was dismayed to discover when his breakfast was carried in that it was almost ten o'clock. He had not rung for a tray, but the nervous maid who brought it whispered that the master was in his study, with the constable expected at any minute, and had asked that the young gentlemen keep to their rooms till the officer of the law had come and gone.

"What a dreffully thing to happen, sir," she quavered, setting the tray on the small table by the windows as he requested, and spilling coffee into the saucer. "If ever I heard of such a thing! All them wicked villins a-bursting in and frighting everyone! Will you like another egg, sir? I declare I never worked in a house where robbers broke in. What my mum will say I doesn't know! There's more toast, if you want."

He assured her that the toast, ham and eggs were quite sufficient, and having ascertained that nobody appeared to have been seriously injured last night, sent her off.

He found it difficult to spread marmalade on his toast, the knuckles of his right hand being scraped and swollen, but the awareness that he'd landed a good one on the nose of one of the thieves was consoling. His head throbbed persistently, but the mirror on his dressing-table told him that, although the cut behind his ear was surrounded by a bruise, his face was not damaged to a degree that would further alarm Minna. A much larger bruise and an ugly graze across his ribs bore mute testimony to his collision with the chair, and when he peered at his back with the aid of a hand-mirror, he discovered a livid welt that would certainly alarm his cousin were she to see it. All in all, however, he'd come off comparatively lightly, which was more, he thought with satisfaction, than the intruders had done.

Before he finished his breakfast the maid returned with an ewer of hot water, his laundered shirt and neckcloth, and the information that the constable was now with the master and that Miss Minerva was down at the kennels.

Adair shaved and dressed hurriedly, then made his way to the back stairs. He heard voices as he approached his uncle's study. Briefly, he hesitated outside the door, then went into the adjoining book room. Uncle Willoughby could have no objection to his hearing what the constable had to report, but if his presence would prove an embarrassment, he'd stay out of sight. The connecting door to the study was partly open and he heard the constable ask for descriptions of the culprits. These details having been rather sketchily provided, the minion of the law was advised that the intruders had been a group of gypsies intent on robbery.

"They were after my ah, sister's jewels," declared Mr. Chatteris. "And—and the silver, of course."

"Oh, I 'spect you're right, sir," said the constable's slow and solemn voice. "Only—I can't quite make out what they was doing in this here room, if they was after valuables. You'd think they'd of gone straight upstairs for the lady's jewels, or into the dining room for your silver."

Adair smiled mirthlessly. It would appear that the constable's wits were faster than his words.

"Well,—er, they did start—ah, into the dining room," said Mr. Chatteris. "But—but then I came—er, into the corridor and—ah, they realized I was the master of this house, so they forced me in here, and demanded I—er, open the safe."

'Safe?' thought Adair. 'What safe?'

"Ah," said the constable. "But I heard as they was tearing everything out of this here desk, sir, which makes me wonder what—"

"Who told you that?" interrupted Mr. Chatteris, his voice becoming strident. "You surely cannot rely on the—ah, the word of the servants! And if my neph——I mean my niece has spoken to you—well, you know how the—ah, the ladies react to any emergency. Fly off into—er, hysterics, or the—ah, the vapours." His laugh was short and strained. "Not reliable as—ah, as witnesses."

Recalling how bravely Minerva had risen to the occasion, Adair frowned.

The constable said mildly, "Then—you're saying as they *wasn't* in this room, sir? I thought p'raps your safe was—"

"I haven't got a safe," exclaimed Mr. Chatteris testily. "But they—ah, obviously thought I had. Now, I've told you all I know of the evil creatures, and I've more—ah, to do than spend the—er, day going over it all again, so you must—must go away now."

"Right you are," said the constable. "Jest one more thing, sir, then I'll have to talk with the gents what come to help and—"

"What *gents*? Now what are you babbling at?"

"Why, I'd understood, sir, as two young gents come in and—as you might say, saved the day. Friends of your nephew, I think?"

"Oh. Er—well, yes, I'll—ah, send for them."

"Thank you, Mr. Chatteris. And if I could just have a list of what were took . . ."

"Took? Oh. Some silver, I believe, and—er, well, my housekeeper can give you the—ah, details. Good day, Constable."

The study door opened. A maid said, "Yes, sir?"

"Please take the—er, constable to Mrs. Sylvan. Oh, and send Mr. Randall to me at once. We must see about—er, installing stronger bolts on the doors."

Adair waited until the departing footsteps were a safe distance away, then pushed the door wider. His uncle was kneeling on the floor, dragging a cardboard box from under the desk. Climbing to his feet, he pulled a thick sheaf of papers from the box and began to leaf through them as though in a frenzy of anxiety.

'His confounded Lists,' thought Adair. As he stepped into the study, the door to the corridor opened and the butler entered.

"You wished to speak to me, sir?"

The Lists were whipped back into the box.

"Yes," said Mr. Chatteris. "Someone told that fool of a constable that—ah, that Mr. Broderick and Mr. Manderville came and—er, helped us last—last evening."

"I don't know who did so, sir. But the constable has asked to see the two gentlemen, and—"

"I want you to hurry up the back stairs and—ah, warn them not to mention my nephew. If the constable knows that—er, the Colonel is here—" At this point Chatteris caught sight of Adair. Every trace of colour vanished from his cheeks, his jaw dropped, and stark horror came into his eyes. "How—long—" he croaked, then, recovering himself, said, "Go, Randall! Quickly!"

The butler hurried out.

Mr. Chatteris remained standing, staring at his nephew with that same expression that put Adair in mind of a trapped animal. He moistened his lips and repeated hoarsely, "How long were— were you there, Hastings?"

"Long enough to hear you fob off the constable with a lot of fustian."

Mr. Chatteris sat down abruptly.

Alarmed by his pallor, Adair said, "Uncle, I've no wish to distress you, but—"

"No wish to distress me?" Willoughby's pale eyes suddenly darted rage. "Am I not to—er, to be distressed when—when my own *nephew* skulks and pries, and listens like any shameful spy to what I say or do in this—this private room?"

Standing very straight, Adair said, "I'll not apologize, sir. I kept out of sight, as you asked, but you know as well as I that those bullies last night were not gypsies and that they made off with no jewels or silver."

Leaping up once more, Mr. Chatteris shouted, "Do you dare call me a liar, sir?"

His own voice quiet but stern, Adair said, "They came here for one purpose only. To take your famous Lists. Why, Uncle?" He stepped closer. "What in the name of heaven is so vital as to—"

"Stay back!" Willoughby's voice rose to a near scream. He wrenched the drawer open and tore out a small pistol. "Another step, and—so help me, I'll fire!"

For a moment that seemed an eternity the two men faced each other in silence. The pistol trembled in Willoughby's hand, his features were flushed and distorted with wrath. Outwardly cool, Adair was astonished by a phenomenon he'd encountered in the past but never expected to find here: a weak man transformed into a veritable tiger when backed into a corner.

He said, "Come now, Uncle. I cannot believe you mean that."

"*Go!*" snarled Mr. Chatteris, gesturing to the door with his pistol. "Leave this house! At *once*, do you hear?"

"I do. Forgive me if I must disobey. Please try to understand. My life is in a shambles, my honour is in the dust, my career ended. Is it so much to ask that you—"

"What—for the love of God, have *I* to—er, to do with your disgrace? *Nothing!* You invade my home, bringing your troubles with you, endangering my—my niece and my—er, servants! Sticking your—your proud Adair nose into personal matters that have nothing whatsoever to do with you! How *dare* you, sir! How *dare* you!"

"I dare, Uncle, because in some way that I don't yet understand, those sacrosanct Lists of yours appear to be connected with my 'troubles,' as you call them!" Adair stepped closer, and leaning forward, placed one hand on the desk. The pistol, which had begun to sag, whipped up again. His uncle's eyes narrowed to a fanatical gleam. Knowing that he had seldom stood in greater peril, Adair said, "If you're going to shoot me, sir, you had best do so, for I mean to find out why a man who attacked me in Bedfordshire was with these same bravos who forced their way in here last night."

Mr. Chatteris looked taken aback, then he exclaimed, "Rubbish! You're likely mistaken. Grasping at—ah, at straws!"

"I grasped his hood certainly, and tore it off. I am not mistaken. It was the same fellow."

"Then he's probably a soldier of—er, of fortune. Willing to attack anyone and—and go anywhere if the reward is—er, sufficient."

"Is it not stretching the bounds of credibility a touch far, sir, that the 'reward' should bring him here?"

"It would stretch credibility farther to—to suppose that my private—ah, hobby, could have any connection with *your* murky business!"

"And what of your connection, Uncle, with the Nunnery of the Blessed Spirit?"

It was really no more than a shot in the dark, but the effect on Mr. Chatteris was devastating. The pistol appeared suddenly too heavy for him to hold. White to the lips, he lowered it to the desk and gasped, "I—I never heard of—of such a place."

"And yet, sir, you appear in a carving in that nunnery. An exceptionally fine depiction of the Crucifixion. You *are* Saint John—no?"

"You're mad . . . ! Your poor mind has—er, has cracked. You don't know—ah, what you're saying!"

"I know that you are in some fashion involved with that nunnery, sir. And with the Mother Superior—who is also, I suspect, a French emigré!"

"A *spy?*" Clinging to the desk with both hands, Mr. Chatteris screeched, "Is *that* what you now imply? Oh—what *wickedness!* That my—my own flesh and blood would *dare* to—to stand here in *my* house and accuse me of *treason!* I cannot—I cannot . . ." He seemed to shrink suddenly; his voice broke, and he bowed forward, putting a hand across his eyes.

Adair ran to throw an arm about him and lower him into the chair. "Oh, Lord! Sir—I am so sorry, but I hoped you would have some simple expla——"

"Uncle!" Minerva came into the room and flew to Willoughby, who at once clung to her, mumbling pleas that she send Hastings away.

"What have you done to him?" she demanded, frowning at Adair. "Surely you can see that he is in no condition to be further upset."

"It's his Lists, Minna. For some reason they're at the heart of all this. I *must* know what—"

"Go *away*!" wailed Chatteris, his voice thready. "Minna—dearest child—make—make him go away!"

Adair threw up a hand as Minerva turned to him. "I'm going—I'm going. But—please try to make him tell you why—"

His uncle moaned pathetically.

With her arms tight clasped about him, Minerva said coldly, "Your friends are waiting for you in the morning room, Cousin. It would be best, I think, were you to leave us now."

Adair bowed, and left them.

11

*cannot force the old fellow to show me his confounded Lists,"
muttered Adair, trying unsuccessfully to find a more comfortable position in a morning-room armchair. "And be damned
if I can think of him as doing anything really havey-cavey. He
may have got himself into some sort of devil's brew, but he's not
a bad man."

Manderville sprawled on the sofa, settled his boots on the
fender of the hearth, and pursed his lips but said nothing.

Half-sitting against the end of the sofa, Toby Broderick remarked that Hasty's reaction could be ascribed to familial instincts. "Agrippina likely thought the same," he said. "And paid
with her life. Not that I mean to imply your uncle has any murderous tendencies, but—"

"Who?" interrupted Manderville rudely.

"Agrippina. Nero's mother. Of course, he wasn't directly involved with her murder. That was the result of Poppaea Sabina's
conniving, and it is said that—"

"How in the name of all that's wonderful did ancient Rome
slither into this discussion?" demanded Manderville, irked.
"That silly apothecary who mauled us about this morning must

not have looked closely at your brain-box or he'd have taken you away under restraint! Do, for once, try to stick to the subject."

"The improvement of your mind is my most taxing subject," said Broderick grandly, and grinning at Manderville's lewd response, added, "It rather sounds as though you are *persona non grata*, Hasty."

"I expect we all are," agreed Manderville, still scowling at him. "But at least we won our little war and—"

"We won a battle," said Broderick. "But I rather fancy the war is not yet won."

"Don't listen to this gloom-monger," urged Manderville. "Whatever he says, last night we were the victors!"

"Thanks to you two intrepid warriors charging to the rescue in the nick of time," said Adair.

"And to Miss Minerva's hounds," said Broderick laughingly.

Manderville said, "Right-oh! We'll be known henceforth as the Canine Corps. Yours to command, Hasty!"

It was all very light-hearted, but scanning them Adair saw that Paige had a puffy and discoloured lip and had arranged his thick locks to conceal the ugly graze on his forehead. Toby had dislocated his wrist, and although the injury had been put to rights, it was swollen, and he also limped slightly, the result of a kick administered by one of the ruffians. "My 'command' looks sadly mangled," he commented.

"Look to yourself," protested Manderville. "You can scarce walk straight. That fool of an apothecary didn't get the chance to practice his alleged skills on you, I collect?"

"I wasn't supposed to be here. No more were you, actually. Which reminds me: Why *did* you come?"

Manderville sat upright. "Dashed if I didn't forget all about it. You'll have to go back to Town, Hasty."

"It's that silly fellow, Webber," said Broderick. "Spreading it about the clubs that you're hiding from him."

"Oh, egad! I'm supposed to meet him. Of all times!" Adair flexed his swollen right hand experimentally. "I'll be able to hold a pistol in a day or two, I don't doubt."

His friends exchanged a quick glance.

"Well?" he enquired.

Manderville pointed out, "You don't have choice of weapons, dear boy. Webber claims you challenged."

"He's right, by George! I did."

"Besides," said Broderick, looking grave. "He knows you're a crack shot."

"Hmm," muttered Adair. "Will you both be my seconds?"

"Well, I don't know," said Manderville, pondering. "How are you with a small-sword?"

"You must forget that I've been in several engagements. I'm not unused to the heft of a sword in my hand."

"A *sabre* and a battlefield is one thing," said Manderville.

"Two things," corrected Broderick sweetly.

"A *small-sword* and a dawn meeting is another," snarled Manderville. "I wouldn't want to stand up with a rank amateur. I have to think of my reputation."

"Best not think of it, old fellow," advised Broderick. "It'll upset your stomach." Over Manderville's spluttered outrage, he added, "I'll second you, have no fear, Hasty."

"Just be sure to write out your will," said Manderville.

"Now that is very bad form," exclaimed Broderick, shocked.

"And quite ridiculous," said Adair. "Nobody fights with swords any more. The fellow will choose pistols."

"We shall hope he does," said Broderick. "He's a damned good swordsman."

Adair stood. "Then, just in case, I shall have to practice."

"If you can find the time between unmasking murderers and cultivating your interest in Miss Cecily Hall," said Manderville.

"What makes you think my interests lie in that direction?" demanded Adair.

"If they do not, old lad, why is your face so red?"

"Probably from the restraint I must practice to keep from strangling you." Adair grinned, and went on hurriedly, "My apologies, but I must rush you off now. I don't want to further upset my uncle."

Their valises were already waiting in the entrance hall. At the foot of the steps a groom held Toreador, and Broderick's phaeton was being driven around from the stables. The butler limped across the hall to bid them farewell, a maid following with cloaks and hats. Adair pressed a generous *douceur* into Randall's hand and exchanged a few words with him about the need for vigilance. Only as they went out into a chilly and overcast morning did he remember to ask, "I believe Paige said that you had something to show me, Toby?"

"So I do, by George!" Broderick threw back his cloak and drew a small box from an inner pocket. "I completely forgot I'd kept this. Should have returned it at once, of course, but—"

He broke off and they all turned as a rider cantered up the drivepath.

Manderville grinned appreciatively. "What a dashed pretty girl!"

"Careful," said Broderick. "It's Hasty's *femme fatale*."

Hurrying to meet her, his heart gaining speed, Adair said, "Miss Hall! Welcome. Oh, you've brought a friend, I see."

Laughing, she leaned from the saddle to hand him the puppy she carried. "I found him while I was out for a gallop with my cousin. I rather suspected he might belong to Miss Chatteris, so—Good gracious!" She looked from one to the other of them, noting the signs of combat. "Have you fought a war here?"

"A small one, merely." Trying to move naturally, Adair put down the puppy and reached up to lift her from the saddle. "I'll call Minerva. You must come in and meet her."

"And—us," said Manderville, stepping forward. "But if you are too selfish to present us, Colonel—"

Adair performed the introductions, very aware of the enchanting twinkle in a pair of blue-grey eyes.

Manderville bowed and touched the lady's gloved fingers to his lips.

Broderick bobbed his head shyly and reached to take her outstretched hand, then shrank back as she gave a shocked cry.

"Where did you get that?"

He looked down at the box he held. "Oh—Jupiter! Well, I—er, chanced to—That is I—I found it, you see, and had meant to—"

"Unless I mistake the matter, Lieutenant, you 'found' it inside my uncle's country house!" She darted a sardonic glance at Adair and her lip curled. "Though—*how*, and why a gentleman would make off with someone else's property, I cannot guess. Since it belongs to my grandmama"—she held out her hand again—"pray be so good as to return it."

Scarlet with embarrassment, Broderick stammered, "Well, I will, of—of course, ma'am. Only—I think Colonel Adair has a right to—er, first see what it contains, because—"

"You *opened* it? Oh, how *dare* you!"

Despite the angry words, it seemed to Adair that her lovely face had lost its colour. He glanced at the interested grooms and said quietly, "Perhaps we should discuss the matter inside. If you will accompany us, Miss Hall, I'll summon my cousin, and—"

"I will do no such thing! Give me back my grandmama's box. At once! Oh, Rufus! Thank heaven!"

Rufus Prior rode up at a thundering gallop, clearly prepared to rescue his beleaguered cousin.

Adair swore under his breath.

Manderville said softly, "This, I take it, is the hothead Adair has got into the habit of knocking down."

Prior flung himself from the saddle and sprang to his cousin's side, eyes blazing, riding crop tight-gripped. "I *told* you how it would be, Cecily! If these clods have dared insult you—"

Broderick opened the small box and shoved it at Adair. "Perhaps I mistake it, Hasty. You'll recall I found this little box in Mr. Prior's cellar. I couldn't get it open and must have popped it into my pocket. Just found it again. Ain't this—"

"My emerald pin!" exclaimed Adair, astonished. "How on earth . . . ?"

Miss Hall said weakly, "You mistake it, sir. My—my grand-mama has—That is—is her pin, and—"

"And that fellow very probably put it in the confounded box himself," blustered Prior.

"Be dashed if I did!" exclaimed Broderick indignantly. "And you should not swear in front of a lady, sir!"

Minerva hurried out onto the terrace. "Oh, thank goodness I caught you, Hasty. Please come back inside before you—" She paused, glancing around the little group uncertainly.

Adair said, "May I present Miss Cecily Hall and Mr. Rufus Prior? My cousin, Miss Minerva Chatteris. Miss Hall returned one of your pups, Minna. It evidently wandered off during—last evening."

"Thank heaven!" exclaimed Minerva. "I have been so worried! How very good of you to return Scamper, Miss Hall!" She picked up the venturesome puppy that was now frisking about her heels. "Forgive me if I must take this rascal to the kennels. We had a little upset here last evening, but it is all cleared up now, so pray don't think you must hurry off. Would you kindly take Miss Hall and Mr. Prior into the morning room, Hasty? It is most rude in me, but I'll not be above a minute, and then we will have a lovely chat."

Manderville volunteered to instruct the grooms to return horses and coach to the stables, Miss Hall and her cousin were ushered into the morning room, and Randall was summoned and instructed to serve refreshments.

As the door closed behind the butler, Prior said heatedly, "Now see here, Adair—"

"It is of no use to bluster," interrupted Adair in a steely voice. "You know, and I know, that this is my emerald. I'd thought I lost it at your cottage, but it is clear now that it must have fallen during my first encounter with you at Singletree. What I do not understand is why it was tucked into this little box and hidden in your cellar."

"No such thing," declared Miss Hall, defiant but obviously shaken. "If—if Grandmama chanced to mistake it for her pin—"

"Is the lady in the habit of hiding her jewellery in the cellar?" murmured Broderick.

"Whatever my grandmother does with her belongings is none of your bread and butter," flared Prior. "And you had no business poking about in our cellar in the first place!"

Adair said gravely, "It would appear to be very much my business. I do not wish to embarrass Lady Prior, but this is a valuable emerald, and I think I am entitled to an explanation."

"I mislike your tone," snarled Prior, his face very red.

Adair nodded. "Then I will say no more, but put the matter in the hands of the constable."

Miss Hall moaned. "Oh, no! Oh, pray do not!"

"Don't let this fellow frighten you, Cecily." Prior folded his arms across his chest and tossed his head high. "I am here to protect you!" He abandoned his gallant pose abruptly, and seemed very much the boy as he said, "What could that dim-witted constable do, at all events?"

"If he puts two and two together, I dread to think." She sank into the chair Broderick pulled up for her. "It's no use, Rufus. We had as well confess."

Adair sat on the sofa and waited.

Prior argued, "I don't see why we should take these fellows into our confidence. And besides, *you* have nothing to confess, Cecily."

"She is my grandmama, and I cannot allow her to be shamed and humiliated, which will surely happen if Adair calls in the constable."

"She is my grandmama too. And if Adair was a gentleman he'd not do so unkind a thing to a little old lady!"

"If we throw ourselves on his mercy, perhaps he will not."

"Throw ourselves on—" spluttered Prior. "Be dashed if I will do so revolting a thing!"

Suppressing a grin with difficulty, Adair stood. "In that case, you've wasted enough of my—"

"No!" shrieked Cecily. "Put your silly pride in your pocket, Rufus! For Grandmama's sake, do!"

"Oh, very well," he said sulkily, and in a last display of drama he lowered his voice and demanded, "But I'll ask for your solemn promise, gentlemen, that what we reveal will not go beyond this room!"

"How can we make such a vow when we don't know what you're going to say?" protested Broderick. "If ever I met such a cloth-head!"

"You are going to have to rely on our judgment, I'm afraid," said Adair. "And you're going to have to do it quickly, for my patience is quite gone!"

Cecily hissed, "Ru-fus . . . !"

Prior said with reluctance, "The truth is, that—that Lady Prior has a—er—"

"A naughty little habit?" Adair murmured.

"Then you did guess! I knew it!" Cecily wrung her hands. "The poor darling simply cannot resist certain—objects. I think it's a sort of—game with her. She is the kindest creature and would not hurt anyone for the world, but—"

"But she appropriates things that catch her fancy. She has done this before, I gather?"

Rufus sighed. "We tried to watch her. If somone complained that they'd mislaid something, we would search her suite and return whatever was taken."

"But she suspected what we were doing," put in Cecily. "And so she now finds hiding places for—for her treasures. It makes things very difficult."

"I should rather think it might," said Broderick, appalled by such a prospect. "Is her ladyship single-minded, Prior? Jewellery only?"

"Usually, but not always. Once it was a charming enamelled snuff-box. Once a very antique pair of silver sugar-tongs."

Cecily spread her hands helplessly. "I feel dreadfully about it. Especially when our guests are the victims, though, so far, we have managed to convince them they simply mislaid things."

Adair said with a smile, "Do not scourge yourself. You have likely warned your close friends, no?"

"Good God—no!" exclaimed Rufus, horrified. "They'd likely have poor Grandmama clapped up, or—or put in Bedlam!"

"Oh, I doubt that," said Broderick. "The lady likely cannot help it, you know. My father knows everything, and he told me there is a new theory, not much developed as yet, having to do with a condition called kleptomania."

"Mania!" gasped Cecily, whitening and clutching her cousin's hand. "But—my grandmother is not mad!"

"I believe it is not judged to be madness," said Broderick, spurred by the frown Adair levelled at him. "Especially since the people who steal—I mean—who purloin the objects are usually not at all in need of them from an economic standpoint. It is more a sort of compulsion, I think. Relatively harmless, provided that the—er, articles can be returned without a fuss."

Miss Hall asked rather tentatively, "Do they know if—if such a condition runs in families?"

"D'you mean like an inherited tendency? Oh, no. I doubt that, ma'am."

Cecily and Rufus looked at each other.

Noting that troubled exchange of glances, Adair asked sharply, "Why? Does some other member of your family share the trait?"

Rufus sighed. "I'm afraid my sister may have the same—inclination."

"Miss Alice? By Jove!" His eyes alight with excitement, Adair sprang to his feet, only to gasp and grip the chair-back.

Cecily jumped up and put her hand on his arm. "You're hurt! I thought you and your friends had been indulging in horseplay, but—"

"It's more than that, I fancy," interrupted Rufus. "What happened here, Adair?"

"An attempted—robbery," answered Adair unevenly. "And I thank you for your concern, ma'am, but I'm not seriously damaged. Luckily, my friends charged to the rescue and between us we managed to put the varmints to flight without anyone getting killed. But we all collected a few bruises."

"How many rogues were there?" asked Rufus.

"Half a dozen or so," replied Adair. "But they didn't make off with anything. And of more importance is the chance that Miss Prior may have left us a clue to this whole ugly affair."

Rufus said slowly, "You think Alice might have found something that spelled danger to someone?"

"Oh, it is possible!" Cecily's eyes sparkled with excitement. "We must hurry home, Rufus, and search her room. There might be—" She left the sentence unfinished as Minerva and Manderville came to join them.

A tray of hot chocolate and little cakes was carried in, and as the cups were handed around, Minerva apologized for her absence. "A dreadful way to treat guests," she said brightly, "but it is Lieutenant Manderville's fault, he begged to go to the kennels with me and see the puppies."

"Miss Chatteris has some jolly fine dogs," said Manderville with genuine enthusiasm. "I've told her I mean to have one, depending upon what Wellington has planned for me."

Minerva beamed at him. "The lieutenant has won all their hearts, I do believe. I could scarce drag him away."

Broderick said, "I didn't know you were such a dog fancier, Paige."

"I didn't know it, either. I think Blackbird Kennels has cast a spell over me."

"Perhaps it is the fair proprietor who has cast a spell," teased Adair.

"Don't doubt it for a moment," said Manderville gaily.

Her cheeks rather pink, Minerva offered the plate of cakes again. "It was so good of you to bring Scamper home, Miss Hall. I expect you will have noticed that our gentlemen bear the marks of violence. Has Adair told you of our intruders? It was a terrifying experience. I am only grateful that he was here. He fought them off very bravely till his friends came, and thank heaven they did, for poor Hastings was outnumbered six to one."

"But how splendid, Colonel," exclaimed Miss Hall.

Torn between gratification and embarrassment, Adair said,

"Splendid that Toby and Paige arrived, for by then I was quite against the ropes."

"Jupiter!" said Prior, his eyes very round. "It must have been a jolly good scrap."

"I hope your uncle was not injured," said Cecily.

"Not—physically." Minerva slanted a sidelong glance at Adair. "But he is of a rather nervous temperament, and we judged it best that he keep to his bed today."

Cecily agreed that this was a wise decision. "I remember that Mr. Chatteris was inclined to be frail. To have strangers invade his home and with such brutality must have been a terrible shock."

"You have met my uncle?" asked Minerva curiously.

"Yes. At a party some years ago. You came with a puppy for Lady Warren-Wyant's son."

"So we did! And somehow Uncle Willoughby became Father Christmas! It was such a jolly party. But—forgive me, did we meet?"

Cecily said with a smile that it had been rather a noisy evening. "I think introductions were lost in the uproar. The children were so excited."

"Even so, I would think I'd remember you both," said Minerva, looking from Rufus's boyish grin to Cecily's lovely face.

"What you mean is that you'd have remembered my carrot top," said Rufus, laughing. "But I wasn't there, ma'am. Still, I did meet your uncle about a year ago. It was at a charity affair of some kind, as I recall. Yes, that's it! A bazaar to raise funds for a nunnery. Quite an interesting old place, though I've forgot the name."

"The Nunnery of the Blessed Spirit, perhaps?"

Adair's voice was bland, but Cecily looked at him sharply.

Rufus said, "By George, but you're in the right of it! In fact, I bought one of their fruitcakes for my grandmama."

"With wonderful foresight," murmured Cecily mischievously.

Adair laughed. Rufus stared uncomprehendingly, then said, "You never mean it was the same one we shared in my cottage?

169

Of all the ingratitude! I gave it to Grandmama months ago!"

"I believe fruitcakes improve with age," offered Minerva soothingly.

"You've likely visited the nunnery, Miss Chatteris," said Rufus. "I gained the impression that your uncle has been a generous donor. Is that the case, ma'am?"

"Why, I've no idea," answered Minerva, surprised. "It's the first I've heard of it. I think he has never mentioned such a place."

Adair thought, 'I am very sure he has not!'

***

"It's not the best part of Town." Julius Harrington wandered around the parlour of Adair's newly rented flat and paused to peer out of the window at the fading afternoon. "You're going to get a deal of noise from Fleet Street. If you'd told me you meant to move, I could have found you a nicer place."

Adair settled himself in the window-seat and began to polish the grip of his small-sword. "I'm sure you could, but I don't want a nicer place—for the time, at least. No one would think to look for me out here, yet I'm just a ten-minute ride from Mayfair."

"Optimist," said Harrington.

"In any case, you've done enough, Julius. I appreciate your having ventured back to my father's house to collect my sword. You escaped injury this time, I hope?"

"Fortunately. But I did not escape some searching questions from your housekeeper. She wanted to know why you needed it. I fobbed her off by saying your nephews wanted to see it. Even so, she gave it me with reluctance, and I'm not at all sure she believed me. She is very devoted to you."

"Yes, bless her heart. Did you chance to see Paige or Toby?"

Harrington pulled up a faded armchair and inspected it through his quizzing glass before sitting down. "Manderville took Webber's seconds in strong aversion. They insisted on delaying to Thursday, and then claimed their principal was generously allowing you time to set your affairs in order."

"Does Webber still swagger about boasting that I've been in hiding and afraid of facing him?"

"He's an unpleasant creature. Why does he hate you so much?"

"An old score. Besides which, I dealt him a leveller in the pride. At the time he accused me of having broken his arm. If he's ready to fight I must have been correct in thinking his shoulder was dislocated merely. Who are his seconds, by the way?"

Harrington sighed and said glumly, "That fellow Nestor who's always fawning around Prinny."

"Oh yes. One of the Carlton House set. Fancies himself a man of fashion."

"A misguided fancy. Brummell used to look at him and shudder."

Adair laughed. "Who's the other?"

"A former East India Captain; rather an odd duck. He must be at least fifty, but has a rosy-cheeked baby face and a great thatch of golden curls. He walks with a sort of roll; very nautical."

Adair's hand stilled. Looking up sharply, he said, "Droitwich?"

"Yes. You know him?"

"By repute only. And if it speaks true, Lord help the poor devils who served under him. It's not surprising that he would cry friends with Webber."

"True. They're birds of a feather, no doubting." Worried, Harrington said, "I wish you had allowed me to second you. Broderick's a good enough fellow, but Manderville—well, isn't he a touch cork-brained?"

It was logical enough that so hard-working a public servant as Harrington should look askance at Manderville's carelessly nonchalant approach to life. Equally as logical for Paige to have remarked scornfully that Miss Minerva deserved better than "a pudgy toad-eating politician who can speak for an hour and say nothing." Stifling a smile, Adair said, "Don't be fooled by his lazy manner. Paige is a very good man in a fight."

"Which is more than can be said for you! No, don't eat me—be honest, Hasty. You're no swordsman, and Broderick says your back is all the colours of the rainbow. If you're slowed, Webber will show you no mercy even though he—"

Flushing angrily, Adair said, "Deuce take you, Julius! Next you'll have me on my knees in front of the clod! I may not be in the same class as Lucian St. Clair, but I've done some fencing and I'm not totally inept!"

"No. Just reckless! You must be aware that you have a vengeful enemy. That fiasco with poor Alice Prior was carefully planned. Had to have been. If Webber's the man who wants you dead, you're granting him a perfect opportunity to achieve his ends!"

"Well, dammit, what would you have me do? D'you suppose I want to fight a stupid duel when I'm bending all my energies to try and find out who stole Miss Prior and curst near got me hanged? I've no choice and you know it! Webber struck me in the face with his horsewhip. In front of all London—or much of it. You were there; you saw it. My honour may be in the dust, but I've not sunk so low that I can let that go by! Nor would you, I'll wager."

Harrington said with a wry smile, "I'd use my wits to avoid such a horrid encounter, else Minna would be a widow before she's a wife! Speaking of my lady, I'm driving down there tomorrow. Any messages, Hasty?"

"Just give her my love, and—well, you might try to discover if my uncle has forgiven me. I'm in his black books."

"Yes. Minna told me it was something about those Lists of his. What did you do, take a peep?"

"Not—exactly. But I'm fairly sure the bullies who broke in were after them."

"What—old Willoughby's *Lists*?" Harrington said incredulously, "Surely you're not serious. Who would want the silly things?"

"I wish I knew." Adair put down the sword and looked out

at the river, his eyes remote. "Have you any idea what kind of information my uncle collects?"

"None. Save that there's a dashed lot of it and he guards those Lists as ferociously as if they were State secrets. Of late I've begun to wonder if he's not—no offence, my dear fellow—but he does seem to be slightly—er, unbalanced."

"You may disabuse your mind of that notion. My uncle is an eccentric, I'll grant you, and perhaps he's not a deep thinker, but he's as sane as you or I."

There was an edge to Adair's voice, and Harrington was relieved when York, the emaciated individual who now served Adair as valet and general factotum, opened the door to announce another caller.

Harrington's brows lifted. "Rufus Prior?"

"Yes. Are you acquainted?"

"Never met the fellow, or any of the Priors, come to that. They're said to be a fiery lot."

Prior came in, a long flat case under his arm. "My apologies if I'm late," he said, with a curious glance at Harrington.

Adair stood and performed the introductions.

As the two men shook hands, Prior said, "You're in Parliament, ain't you? My father took violent exception to your speech about the improvement of the road through Hyde Park."

Harrington smiled good-naturedly. "It's difficult to please everyone."

"True enough." Prior opened the case to reveal two small-swords. "I've come to give Adair a lesson."

"Good Lord!" exclaimed Harrington, recoiling in horror.

Adair chuckled. "No cause for alarm, Julius. Mr. Prior is an expert fencer and has kindly offered me some instruction in the art."

Harrington stared. "*Prior*? But I thought . . . that is—"

"Oh, we've acquitted him of any guilt in the abduction of my sister," said Prior. "At least, my cousin and I accept his version of the business. We are, in fact, all working together to try and find poor Alice."

173

"You are?" Fascinated by this new development, Harrington asked, "Have you had any success?"

Adair took off his coat and rolled back the wristbands of his shirt. "Let's say we have unearthed some promising clues. And now, Julius, I must very impolitely ask you to leave. There's little enough room for the lesson and you'd be at considerable risk if you stayed to watch my clumsy efforts."

"Actually, he's remarkably quick," said Prior, helping Adair move the sofa to the wall. "I doubt you'd be in danger of being badly cut if you wish to stay, sir."

Harrington refused this golden opportunity, however, and took his leave, promising in the tiny entrance hall to let Adair know "how the wind blew" at Blackbird Terrace.

Adair returned to the parlour to find Prior flexing the blade of his sword. "This is a jolly fine weapon. If the seconds agree, you'd be well advised to use it on Thursday." He tossed the sword and snatched up his own. "Off with your shoes. Ready? *En garde!*"

For the next hour the air rang to the beat and scrape of steel on steel, the stamp of stockinged feet and the occasional breathless shouts of the two men.

"C'est assez, merci!" gasped Adair at length, stepping out of distance. "Phew!"

"I agree," panted Prior. "You're a sight better than I expected after only two lessons. In fact, you dashed near had me with that thrust in low *carte*. I think you've hoaxed me, Adair. You've fought before."

"I've fenced before, and I've had some challenging battlefield encounters. I've never fought a duel. And if we hadn't put buttons on the points, that brilliant time thrust of yours would have written my *finis*! I'd like to practice that manoeuvre, I've never been able to master it."

"Don't. It's deadly dangerous." Mopping his brow, Prior sprawled on the sofa. "Better that I show you how to counter it."

Adair shouted for York, and ordered ale.

Prior said, "Your new man looks like an undertaker. Where did you find him?"

"He was a chef. A good one. But—he served some—er, unfortunate shellfish, and was held accountable."

"Jove! D'you mean he *poisoned* someone? I wonder he wasn't transported at the very least."

"They couldn't prove it was deliberate, and he swore it was not, but of course, he was ruined. I know the feeling. So I took him on. I begin to think I'm very lucky to have found him."

"Trusting of you," said Prior. "But I think I'll not stay for dinner!"

"And I think you lack an adventuresome spirit!"

York carried in wine and a tray of sliced cold meat and cheese.

When he had gone away again, Adair asked, "Tell me what you found in your sister's suite. Anything useful?"

"I found nothing. Cecily came across a reticule that had a lot of bits and pieces inside. Not much help, I'm afraid."

"What kind of bits and pieces?"

"Let me think—there was an earring set with aquamarines, a Spanish hair comb, a small pair of scissors. I believe that's all, except for a few buttons."

"Buttons?"

"They can be quite ornate, you know. I've an aunt collects the things. Has boxes of 'em. I've often wondered what in the world she means to do with 'em. Cecily thought you might like to see for yourself what she found."

"I would indeed, but I don't dare show my face at your house. Confound it! I wish I might call on her. Does she ride in the mornings? Would you be offended if I met her in the park?"

"I would not. But if my papa were to hear of it—awful!"

"Yes, and I'm a fool, for she should not be seen in my company." Adair frowned and was silent.

Watching the strong face, Rufus murmured, "I think you're another victim. Have a care. My cousin is quite an enchantress."

175

"She is very lovely." Adair reddened. "I gather I am obvious, but rest assured—I know I'm not the first to admire her. Certainly, I must be the least acceptable, even were I not the prime suspect in the disappearance of your sister."

"Acceptable in what sense? Would you court Cecily under different circumstances?"

"The lady can look as high as she pleases, obviously. At best I had a comfortable competence and my army pay." He shrugged ruefully. "Less than a scintillating *parti* for your beautiful cousin."

"Who is also," said Prior idly, "a considerable heiress."

Adair shook his head. "And that should properly drive me to the ropes. But I'll be honest with you. When I clear my name I shall pursue your beautiful cousin despite her fortune. What do you say to that?"

Watching him thoughtfully, Prior said, "You evidently enjoy battling against long odds, Colonel."

12

Looking up from the walnut he'd just cracked, Paige Manderville declared indignantly, "I shall do no such thing! Lord Ignatius Dale rarely hosts a party, but when he does stand the huff, it's a jolly fine show. Get your own invitation, you unprincipled pirate!"

"You are all heart." Adair threw another log on the fire and crossed to re-fill Manderville's wine-glass. "I should have told York to serve kippers for dinner!"

"What—after I'd condescended to take a draughty hackney coach all the way to the hinterlands on a wet evening? Had you done so savage a thing I'd have added my name to your list of enemies. And you've more than enough of those to be going along with. Still, I'll have to admit you were right, Hasty. Your aspiring undertaker is a splendid cook. That beef was tender as butter and I liked his way with the crab."

"Then, since you are sufficient of an ingrate to refuse to give up your invitation, will you at least grant me a favour?"

"Not if it's going to result in more assault and battery on my very nice self. I value this body almost as much as the ladies do."

Adair offered an audible prayer for strength. "I ask only that you get word to Miss Hall that tomorrow evening I shall be at the Dales' masked ball, and beg her to meet me there."

Manderville shook his head. "Objection number one: You are fighting a duel early the following morning and have no business cavorting about at a party for all hours of the night. Take my advice, my lad. I've been out twice and I know. Get to bed early, else your courtship of the lady may cease before it is properly begun."

"Good advice, I've no doubt, but—"

"But you're a colonel and don't take advice from a lowly lieutenant. I knew I was wasting my breath, but I tried. So be it. Objection number two: You have no invitation and you may disabuse your mind of whatever slippery schemes you're hatching to appropriate mine. I have my own—er, fish to fry."

"I've no doubt of that, but with or without an invitation, I shall attend."

Manderville sighed. "Third objection: How will you find the lady? It'll be a crush, I promise you, and with everyone masked—"

"Ask that she wear a blue flower, and I'll find her."

"But—"

Adair's jaw set in the way that Manderville had come to respect. "No, do not try to turn me aside, Paige. I go only to meet the lady and will not stay for the unmasking, I promise you. If there should be trouble, steer clear of it. What do you know of my reluctant host, by the way?"

"He is very plump in the pockets—and in his person. His hauteur is legendary—a frightful snob. There's a rumour that his lady holds her nose up so high that she frequently trips over her own feet, though I've never seen her do so. Lord Iggy has a grand mansion in Mayfair, and a large and impressive country seat in Sussex to which no one below the rank of baronet is ever invited."

Amused by the irreverent abbreviation of the proud peer's

name, Adair said, "If the Dales are so high in the instep, how did *you* ever wangle an invitation to their ball?"

Manderville grinned. "The invitation was sent by Lady Dale, who is madly in love with me, of course."

"What you mean is that the invitation was intended for your father. Rumour has it that he was quite the Don Juan in his day and is doubtless acquainted with the lady."

"With many ladies, and his day is not done, I promise you. He taught me all I know and I very comfortably continue in his footsteps and add lustre to the Manderville reputation."

"I think you could delete the final two letters of lustre . . ." Adair laughed and caught the nut Manderville hurled at him. "No, seriously, Paige, is it truth that Lord Dale is in some fashion powerful in Whitehall?"

"If he is, it must be an extreme deep secret. I'd have judged his head to be one of the emptiest in the southland. Though, now I come to think on it, that description would fit many of the esteemed diplomatists who guide the affairs of our hapless nation! Well, never mind about that. If I'm to call on your admired lady, I must be on my way. Mr. Prior's as top-lofty as old Iggy and will likely deny me, but I'll get your message to her somehow—since you didn't serve me kippers for dinner!"

Risking the ire of his family, early the following morning Adair paid a quick visit to his faithful friend Mrs. Redditch. The housekeeper was delighted to see him, and in spite of her obvious apprehension did not hesitate to offer her help. She managed to retrieve an invitation to the masked ball which Lady Andrea had thrown away. Her ladyship had been heard to say that it had been sent with the malicious awareness that nowadays she and the Viscount would not dare show their faces to the "almighty Dales."

Adair gave Mrs. Redditch a hug and left by a rear door, troubled by the knowledge that because of his disgrace his mother must be shunned by the society she loved. He harboured no illusions; Lady Andrea was a selfish and foolishly proud woman. But the ties of blood could not be denied, and when he'd pleased her she had shown him a warm affection. Now and then while he was in school, and later, during the Peninsular campaign, she had taken the time to write chatty little letters that had meant a great deal to him. Knowing her, he knew how deeply she must be grieving, and if that grief was for her own ostracism rather than for his ordeal, he could not like to be the cause of it, and prayed that he might very soon dispel her unhappiness.

"Well? Well?" snapped Lady Abigail Prior irritably. "Have you never before rested your eyes upon a lady of Quality?"

Having admitted this unorthodox caller to the front hall of his employer's house, the elderly butler's hand lingered on the door-latch. "I've—er—that is to say, I wonder if there is some mistake, my lady? This is the residence of General Sir Gower Chatteris, and he did not say he was expecting a—er, visitor."

Lady Abigail shook out her umbrella and as the butler moved out of range, said, "What you mean is that a lady don't call on a gentleman unaccompanied, unexpected and after dark. Well, I *am* a lady, and I *am* unaccompanied *and* unexpected, and whether it be dawn or dusk is all one to me. Take this"—she thrust the dripping umbrella at him—"and give him my card. At once!"

"But—but he is at his dinner, ma'am."

"Better and better. With luck I'll give him a fine case of indigestion. Go on, go on! Don't just stand there chewing your teeth!"

"Yes, milady. I mean—no, milady. I'll take your card up and tell the master you wish to see him." He started off, only to reel to a halt as his coat-tails were seized and tugged violently while his name was demanded.

Affronted, he said icily, "It is Polebrook, madam."

180

"Well, Polebrook, you will do no such thing," barked Lady Abigail. "What you will do is tell Sir Gower that I *insist* on seeing him, and if he keeps me waiting above five minutes I shall come up. Screaming!"

"Goodness gracious me," muttered the unhappy butler, making his rheumaticky way up the sweep of the grand staircase. "Whatever next!"

His employer was less timid. "*Insists* on seeing me?" he roared. "Devil take the woman! Didn't you tell her I was dining?"

"I did, sir. But—but she is most—forceful."

"Then force her out! I don't know any Lady Prior . . ." The General paused, scanned the card through his quizzing glass, and grunted. "I take it the woman is that poor child's mama. Well, I've no wish to have her weeping on my shoulder. Send her away, Polebrook. Tell her I've dinner guests. Now why in Hades do you show me that Friday face?"

"The lady is—is quite elderly, sir. And—and she said if we kept her waiting above five minutes—"

Polebrook was interrupted by a piercing shriek.

"Good God!" exclaimed General Chatteris, leaping to his feet.

"—she would come up—screaming," finished the butler.

The door burst open. In full scream, Lady Abigail stamped into the dining room. "On second thoughts, I'll keep this," she said, snatching her umbrella from Polebrook's hand.

The General bowed stiffly and said at his most crushing, "I believe I have not the pleasure of your acquaintance, madam, but—"

Lady Abigail advanced, her umbrella scattering raindrops as she levelled it across the table at the old soldier. "Don't remember me, do you, Gower Chatteris?" she snapped. "Well, I remember you, *and* that Midsummer's Eve under your father's apple tree! Well you may blush, sir! And I will tell you without equivocation that had I dreamed you would turn into a stiff-rumped, high-in-the-instep, hard-hearted old curmudgeon, you'd have collected a boxed ear instead of the kiss you stole! Now sit down, Sir Gower, while I tell you something about yourself!"

181

Scarlet and speechless, the General, who had jellied the knees of countless junior officers, collapsed into the chair.

The butler tottered away and left them together. Before he was half-way down the stairs, however, he was giggling uncontrollably. It was, in fact, a full minute before he could command his voice sufficiently to advise the various members of the household staff, who had gathered apprehensively in the hall, that the lady had been frightened by a mouse.

No one believed him, of course, as a result of which General Chatteris gained considerable stature—at least in the eyes of the male members of his staff.

In spite of a cold drizzle, Dale Hall, an enormous Curzon Street mansion, presented a brilliant picture when Adair arrived the following evening. Candle- and lamplight shone from the windows, and on each side of the wide front doors flambeaux blazed, reflecting on the wet flagway and lighting the faces of the curious who had gathered under umbrellas or pieces of oilcloth to watch the stream of arriving coaches. Lackeys held up large umbrellas to protect the guests on the brief journey from their carriages to the awning that had been erected across the pavement. Most of those arriving were already masked, and the onlookers shouted guesses at their identities, this lending an extra air of excitement to the occasion.

Having arrived by hackney coach, which branded him a nobody, Adair gave his invitation to a footman whose hands were already full of similar cards. The man scarcely glanced at him, and he sauntered into the crowded entrance hall. He wore a plain black domino and York had purchased a large mask, trimmed with black ruffles that effectively concealed his brows and cheekbones. He had brushed his dark hair into the tumbled untidiness now popular. It was a departure from the neat military style he usually affected and he thought it made him appear younger, but he felt exposed and vulnerable and was enormously relieved when other guests glanced at him without recognition.

The strains of one of the new waltzes drifted from the ball-room. He edged through the crowd and then paused, tensing, as a tall angular lady rapped his arm with her fan. Laughing, she said shrilly that she hoped she knew "Cam," mask or no mask. She had taken him for Camille Damon, probably. A compliment, for the young Marquis, though something of a hermit who seldom went into Society, was said to be the handsomest man in the southland. Adair smiled and bowed, but walked on without speaking, paying no heed to her loud complaint that he might at least admit she was right.

The dance floor was crowded with couples safely hidden behind their masks, attempting the daring and frowned-upon waltz. Adair strolled among the onlookers, searching unsuccessfully for a slender lady wearing a blue flower. Several girls who were not dancing eyed him hopefully. He was painfully reminded of the last time he'd rescued a lonely damsel from just such a predicament and of the nightmare results.

A hand clamped onto his shoulder. His heart sprang up behind his teeth as he jerked around. A young man of average height, with light brown hair, a scar down one side of his brow, and eyes that shone a tawny gold behind his mask, gripped his hand and said in a low voice, "Are you quite demented? If you're recognized here, there'll be—"

"The devil to pay," finished Adair, as softly. "I know, Jack. But I had to come. And I'm glad you're here so I can thank you for your hospitality."

Captain Jack Vespa, who had been one of Lord Wellington's prized aides, led him aside. "I just saw Manderville. He tells me you've removed your notorious self from my house, which was as well, because a damned crusty major brought a troop to search for you this afternoon."

Adair stiffened. "Gad! Am I a wanted man, again? My apologies if you were embarrassed. I suppose they believe I've done away with poor Miss Prior?"

"Be dashed if I know. I understand his lordship is vastly put out with you. He don't like losing good officers, especially now."

Adair said drily, "Aside from that letter he writ to his brother, Wellington didn't bestir himself to help me."

Ready as always to defend his General, Vespa pointed out, "You're still alive. Who knows what he's been 'bestirring.' Paige says you're making progress and that you've formed a tendre for Cecily Hall. She's a rare beauty." A grin curved the fine mouth. "I'm glad you've turned your unwelcome attentions from my lady!"

Adair chuckled. "I gave you a short run for your money, didn't I? Is Consuela here tonight?"

"If she were, I'd not tell you. But—to say truth, Hasty, she has been extreme anxious for you, and I know she holds you in her prayers."

"God bless her. Thank her for me, and—"

A lady wearing a rich blue gown and with a blue flower in her fair curls danced by in the arms of a naval officer. Adair swore softly. "I'd like to know who gave that fellow the right to hold her so close!"

Vespa glanced around. "Is that the 'heavenly Hall'? Trust her to flout convention by dancing the waltz in public. No, you really must not glare so murderously, my dear chap. I'm told that every bachelor in Town—and a great many men who are no longer bachelors—yearn to hold Miss Hall in just such a way. Now where are you going? Don't be a fool! You can't—"

"Devil I can't!" growled Adair and dodged his way through the dancers to tap the naval officer on the shoulder.

"Be off with you, Mister Impertinence," said the Navy, whirling his partner away. "You cannot cut in on the waltz!"

Adair pursued them. "Your Admiral wants a word with you. He's waiting by that potted palm."

The naval officer glanced where Adair indicated. "I don't see—"

"He's stepped into the corridor. Best hasten, old man. He's boiling about something!"

"Oh, my!" Behind her lacy mask, Cecily's eyes danced with

laughter. "Do go, Monty. I'd not have you in his black books. I'll try to save you a dance later. This gentleman may finish the waltz."

The Navy muttered angrily, but gave Adair a curt nod, then hurried off the floor.

Adair gathered Cecily's fragrant and willowy figure into his arm and smiled down at her as he guided her into the dance.

"I think you told that nice lieutenant a fib," she accused.

"Another crime to be added to my infamies! But the end justifies the means."

"Does it?" She said, "Oh, you dance so well! But what a risk, to draw attention to yourself."

"I'd risk more than that for the pleasure of dancing with you."

She looked up and met his eyes. The crowded room and the guests faded and they were alone in a haze of contentment.

After a timeless and blissful interval, Adair was startled to hear laughter.

The music had stopped. Other couples were leaving the floor and watching them in amusement. There was a smattering of mocking applause.

"Oh, Jupiter!" he gasped, drawing Cecily to a halt.

Flushed with embarrassment, she tugged at his hand. "Not that way!"

Her naval admirer was at the edge of the crowd. He looked furious and was obviously searching for them. Adair reached up quickly and snatched the blue flower from Cecily's hair.

She said, "Come. Hurry!"

They blended with the chattering crowd and Cecily led the way into a wide corridor and thence to a passage along which were several ante-rooms. She chose one that was unoccupied and Adair started to close the door but paused to ask, "You permit?"

She knew as well as he that this was most improper, but she nodded without comment and he closed the door.

"Thank you," he said, taking the hand she held out to him.

185

"You are very good to have come. I didn't know how else to meet you, but I'm afraid you run a risk by talking with me, so we must make this brief."

They sat side by side on a gold velvet sofa. The scent she wore was elusively intoxicating; the low-cut blue velvet gown clung revealingly to her superb figure. Adair had to fight the need to hold her again, to kiss that soft and vivid mouth.

Cecily was accustomed to being admired, but his ardent gaze flustered her and she gave a nervous little ripple of laughter.

He flushed. "I'm sorry. I said we must hasten and here I sit like a tongue-tied idiot. Very well, to business." But the firelight was glinting on one little curl that clung to the edge of her mask. Watching it, knowing what he meant to ask her, he heard himself murmur instead, "You have glorious hair, Miss Hall."

"Thank you. If that is your way of being tongue-tied, I think you must be—"

"Bewitched?" He looked at her steadily. "I am. No point in denying it, is there? Are you offended?"

Her smile was faint but betrayed no sign of annoyance. "I rather gathered you had revised your first impression of me, now that I am no longer trying to shoot you."

"You levelled me without firing a shot. I am captive and—completely captivated."

She leaned closer and asked huskily, "So what do you mean to do about it, sir?"

"What can I do? Even if I dared hope you feel the same, I am liable to arrest and deeper disgrace. How could any man ask a lady to share such a future?"

"But when your name is cleared—as it will be—"

He took up her hand again. "Thank you for your confidence. In that event, I would hopefully be reinstated and could offer you a name not tainted by desertion and murder." He shrugged wryly. "But precious little else. Oh, I'm not a pauper. My maternal grandmama has promised me a very nice estate in Gloucestershire—provided I survive the war and do not bring disgrace

186

on the family name. I have a competence that I judge comfortable, but it must appear insignificant when set against a great fortune. Besides which, I am very sure you are besieged by far more illustrious suitors than I."

She said carelessly, "Oh, yes. I am offered an even larger fortune than my own, or to become a countess, or even a marchioness, though with somewhat lesser fortunes."

It was no more than Rufus had implied, but his heart sank. She was beautiful, spirited, rich and intelligent; of course she would be admired and courted. He drew a deep breath and said with forced lightness, "And I am a sorry fool who had no right to speak as I did. Forgive, and tell me—"

"About myself?" She said with wide-eyed innocence, "But of course, you know very little of my background. If you are really interested . . . ?"

"As well ask if I am interested in breathing! Start at the beginning. I picture you as a lovely little girl who—"

"Who was very unhappy," she interposed, the smile leaving her eyes. "I can scarce remember my father; he was killed in a great storm when I was not quite five years old. My mama was the angel in my life. Lovely, gentle, always kind. I adored her. She remarried a year after my father's death. My stepfather already had three small daughters. He was extremely handsome. Tall and fair, a very informed mind, and cold as ice. I think he cared for Mama, insofar as he was capable of it. To me he was polite. He demanded respect and absolute obedience. Neither of which I granted him."

Adair found that he was still holding her hand, and he made no attempt to relinquish it. "Never say he was cruel to you?"

"If you mean did he beat me—no. I'd not have minded that, for at least he would have shown an interest. He simply ignored me, and my stepsisters were just like him. I was kept away from Mama. I could scarce have been more isolated on a desert island. I know Mama grieved and wanted me by her. She was always frail and she died of an inflammation of the lungs two years later. Along with my stepfather's children, I was put in the care of a new governess. She soon realized that I was not valued, and played her cards accordingly. Once again, I was the unwanted outsider."

Adair patted her hand. "Poor things, they were likely very jealous, for you must have been far more lovely than any of them."

"They were jealous, true, and lost no opportunity to sneer and make my life miserable. Still, I saw enough of the outside world to understand that I had very much to be thankful for, a beautiful home, servants, pretty clothes, and I certainly never went hungry. All I lacked was the kindness and affection I longed for. My grandmama rescued me, bless her. She is the only person I ever saw best my stepfather in an argument. One morning she came calling. I was sent for and she talked to me for a few minutes only, but it was enough. She and my stepfather went into his study. I heard their voices begin to rise. He had no chance, poor fellow. That afternoon Grandmama carried me off to Singletree. Alice and Rufus were waiting. For the first time since my dear mama died I was greeted with love." She smiled mistily. "It was the—the happiest day I had known for years. I lived with them until my stepfather removed to our consulate in Denmark. Grandmama refused to allow me to go with him, and I doubt he cared except for appearance's sake. Alice and I were sent to a Young Ladies' Seminary for two years. Afterwards, being the elder, I was brought out first. I loved the busy social scene, whereas Alice was shy and really wanted no part of it. We have seen less of each other this past year or so, but I never dreamed . . ." Her voice broke.

Adair pressed her hand to his lips and said gently, "You must feel you have lost a beloved sister. I am so sorry."

"Thank you." She said with a faint sigh, "You do understand. I knew you would."

"I'm glad of that. And I beg you will not give up hope. We'll find her yet. In that connection, I must ask you—did you know that Miss Alice was slipping out at night to meet my brother?"

"No!" She drew back, her eyes at once stormy. "And I don't

believe a word of it! She would never do such a disgraceful thing! Besides, Hudson Adair is a very attractive gentleman, but scarcely the type to appeal to a young and romantical girl."

"Not Hudson. My younger brother. Nigel. And I am sorry to say he has made it clear that he is deep in love with your cousin."

She stared at him with shocked eyes. All the colour drained from her cheeks, and she exclaimed in a half-whisper, "*Nigel* . . . ? Oh! My heavens! I—we . . ."

"What is it? If he has—"

"No, no, he has not—That is—Oh, Hasty! What a dreadful mistake for us to make! Yes, I know you don't understand. But did it never occur to you to wonder why we were all so sure you were guilty?"

"You trusted in your coachman and the testimony of the people at the hotel. I can scarce blame you!"

"It was damning, true. But we might have investigated more thoroughly had it not been for . . ." She fumbled in her reticule and took out a creased piece of paper. "I intended to confront you with this. I found it on my cousin's writing-desk after she disappeared. It was never introduced into evidence because we feared it would damage her reputation. We knew you had been in England on several occasions last autumn, and this little re-minder that she had writ to herself convinced my family that you had indeed met Alice prior to the ball, and were lying about it, and about everything."

She handed him a note, written in a careful copperplate hand.

Meet Adair Tuesday. Same place and time.

He said slowly, "You thought I was the 'Adair' in question."

"I—we—never doubted it for a moment. You were the dash-ing hussar who would easily win a young girl's heart. I did not dream she cared for Nigel! They are just—children! Oh, if *only* we had not rushed to condemn you! I am so ashamed!"

"Don't blame yourself. It likely wouldn't have made any dif-ference, as things turned out." But he thought, 'Would it? If the note had been produced in evidence, would Nigel have realized that Alice had been referring to him? Might he then have come forward to confess his relationship with her?'

Troubled, Miss Hall said, "Surely, he wouldn't have eloped with her?"

"He's a good lad and has been bred up to be very aware of the proprieties and he goes in awe of my grandfather. I think this is his first love. My family brush it off as 'puppy love,' but youngsters feel things very intensely, you know."

After a pause she asked, "Did you, Colonel? Or can you remember back that far?"

He looked at her sharply. A dimple trembled beside her mouth, but her thick lashes were lowered.

"I think I am being called elderly," he said with a grin. "But I can certainly remember my first love. The lady was my mama's French maid and quite the loveliest creature I had beheld in all my sixteen years. I would have died for her, and I'm very sure I plagued her to death with my passionate poems and the little bunches of flowers I would smuggle to her." He smiled, remembering. "She was ten years my senior, and very patient and kind. I was hopelessly enamoured for upwards of a year until she married the under-butler and they emigrated to the New World."

"Poor boy. Were you shattered?"

"I probably would have been, had I not found a new love; a superb dapple-grey mare my grandfather was so kind as to give me."

"Aha! Would your present mount be related to that lady?"

"Toreador is one of her sons—yes. Thank you for noticing him."

"How could one avoid it—he's a beauty. And I'm glad you recovered from your lovesick state. But I believe you side-stepped my question about your brother. *Do* you think he is so deep in love that he might have persuaded Alice to go to Gretna Green?"

Adair said slowly, "No man who really loves a lady could persuade her to an elopement that would lead to her disgrace and social ostracism."

"But he is very young. If he *is* so enamoured and Alice agreed to an elopement, what then?"

"I might own it to be possible save for the fact that Nigel has made it clear he believes I have lured the lady away and keep her in hiding. He's ready to call me out, I'm afraid." And he thought that he must find Nigel as soon as possible.

Cecily saw his rare frown and asked, "Do you make a habit of duelling, Colonel?"

"Not with my own brother, certainly." He spoke lightly, but she looked so grave that his smile died. "You do not approve of the *affaire d'honneur*, I take it."

"I think it a primitive and stupid way of settling a quarrel. Duelling should be strictly forbidden!"

"I agree. And it is against the law, you know."

"A law *you* mean to break, do you not? Oh, never look so startled! I know Rufus has been fencing with you daily."

Uneasy, he said, "He's very good, and because we fence doesn't mean that—"

"That you're going out with that horrid Thorne Webber?"

He groaned. "Rufus had no business telling you of it!"

"Nor did he. Mr. Webber has been pursuing me—very clumsily, I might add—for some time. I allowed him a dance one evening and had only to mention your name to send him into a rage."

"Whereupon you coaxed the details out of him, did you?"

"It took very little coaxing. He is a boastful creature. But I've heard he is also very dangerous and has killed his man."

Adair was silent.

"Good heavens, Colonel! I'd think you have seen enough of blood and killing during the war! Do you so enjoy fighting?"

"I am no longer a colonel, you know," he evaded whimsically, but seeing her irked frown he answered, "There are insults, Miss Hall, that a gentleman cannot overlook."

"Such as being struck in the face with a horsewhip while others looked on."

He flushed hotly. "As you say, ma'am."

191

"So, to mend matters, you must needs go out and try to cripple or kill each other! What utter folly! How many children have been left fatherless, I wonder, or sweethearts and wives heart-broken, only to appease your stupid male Code of Honour!"

She looked and sounded very upset, with the result that his own heart lifted. "Be honest, Miss Hall. Would any one of your brothers swallow such an insult?"

"I have no brothers. You confuse me with another lady, no doubt."

"Not so! You distinctly warned me when first we met that you had five brothers who were fine shots."

She moaned and put a hand over her eyes, then, peeping at him through her fingers, said, "Oh, but you are unkind! Must you remember every foolish thing I say and then shame me by repeating it?"

He chuckled. "You were seeking to ward off any improper advance I might make. Understandable, under the circumstances. But you will own that you ladies are not without pride."

"I'll grant that. If another lady were to strike me in the face, I might very well strike her back, but—but I'd not take a pistol and try to blow her br-brains out, or run her through with a sword in some—some muddy field at d-daybreak!"

Suddenly her eyes were glittering with tears. Ecstatic, Adair lifted the hand that now clung to his so tightly, and pressed it to his lips. "Perhaps not. Yet you did not hesitate to take a pistol to me not so long ago."

She said with a sob in her voice, "Do not . . . change the subject!"

Somehow, his arm slipped around her. He murmured, "Dare I hope that you might care if I should fall?"

She swayed to him and murmured unsteadily, "You stand in so much danger already. If you should be killed . . ."

He brushed his lips along her cheek. "Then it *would* matter to you?"

She wailed, "Oh . . . Hasty . . . !"

Those were the last words she uttered for a short, heavenly space, during which she was crushed to his heart and kissed as she had hoped someday to be kissed. She was breathless and starry-eyed when he drew back, whispering the tender words of love every woman longs to hear.

"Whatever . . . has happened to us?" she asked dreamily.

"We have been blessed. We love each other, my very dear."

"Do you think it really a blessing? Should we be grateful, then?"

He kissed her ear. "Exceeding grateful."

"It would be very wicked to—to throw away such a magnificent gift, no?" She felt him tense and her hands tightened on his cravat. "You have kissed me, Colonel Adair! If you really value your honour you must—must make an honest woman of me!"

He detached her hands but held them enfolded within his own. "It is the dearest dream of my heart to be able to offer for you, my beautiful blessing."

Cecily frowned and stood, tidying her gown and straightening her mask. "But you will not."

"My dear." Standing to face her, he said quietly, "You know I cannot."

"Why? You love me. You admitted it. And Grandmama knows that I love you!"

At this, he reached out to the peerless lady he had found so unexpectedly, but she stepped back, regarding him with cold angry eyes. He let his hand fall, and asked, "And does she approve, Cecily? Of course she does not. Your uncle holds me to blame for his daughter's abduction. Can you imagine his reaction were I to knock on his door and ask for the hand of his lovely niece? He'd likely shoot me on the spot."

She bit her lip. "When you are cleared he will welcome you." Adair started to speak and she put her fingers over his lips, silencing him. "Meanwhile, we can plight our troth. Here. Now."

He kissed her soft fingers but shook his head. "Not until I can approach your family openly. As it is, I should not in honour

193

have spoken at all. I have told you of my prospects—or lack of them."

"Oh, how stubborn you are! Do you say you would throw away happiness because I have a large fortune? Are you so despicably proud, Hastings Adair?"

"No." He pulled her close and despite her struggles held her in an iron grip. "Your fortune is not a lure but I hope I'm not such a fool as to sacrifice my every hope of winning you because of it. Think, lovely one. If I should be cleared, I'll go back to the army. That is no life for you."

"Better than emptiness without you." She stopped struggling and her arms slipped up around his neck. Pressing tight against him, she said, "Are you afraid I'll disgrace you in front of your almighty General? You should have thought of that before you kissed me, sir."

He sighed. "Very true."

"Oh! Brute!"

"No, no. I would be the proudest man in the world to present you to Lord Wellington as my wife. But—"

"But—but—but! Then let us at least tell Grandmama and Rufus that we are unofficially betrothed. Oh, you wretch!" She seized his ears. "Do not shake this handsome head again! If you really loved me—"

"*Because* I do so love and honour you—"

"You will not offer for me! Famous!" She flung around, presenting her back to him. "So much for honour!"

"Yes. I have disgraced myself once more. I'll leave you."

He kissed the nape of her neck and turned to the door.

Like a flash she was before him, leaning back against it, her wide gaze fixed imploringly on his face. "Let us not part like this. Please, Hasty, at least promise you will not fight that horrible man."

"I have no choice. You know that."

"I know that your alleged love must be feeble indeed, since you deny every request I make of you!"

His jaw set. "Could you respect a man who did not defend his honour? I think rather you would come to despise him!"

"Go, then." She turned away and muttered bitterly, "I had heard the Adairs were a proud lot. It is truth, indeed. I am only ashamed that I have humbled my own pride. Do me the favour, sir, of forgetting my foolishness and not boasting of your conquest."

He whitened. "Cecily! Don't say such things! You've given me a gift I'd not dared to hope for and that I'll cherish as long as I live. How could I ever forget it? When I can come to you without shame, I'll remind you—"

"Do not bother! Long before that day dawns I will have quite forgotten you!" With a toss of the head she wrenched the door open and swept into the passage.

Adair gazed after her, torn between the ecstasy of knowing that he had found his true love, and despair that he might also have lost her. He saw on the sofa the blue flower she had worn in her hair, and stooped to take it up. A faint fragrance lingered about it. He was putting it carefully into his pocket when he heard a great roar of excitement from the ballroom.

Through the hubbub, one cry was repeated, "The unmasking! The unmasking!"

13

~

*A*dair opened the door with caution. There was great deal of excitement nearby, but the passage was clear. He strode along quickly and silently but halted as a crowd of merry-makers appeared, blocking his way and searching the various anterooms to "capture" those who had not yet unmasked. They whooped and cheered as a pair of "culprits" were surrounded, masks removed and friends identified.

Adair retreated, but from the other end of the passage came more guests, and the tall lady who had challenged him earlier swept towards him.

"There you are, naughty boy," she cried playfully. "Come, everybody, and see that I was right! Off with it, Cam!"

"No, but Damon's hair is darker," argued a fat but jolly maiden. Adair moaned inwardly. Miss Pauline Jameson was the daughter of one of his mother's close friends. At one time Mrs. Jameson and Lady Andrea had their hearts set on a marriage between himself and the young lady, and Miss Jameson had made it clear that she was not averse to the match. It was another instance in which he had displeased his mother by quietly but firmly resisting her plans. Mrs. Jameson had been one of the first who "ceased to know" Lady Andrea when the scandal of his arrest had become public knowledge, and Lady Andrea had been heard to remark bitterly that Hastings had been "right for once" in refusing to offer for the child of such "a fair-weather friend"— whom she would "never forgive. Never!"

There were hoots of mirth, demands to be told how Miss Jameson knew the elusive Camille Damon, and more laughter when she declared defiantly that she had met the young Marquis during a family visit to Copenhagen.

"When you were ten" chortled a Dandy who wore an enormous bouquet in his buttonhole.

This evoked more laughter, under cover of which Adair edged towards the ante-room he had just left.

Not to be deprived of her triumph, the tall lady had been watching him and suddenly swooped to snatch off his mask.

The laughter ceased.

There were gasps and cries of outrage.

The tall lady exclaimed, "Oh! My heavens!"

Adair said, "You were mistaken, you see, ma'am." He stepped back into the ante-room, slammed the door shut and propped a chair under the handle.

Pandemonium raged in the passage. Fists pounded at the door. There were conflicting shouts that he be thrown out, and that the Watch be summoned to haul him back to gaol where he belonged.

He ran across the room and flung open the window. The ballroom was on the first floor of the mansion and there was quite a drop to the gardens below, but he climbed out, hung by his hands from the sill briefly, then let go and landed in a flower bed without mishap.

From above someone shouted, "He'll climb out of the window! After the scoundrel!"

As he ran, those words seared Adair's mind. "The scoundrel . . . ! The scoundrel!"

The wet weather had prevented decorative lanterns being hung from the trees and he blended with the deeper shadows and made for a rear gate that gave onto the alley. A door on the terrace was flung open, sending a bright beam across the lawns. At least a score of men ran outside. They were all shouting at once, seemingly united in the desire to "teach the filthy swine a lesson." It was a voice Adair had heard before—the voice of the mindless mob, and when a howl of "There he goes!" rang out, he abandoned the trees and cut across the open grass. They were after him at once. If he were caught, his family would be in for more humiliation at the very least. He ran faster and was almost to the alley when the back gate was flung open and a liveried footman, alerted by the uproar, rushed at him.

"Did he pass you by?" howled Adair, and when the man halted, shaking his head uncertainly, he commanded, "Try the west gate! I'll get this side!"

"Who is it, sir?"

"A thief! A guinea to you if you catch him!"

The footman tore off. Some of the pursuers, confused, followed him, but most were still hot on Adair's heels as he sprinted through the gate.

He swore in frustration as a closed coach pulled up, blocking his way.

The vengeful crowd was almost to the alley.

He started toward the horses' heads, but the carriage door was flung open, cutting off his retreat in the narrow alley.

"Get in! Quickly!"

There was no mistaking that clear voice. Adair sprang inside and slammed the door and the coach raced away.

Sitting back, he panted, "Phew! I thank you, ma'am."

As though there had been no interruption in their previous conversation, Cecily said composedly, "Were I to wait until you feel inclined to offer for me—"

"Feel *inclined*? You know very well—"

"And was I so fortunate as to become your wife before I am old and grey—would my life always be like this? One desperate melée after another?"

He took up her hand while he considered, then he said with a slow smile, "Army life is seldom tranquil, my dear." Kissing each finger, he added, "But I thank you for . . . riding to my rescue. They were not . . . very kindly disposed . . . I fear."

Watching with interest as the little finger was attended to, she observed, "Only set loose a group of male animals and they revert to naughty little boys." She reclaimed her hand. "The tale will be all over Town by morning, you know."

"Yes. Might your coach have been recognized?"

"I doubt it. The light in the alley was not good and there is no crest on the door panels. Tell Peters your direction, and then I'll show you my cousin's ill-gotten gains."

Adair leaned from the window and called to the coachman. When he sat back again, Cecily handed him a small velvet bag. "These are the only things we found," she said regretfully. "I'm afraid they're of no help, Hasty."

They inspected the various items together. In the dim light it was difficult to see details, but in addition to some small items of jewellery, a pair of scissors, a comb and an elaborately embroidered handkerchief, there were several buttons, as Rufus had said.

When the coach pulled up on the corner of Fleet Street, Cecily told him he could keep the bag and inspect the contents in his new home. "You are not fighting your beastly duel in the morning, I take it," she said, watching him suspiciously. "Else you'd not have gone out tonight."

"I shall start a new fashion," he teased, "and send out written invitations to witness our meeting."

She was not amused and declared her intention to pester Rufus until he told her where and when the duel was to take place. "And I shall notify Bow Street at once."

Adair swung open the carriage door. "In which case I shall probably be tossed into gaol," he said. "With even less chance of proving my innocence."

He stooped to kiss her cheek. "Try to remember me kindly."

"I shall remember that I hate you," she retaliated, but she leaned to his kiss and as he sprang from the coach she called, "Hasty! Do *please* take care!"

He stood on the dark rain-swept street and watched the carriage out of sight. Walking on towards his flat, the smile died from his eyes. It was all too clear that public sentiment was running high and that if he was caught he was more likely to be dealt summary justice than be handed over to the authorities. He unlocked the outer door and walked slowly up the stairs to his flat. He felt tired and dispirited and with every step he heard again those enraged voices: "The scoundrel! The scoundrel!" But routing despair was the glowing recollection of the beautiful Cecily coming to his rescue. Impossible as it seemed, she had admitted that she cared for him and that when he cleared his name . . . He smiled the tender smile of lovers. Truly, to every cloud there was a silver lining.

York answered his knock. His face was as closed as ever, but he enquired mildly if the Colonel would wish that a Cognac or a glass of port be carried to his bedchamber.

Adair noted the oblique glance that came his way and requested with a smile that the Cognac be served to him in the parlour. "Is the fire still burning?"

"I fear it is almost out, sir. I assumed you would be retiring early. There is a warming-pan in your bed and—"

"Thank you. But first, let's have another shovel-ful of coal on the fire, and light some more candles, if you please. No, don't look at me so reproachfully. Truly, I am grateful for your concern, but there's something I must do before I go to bed."

York bowed and attended to the fire. Adair went to his bedchamber and changed quickly into his night-shirt and dressing-gown, reflecting that his "aspiring undertaker" was already starting to act like a long-time retainer. He had not the least objection. It was, in fact, a rather comforting thought.

His glass of Cognac was presented on a silver tray. He told York to leave both, and spread Miss Alice's little hoard of treasures on the tray.

The Spanish hair-comb was an elaborate affair but the only clue to its owner's identity was a faint scent—nothing like that worn by his beloved Cecily. One blade of the little scissors was chipped at the end, and an ear-ring was set with sapphires rather than the aquamarines Rufus had supposed. There was also a delicate gold bracelet with a beautiful miniature painting in the centre. Adair looked eagerly for some identification on the back of the painting, but the inscription noted only the name "Ada," and rack his brains as he might, he could think of no lady of his acquaintance who was so named. With a sigh of frustration he examined the buttons. There were seven, some obviously having come from feminine attire, and two of a larger size from a man's coat or waistcoat. The female articles were pretty and one looked to be set with a nice topaz, but none was identifiable. Of the large buttons, one was covered with a rich silver brocade and had likely fallen from the evening coat worn by some elegant Georgian gentleman. The remaining button was of tarnished silver, and was bent, as if it had been stepped on. There was the faint indication of some embossing, and he was peering at it curiously when York again appeared at his elbow and with an apologetic cough enquired if the Colonel would take another glass of wine before retiring.

Adair said with a chuckle, "All right, all right. I'm going to bed. Be sure to wake me at five." He stood and stretched, suddenly aware that it was close to one o'clock. "By the by," he added, handing York the silver button. "What d'you make of this?"

The valet inspected the button closely. "It is from the garment of a gentleman of Quality, that much is sure, sir. And there was some sort of crest engraved. It—looks like an . . . umbrella, perhaps, and I think there might be a letter here . . . It's hard to tell. A *T*, possibly?"

His remarks echoed Adair's conclusions. Webber's family had a profitable trade in umbrellas, and Webber's first name was Thorne. He said, "I agree. Have you ever before seen such a design?"

York admitted he could not recall having done so.

Yawning, Adair sought his bed. He had thought he'd fall asleep at once, but the moment his head hit the pillow, Cecily's image was before his mind's eye, her musical voice in his ears, and love for her warming his heart and causing him to envision wonderful and highly improbable images of their future life together. He was smiling when at last he drifted into sleep.

Dawn was lighting a grey morning and the copse of trees in the fields beyond the Foundling Hospital was lit by two pairs of carriage lamps when York guided Toby Broderick's pair towards the other coaches and reined them to a halt.

Adair groaned.

Manderville, never at his best in the early morning, muttered disgustedly, "If ever I heard of such a thing! Nobody oversleeps the night before a meeting! What it is, you lack sensitivity, *mon Colonel!*"

"Well, he certainly don't lack gumption," said Broderick. "Trouble is, Hasty, dear old Webber will claim you're late because you were scared."

"If he don't, that wart Droitwich will," agreed Manderville.

Their surmises proved well-founded. Adair's apology that he had overslept was received with a disparaging snort from Thorne Webber and a sneer from his pale and languid friend, the Honourable Millard Nestor. Captain Droitwich, golden curls gleaming under his rakishly tilted hat, smiled his broad and perpetual smile and remarked that there was no disgrace in being a tiny bit late, so long as a fellow was able to get himself to the ground eventually.

Manderville demanded haughtily, "Would you care to speak more plainly, sir?"

Adair said, "Let it pass, Paige. Poor fellow likely couldn't speak plainly if he tried."

"It's still damned dark," grumbled Webber, peering at the sword-box by the light of his carriage lamps.

"And it's beastly well freezing." Mr. Nestor drew his cloak tighter about him, and simpered, "If it means to rain, I shall go home. I'm sorry, Thorne, but my constitution—"

"Devil with your constitution," snapped Webber. "We'll be able to start in a few minutes."

Broderick and Manderville went over to inspect the weapons, and Adair's sword was compared to the other two and accepted by the seconds.

"Much difference it would make was it a foot longer," boasted Webber. "The poor fellow is doomed and knows it. That's why they'd such a time getting him here."

Adair held out a hand that was steady as a rock. "As you see, gentlemen," he drawled. "I am all a-quiver! But you should not have your crest emblazoned on your buttons, Webber. The umbrella identifies you for the scheming rogue you are!"

"By God, you really are wits-to-let!" Webber stared at him, then turned away, shaking his head, and voicing his opinion that for the first time he would fight a lunatic.

Returning to his principal's side, Broderick muttered, "The weapons are the exact same length. More's the pity. Webber has the longer reach and he's counting on it. For the love of God, keep your wits about you!"

Adair said grimly, "I've more reason than ever for besting him now."

"Then don't let him drive you into losing your feet," urged Manderville. "It's damned easy to do and once your position is lost—"

Droitwich called dulcetly, "Are we ready, gentlemen?"

"I doubt it," sneered Webber, flexing his blade between his hands.

Adair walked to face him.

The seconds drew their swords and stood watchful and ready.

The salute. Adair offered the customary brief raising of the sword hilt to his lips. Webber, however, executed an involved old-fashioned series of Italianate flourishes culminating in his holding his hat at arm's length and bowing. Adair was not a little astonished by these antics and was almost caught off-guard when Webber suddenly hurled his hat aside, yelled, *"En garde!"* and sent his blade in a flashing thrust in *carte* that Adair was barely in time to parry.

Broderick shouted angrily, "Unfair! A foul!"

Manderville whispered, "Blast! Hasty'll have to do better than that, else he'll not last five minutes!"

Five minutes later Adair was still on his feet, but he was all too aware that it had been a desperate struggle to defend himself, and that he'd had no opportunity to attack. Webber was truly a splendid swordsman and was clearly enjoying himself. Resorting to an outside guard in *tierce*, Adair was once more almost overpowered when Webber reversed his wrist in a brilliant *carte* over the arm. A long rent was opened in Adair's shirt-sleeve, crimson splashed onto the white linen and the opponents stepped out of distance as Manderville leapt to strike the swords up.

"First blood!" he cried.

"Stuff!" howled Webber. "I barely scratched the poltroon! Besides, we did not agree to first blood!"

"Gently, gently," murmured Droitwich, smiling. "We must not frighten the poor fellow."

Broderick asked anxiously, "Is it deep, Hasty?"

"Do please allow them to bind it up," wailed Nestor. "I knew this would happen and I cannot *stand* the sight of blood!"

Broderick ripped Adair's shirt and revealed an ugly gash above the right elbow. "Your sword-arm," he growled. "And that's no 'scratch.'"

"Nor is it sufficient for me to surrender," said Adair grittily.

Manderville hurried up with the surgeon, a pompous little man who clicked his tongue and chattered continuously to himself in an under-voice, but moved with swift precision to bandage the cut.

Webber shouted an enquiry as to whether they meant to

delay till the Watch discovered them and stopped the duel. The little surgeon surprised everyone by bellowing fiercely, "In a hurry to meet your Maker, are you, sir? You must have led an examplary life, sir! Very well—have at it!" He went stamping back to his coach, grumbling all the way about "stupid, hot-at-hand ninny-hammers," and the duel resumed.

Webber was more aggressive now and set a furious pace that taxed Adair's uncertain skills to the limit. Broderick let out his pent-up breath in a gasp of relief when Webber at length jumped out of distance and threw up his left hand for delay.

Adair lowered his weapon immediately and wiped his sweating hand on his breeches. As if he'd seized the opportunity to attack, Droitwich leapt between them flourishing his sword dramatically and roaring, "A halt! A halt! At once, Adair! You must obey the rules!"

Manderville shouted, "He *did* halt, damn your eyes!"

Broderick demanded, "What's to do?"

Webber's answer was to roar a sneeze and resort to his handkerchief.

Adair waited, glad enough of the chance to catch his breath.

Manderville grumbled, "Nine men out of ten would have run the makebait through while they'd the chance!"

"It may have been his last chance," said Broderick. His pleasant face was unwontedly grim and as Webber suddenly leapt to the attack, he added, "Hey! We're off again!"

Manderville shouted, "Give fair warning, blast you!"

Adair had anticipated such a breach of the rules and he parried a thrust in *seconde* neatly. Webber immediately attacked in *tierce*. Adair's feather parade succeeded only in turning the blade and again he felt the sharp burn of pain, this time across his ribs. He retreated, gasping, but waved off Broderick's attempt to intervene.

"Webber means to cut him to ribbons," groaned Broderick. "This is plain murder, Paige. We must stop it!"

As he spoke, Adair was making a clumsy business of parrying a thrust in low *carte*, and Droitwich called mockingly, "Give you odds, Manderville. Eighty to one against your pathetic amateur!"

Manderville's response was to spring at him and in a flash a second duel was raging.

Supremely confident, Webber laughed and thrust to the left, leaving his right side exposed. Adair guessed it for a *feinte* and managed to counter Webber's lightning reversal to the right by essaying a half-circle parade. The manoeuvre spared him the thrust that would have pierced his lung, but it was awkwardly done and his attempt to force Webber into a disengage failed.

Webber gave a whoop and a moment later a *glizade* almost tore the sword from Adair's hand. His breath was coming hard and painfully now, and his face was streaked with sweat, but he fought on doggedly, defending himself as best he might, praying for a chance to attack.

Anguished, Broderick mopped his own wet brow and swore helplessly.

Adair somehow survived a sizzling thrust in *tierce*, bungled an attempt at an *appel* and barely parried another *feinte* in *carte*. The cut on his sword arm ached fiercely, and Webber's blade was like a thing alive, malignant and merciless that came at him so fast and furious that he was constantly having to shift from *tierce* to *sexte* to *seconde* to *prime*, essaying at last a *volte* that made Broderick shudder.

"Paige" howled Broderick. "Stop playing with that clod. We must end this! Hasty can scarce stay on his feet."

It was an opinion Webber shared. He had driven his enemy to the end of his endurance. Adair was swaying, and although it had been good fun and the fool had actually lasted much longer than he'd anticipated, he himself was tiring and he had no intention of allowing the duel to end with Adair collapsing from nothing more deadly than exhaustion.

"Oh, well," he murmured regretfully. "My brother will be avenged, at all events."

Adair reeled back a pace but managed to parry Webber's half-thrust. "Have—the decency," he panted, "to at least own that—*you* staged Miss—Miss Prior's abduction and—and tried to have me—hanged for it."

"*Paige!*" roared Broderick, starting forward.

Webber chuckled. "Oh, no, my poor dupe. I'd have been delighted to see you a-swing at Newgate or the Tower, but—the fellow who planned that business is more ruthless than I. You should have looked closer to home for him." His blade swung into a low *feinte* preparatory to the thrust to the stomach that would, with luck, paralyze Adair for life.

Even as Manderville abandoned his own fight and ran to join Broderick, Webber stepped closer. "Stupid fool," he murmured.

Adair stared at him numbly.

Grinning, Webber lunged hard and true.

Adair's right foot stamped forward. His left leg stretched back. Crouching, he ignored the menace of Webber's blade and thrust to the length of his arm. Steel sliced through his hair and nicked his ear, sending blood streaking down his jaw. His own sword had gone home and he wrenched it free as Webber cried out shrilly and sank to his knees.

Through an instant of stupefied silence, Webber gripped at his chest with reddening fingers and stared in a mixture of disbelief and hatred at Adair's blood-streaked face. "Tricked . . . me . . ." he gulped chokingly. "Damned . . . cheat . . ."

Then Droitwich and the surgeon were running to him, stepping over the Honourable Millard Nestor, who was stretched on the turf in a dead faint.

Broderick took Adair's sword and threw an arm about his shoulders. "Excelsior!" he exclaimed.

"You're insane," beamed Manderville, wringing Adair's hand. "But—by Jupiter, you're alive still! Well done, Hasty! Jolly well done! I thought you were spent!"

"Damn near was," Adair panted. "I knew—early on—that—that I couldn't hope to out-fence him. My only hope was to—

outwit him. I just had to—to wait till he was so sure of my 'inexpertise' that he'd not expect such a—a manoeuvre. Rufus Prior warned me not to try it."

"Small wonder," agreed Manderville. "I'm quite good, but I'd not attempt a time-thrust."

"You dashed near waited *too* long," scolded Broderick.

Manderville glanced towards the waiting coaches, and muttered, "Whose carriage is that?"

Adair said, "I must see how Webber goes on."

"Not well," said Broderick, handing Adair's sword to Manderville and walking towards the little knot of men gathered around Webber.

Droitwich, on one knee, glared up and snarled, "You won by a foul, Adair! And so I shall declare to the *ton*."

"Then you'll make an even bigger fool of yourself," said Broderick coldly. "The rest of us saw Webber's ugly tricks. Had he not enjoyed himself by playing with Adair, he might have won. But he was defeated fair and square."

Adair looked down at Webber's ashen and contorted face and asked quietly, "Will he live, Doctor?"

Webber tried to speak and choked horribly.

Without looking up, the surgeon replied, "He's a strong constitution, but your blade took him through the lung. He'll recover—with time." His bright eyes slanted briefly at Adair. "That was the most astonishing finish I've ever seen. You're the one who should lie here, sir! It was a desperate chance to take. I felicitate you on having survived it. Now go away. I can't have my patient further enraged."

The two friends moved towards the waiting coaches. Adair said, "Gad, but I'm ravenous. Breakfast, Toby?"

"I endorse the motion. Heartily! Hi, ho, for a few rashers and some smiling eggs! Where the deuce has Manderville taken himself?"

"He's over there, talking to . . ." Adair broke off, gazing in disbelief at the large carriage and the white-haired gentleman who sat on the steps by the open door, drinking from a flask. *"Grandfather?"* he whispered.

"You may well stare," barked General Sir Gower Chatteris. "Much you care if I suffer a heart seizure! Of all the ridiculous capers to cut!"

Adair hurried to him. "You came, sir! But—how did you know—"

"I may be an ancient figure of fun to you young sprigs, but don't make the mistake of thinking you can write me off as being out of touch with what goes on in my own City." The General stoppered the flask and handed it to the stockily built ex-soldier who had lost an eye during the retreat from Corunna and had served as his major-domo ever since.

"You two fellas," the old gentleman said, fixing his piercing gaze on Broderick and Manderville, "encouraged him in this reckless folly, I collect. You should have known better than to let a novice fencer go up against a man of Webber's mettle. Still, I thank you for standing by him. Not many would—with his reputation!"

"But you see, we do not believe his reputation, sir," drawled Manderville, assisting the General to his feet.

"Then you must know more than do I," said Sir Gower, who had leaned heavily on his arm. "And I don't need to be lifted, thank you very much! Now I want a word with this crazy fire-eater. Pray excuse us for a moment."

Manderville and Broderick exchanged an amused glance and walked out of earshot.

The General demanded, "What did you say to Webber—at the end there?"

"I accused him of having laid the trap to ruin me, sir. He denied it, and said I should look—closer to home for the man who plotted the ugly business."

"I see. So you still maintain your innocence, and now you mean to start accusing each of us! Starting with your Uncle Willoughby, no doubt!"

Startled, Adair asked, "Why would you think that, sir?"

"I know you went down there and found his home full of thieves, and that you jumped to the conclusion they were seeking out his stupid Lists! Oh, yes, I have spoken with your uncle, and listened—with very little patience—to his nonsensical account of the business. Let him be, Hastings. If he's concealing something from you, it's not—Well, whatever it is, it don't have to do with your imbroglio."

"Your pardon, Grandfather, but I believe the Lists have a great deal to do with my 'imbroglio,' and I must—"

"You must look *elsewhere* for your scapegoat, I tell you!"

Adair stiffened. "I mean to find the rogue who has ruined Miss Alice Prior and me. I do not seek a *scapegoat!*"

His icy response seemed to please rather than offend the General, who grinned and said, "Got back on your high horse and have the bit, 'twixt your teeth, have you. Well, I cannot blame you. But I won't have Willoughby's Lists made public. Mind me, now! The contents would most certainly land the fool—I mean your uncle—in Bedlam, and this family has had enough of notoriety." He paused, and said as if the words were torn from him, "I'm told we have treated you unfairly. If that's the case, I'm sorry for it."

Adair gazed at the large hand that was thrust at him. For so long he had prayed for such an admission, and in the misery of his ostracism and rejection had pictured the depth of his joy if it should come. Well, it had come. The old gentleman had humbled his pride and apologized. And perversely, he felt neither joy nor relief, but rather a surge of rageful resentment. It was an apology too long overdue. His family—especially this man, to whom he'd always been so close—should have never doubted him, or even if they did, they should have stood by him.

Glancing back, Broderick saw the two motionless figures, the tall old man's outstretched hand, the slim young man's frozen hauteur. And he halted and stood very still, holding his breath, waiting.

General Chatteris let his hand fall. He turned away, as erect and fierce as ever. And suddenly the broad shoulders slumped, the proud head was bowed. He mumbled hoarsely, "I cannot blame you if—if you cannot forgive. God knows, I—we all of us—let you down shamefully. I'd like you to—to believe, boy, that when I was first told, I denied the whole ugly business. I wouldn't accept that you were guilty until—until that fellow Prior came and showed me the note his lost daughter had writ. And then . . ." He sighed heavily. "But you know about the 'then,' poor lad. I think—I know I shall never forgive myself for—"

He was seized and whirled around, then crushed in two strong young arms.

Holding him close, Adair said brokenly, "Of course I forgive you! What else were you to think in the face of—of such damning evidence? You cannot know what it means to me that . . . you cared enough to come today."

A short distance away, Manderville, who had also watched the emotional scene, exchanged a look with Broderick. "Phew!" he said.

"Very phew!" agreed Broderick, and they walked on together.

The General had stepped back and made a great show of blowing his nose, and Adair drew a hand quickly across eyes that were suddenly dim.

"No—no matter what the evidence," persisted the General, abject in his contrition, "I should have known—It is to my everlasting shame that I failed you at the start."

"Stop scourging yourself, sir," said Adair bracingly. "The most important thing is that you believe me now, although I've still not cleared myself, you know."

General Chatteris put away his handkerchief and said with a return of his usual brusque manner, "You will, Hastings! And I shall be the proudest man in all England when you can prove your innocence to those blockheads in Whitehall! Oh, Gad! Enough of this! I despise maudlin sentimentality! Now what's the time?" He groped in his waistcoat pocket.

Adair pulled himself together and managed to impart that it

was almost eight o'clock. "Sir, I am most anxious to talk to Nigel. Is he in Town still, do you know?"

His grandfather scowled. "If he is, he's damned well hidden. I've tried to corner him, but to all intents and purposes, he's disappeared. I suppose he's the one the Prior gel was meeting on the sly. Is that your thought?"

"I'm afraid it is, sir. But Nigel's not responsible for her abduction. Of that I'm very sure."

"Blasted young cub! He's not up at Oxford, I can tell you. If his friends know where he is, they're keeping his secret."

"Speaking of secrets, Grandfather, I gather that others in Town knew of this meeting. I had supposed it to be a well-kept secret."

"Not from the harridan who invaded my house last night! Gad! I didn't recognize the woman, but after all these years her tongue is as tart as it always was! Put the fear of God into me, I don't mind admitting."

Adair said incredulously, "You surely cannot mean Lady Abigail Prior?"

"That is exactly who I mean! Dreadful termagant—and she was such a lovely young thing when we—" He coughed and broke off, his colour heightened. "What the deuce can I have done with my watch? I know I wore it last evening and I was sure I left it in this pocket. Must have mislaid it somewhere, I suppose."

His lip twitching, Adair said gravely, "Very likely, sir."

<hr>

Lady Abigail looked out of the window of the fast-moving carriage and said plaintively, "Why ever you should think I would be informed of such abominations as duels, when you know how I despise such murderous stupidity, is beyond me. And furthermore, to drag my poor old bones back into Sussex again in this frightful weather is not kind!"

Under a cloak of scarlet velvet, her ladyship had chosen to wear a travelling-gown of bright orange wool, trimmed with red French beads. A necklace of elaborately scrolled gold and rubies was about her throat, and a bonnet with an enormous poke completed her costume.

"Your poor old bones, indeed! Eyeing her grandmother's finery with faint amusement, Cecily said, "It is neither snowing nor raining, and you are sprightly as many a lady half your age, so do not think I don't know it. I believe you found out about the duel because Rufus brought Adair's man out to your coach yesterday afternoon, and you were clearly bullying the poor—"

"By thunder, miss! Have you been so impertinent as to spy on me?"

"But of course. You refuse to tell me anything, so what other recourse have I? You did find out about the duel, didn't you? And last evening you went out all by yourself and came home looking like the cat that swallowed the canary. When is it, Grandmama? Tonight? Tell me, I beg you!"

Lady Abigail turned her head and frowned into the lovely eyes that watched her with such anxiety. "Assuming that I knew, child, I most assuredly would not tell you, for I can see you mean to worry yourself into a decline over this most ineligible young hussar."

Cecily drew back with a little growl of frustration and for a few moments the only sound in the carriage was the rumble of wheels and the clatter of hooves.

"Don't sulk," said Lady Abigail.

"I am not—And why—And besides, he is *not* ineligible, Grandmama. At least, he won't be when he has cleared his name."

"And come into a nice fortune and a title and will leave the army—eh?"

Cecily's chin lifted. She said defiantly, "He has what he calls a comfortable competence, plus his army pay. And—and his grandmother has promised to leave him a very nice property in Gloucestershire, when she goes to her reward."

"His . . . grandmother," mused her ladyship, taking a mental inventory of the elder *ton* dowagers. "That would be Lady Adair's mama, who lives 'out of the world' in Gloucestershire as I recall. . . . *Rondelay?*" Her lips pursed and her brows lifted. "Oho! A

213

'very nice property,' indeed! But nothing to your own fortune, my love. And you may aim as high as you please."

"I have," said Cecily, her eyes becoming very tender.

Lady Abigail shook her head. "People who fall in love so quickly very often fall out of love just as quickly. It will pass, child. You are dazzled by a handsome young soldier who is the more romantical because the world has treated him cruelly."

"The world and his family," muttered Cecily, frowning at a tree that had fallen by the side of the road.

"Hmm," said her ladyship smugly. "Well, I think I have put a spoke in that particular wheel."

Cecily's face lit up. "You have? Is that where you went last evening? To talk to his father?"

"His father—pish! I've no patience with the Viscount or that selfish wife of his. Don't *tug* at me, child! Oh, very well—if you must know, I went to see the General. And you may believe I put a flea in his ear!"

Awed, Cecily half-whispered, "You never did! How brave you are! Did he listen to you?"

"If he hadn't I'd have boxed his ears, as I should have done fifty years ago when he—But never mind about that. Now tell me why I am here, and what you mean to—Good gracious, has Peters lost his wits? Why do we turn into a nunnery?"

"Because," said Cecily conspiratorially, "I believe there is something very odd going on here—something that Hastings is trying to find out about."

"What possible connection—Here comes someone. Now that is a fine-looking woman!"

The footman opened the carriage door and let down the steps.

"But how nice that we shall have the visitors," said the Mother Superior, coming gracefully towards them.

"Heavens!" hissed Lady Abigail. "She is French! You never think . . . ?"

"We'll try to find out," said Cecily.

214

14

I apologize for calling at the Hall, sir." Hastings had not expected his father to be up at this early hour, and seated opposite him in the morning room he said, "I promise I won't disturb you above a minute, but—"

"I am disturbed to hear of one lurid escapade after another." Lord Esterwood, immaculate in morning dress, laid aside *The Times* and asked coldly, "Is it truth that you are to meet Thorne Webber?"

"Actually, sir, we—er, already met."

"Ah." His lordship said drily, "Knowing your marksmanship, dare I hope that you refrained from killing the fellow? Or are you on the point of flying the country?"

"Neither. Webber had choice of weapons, you see, and—"

"He'd have been a fool to—" His lordship's eyes widened. "Good God! *Swords?*"

Adair nodded.

"And you survived? You must have polished your skills considerably since the last time I saw you fence! But I could wish you'd come to tell me of it before the fact, rather than after."

"To say truth, father, I did not come to talk about the duel. I am most anxious to talk to Nigel. The General tells me he is from Town. Do you know if he has returned to Oxford?"

"I think not. Nigel has not been seen for days. I sent a message to his Tutor, and he's evidently not been in Oxford either." His lordship hesitated, then said frowningly, "He may be drowning his sorrows in dissipation, I suppose. But my enquiries have turned up no trace of the tiresome boy."

Hastings rose. "I shall hope to have better luck, sir."

Standing also, Lord Esterwood said, "If I were you, I'd give him time to cool down. The General thinks he is enamoured of this poor Prior girl, and that he holds you responsible for her disappearance . . ."

"He does, sir." Hastings muttered, "If only he had confided in me . . ." He shrugged impatiently. "Well, he didn't. The poor lad is probably searching for her. I must find him, so with your permission, I'll take myself off."

"To go—where?" asked Lord Esterwood, accompanying him into the corridor.

"First, to see my Uncle Willoughby."

"I doubt you'll find Nigel there."

Adair doubted it, too. But he had other reasons for riding down to Woking.

———— ❧ ————

Professor Anton Broderick was tall, thin, and stoop-shouldered. His luxuriant grey hair was worn short but contrived to curl despite his efforts, which were not very stringent, since Mrs. Broderick liked his curls. Behind his spectacles his pale blue eyes were shrewd. He was thought by many to be inflexible and autocratic, but his wife, to whom he was devoted, loved him, and, although he was a stern disciplinarian, his children respected and were fond of him. In one sense he was a rarity among learned gentlemen, for he was tidy and well organized and not in the least absent-minded. Seated at the neat desk in his study, poring over an account of the death of Socrates as

216

recorded in the original Greek, he looked up when a familiar voice called a cheery "Good morning, sir. May I come in?"

"Now there's a damn-fool question!" The professor, who was famed for his salty language, set aside the manuscript and stood to welcome his son with a strong handshake. "Of course you may, Tobias. I thought you'd gone back to France. Never tell me the war is over?"

Toby said with a grin that it was not, and that he was in England on detached service.

"Ah, yes." The professor walked around the desk and occupied one of the armchairs before the hearth. "That ugly business with Sir Kendrick Vespa, I take it? One might think that a bright fellow like Jack would do better than have a murderous traitor for his father. You have to testify, of course. Give that curst bell-rope a tug, will you? Now come and sit down, my boy, and we'll have something to eat. Or would you prefer a flesh-and-blood or some less gut-rotting liquid libation?"

Perfectly aware that his father would have been shocked had he asked for so potent a drink as gin and port at this time of the day, Toby laughed and when a housemaid bobbed a curtsy and asked their pleasure, he put in a bid for hot chocolate and toasted crumpets. His father's eyebrows lifted, and he said by way of explanation, "Beastly cold out, sir. And it's a long drive from Town."

"It is," agreed the professor, lighting his clay pipe with a taper from the fire. "I wonder you essayed it. Seen your mama and the girls already, have you? So now it's my turn. Are you here to tell me you've wangled your way closer to becoming a Don?"

Tobias thought it best to evade that question and said he hoped his sire was not so disappointed in him that he was an unwelcome visitor. "Don't mean to disown me because Oxford doesn't want me, do you, Papa?"

"As your friend Adair has been disowned? The hell I do! I expect great things from you, my boy. When you've matured sufficiently to listen to your brain cells."

In another rather desperate evasion, Toby said, "So you know about Hastings Adair."

His father shrugged. "I'd suppose all England knows. Some vindictive bastard has certainly gone to great lengths to ensure that fact."

"Jupiter! Guessed that, did you? I'm not surprised; you don't miss much. It's a strange business, sir. Hasty's a good man and don't deserve the trap he's been caught in."

"You really believe him innocent, then?"

"Oh, absolutely. He'd no more harm a young girl than you would!"

"Your filial loyalty is touching," said the professor drily. "I shall endeavour to live up to it. What do you want of me?"

At this point the maid returned with a laden tray, and both men applied themselves to the contents.

After a comfortable interval, Tobias said around a buttered crumpet, "I'd like your opinion, sir. If I lay it out before you, I'll go bail you'll solve the riddle in jig time!"

This blind trust so pleased his parent that aside from a request that Tobias be as brief and succinct as possible he listened politely while the facts were made known to him. "The thing is," his son finished, "Adair believed Thorne Webber was behind it all, only Webber laughed at him and said he'd had no part in it."

"And why in Hades would Adair pay heed to what a clod like Webber said?"

"Oh—well, they were—er, engaged in a beast of a duel at the time, and Webber meant to despatch Hasty, and we think he'd have been more likely to crow at that point than—"

"Adair fought *Webber*? I wonder Webber had time to say anything, much less have the slightest chance of putting a period to your friend. I have it on excellent authority that Colonel Hastings Adair is such a good shot that few men in London would care to face him."

"That's quite true, sir, but Webber chose swords and Hasty's at sixes and sevens with a small-sword."

218

"Good God! You were at this debacle, I take it? You're bloody well fortunate that you weren't all hauled off to the Watch House! Was Adair much hurt?"

"No, very slightly," Tobias said with enthusiasm. "We were sure he'd fall but he kept going like a dashed Trojan, and when we thought he was quite against the ropes, managed a Time Thrust! Gad! If you could have seen it—"

"Had I known of it I'd have called in the Runners at once! Trojan, indeed! Of all the confounded ridiculous and outmoded exhibitions of male egotism, dueling is—" The professor took a deep breath, and said in a calmer tone, "But I'd best not get started down that road! Does Adair still hold Webber to be his secret enemy? If he does, he's a fool. I observed Thorne Webber during his brief and deplorable sojourn at Queen's. The fellow is a crudity who hides abysmal ignorance by charging through life like an angry bull, though with a deal less sense. He'd not come up with a devious plot like that in a million years!"

"He told Adair to look closer to home, and Adair now suspects—er, well, in strict confidence, sir, he's troubled because his Uncle Willoughby keeps all those Lists and—"

Professor Broderick gave a shout of laughter. "Balderdash! If ever I met a thimble-wit, it's Willoughby Chatteris! The fellow's head is full of maggots! The best one could say of him is that he rarely opens his mouth and is kind to his late brother's family— or whatever they are." Toby looked at him sharply, but he went on, "No, no, my boy. Adair will find no fish to fry in that direction. I'm sorry for his boringly stiff-rumped diplomatist of a brother. Hudson Adair wanted that Cabinet appointment to distraction, and I must own he worked for it. Lost it now, of course."

Surprised, Tobias said, "What, have they chose someone else?"

"I had it from Holland that there were three contenders."

"You wouldn't know—er . . . ?"

The professor reached for a tablet and pencil and wrote down three names, then handed the paper to his son.

219

"Dash it all!" exclaimed Tobias, deeply shocked. "Do you say this fellow atop the list is a favoured candidate? You can't be serious!"

"As I understand it, he may very well have been confirmed by this time. And why that should surprise you I cannot imagine."

"But—but the holder of that position wields great influence in Whitehall! Hudson Adair may be stiff-rumped, as you say, sir, but he knows what international diplomacy and financing is all about. A few cork-brained mistakes in that quarter could affect the entire war effort!"

"But, of course! My poor boy, did you really expect a sound and sensible choice?"

Tobias whistled softly and repeated, "Dash it all!"

Adair reached Blackbird Terrace early in the afternoon only to be denied entry by the gatekeeper. Bailey apologized profusely; he couldn't guess what maggot had got into the master's head, but he had his orders.

Irritated, Adair turned Toreador aside and rode a quarter-mile to a lower part of the wall. The dapple-grey cleared it neatly and Adair cantered him across the park quite aware of the faint cheer that emanated from the gatekeeper. He left Toreador in the care of a scared-looking stable-boy and entered the house by the rear door. There were some squeaks from the kitchen maids, which he ignored, and he was glancing into the drawing room when Willoughby Chatteris came running down the stairs, waving his arms and shouting his resentment that Hastings dare defy his orders to keep away.

"I saw you jump our, ah, wall, and I know—er, why you're here," he shrilled. "You mean to read my Lists! Well, you'll—you'll set eyes on them over my—er, dead body! Go, confound your impudence! Leave this house before I—er, fetch my pistols and—"

Still baffled by this militant stranger, Hastings said icily,

"Then you had best get them, Uncle. I've every reason to believe your Lists are in some way a threat to this nation, and I mean to see for myself what treachery you've been about!"

Willoughby's jaw dropped. "You've lost your wits!" he gasped. "Mad! Stark-raving—"

"*Bonjour, mon cher* Will," called a musical feminine voice.

Both men turned. Adair was taken aback to see the Mother Superior from the Nunnery of the Blessed Spirit standing in the open doorway, as poised and gracious as ever. She had said "Will"; he glanced at his uncle curiously.

Mr. Chatteris was white as a sheet and stared at the lady in obvious stupefaction.

Advancing, she held out her hands. "Will? Can you find no welcome for me?"

"LaVerne," he gulped hoarsely, taking both her hands. "*You? Here?*"

She nodded. "It is, I think, time." She turned to Adair, who had watched this meeting in frowning silence. "Pray be so good as to for just a little time excuse us, Colonel."

He bowed, and did not follow when his bewildering uncle led the nun towards the morning room.

"And what do you have to say about that, Hastings Adair?"

The laughing question brought him to the open front door in two swift strides. The lady who now stood there wore a cloak of rich mulberry over a light pink gown. Her eyes were alight with triumph, and she was, he thought with a jolt of the heart, the most beautiful creature he had ever seen. "Cecily!" He pressed her fingers to his lips. "How wonderful to see you! But what on earth are you doing here, and with the Mother Superior?"

"We have been contriving in your behalf, Colonel," said Lady Abigail, from the terrace.

Cecily chuckled. "Grandmama certainly has. She called upon your grandfather, though she will not tell me what she asked of him."

"He—er, came to see me." Adair hurried to bow over the

old lady's hand. "For which I am more than grateful, ma'am. Pray come in, and I'll call for refreshments."

Lady Abigail refused this offer, however, saying that she had glimpsed Miss Chatteris down at the kennels and meant to join her and see the puppies. "I presume," she added, rapping her fan on Adair's wrist, "that since there is a nun in the house you are to be trusted with my granddaughter?"

"With or without the nun," he answered with a smile.

"Not too long, mind, Cecily," she called. "We must be back in Town before dusk if we're to go to the Tenbury ball tonight."

Adair closed the door behind her and led Cecily to a comfortable if rather faded sofa. "You are lovelier each time I see you," he said, sitting beside her. "Do I take it that you brought the Mother Superior here?"

"Grandmama and I." She added with a twinkle, "I didn't know how we would manage it, but I knew you suspected some connection between your uncle and the nunnery, so I asked Grandmama to drive down there with me this morning." She paused, smiling fondly at Adair's down-bent head as he took up her hand and kissed it. "Between us, we were able to persuade the Mother Superior to come here and talk to your uncle. But I must say, Hasty, I cannot believe the lady is a French spy. She is much too delightful."

"I think spies very often are. I own she has great charm, but it is very obvious that she is well acquainted with my uncle. She called him 'Will.' I've never known anyone to use his name in that way."

"She implied that they are simply old friends."

He was silent, thinking that there was nothing simple about this remarkable uncle he had once thought he knew well.

Cecily said lightly, "The lady appeared to be genuinely distressed when I told her of the fix you're in and how desperately you are striving to clear your name. You have made a great impression on her, you know, and although she was reluctant at first, she eventually said she would try to help and asked that we bring her here."

"Bless you, my darling girl! And your splendid grand-mother!"

"Thank you, kind sir. How wonderful it will be if she can really help! Well, you will soon know. And now, Hastings Chatteris Adair, be so good as to answer me a question. When is your horrid duel to take place? Rufus has taken himself off somewhere and I could get nothing from him before he left."

"Oh. Well—er, to say truth, it took place. Early this morning."

She gave a little shriek and paled, turning to grasp his arm and search his face anxiously. "My dear heavens! After staying up half the night—"

"And dreaming of you the other half."

"I wonder you are alive! And I knew nothing of it! Oh, you wretch! If I had—What is it? You're hurt!"

"Only slightly," he said, wincing away from her gripping hands.

"Your arm! Oh, mercy, I shall swoon! No—I haven't the time! Here?" She was unbuttoning his shirt-sleeve and turning back the cuff, slapping away his hand when he attempted to restrain her. "Bandages! I can feel them! Oh, *Hasty!*"

The fear in her eyes warmed his heart, but he said with mock severity, "Do you mean to remove my shirt, ma'am? I am shocked! No—stop, do! Really, my love, poor old Webber managed to scratch me—nothing more, and it is, as you can feel, above the elbow, so do not ask that I take off my coat. Remember, I told your grandmama that I was trustworthy!"

She blinked and sat back, staring at him. "You may laugh, but—what do you mean when you say *poor* old Webber? Did you put that nasty man into his grave?" Springing up in renewed agitation, she exclaimed, "Oh, what next? Then you must fly the country! Today! At once, or—"

"Hush." Standing also and pulling her into his arms, he said laughingly, "Gad, what a dramatic scenario you paint! I was lucky is all, and Webber was—not. He will be safe abed for several weeks at least, by which time his temper may have cooled. Now do pray tell me—exactly how does the Mother Superior mean to help me?"

Cecily glanced past him. "I think she will answer that question herself."

Willoughby Chatteris looked worried as he accompanied the nun into the room, but the lady's lovely face was as serene as ever. She said, "I have talked with my dear friend, Miss Hall, and I can do no more. So now, I ask that you will please to take me back to my nunnery. If I am away, you see, my little ones—they tend to get into the difficulties."

Adair ushered both ladies to the door and was surprised to see Lady Abigail being escorted across the lawns by Paige Manderville. When the coach departed, with Cecily waving a lacy handkerchief from the window, Manderville refused an invitation to come into the house, saying with a sideways glance at Mr. Chatteris that Miss Minerva awaited him at the kennels.

Adair closed the door and turned to his uncle.

Willoughby said unhappily, "Well, you have—er, won, Nephew. That lady I cannot deny and she—ah, she has convinced me that your—your reason for demanding to read my Lists is—er, is of an urgency. You may come to my study. I ask only for your word that should you indeed find something vital to the well-being of our nation, which—er, which is quite ridiculous, you will report on that subject only and reveal nothing else."

"I give you my word of honour, sir. And thank you."

Stamping off down the corridor, Mr. Chatteris grunted, "You are far from welcome. And I want to hear no snide comments. These papers are extreme private and were intended for no other eyes than my own."

An hour later, however, Mr. Chatteris wore a very different expression and he watched avidly as Adair turned a page and uttered another whoop of laughter.

"What? What?" Chatteris demanded.

Not for an instant had it occurred to Adair that his uncle's Lists were in fact observations upon the character, romantic escapades and foibles of many leaders of the *haut ton*. The notes of this shy and usually mild-mannered gentleman revealed a biting wit, and his barbs were often so close to the mark as to reduce his nephew to tears of mirth. "Oh, egad, Uncle!" gasped Adair, wiping his eyes. "What a rare gift you have! If this were to be printed—"

Grinning delightedly, Willoughby exclaimed, "I would be lynched! And rightly—er, so, for I've no business pointing out the failings of others. Except in private."

"You have an incredible eye for detail. This note about the Regent and Mrs. Fitzherbert at that Carlton House dinner party is truly hilarious! Were you there, sir?"

His uncle shook his head. "Much of what I've written was relayed to me by friends or—ah, overheard about Town. People like to talk, you know. As to the Carlton House fiasco—yes, that was the actual cause of their separation; because he had her—ah, moved to a less distinguished place at table."

"The straw that broke the camel's back, perhaps," said Adair, turning several pages at once. "How I'd love my grandfather to . . ." His light words trailed into silence and his smile died. He had come upon a long evaluation of a young lady who would seem to have been the epitome of beauty and purity. Expecting cynicism, he found only adoration, but not until he read the name "LaVerne" did he realize the girl's identity. "Jupiter," he said, his face hot with embarrassment, "I do beg your pardon, sir. I'd no intent to pry into your personal—"

Chatteris shook his head. "LaVerne wanted you to understand. Read on."

"No. To put it mildly, your Lists are not what I'd expected, but this is—"

"It is the tale of the happiest—er, time in my life," said Willoughby simply. "We met in Hookham's Lending Library. I walked around a bookcase too rapidly and we—er, collided. When I retrieved her books and looked up, she was smiling down at me. My—my heart just—it turned over." He sighed and said nostalgically, "I am older now, and I know you and—and

225

the rest of the family look on me as a—er, milquetoasty sort of fellow." He raised a hand to halt Adair's attempted protest. "No need to deny it. I know. But then—then I was young and—and my hair was not thinning, or my—ah, shoulders so stooped. Not that I was ever a dashing fellow like you, of course."

"Uncle!" exclaimed Adair, squirming. "For Lord's sake!"

"But LaVerne thought I was," went on Willoughby, lost in the past. "We fell deeply in—ah, in love. She was French-born and my father—your grandfather, you know—straitly forbade the match. LaVerne also resisted my pleas for a while, but at— er, at last she consented. We were married secretly. I had not come into this estate then, and I leased a cozy cottage near Lewes. We were so—ideally happy. When LaVerne found she was with child, our union seemed blessed. She gave me a little girl . . ." He sighed again and lapsed into silence.

Adair found he was holding his breath, and after a moment prompted gently, "It sounds to have been a blessed union indeed, sir. What went wrong?"

"Eh?" Willoughby started. "Oh—well, it—ah, it did, of course. Go wrong, I mean. I had decided to bring my little family up to Town to confront the General. We chose Christmas-time, thinking everyone would be in a—er, more charitable frame of mind. But—the weather, alas, was not kind."

"Your babe became ill?"

"Not ill, Hastings. There was ice. A horse stumbled, the coach slid off the road and overturned. I was unhurt, but—my wife and the baby . . ." He drew a deep breath and went on in a low voice, "All that night I feared for their lives. LaVerne regained consciousness at dawn, and was frantic when she heard about our—er, child. She blamed herself and in a frenzy confessed to me that she had been a novice nun and this was God's punishment because she—she had renounced her vows."

"Surely, that was not the case, sir. Even with the tragedy of the loss of your child, could you not convince her—"

"We did not lose the child. LaVerne prayed and prayed and took a sacred oath that if the Lord would but spare our babe, she would complete her vows and—and spend the rest of her life in His service."

Awed, Adair said, "Then her prayers were granted?"

"They were, thank heaven."

"But—you lost your wife."

Willoughby sighed. "I did—in a sense. It was not—not easy for me. But at least I could see her now and then. And—it was her wish. How could I go against it?"

After a moment, Adair asked, "And none of the family knew anything of it? Is your little girl now one of the nuns, sir?"

"One of our family knew of my marriage," corrected Willoughby. "My brother Jerome."

Major Jerome Chatteris . . . who had fallen during the retreat from Corunna . . . and whose widow and children Uncle Willoughby had taken in to live with him as if they were—Adair gave a gasp. The Mother Superior's beautiful grey eyes had reminded him of someone . . .

He said incredulously, *"Minerva?"*

"You are very quick," said Willoughby, smiling.

"Does she—know?"

"No. Hilda had suffered a miscarriage a few months earlier, and was delighted to welcome my child. Out of respect for my wishes, Jerome told the General they had decided to adopt the daughter of an impoverished friend, and to bring her up as their own. He agreed to keep their confidence. If he noticed a family resemblance, he never mentioned it. Perhaps he thinks Minerva was Jerome's child, born 'on the wrong side of the blanket.' "

In Hastings' opinion, Uncle Willoughby had denied the General the joy of knowing that Minerva really was his granddaughter, and denied the girl the truth of her parentage. But, how easy it was to make such judgments for others; how difficult to resolve problems that were one's own. Accepting that awareness, he made no comment.

As if sensing his reaction, Willoughby said defensively, "My sister-in-law has been a wonderful mother to her; Minerva thinks Hilda *is* her mother. And I have—er, have had the joy of watching my child grow up. Though . . ." His face clouded and he said hesitantly, "It does—you know—seem unfair to LaVerne, though it was as she desired."

Adair waited through the pause, then began to tidy the Lists.

"Why do you frown, my boy? Do you think I am wrong in concealing the truth from Minerva?"

"Jupiter, sir! I'd not presume to judge. That decision, I think, could only be made by the people involved. No, if I am disturbed it's because for the life of me I cannot understand why men would risk imprisonment and even hanging to get their hands on your Lists. There's nothing here of any military significance."

"So I thought. Do you suppose someone—er, might fear I intend blackmail?"

"I don't see how anyone could know what you've written, and even if they suspected, you've not published any of it. Your wife has evidently lived in England for many years, and at all events, if she were an agent for Bonaparte—forgive the suggestion—she would scarcely have urged that you let me read something that might be damaging to her."

Through a brief silence both men pondered the matter. Then Willoughby said with a determined nod, "Even so, Hastings, I think you must finish reading my—my foolish Lists."

"Far from foolish, Uncle! Say shrewd and witty, rather!"

Blushing with pleasure, Willoughby thanked him but persisted, "Still, I may perhaps have written of something that *could* prove damaging to some unknown individual. I think I will not— er, rest easy, my boy, till you tell me you've perused it all."

Since Adair was inclined to agree, he did not protest too vehemently, and when dusk fell he was still busily and, for the most part, enjoyably occupied in reading his uncle's observations on the world of London fashion.

Randall came in and was lighting candles when he heard Adair utter a stifled exclamation. He moved a candelabrum closer to the engrossed reader and by that golden light he noticed that the young Colonel looked very stern. It would be interesting, thought the butler, to know what was in the master's Lists to inspire such an expression.

———~∞~———

"Never have I changed my dress in such a scrambling way," complained Lady Abigail Prior, peering at her reflection in the carriage window and patting the convolutions of her alarmingly tall wig. "I begin to think I should have insisted on the white doves rather than this bluebird." She fingered the adornment cautiously. "The wretched creature looks to be moulting!"

"No, it looks charming," said her granddaughter. "And it won't moult if you just stop mauling it about."

"I would go back and change the little beast," said Lady Abigail fretfully, "save that it is nigh eleven o'clock, and we would be judged extreme rag-mannered to arrive so late to a ball."

"We are not unconscionably late, Grandmama," soothed Cecily. "And besides, you sent Rufus on ahead to convey our apologies. I am sure Lady Tenbury will not regard it, if she even notices that—" She was interrupted by a scream.

"My *feathers*! Only see how they droop! Oh, I shall look a quiz, I know it!"

"Good heavens! How you startled me! Let me see. They look very well and—"

"You say that to put me at my ease, which I am not and could not be, what with moulting birds and wilting feathers, and galloping from one end of England to the other to help your so admired Colonel. I vow there is no rest for a frail old lady. Much you care if I am exhausted!"

Cecily laughed and hugged her. "God grant I am as frail when I reach your age, dearest. And we are doing whatever we may to help Adair because we believe in that way we may also help our darling Alice. Now—show me your poor feathery disaster."

Her ladyship turned back to her reflected image and poked at one very slightly tilted feather. "See it! Perfectly disgusting!"

Peering around her, Cecily said, "It just needs to be—" She broke off, her gaze passing her grandmother's reflection and resting on the gentleman who was walking around the corner they'd just passed. Jumping up, she pulled on the check-rein and tugged at the window.

"What on *earth* . . ." cried Lady Abigail, drawing her cloak higher about her chin. "It is freezing! Are you run mad, child?"

"Peters!" called Cecily. "Turn around at once, and follow the man who just turned down Grosvenor Street!"

"Why should we do so crazy a thing?" demanded her grandmother irritably. "We're late as it is! Who is that fellow?"

Sitting down again, Cecily said, "It's Nigel Adair! I'm sure of it! Hasty has been trying and trying to find him, and I want to ask him—" She broke off as another coach turned the corner and pulled into the kennel.

"You can't ask him now," said Lady Abigail, peering into the darkness. That carriage has taken him up."

"Oh, confound the creature!'

"Cecily Hall!" exclaimed the old lady, scandalized. "Because I sometimes use a naughty word is no excuse for you to—"

"I know, I know, Grandmama, but—Oh, whatever is he about? He surely must know the nasty creature is no friend to Hastings!"

"What 'nasty creature'? What are you babbling at? *Now* what are you doing? Oh, I shall go distracted!"

Cecily was letting down the window again, and calling to Peters to follow the other carriage."

Lady Abigail moaned, "We shall *never* get to this wretched ball! And just as I had my feathers decently arranged!"

"I'm sorry, dearest," said Cecily breathlessly. "But it's the coach of that horrid Captain Droitwich, who seconded Thorne Webber in his duel with Hastings."

"Good gracious me! Why would Nigel Adair associate with such a ruffian? You never think—*Nigel* . . . ?"

"I don't know! I don't know! But—oh, I cannot like this! Grandmama, we *must* follow and see where they go! We *must!*"

"You're demented! They'll see us!"

"They may not be going very far, and they won't see us if Peters stays well back. Dearest, if we help Hastings, we help Alice!"

"Oh, very well," said her ladyship in a martyred tone. "Have your way! We shall both likely be found floating in the river with our throats cut from ear to ear before we see the end of this horrid business! But I don't complain, however old and infirm I may be."

Her lack of complaint was lost upon Cecily, who was already leaning to the window and calling further instructions to Coachman Peters.

"If you must know," drawled Paige Manderville, stretching his long legs to the hearth and blowing cigar smoke at the ceiling, "I come down here now and then. To see the dogs."

With just one branch of candles augmenting the leaping glow from the fire, the drawing room was a cozy and comfortable chamber on this cold winter evening. Dinner had been a merry meal, with the widowed Hilda Chatteris acting as hostess for her brother-in-law, and Minerva aglow with happiness because her favourite cousin had clearly won his way back into Uncle Willoughby's good graces. The ladies and Mr. Chatteris had retired half an hour since, but the two young men lingered, each pondering a vexing, though vastly different, problem.

A log shifted. Adair watched sparks fly up the chimney, and murmured idly, "To see the dogs, eh?"

Manderville turned his head against the sofa cushions and declared with a trace of defiance, "I am a dog lover. I thought you knew."

"There are likely hundreds of dogs between Woking and Town."

"Probably. But I find this house pleasant. And I think your cousin a jolly nice girl, with no simpering affectations about her."

Adair thought of the many London beauties who adored his

handsome and sophisticated friend, and of his plump and far from sophisticated cousin. He said, "Oh, I agree," and added without emphasis, "She is also betrothed, you know."

"So you say. It has not been published as yet."

So he'd actually gone so far as to do some digging! Amazed, Adair murmured, "My grandfather doesn't approve. Harrington's lineage is—er, 'unsuitable,' he says."

"I'd thought Julius your good friend. A bit of a dull dog, but a nice enough fellow. If Mr. Chatteris approves . . . He—does, don't he?"

Uncle Willoughby's notes under the heading: "Harrington, Julius," flashed before Adair's mind's eye. He said with a shrug, "Minerva certainly approves. But she's never been besieged by a dashing man-about-town, and if you mean to—"

"Good grief, man! I find the lady charming. No more, no less. Don't build the eternal triangle around it! What the deuce is that you're playing with?"

Adair tossed him the button he'd been turning in his hand. "Miss Hall found this among her cousin's belongings. She—er, evidently collects such things."

"No need to wrap it in clean linen, old boy. Toby told me about the odd habits of the Prior ladies." Manderville roused himself and sat up straight, holding the button to the candlelight. "This battered object came from a man's coat. Her sire's, perhaps."

"Perhaps. Save that there seems to be some kind of crest or heraldic device and a pair of initials. D'ye see?"

"Not exactly." Peering at the button, Manderville said, "Can't make head nor tail of the initials. What's that thing in the middle?"

"It's an umbrella." Adair went to take the button. "Look here . . . That's the handle."

"Are you sure? It don't look like an umbrella to me."

"Probably because you're holding it upside down. This way, gudgeon. This way!"

Manderville yawned. "That fella we just fought . . ."

"Thorne Webber."

"That's the one. Don't his family have something to do with the manufacture of—"

"Umbrellas," said Adair.

"Well—there you are then. Neat and tidy, eh, *mon colonel*?"

"Hmm," muttered Adair.

15

⁓⁓⁓

General Chatteris has not yet taken his breakfast, miss," said Polebrook, his disdainful gaze fixed on a point some twelve inches above the head of this lovely but shockingly fast young woman.

"And so I told her, sir," murmured the footman, taking refuge behind the elderly butler.

"I do not care if your master is in his bed," declared Cecily, raising her voice and pushing impatiently at the front door. "I demand that you announce me. At once! It is a—a matter of life and death!"

Polebrook curled his lip, his manner saying clearly that he'd heard that tale before.

"I believe," said Cecily, raising her voice to an even more shrill pitch, "that you're the silly man who attempted to deny my grandmama a little while ago. If I am forced to bring her here again, General Chatteris will not be pleased, I am very sure!"

Staring at her, the butler lost a little of his colour. "Your—grandmother, miss?"

"Lady Abigail Prior," shouted Cecily at the top of her lungs. "Now shall you open this door, or—"

"What the devil is going on?" Clad in his dressing-gown, General Sir Gower Chatteris stamped down the stairs, roaring. "I rang for you twice, Polebrook! What is that young woman screaming about? I declare there's no longer any peace to be had in a gentleman's home! I'd have a more serene life were I in France with that young rascal, Wellington! What does she want?"

Polebrook turned from the door and offered Cecily's calling card. "Miss Hall says she is the granddaughter of Lady Prior, sir."

"Is she, by God!" The General took an involuntary step to the rear. "She has the voice for it, certainly!"

"And you are discourteous, sir," announced Cecily, for the benefit of any neighbours who might be eavesdropping. "Else you'd not keep a lady waiting on your doorstep!"

"A lady would not call on a gentleman at this hour," retaliated the General, but casting an uneasy glance at the street. "Is your grandmama with you?"

"No. We were out late last night, and—Oh, I'll tell you all about it, but for goodness' sake order this idiot to stand aside, sir! I am come on an urgent matter concerning your grandson."

At the General's gesture, Polebrook and the footman retreated. "I presume you refer to Hastings Adair," he said, frowning. "Did I hear you say a matter of life and death?"

"I should think the whole street heard me say it," said Cecily, taking off her cloak and thrusting it at the footman. "Now you will want to finish your breakfast, I expect, sir, while I tell you why I have invaded your home in so rude a fashion." She smiled in a way that caused the General to be carried back to other times, and his ire faded. "I trust you can spare some food for me," she said mischievously. "I'm absolutely famished."

General Chatteris laughed, and offered his arm. As they went up the stairs together, he said, "I take it that you share your grandmother's conviction that Hastings is innocent."

"Absolutely. And her regret that we added our mite to his misery."

He pushed open the door to the breakfast parlour. "I find that remarkable. Under the circumstances. I understood your grandmother to say that you and Miss Prior are like sisters."

"So we are, sir, and I love her dearly. But"—she paused as he drew out a chair for her—"but I also love—your grandson, you see."

"Bless my soul!" exclaimed the General, and rang for the maid to set another cover.

When the servants had been dismissed and Cecily was depleting the plate of haddock and toast set before her, she said, "I have come to you because I've learned something that Colonel Adair must be made aware of. He is not at Adair Hall, nor at his flat. I'd hoped you might have seen him."

The General shook his head. "Perhaps he's with his friends at Jack Vespa's house."

"My cousin went there, but Broderick has evidently gone to visit his father, and Paige Manderville is down at Blackbird Terrace. Hastings was there yesterday. I'd thought they would have returned, but they may have been delayed by this fog. Or perhaps Mr. Chatteris was really able to help."

"Willoughby? By Jupiter, I *told* Hastings to pay him no heed! If you're relying on my son, you waste your time, my dear lady. There's small chance that poor Willoughby has wits enough to help himself—much less anyone else!"

"I believe Hastings thinks otherwise, sir. But at all events, I thought I should approach you with the nasty business before I go down there."

"What 'nasty business'? And why should you go down there in this weather? Surely, it can wait till Adair comes back to Town?"

"No, sir." Cecily met the General's eyes gravely, and waving a slice of toast to emphasize her remarks, said, "It must not wait. I'll tell you as quickly as I can, and then I must find Hastings!"

Ten minutes later the house of General Sir Gower Chatteris was a busy place as the footman raced to the stables, the General went to his room to summon his valet and dress for travel, and

Cecily scribbled a note to her grandmother and another to be delivered to Adair's flat. Very soon afterwards a fine coach and four was being tooled through the traffic that thronged London Bridge. The coachman paid little heed to the thickening mists that drifted about the great City. His thoughts were all on the relationship between his rigidly proper master and the beautiful young woman who now sat beside him in the carriage.

"I thought she'd never leave us," muttered Broderick, returning from having closed the drawing-room door behind Minerva.

Paige Manderville fixed him with a frosty stare. "Well, that's a charming remark to make, I must say. This happens to be the lady's home. You're the intruder!"

"So are you, for that matter." Broderick sank into a fireside chair and accepted the mug of hot cider Adair handed him. "Why are you cluttering up the place, anyway?"

Adair intervened quietly, "Have you ridden from Town, Toby? You must have set out early. It's not yet eleven o'clock."

"Actually, I came from Thames Abingdon. I'd have arrived sooner, but I'd to contend with this devilish mist all the way."

"Visiting your papa?" enquired Manderville.

Broderick nodded and gave Adair a sober look. "Needle-witted is my sire. He gave me some news I thought you should know about, but I couldn't tell you while your cousin was present."

"Sounds intriguing," said Manderville, amused. "But if your combined great brains have led you to believe that Mr. Chatteris is our murderous abductor, you're far off the mark, old lad."

"It would be fun to know what your own 'great brain' has deduced. No doubt you have solved the entire puzzle, thus making my small discovery worthless."

"Not that, perhaps, but I've helped. We found a clue. Tell him, Hasty. Better yet—show him."

Staring blankly at the fire, Adair was silent.

Paige and Toby exchanged glances. Broderick mouthed a

soundless "More trouble?" Paige shrugged and half-whispered, "Something has him in the hips."

The quiet words broke through Adair's dismal introspection. He forced a smile and said, "Gad, but I'm a clunch! My apologies. You were saying, Paige?"

"We were wondering what has you looking so Friday-faced. I'd thought we were making progress."

Broderick said soberly, "Perhaps we progress in a direction Hasty don't want to follow."

Darting a keen glance at him, Adair said, "You've turned up something, Toby?"

"I have, but lest you're inclined to kill the messenger, I'd like first to see whatever it is Paige wants you to show me."

Adair looked at him steadily, then took the button from his waistcoat pocket and handed it over.

Disappointed, Broderick said, "This is your clue?"

"The mystery of the purloined button," said Manderville lightly. "Miss Prior evidently 'collected' it. There's a crest or escutcheon or whatever engraved on the front—see, here."

"So there is." Broderick peered near-sightedly at it. "An anchor."

Adair started and caught his breath in a faint hiss.

"It's an *umbrella*, you cloth-head," exclaimed Manderville, exasperated. "Which ties the button directly to Thorne Webber and the fact that he must be acquainted with Miss Prior. Lord save us all, you're holding the stupid thing upside down; no wonder you can't see straight! Look, here's his initial—*T*. You really should buy yourself a pair of spectacles! When we go back to France, be damned if I want you riding behind me with a musket in your fist!"

"It don't look like an umbrella to me," argued Broderick doggedly. "It's an anchor plain as day. Nor does that look like a *T*. I'd say rather—"

"Spectacles," decreed Manderville firmly.

Adair asked, "You said you brought some news, Toby?"

Broderick nodded. "My father seems to have some private source of information on behind-the-scenes frolics at Whitehall. He found out that three gentlemen are being considered for the Cabinet post your brother Hudson hoped to win." He handed Adair a slip of paper. "The first name is apparently all but confirmed. My congratulations. I'm sorry that your brother must be disappointed, but you'll keep it in the family at least. I didn't want to say anything in front of Miss Minerva, because her betrothed will likely want to give her that piece of good news himself."

Adair gazed at the printed name.

"You never mean—*Harrington?*" Springing up, Manderville snatched the paper. His eyes widened. He gave a sudden shout of laughter. "I *knew* they were all bacon-brained in Whitehall!" Becoming aware that Broderick looked censorious and that Adair was remarkably white about the mouth, he added uncertainly, "I say—I don't mean no offence. It's—it's a feather in his cap to win such a dashed important position."

Broderick said, "His lady will surely be very pleased. D'you think the General will sanction the match now, Hasty?"

Adair stood and paced to the window. Looking out at the misted air unseeingly, he did not at once answer. Then he said slowly, "I'll ask him. I must be getting back to Town at all events, and since my uncle has allowed me to read his Lists—"

"Good Lord!" cried Broderick, taken aback. "He has?"

"Yes. I'm sorry, Toby. I forgot you weren't here at the time."

"Hasty says they were not at all as he'd expected," said Manderville. "And that they were more after the style of a London diary and in no sense treasonable. Correct, Colonel, sir?"

"More or less. Do either of you ride with me?"

"What d'you mean—'more or less'?" demanded Broderick. "And where's the rush? I'll tell you what, Hasty, my mama has charged me to deliver a parcel to my eldest sister. She lives near Farnborough. I'll be lucky if I can break away inside an hour. There's a new little niece to be admired and I'll have to relay all the Society gossip. If you'll ride down there with me, it'll give me an excuse not to linger. Then I'll go back to Town with you." He added with an air of tragedy, "But I had hoped to be offered a crust of bread here, at least!"

"Of course. I'm a poor host. I'm sorry." Adair tugged on the bell-rope. "You stay and enjoy your 'crust,' Toby, but forgive if I don't visit your sister. I really must get to Town. What about you, Paige? Do you go with me?"

Manderville said lazily that he wouldn't mind a "crust" himself, and that he'd then keep Toby company on his errand.

Within minutes, Adair rode out alone.

In the house he'd left, Manderville toured the breakfast parlour, then returned to the drawing room. "They've brought our 'crusts,' Toby. Some jolly nice cold roast pork, fried potatoes, asparagus, and scones with honey. I'm not going to await your pleasure, so you'd best come."

"Mmm."

"Succinct and to the point, I suppose. If one knew what you are mulling."

Broderick turned from the window. "I've not cried friends with Adair for a great time," he said thoughtfully. "But I saw him often on the Peninsula, of course, and I've always fancied him to be well-bred."

"Have you now. Pray tell how he has fallen from grace."

"Didn't you notice? The lad he sent for Toreador was running."

Manderville clapped a hand to his brow with theatrical drama. "Infamous behaviour to demand such an effort! He was in a hurry, you great gudgeon."

"In so much of a hurry that he couldn't spare the time to say his farewells to his uncle, or to Miss Minerva? Simple courtesy, Paige."

"How the devil d'you know he didn't see them? Been watching him?"

"Yes. I'd swear he deliberately avoided Minerva, and he rode out as though the devil himself was perched on his shoulder."

240

"Not like old Hasty," agreed Manderville uneasily. "What d'you think we should do?"

Broderick hesitated. "Think on it while we eat our 'crusts'?"

"Jolly good tactics, dear boy!"

<hr />

Adair set a steady pace and wasn't sorry that his friends had not accompanied him. He had much to think about, and besides, he would travel faster alone.

Yet he was not alone. Beside him, all through that mist-shrouded early afternoon, rode the Daemon Suspicion.

He tried not to heed the sly whispers. It was, he told himself, despicable to think for a moment that a close friend might be capable of treachery. Harrington had proved his loyalty in countless ways. "He stands by his friends . . ." Minna had said that. Certainly, Harrington had not hesitated to side him when Webber had attacked him in front of that hostile London crowd. He'd risked condemnation by championing the Adairs while the rest of the *haut ton* turned their backs on the family. And even after the man had been injured when calling at Adair Hall, he'd appeared to be as staunchly supportive as ever. He was in love with Minna, and she with him. Adair thought wretchedly that if his half-formed conclusions proved to be fact—Lord! It would break Minna's heart!

Rounding a bend, he had to rein Toreador onto the grassy verge as a heavy-laden waggon pulled out from a misty farm gate. The cart-horses snorted and reared with fright and Toreador shied. Adair swore and urged the dapple-grey onward again, and with a thunder of hooves they swept past, leaving behind eddying swirls of grey vapour and the angry shouts of the waggoner. But the Daemon was not left behind.

". . . Be sure of your sources, Colonel!"

Another voice invading his thoughts; this time the strident tones of Field Marshal Lord Wellington. The remark had been made after an incident in Spain when, during a perilous advance through enemy territory, Adair had begun to question their guide's loyalties. He had acted on his suspicions at once, which had spared them from what would have been a deadly ambush. Not expecting praise from Wellington, he'd been somewhat taken aback when the General had fixed him with a stern stare and warned, "You were lucky this time, Colonel. But you should always be sure of your sources before rushing off half-cocked." Since he was not responsible for having hired the guide and had, in fact, been instrumental in averting disaster, the scold had seemed unjustified. Might it apply today?

The truth was that he had precious little evidence against Harrington. A battered old button; Uncle Willoughby's possibly prejudiced Lists; and now the Cabinet appointment that had been so completely unexpected.

He could all but hear the Field Marshal; sneering . . .

Very well. He would not "rush off half-cocked" but would consider his sources.

To judge Harrington guilty must be to assume that he was capable of betraying the lady who loved him, and whom he professed to love; to hold him responsible for the seduction of an innocent young girl and to have cunningly contrived that another man would be accused of the crime. Could Harrington have so convincingly feigned grief and sympathy when—thanks to his own scheming—his "good friend" and future cousin faced ruin and disgrace and a shameful execution? Surely no man could be so sly?

He'd inspected the button again while waiting for Toreador to be saddled up, and he'd seen that Toby had been right, as usual: Battered as it was, the "umbrella" was, in fact, an anchor, and the initial he'd taken for a *T* became a *J* with the loop almost obliterated and the second initial so unreadable it could have been an *H*, an *M* or a *W*. If he'd not been so ready to believe the worst of Thorne Webber, he would have recalled a similar crest on Harrington's cane. Which raised the question of how a sheltered damsel like Alice Prior had come by the button. Harrington had said he was not acquainted with the Prior family, so it was unlikely that he'd ever called at their home. Besides, when he himself had told Cecily and her grandmother that Minna was betrothed to Harrington, Lady Abigail had said that she'd "never heard of him." Alice would certainly not have picked up the button in the street, or at some Society function. Even more unlikely was the possibility that an acquaintance, aware of her "gleaning" habits, would have given her so trite an object. Logic said that she *must* have met Harrington somewhere, in which case why had he denied it?

Next, and far more damning, was the matter of Uncle Willoughby's notes. Most of the famous Lists were concerned with illicit romantic liaisons or the amusing personal idiosyncrasies of members of the *ton*. Some of the caustic comments on various social entertainments had made him laugh aloud. But there were also a number of more sober accounts of cheating at cards, poor sportsmanship, or underhanded business dealings. Included in this sorry group were several highly respected names that had caused Adair's brows to lift in shock. This was volatile material indeed. If the details were accurate and the information should fall into dishonest hands, it could provide a lucrative source for blackmail, and if those items were ever made public, the results could be devastating. Envisioning famous families disgraced, suicides, marriages destroyed, charges of libel, court proceedings and notoriety, Adair could well understand why his uncle had guarded the Lists so zealously.

The summary on Harrington was involved and of an even darker nature. There were several entries, none favourable. One concerned the competition for the Parliamentary seat to which Harrington had aspired. His opponent, a popular banker, was widely held to be most likely to win, until he had been accused of embezzlement. He'd denied the charge under oath, but had been unable to prove his innocence. When missing bonds had been discovered in his home, the scandal had so wrought upon him that he had shot himself. Here, Uncle Willoughby had penned a comment at the side: ("Or did he?") that had caused Adair to utter a startled exclamation. Rumours of fraudulent vote-counting had faded away and Harrington had won the election. Willoughby had noted:

Since taking up his seat in the Commons he has managed to make himself indispensable to gentlemen of influence. As a result, he often is given the awarding of choice contracts (over the head of some more experienced and worthy fellow). Nota bene: *the building of the new steam packet. He awarded this prize plum to Barnabas Fulmer & Sons—a comparatively new concern whose major stockholders cannot be identified. I'd wager my estate that it is actually a subsidiary of Harrington Shipbuilding!*

Clearly, Willoughby had been unable as yet to confirm his suspicions or verify the fact that lucrative bribes were whispered to have changed hands, and that exorbitant fees had been paid for materials—said to be inferior—that had gone into the building of the vessel.

There had been more incidents, not all so flagrant, but forming an ugly pattern, and Willoughby had noted:

My earlier apprehensions concerning this young man were justified. I believe that far from being amiable, as most people judge him, he is an unscrupulous rascal consumed by ambition. I doubt he has gone near his home district since he was elected, and he ignores the needs of his constituents while assuring them through his assistants that he is working night and day in their behalf. One might suppose that such behaviour would hinder his chance for re-election—but perhaps Mr. Harrington has loftier goals in mind.

There was a more recent entry:

Disaster! This creature is now courting my precious Minerva! I have tried to influence her against him, but he is so cunning as to pretend affection and admiration for me, and she is distressed if I speak, as she says, unkindly of her "betrothed." The dear innocent has had so few beaux that she is quite taken in. Also,

244

he has gone out of his way to befriend Hastings, who appears to like him, thus further influencing Minerva; she has always looked up to her cousin.

By this time deeply disturbed, Adair had confronted his uncle on the subject. "If you really believe all these charges, sir, you could have gone to my grandfather, and—"

Willoughby had given a derisive snort. "The General would have laughed at me, as he—er, always does. And after all, what can I prove? For what reason would an ambitious man pursue a sweet child who is not a great beauty and who has lived mostly in the country? Minerva would not know—ah, how to go on in the home of a statesman, and though my fortune is comfortable, it is scarcely worth such deception—for deception I—er, believe it to be. I can only surmise that he craves the social prestige of marrying into our family, and thinks your present—ah, embarrassment will soon be forgotten. My sister Hilda is well pleased with the prospective match because she feared she would never be able to fire Minerva off. Such nonsense! But I'm outnumbered and outmanoeuvred, for if I reveal the extent of my—ah, private investigations, I run the risk of turning the child against me."

Pondering all this, he'd asked cautiously, "Sir, do you think Harrington might be aware of your investigations? Could that account for the attempt to steal your Lists?"

"It has crossed my mind. But I am prejudiced, and I suppose I could be wrong."

"But you don't believe you are wrong, do you, Uncle?"

With a deep sigh, Willoughby had said, "No, Hastings. I'm sorry to judge your friend harshly, but—in the light of all the facts I've unearthed about him, how—ah, how could I be wrong?"

But he *could* be wrong. Doubtless the Field Marshal would say that most of the "facts" Uncle Willoughby had uncovered could be set down to hearsay, or the prejudices of a devoted father who believed his daughter to be making a disastrous marriage. Harrington's rival for the Parliamentary seat might really have embezzled funds and committed suicide. Willoughby had himself admitted that the vote-counting frauds had "faded away"—probably for lack of substantiation. Nor had he been able to verify the true ownership of the shady Barnabas Fulmer shipbuilding company. The verdict would be that it was all conjecture; much of it based on the reports of hired investigators who may have been willing to report whatever they thought their employer desired to hear.

And how would the Field Marshal explain the Cabinet appointment, pray? Julius knew how hard Hudson had worked to win the post, yet had never even hinted that he himself had ambitions in that direction. He must have been aware that he was being considered. In view of his close connections with the Adairs, simple courtesy should have demanded that he inform them of his hopes. Instead, he had kept the matter a close secret even while he must have been working hard behind the scenes to ensure his nomination. If confronted with this, Julius would probably claim that he'd refrained from mentioning his ambitions for fear of upsetting Hudson and the family. And under the circumstances it would have been an awkward topic to raise.

But if Harrington really was guilty, where was the motive for such appalling behaviour? A long-held grudge? A slight some member of the family had dealt him? An obsessive determination to remove Hudson Adair from his path to winning an influential Cabinet post, and to do it in such a way that he himself would not come under suspicion? Was any political career so important as to justify two murders, the ruination of a close friend, the destruction of a proud old family?

Thus the miles passed while Adair fought against believing what the Daemon Suspicion whispered in his ear, and was plagued by a familiar and disquieting sense of impending disaster.

Despite the fog and the fact that he had to stop twice to rest Toreador, he reached Town shortly after two o'clock. He went straight to Julius Harrington's house on Clarges Street and was advised by the soft-voiced young gentleman who was secretary to the Member of Parliament that his employer was not at home, but expected to return this evening. No, he did not know where Mr. Harrington might be found but he rather thought he had gone out of the City.

The information was relayed in nervous little rushes of words. Adair scrutinized him grimly and the glare in the narrowed blue eyes caused the secretary to pale and draw back, babbling that he'd tell Mr. Harrington the Colonel had called. He was obviously panic-stricken to be faced by so notorious a soldier, and was probably telling the truth. In which case there was nothing to be gained by waiting there and wasting hours that could be better spent.

Frustrated, Adair rode to his own flat, keeping his hat pulled low and turning up the top cape of his cloak since the fog was not sufficiently thick to conceal his identity. He gave Toreador into the hands of the lad who served as messenger for the four flats in the building, with instructions that the tired horse was to be taken to the stables and pampered.

York answered the door and took Adair's saddle-bags, asking solicitously, "Have you ridden from Woking, sir?"

Adair was tempted to answer, "No, you fool! I walked!" But he mustn't vent his mood on poor York, and he answered, "I have. What are you cooking? It smells delicious."

"I thought you might come home and want some luncheon, so I've potatoes au gratin in the oven, and we've some cold chicken and a sallet, if that would suit?"

Until that moment, Adair hadn't realized how hungry he was. "It will suit splendidly," he said, making for his bedchamber. "And I'll take a glass of claret now, if you please."

Dismayed by his employer's look of restrained ferocity, York lost no time in providing a glass of wine and a ewer of hot water. Having sampled the first and washed with the second, Adair felt refreshed. He was brushing his hair when York set out a clean shirt, murmuring that this fog put a layer of grime on everything, and would the Colonel wish his boots to be pulled off?

Adair growled that he would be going out again shortly, and when he'd changed his shirt and shrugged into a comfortable old corduroy coat, went into the dining room. His luncheon was on the table, and beside his plate were three newspapers atop a small pile of what looked to be York's accounts of household expenditures. He delayed wading through the collection till he'd finished his lunch. York's culinary skills were as satisfactory as ever, and his dark mood had eased slightly by the time he set aside the newspapers and took up first a listing of amounts expended upon such vital necessities as coal, candles, soap, beeswax, and silver cream; and next, a butcher's bill. Reaching for another bill, he saw instead a fine paper inscribed in a neat feminine hand to "Colonel Hastings Adair." He broke the seal eagerly and read:

Dearest Hasty:

Late last evening Grandmama and I saw Talbot Droitwich take up your brother Nigel near Adair Hall. I know how you've been trying to find Nigel, and I am anxious to talk to him, as you know, so we followed their coach. Nigel was set down at the Madrigal Club. Mr. Droitwich drove on to the house on Clarges Street now owned by your cousin Minerva's fiancé. He was admitted at once.

I crept to the window. I couldn't see inside, but I heard a lot of hearty talk and laughter, which puzzles me.

If Harrington is your friend, what was he doing with that nasty Talbot Droitwich? And why was your brother with the creature?

I knew you were still at Woking, so I called on General Chatteris early this morning. Perhaps I am making mountains out of molehills, but I thought you must be told of this at once, and since the General also wants to talk to your uncle about his Lists, we are driving down to Blackbird Terrace together.

I will send this note round to your flat in case you are already en route to Town and pass us on the road in this beastly fog.

Bless you, my dear.
In haste
Cecily

"Droitwich . . . !" muttered Adair, scowling at his letter.

York's hand jerked and the coffee he'd started to pour splashed into the saucer.

Glancing at him, Adair surprised a look of stark terror.

"Sir," said the valet, suddenly deathly pale, "I beg you will not allow—I mean—If the gentleman has complained . . ."

"Why should Mr. Droitwich lodge a complaint against you?"

"So he has done so!" York's bony hands were wrung. "Again! It is always the same. When I finally win a new position I try my best to please, but then—he writes to my employer, and—" He shrugged helplessly. "He won't be satisfied until I am in the gutter or my grave! But I didn't mean it, sir! As God be my judge—"

"Ah," said Adair, the light dawning. "Mr. Droitwich was one of the gentlemen who became ill after the accident with your shellfish, is that the case? Did anyone actually perish in that sorry affair?"

"No, sir, thank heaven. But three guests were made very ill and—and Mr. Droitwich tried to—to have me transported, though I *swear*—"

"Yes, yes. I quite believe you." York's eyes were on the letter in Adair's hand. He said, "Miss Hall wrote on another topic. Are you aware that Droitwich seconded Mr. Thorne Webber in my recent—'outing'?"

York looked relieved. "I wasn't, sir. May I take it that you are not close friends?"

"You may take it that we are not friends in any sense of the word." His thoughts turning to his beloved and her heart-warming efforts to help him, Adair heard York mutter something under his breath as he prepared a fresh cup of coffee. "What was that?" he asked sharply.

"I should not have spoken. I apologize, sir."

"You said, I believe, 'Just as well'?"

The scared expression returned to the valet's cadaverous

249

features. "I had no right to have done so. But—well, I know Mr. Droitwich, you see."

"Do you, indeed! Sit down, man, I'm not going to eat you. In point of fact, you may be able to help me. Tell me all you know of Mr. Talbot Droitwich."

16

This time Adair gave not a thought to the risk of being recognized as he guided Toreador along London's fog-draped streets. A loaded pistol was in his saddle-holster, another in the pocket of his cloak, and vengeance was in his heart. His conversation with York had left little room for doubt that at the very least Julius Harrington was involved in the plot against him and he was determined to call the devious politician to account.

Before his shellfish disaster, York had been a respected member of the social world of London's superior servants. As such, he had often shared a laugh at the stories which Mr. Talbot Droitwich's valet had related about his master. Mr. Droitwich, it seemed, had two major weaknesses—the Fair Sex, and gaming. Some of his "ladies" and card parties were of a type not smiled upon by the *haut ton*, and Mr. Droitwich had judged it expedient to hold his revels away from the hallowed halls of Mayfair. To this end he frequented a house in the back streets of Westminster. It was a district never visited by Society, and Mr. Droitwich had thought his identity well concealed. While this had been a wise move, he had lacked the wisdom to treat his servants kindly. His valet despised him, and had suffered no qualm of conscience in describing his employer's hideaway. It was, the valet had said, "a dirty little red brick house on a dirty little street in Westminster, to which gentlemen drove in closed unmarked coaches, and 'ladies' came unescorted by maids or chaperons."

Pressed for the identities of some of these "gentlemen," York had named some hardened gamesters, and with reluctance had admitted that Mr. Julius Harrington was known to visit the house often, though always under cover of darkness.

For Adair, it was the last straw. Why Nigel should be on friendly terms with a rogue like Droitwich was baffling, but for Droitwich to have called upon Harrington and received an apparently cordial welcome bore all the appearance of duplicity at the very least. While professing to be his own "good friend," Harrington had spoken contemptuously of Droitwich, and was well aware that the man had seconded Thorne Webber in that infamous duel. It would be interesting, thought Adair, his jaw tightening, to hear his "good friend's" explanation, and also to learn why Harrington, a Member of Parliament who had just won an influential Cabinet appointment, should risk frequent visits to a "dirty house" in a most unsavoury neighbourhood.

Soon, carriage traffic thinned. They were coming into the dismal Westminster slums; a shameful blot on this part of the city that was so steeped in history. The daylight was fading, the foggy air and low-hanging grey clouds combining to make the hour seem more like six than four o'clock.

A few roughly dressed men sauntered along the narrow streets or gathered about the doors of corner alehouses. An occasional rider peered at Adair curiously; a shabby individual pushing a reeking barrow howled an offer for a "pint o' winkles" that was greeted by a shrill cackle from a woman carrying a bottle and obviously the worse for drink. "I'll lay your pint 'gainst mine as that there nob don't even know what a winkle is," she screeched, and they both laughed uproariously.

Adair failed to notice the mirth of the winkle vendor and the lushy lady; he also failed to notice the rider who—although keeping some distance behind—had turned each corner he'd turned, and followed with stealthy persistence. He was thinking that for members of the *haut ton* to enter this district was risky business, and that Droitwich and his gamester friends must come well-armed. Searching about for such individuals or for unmarked coaches, he was haunted by one of Uncle Willoughby's remarks: "Perhaps Mr. Harrington has loftier goals in mind . . ." What "loftier goals"? A powerful position in the Cabinet that might perhaps lead to knighthood? He'd achieved that. The opportunity to amass a fortune by way of bribes and corruption? It appeared that also was within his grasp. What more? To reach a higher office? Perhaps—Lord forbid!—to become Britain's Prime Minister?

Telling himself sternly that he mustn't let imagination run away with him, Adair hailed an urchin who was trotting along in the littered kennel and watching him hopefully.

"Yus!" The lad "knowed where there was parties fer flash coves on dark nights. It were a proper nice house; the only brick house on that pertic'ler street, but there wasn't no party there terday, nor hadn't been for nigh on a month." Bribed with a promise of sixpence to lead the way to the "proper nice house," he set off eagerly.

They soon arrived at an unlovely thoroughfare optimistically named Appletree Place. The urchin halted and indicated a dirty two-storey brick house several doors from the corner. It was undoubtedly the finest residence on this alley of tumbledown houses that should long ago have been condemned. Scanning it, Adair detected a faint glow emanating from behind stained window curtains and his pulse quickened. It would be asking too much of Lady Luck to hope that Harrington was inside, but someone was there. And even if Talbot Droitwich was the only occupant he might be persuaded—after being slightly throttled—to volunteer some information about his Cabinet Minister friend.

Adair had to fight his need for immediate and violent action. If Harrington really was behind this whole ugly business and Droitwich in league with him, then they were very dangerous men who did not draw the line at murder. That dirty house could well contain armed ruffians hired to guard them. There were few people about and those few were not likely to come to his aid if he burst into the house and was overpowered. To attempt such an attack alone would be folly, but to send for Bow Street or the Watch would be as useless.

Wisdom dictated that he withdraw and gather reinforcements. He gritted his teeth against "wisdom." No doubt he was "rushing off half-cocked" but, by heaven, he meant at least to take a closer look at that wretched little house! He dismounted, therefore, to confer with his small guide, who waited and watched him patiently.

Relying on the probability that Paige and Toby had returned to Town by this time, and very sure they would be willing to help, Adair tore a page from his tablet and wrote a quick note to York. "Find Mr. Broderick and Mr. Manderville at once, and send them here with their pistols. I promised this lad a shilling if he would guide them to me. Hurry!" He signed his name and gave the folded paper to the urchin, with strict instructions on how to reach his flat.

"Yus!" Billy New could run good and carry a message; and "Yus!" he knowed where Fleet Street were. His eyes lit up when the silver sixpence was placed in his grubby palm, and he whispered breathlessly that for the shilling reward he'd do whatever the "Guv'nor" wanted. "Murder 'n' all!"

Adair watched the small ragged figure scamper off, then he mounted up again. Between the fog and the rapidly deteriorating daylight he might be able to approach the front of the house unseen, but this was not the neighbourhood in which a well-dressed gentleman and a fine horse could linger unmolested. He turned Toreador into the adjoining lane, therefore, and came around to an alley from which he could look over a sagging fence into the area behind the red brick house.

No attempt had been made to plant a garden. The only growing things were a few dandelions and a thriving patch of nettles. Discarded objects were strewn about: a broken chair, a wheel, some empty bottles, rusted pails and similar debris. But to one side was a respectable shed that probably sheltered the mount of anyone not conveyed there by coach or hackney carriage. It was too providential to be ignored. Adair dismounted and, a quick glance up and down the alley revealing no sign of life, opened the back gate and led Toreador inside. The shed was unoccupied but there was an empty water trough, and several nose-bags were hung on nails.

"You'll be out of sight here, while I have a look round," he murmured, loosening the saddle-girths and patting the dapple-grey's smooth neck. "I won't be long."

Leaving the shed, he heard a horse whinny. It wasn't Toreador; the sound had come from the next yard. He looked over the fence. The house was dark and appeared abandoned, but there was a lean-to large enough to house several hacks. It was unlikely that their owners were inside the crumbling ruin; far more probably, they were in the brick house. Caution was indicated.

There came a sudden brightness above him. He turned swiftly. A hand had drawn aside a curtain of the first-floor window. Very briefly, someone looked out. A lady, with a pale sad face and a drooping mouth.

Adair stood rigid, his breath momentarily snatched away.

It was Alice Prior!

─────◦∾◦─────

Billy New jumped over a pile of rotting rubbish. The tattered sandals he'd prigged slipped on the wet street, but he picked himself up, undismayed. "New" was not his real name; he'd never known who had fathered him. He'd been born under a hedge and the prostitute who'd taken him from the arms of his dying mother had named him for the alley in which he had entered this world. His life had not been joyous. With little of kindness, the prostitute had reared him until he was old enough to be sold to a chimney-sweep. Escaping the living death of a "climbing boy," he'd fallen prey to a thief who had taught him how to steal, but had not been as cruel as the sweep. Despite life's hard knocks, bitterness had not touched him and he looked at the world with unfailing optimism—a trait that had once caused the prostitute to say grudgingly that the brat must have good blood in him. For the last year, Billy had made shift for himself, and though he often went hungry and was always cold in wintertime, it had been the happiest year he'd known. Today was the best. Today, with a silver sixpence in the one pocket without a hole, and a shilling promised, he was rich! He'd be able to buy a pasty from the baker's shop and—

His rosy dreams were cut off as a rough hand seized his collar. " 'Ere! Wotcha doin'?" he screeched, struggling madly.

A cultured voice said, "Quiet, nipper! What mischief are you about?"

Wise in the ways of men, Billy summed up the cove who'd grabbed him. A nob; a young nob what had a handsome phiz in spite of a bitter mouth. He said in an ingratiating whine, "I ain't done nuthink, Guv. Don't bash me! Don't you never!"

Nigel Adair held this scrawny wisp of unwashed humanity away from him but did not relax his grip. "I saw that gentleman hand you a paper. Give it to me."

"It ain't yourn!" shrilled Billy, all righteous indignation. "I'm ter take it to a cove what's gonna gimme a borde fer it. You got no right ter take away me liveli'ood. 'Ighway robbery is wot it is! I'll cry rope on yer, so I will!"

"Nonsense," said Nigel, who had a brushing acquaintance with thieves' cant. "If you managed to summon a Watchman in this neighbourhood, which I doubt, he'd likely haul *you* away—not me. And if you were promised a shilling—or, as you say, a borde—you shall have it without the need to run all over the City to earn it. Now will you give me the paper, or shall I take it?"

"I were paid ter take it to a gent," said Billy steadfastly. "An' you ain't that gent."

"Yes, I am. In fact, the man who gave you the paper is my brother."

Billy searched the proud young face narrowly. This cove did look a bit like the nice gent. But . . . "It ain't right," he muttered uneasily.

Nigel took a shilling from his purse and offered it, only to withdraw his hand quickly as the boy snatched for the coin. "The paper first," he said.

There wasn't no gettin' round it. A borde was a borde. And if he didn't hand over the paper the gent would likely take it anyway, and there'd be no borde to show for it.

Shilling and note changed hands, and Billy darted away, to vanish almost immediately into the misty darkness.

A blind fury sent Adair charging up the step to crash full-tilt against the back door of the red brick house. He was mildly surprised when the door burst open at his onslaught. He entered the house at speed and tore along a dimly lit but richly carpeted passage.

A startled yell rang out.

Ahead now, a light glowed, illumining the golden curls of Mr. Talbot Droitwich, who held a lamp high. Momentarily stunned by the sight of a dark figure racing at him with boots stamping and cloak flying out, he gawked stupidly, then howled, "It's *Adair*! Stop him!"

"You filthy bastard!" In the red heat of his rage Adair forgot his duelling pistol. Only his bare hands would suffice for this. Leaping forward, he seized Droitwich by the throat.

The lamp crashed down and flames started to creep along the floor.

Droitwich fought madly, but was no match for Adair who, strengthened by fury, tightened the steely grip about his throat and growled, "You slimy, scheming—"

"*A moi!*" squeaked Droitwich chokingly. "*A moi!*"

A corner of Adair's mind registered a startled, '*French?*'

Running boots, and another voice cried authoritatively, "Put that fire out! Move!"

The voice was all too familiar.

Adair hurled Droitwich aside and turned, crouching, the pistol whipping into his hand.

Julius Harrington was hurrying down the stairs, holding up a branch of candles, their light revealing fine paintings and beautifully carven banister rails. From somewhere at the front of the house, three men ran along the passage. Two threw a rug over the shattered lamp and stamped the flames out. The third started for Adair, a long knife glittering in his hand.

Aiming his dueling pistol steadily at the man he'd thought his friend, Adair said icily, "Come one step closer, ruffian, and I'll shoot your master for the murdering traitor he is! Stay back, Julius!"

Harrington checked and stood rigidly still. Briefly, his eyes glared anger, then his easy smile dawned. "Now, now, Adair— Hasty as ever! You're well-named, dear boy. Of what do I stand accused? To come to an admittedly unfashionable area for a little game of chance? Hardly enough to warrant—"

His back against a corner of the wall, Adair said. "Have done! I know what you are, and now I've proof of your treachery." He raised his voice. "Miss Prior. You can come down now."

"But you are mistaken," purred Harrington. "There is no Miss Prior in this house."

"Liar! I saw her at the upstairs window!"

Even as he spoke, the hem of a lady's gown came into view and Alice Prior crept down the stairs, pale and trembling, to pause behind Harrington.

"Stand aside, traitor," snapped Adair. "I need no excuse to put a bullet through your rotten heart!"

"Well, I will do as you say, of course, my poor fellow. But I don't want you to labour under a misapprehension. I am no traitor. You and I merely serve on opposite sides."

Trying not to reveal the depth of his astonishment, Adair said, "I guessed as much when your chubby cohort called to you in French. Admire the Little Corporal, do you? If that's not being a traitor—"

"Droitwich is half French, but he worships at the shrine of the great god Mammon," said Harrington. "As for me—yes, I admire Napoleon Bonaparte. I more than admire him—I would proudly die for him! I have been his man these ten years and more. Doing whatever I may for la belle France."

"So that's why you schemed and stole and murdered to get the Cabinet post that should have gone to my brother! By God, my uncle was right about you!"

"*Dear* Uncle Willoughby," said Harrington softly. "I really should have dealt with him less charitably. I knew he had agents snooping about. I thought if I pursued his dumpy niece I could make sure of his Lists, but the old curmudgeon guards them like a dragon. I believe whenever I was in the house he took the blasted things to bed with him. I suppose it would take quite some time to persuade you to reveal what he has writ about me, Hasty. And time I cannot waste, so I must adopt more stringent measures."

Hastings said through gritted teeth, "Minerva Chatteris is a gentle and trusting lady you aren't fit to touch, you miserable turncoat."

"Yes, I know." Harrington sighed. "And she loves me, poor girl. One thing, though, she'll have too much to think about, if she survives this night, to worry about me, especially when she learns I have wed another lady."

Infuriated, Adair started for him, but checked as Droitwich lunged forward. "No, you don't! Stay back, Droitwich! I'd as soon shoot that miserable traitor on the stairs as step on a cockroach. Come down, Harrington. Over there. That's right. Now you follow, Miss Alice, but keep well clear of the creature!"

A little nerve throbbed beside Harrington's jaw, but as he stepped aside obediently, he said, "Your advice is rather belated, Adair. The lady has lived with me for several weeks, you know.

With tears streaking her cheeks, Alice mumbled, "I am—I am quite ruined, Colonel Adair."

Shocked by the glare in Adair's eyes, Harrington raised a hand and said, "No, before you shoot me, please be at ease.

Tonight, I mean to make an honest woman of her. Miss Alice will become Mrs. Julius Harrington."

Adair's pistol jolted. He stared at Harrington, speechless, even as he stretched out one hand to the frightened girl.

A shattering crash. A billow of icy soot-laden fog. Sprinting along the passage, Nigel Adair saw his brother, pistol in one hand, the other reaching out to the lady he adored. He gulped an anguished "So you *did* take her!" and levelled his pistol.

Hastings kept his Manton trained on Harrington, and shouted urgently, "Nigel, wait! I'm not—"

"Oh, are you not! Am I to disbelieve my own eyes? Worthless villain! Lying cheat! You deserve—" Maddened with rage, he pulled back the trigger, but the powder was damp and there was no following shot.

Harrington screamed, "Save her, Nigel! Save the poor lady!"

Nigel uttered a strangled sob and flailed the heavy pistol savagely. Hastings, struck squarely on his injured right arm, reeled, and the Manton fell from his nerveless hand. For a minute the scene before him was an echoing distortion. He heard a scream and a lot of shouting. When his vision cleared he was slumped against the wall, Harrington had an arm about Alice, and Droitwich was training a pistol on a white-faced, bewildered-looking Nigel. The tallest of the cutthroats, with a face Adair had confronted in Bedfordshire and at Blackbird Terrace, was stamping towards him, grinning hungrily, one large fist drawn back.

Alice sobbed, "Don't! Please don't! He's hurt. Julius—"

Harrington glanced at Adair. "No need for that, Mel. I think we've drawn the persistent Colonel's fangs. He won't bother us any more."

"Are you gone daft?" Droitwich snarled, "You know damned well how hard we tried to be rid of the pest. D'you fancy he'll give up now that he knows it all? We can't leave witnesses littered about all over Town. We have to finish him. I owe him. I'll do it."

"No," begged Alice. "Please, Julius. You—you could have

260

Colonel Adair pressed aboard ship, or—or something. And I won't give you away—I *swear!*"

"But of course you won't, my sweet." Amused, Harrington drew her closer in his arm. "By then you will be my wife."

"Oh, God!" Nigel groaned. "And a wife cannot testify 'gainst her husband!" He looked at his brother and said wretchedly, "What a fool I am! Hasty—I am so very sorry."

Trying to gather his wits, Adair said breathlessly, "I know, lad. How . . . could you guess any man would be so treacherous? I was . . . taken in also. Like a fool I—I introduced him to poor Minna."

Droitwich laughed and said in fluent French, "You played your part to perfection, Cabinet Minister."

Harrington said, "I really am fond of you, Adair. But—*c'est la guerre*, you know." He shrugged apologetically. "Alas, but the life of a spy is not easy."

"It certainly won't be easy to explain away a wife," said Hastings contemptuously, "when you are . . . already betrothed to my cousin."

"Ah, but keep in mind, Colonel, that the betrothal has never been published. And when I rescue poor Alice—"

"Rescue her?" cried Nigel. "You damned nail! You've ruined her!"

"Well, actually, your brother here did that." Harrington glanced at Droitwich. "As we shall prove, eh, Talbot?"

"Decidedly." Droitwich chuckled. "And ain't it obliging of the gallant Colonel to have visited his own house. Save us the bother of collecting him."

Nigel tore his gaze from Alice's pale tragic face. "You won't get that kite to fly, Harrington. My brother doesn't own this filthy hovel."

"To the contrary," said Droitwich, grinning broadly. "The records will show that it was leased in the name of Colonel Hastings Chatteris Adair."

"And it was in this—er, 'filthy hovel'—though actually it has

261

been completely refurbished, you know—that he held Miss Prior captive." Harrington pulled on the gloves one of his hirelings brought him. "These last few weeks a man riding a dapple-grey horse has come here repeatedly, after dark. Many people will attest to your identity, Adair."

Droitwich tugged at his lower lip and said frowningly, "Still, we shall have to change our plan, now that the halfling has arrived. You surely don't mean to claim you overpowered the pair of 'em?"

For a moment Harrington pondered, looking thoughtful. "Do you know," he said, "it will be better this way. You saw how young Nigel came charging in here. All London knows he has a *tendre* for the lady and holds the Colonel responsible for her abduction. Now, if Nigel followed his brother and caught him with poor Alice, is it not likely he would shoot him out of hand? Indeed, he tried that very thing, so—"

Nigel sprang for Harrington, only to be wrenched back by Droitwich and one of the guards. "You slimy toad," he raged, struggling fiercely. "I might be stupid enough to shoot my brother, but Hasty would never fire back! Everyone knows—"

"Everyone knows you for a hot-headed young fool," said Harrington. "We can arrange the details satisfactorily, eh, Talbot?"

Looking far from satisfied, Droitwich muttered, "I collect that you arrived in time to despatch the murderer and carry the lady to safety. Is that your scheme?"

"To safety and to the man who will wed us. I become a hero for not only having rescued Miss Prior but offering her the protection of my name despite her—er, sullied purity. My cloak, Stark."

The unlovely ruffian who had stood holding the cloak came at once to offer it. Pulling the warm garment close about his throat and fastening the three top buttons, Harrington murmured, "Yes. It will serve nicely."

"It will serve *you* nicely." Droitwich glared at Alice, who had sat down on the stairs and watched them with dull resignation. "She may not be able to testify against *you* in a court of law, but she can implicate *me*, by God! And what's to prevent her from telling the whole to her family?"

"The sure knowledge that whoever she confided in would have to be silenced. You do understand that, don't you, my love?"

Alice nodded. Her tearful eyes were full of fear, but it seemed to Adair that Harrington's eyes held a deep tenderness. He thought, 'By Jove, but the swine really cares for her!'

"There you are, Talbot," said Harrington blithely. "As I said—it will serve."

Adair said, "It will serve to send you both through Traitor's Gate. I'm not the only one to suspect you, Harrington. I've sent a message to my friends who will bring the Runners here at any minute. You'd do well to make a run for the coast before—"

"This message?" Harrington held up the note Adair had given to Billy New. "Another disappointment for you, alas. I think you were not quite aware at that moment, but when my fellows removed your brother's pistol, they also found your message. It appears that your messenger was intercepted."

His heart sinking, Adair slanted a glance at Nigel. The boy looked anguished and met his eyes in a silent pleading for forgiveness.

Harrington chuckled and called, "Mel! Get the hacks put to. And one of you, fetch Miss Prior's cloak and gloves."

Alice asked in a voice that shook piteously, "What—what are you going to do with me?"

"Convey you to your bridal ceremony, my love."

Hastings said, "You're forgetting, I think, that the lady is under age—or do you mean to make a dash for the Border?"

"I forget nothing. An obliging Justice of the Peace agreed to wed us when I told him her sad story—with a few embellishments, of course. And the Special License in my pocket obviates the need for a trip to Gretna Green." Harrington turned to Alice. "Afterwards, I must tidy up some unpleasant business, but it won't delay us for very long, and then it's off to see your father and explain your rescue and my gallant offer of marriage. I doubt he will object; more likely he'll fall on my neck with gratitude."

Frowning, Droitwich grumbled, "You said midnight. Our fellows have likely got things under way by now."

"Yes. I must get down there."

"In this blasted fog you'll be lucky to reach there in time, let alone delay for your foolish nuptials. Why not stay with our original plan and—"

Harrington turned on him like a striking snake, the smile wiped from his face, his expression one of livid fury. "Damn you! No one will harm her! I told you—"

It was the opportunity Hastings had waited for. "Mel," who appeared to be a trusted aide, had gone to pole up the horses; another of the ruffians was above-stairs collecting Miss Alice's cloak. That left only the bully named Stark to cope with while Harrington's attention was on his rebellious cohort.

Adair sprang. One hand fastened in the collar of the cloak Harrington had just secured around his neck, and Harrington was jerked back, then hurled at the wall, barely missing Alice.

With a shout, Stark plunged for Adair and received a flashing uppercut that stretched him on the floor. Nigel had also entered the fray, but turning to him, Adair saw that Droitwich stood behind the boy, an arm across his throat and his pistol pressed to Nigel's temple.

"Now—or a half-hour from now," said Droitwich silkily. "It's all one to me, Colonel."

"Shoot, then," gasped Nigel. "And—he'll have no other weapon, Hasty!"

"No. But—I will." Harrington had clambered to his feet. There was a reddening patch on his forehead from his collision with the wall, and he walked forward, dabbing a handkerchief at his mouth. "So now," he said bitterly, "I must have a swollen lip on my wedding night. I was sportsman enough to stop my fellows from mauling you, Adair. But for this you must pay."

He swung his gloved hand back and smashed it hard across Adair's face.

17

*M*ove your lazy arse!" Straddling a wooden chair that had been brought into the passage, Talbot Droitwich bellowed, "I want all my belongings and Mr. Harrington's belongings packed up and ready to be loaded in the coach within the hour. Be warned, all of you—I'll inspect every drawer and cupboard before we go, and if I find anything has been left—Lord help you!"

The balding savage they called Stark grumbled, "We're doin' as best we can, Guv'nor. If we'd knowed earlier—"

"Nobody knew earlier, gallows-bait. We didn't expect the Adairs to crash in here so that we must change our plans."

"Lob," stout and dim-witted, came down the stairs, balancing several coats against a large box. "All as I could find up there, sir," he declared, making a futile snatch for the razor that toppled from the box.

"Well, don't drop 'em, idiot!"

"Sorry, sir. The rest is her things. What about them two, sir?"

Droitwich glanced to where Adair lay propped against the stairs with Nigel kneeling beside him holding a gory handkerchief to the side of his head. "I'm watching them," he growled. "Tend to what you're about."

"Aye, sir. But if I was to tie 'em up—"

"Our gallant Colonel's going nowhere. When I hit a man he don't get up. His brain-box is likely stove in."

Nigel looked up and said with loathing, "How proud you must be that you had the courage to kick my brother when he was down. Your reputation speaks truly."

"So it does," Droitwich agreed complacently. "I don't hold with all that rubbishing stuff about 'playing the game' and mollycoddling the enemy. I'm French, and this is war, my lad. And in war it's the man who hits quickest and hardest who's the victor and to hell with so called 'good sportsmanship.'"

The words came dimly to Adair's ears as he drifted back to consciousness. He had a confused memory of crashing into the stair railing when Harrington had hit him, and of trying to get up. Harrington had been saying something about Blackbird Terrace, and "what a pity" it was that Willoughby had guarded his damned Lists so fiercely. But then something had slammed against the side of his head. One phrase. ". . . fuel for the fire" had echoed and re-echoed in his ears before sight and sound had melted away for what seemed a very long time.

Nigel spoke, then Droitwich was braying again, his harsh voice hurting Adair's throbbing head.

". . . not my master, damn your eyes! Watch that insolent tongue, else I'll give you a taste of what your brother got! Take that stuff out to the cart, Lob, and tell Stark to saddle up my hack."

Hastings made a supreme effort and said feebly, "If Harrington's not—not your master, how is it that . . . he commands and—and you obey?"

Droitwich sneered, "Well, well, if our war hero ain't awake again. You've a hard head, Colonel. Pity it's so full of maggots. Julius Harrington don't command *me*, I promise you. We'd worked out a good plan between us." He scowled and muttered broodingly, "A plan that would've worked, if he'd listened to me . . ."

"But he didn't," mocked Nigel, taking his cue from his brother.

"Harrington's not such—a fool," managed Hastings, wishing he could see clearly.

"He's played the fool over that damned chit," said Droitwich broodingly. "We had it all going along smooth as silk. He'd cleared the way to his blasted Cabinet appointment. The girl was here. You were the secret owner of the house, and he followed you—"

"And rescued the poor lady?" Nigel laughed. "What stuff! It wouldn't have worked, because—"

Droitwich took the bait and interrupted with a triumphant grin, "It would have worked when our Minister found Miss Alice had killed herself from shame, and he shot down the man who'd driven her to her death. Aye, you may stare, but find fault with it, if you can! Neat and tidy, and no one the wiser!"

All the colour drained from Nigel's face and he was stunned into silence.

Horrified, Adair exclaimed, "I judged him ruthless, but he was bred up a gentleman. I can't believe he would have murdered that innocent child!"

"Can you not?" Droitwich laughed. "Then wake up, soldier boy! You live by your antiquated Code of Honour, I'll warrant— which has killed more fools than I could guess. Harrington has a different code. Oh, very different! He's a fanatic, is what! In his view Napoleon Bonaparte is a saint, and there's *nothing* he won't do for the bloody little Corsican! Pretty Miss Alice wouldn't have been the first he's done for. And she ain't so innocent now, is she, Colonel, sir? He had the stupid chit, but what must our almighty Minister do but fall in love! So now he's off making her his wife. Much good may it do him! I never knew a woman yet could keep her mouth shut, and he's not going to play fast and loose with *my* head at stake. When we're done with tonight's work—not too soon, mind—there'll be a sad case of a new bride surprising a thief and getting her pretty neck wrung!"

Enraged, Hastings sprang to his feet, but his battered head betrayed him and he staggered.

Droitwich chuckled and levelled the pistol at him.

Maddened by such callous plans for the lady he adored, Nigel leapt to the attack.

There was a flash, a sharp explosion and a puff of smoke.

Nigel's slim body jolted violently; he reeled back and fell.

A blazing fury seared away pain and weakness, and uttering an incoherent snarl, Hastings lunged forward.

Droitwich saw his face, but his attempt to retreat was not fast enough and Hastings' fist struck his jaw with such force that his feet left the floor.

Hastings didn't wait to see him crash down, but turned to kneel beside his brother. Nigel's eyes were closed and his face was without a vestige of colour. He looked dead and Hastings whispered a fervent "Thank God!" when he found a pulse; faint but steady. A moment later fear was a lance transfixing him and causing his hands to tremble as he unbuttoned the waistcoat and saw the spreading stain on the white linen of the shirt.

From outside came shouts and running footsteps. The other ruffians would have heard the shot, of course. He relegated that awareness to the back of his mind, and concentrated solely on helping this brother he loved, knowing that the ball had probably torn its way through a lung.

"Hasty! Are you—Oh, my Lord!" Toby Broderick's voice.

Not looking up, Adair reached out. "Your handkerchief or a neckcloth. Quickly! And I need water and something for bandages."

A neckcloth was handed him. Manderville said, "We've a coach outside. York has my pistol on the scoundrels, and says he knows how to use it."

Broderick hurried away and came back tearing a tablecloth into strips. "Who shot him?"

"That carrion over there. I think I've broken his jaw, but he should be tied up. He's an accomplice in treason and murder."

Paige carried in a bowl. "Luckily, there was some hot water in a kettle." He stepped over Talbot Droitwich and peered down at him curiously. "The things you see when you haven't got a stick," he muttered, setting the bowl down beside Adair.

Watching his crude surgery, Broderick shuddered. "Lord knows what's happened here, but it looks as if you've been put through the wringer. We'll get you both to a doctor as soon as you're finished."

Billy New ran along the passage, then halted, staring at Nigel. "Crikey! It's the gent what took yer message away from me, Guv. Did you scrag him?"

"No, and he's not dead," grated Adair, praying.

"Oh. Well, if he's really yer brother like what he said, I 'spect it's a good thing as I went and told the skinny gent in Fleet Street where you was."

"A—a very good thing. Thank you."

" 'S all right." All too familiar with the sight of blood, the boy said with a grin, "I got another borde."

Broderick peered over Adair's shoulder. "What's that thing round his neck?"

"A locket, I think." The locket had been driven in with the bullet, but this was no time to try and remove it. Striving desperately, Adair said, "If we're lucky it may have deflected the ball. There. That's the best I can do till—"

Nigel groaned and his eyelids fluttered open. His attempt to speak caused his face to contort with pain.

"Easy, lad," said Adair. "Toby's going to lift you a little. Just so I can tie you up." Broderick raised the boy gradually, but despite his caution Nigel swooned away again. Adair set his teeth and bound the makeshift pad over the wound as tightly as he dared. Nigel looked up as Broderick lowered him, and Hastings said in a very gentle voice, "We've help now. Our friends have come. You're safe. No, don't try to talk. You're going to be—"

"Must . . ." whispered Nigel. "Did—did you . . . hear? About Black—Blackbird Terrace?"

269

"I heard Harrington mumbling something about being sorry, and—'fuel,' I think."

Manderville, who was using strips of the tablecloth to tie up Droitwich, whistled softly. "Harrington? Then York was right, by Jupiter, and this house belongs to crow-bait Talbot!"

"They claim it was bought in my name," said Adair, dabbing gently at the sweat that beaded Nigel's face. "Our fine Cabinet Minister held Miss Prior captive here."

"What?" Broderick exclaimed thunderously, "The black-hearted rogue! Is she—"

Nigel was gazing at his brother imploringly, and Hastings raised a silencing hand. "A moment, please, Toby. What is it, old fellow?"

"He couldn't find Uncle's . . . Lists," panted Nigel. "So—so he means to burn down the—the whole house." He moaned and his eyes closed, but then he roused a little and whispered, "Says Uncle will surely . . . try to save . . . Lists. Droitwich told him to—to leave no . . . witnesses . . ."

<hr>

"We didn't want to tell you, Willoughby, while Minerva and Hilda were with us." General Chatteris leaned back in the armchair and nodded at Cecily, seated beside him in his son's study. "You likely thought I came down to comb you out, eh?"

"I did at—er, at first, sir," Willoughby admitted shyly. "But when I saw Miss Hall alight from your coach, I—ah—"

"Felt reprieved, I don't doubt. Well, and so you are, my boy. It seems to me that of all of us you were the first to see through that cheating varmint! By God! When I read some of your notes just now, I could scarce believe the cunning of it. If your suspicions are justified, he's one of the greatest villains unhung!"

Cecily said, "Sadly, we have no proof of any of that, do we, sir?"

The General gave her an irked frown and said, "If I know Hastings, he's gathering proofs at this very minute!"

Cecily glanced at the window. It was dusk now, and a little

wind had come up. "I wish we hadn't missed him," she said. "The fog is beginning to blow away, I think. Perhaps we should start back to Town, sir?"

The journey down had taken much longer than usual, the fog so thick in places that the footman had been obliged to get down and guide the leaders. Nothing would have induced the General to admit he was tired, however, so he said with a chuckle, "Worrying about him, are you, m'dear? Don't. That fighting grandson of mine is like a cat—always manages to land on his feet, whatever the odds against him."

"No, really you must—er, must not think of travelling any farther tonight, Miss Hall," urged Willoughby. "Broderick and Manderville are likely already back in Town and will support Hastings if he pursues the—ah, business. Besides, my sister and Minerva are so—er, pleased to have company, they will be greatly disappointed if you leave us. I'm sure they are even now helping the servants to prepare guest chambers for you, and— and I've no cause to—er, apologize for our cook!"

"You are very good, sir." Cecily dazzled him with her smile. "Thank you. I cannot help but wonder, if our suspicions prove true, do you intend to warn your niece?"

Willoughby answered hesitantly, "She becomes upset if I even hint against him. And—and it would be dreadful if my information is—is at fault, wouldn't it? What do you think, Father?"

The General pondered. "I suppose it's a case of 'sufficient unto the day is the evil thereof,' or however that goes. But we'll have to watch the bounder. And thanks to you, we're fore-warned."

Willoughby became quite pink with gratification and muttered something unintelligible.

"Sir Gower says that your Lists are truly remarkable," said Cecily.

The General nodded emphatically. "So they are. What baffles me is how the deuce you were able to gather all those snippets of information. I hadn't thought you went about Town very often."

271

"More often than you think, sir. But I'm a rather—nondescript sort of fellow, you know; people tend not to—to notice me."

"And you keep your ears on the stretch, eh?"

"That, and I have three—ah, investigators who gather interesting—what you call 'snippets' for me. I pay them well, but I insist that they only supply me with factual information and they—ah, they know they will cease to work for me if—if they invent stories."

Intrigued, Cecily asked, "Are your 'investigators' policemen, perhaps? Or Watchmen who have retired?"

A twinkle crept into Willoughby's eyes. "To say truth, Miss Hall, two are highly respected Mayfair dowagers, and one is an eminent modiste."

General Chatteris gave a bark of laughter. "Do you say these 'highly respectable ladies' actually take payment for their gossip?"

"It is my experience, sir, that few people, whatever their station in life, can resist a little extra cash in the purse."

"But whatever do you tell them, Mr. Chatteris?" asked Cecily. "Aren't you afraid they'll give you away?"

"They believe I am preserving for—ah, posterity a record of today's Social Scene," Willoughby said with a shy smile. "I suppose in a sense I am. And they cannot very well give me away without the risk that I'll reveal my—ah, sources. Do you see?"

"I see that you're a crafty rogue," said the General, laughing and revising his opinion of this son he had always judged a bacon-brain. "I'll tell you one thing—it would make a dashed good book, not that you'd dare publish it, of course."

"Thank you, sir." Pleased, Willoughby asked, "Now may I tell my ladies that you will overnight with us?"

"Indeed, you may, my boy. Provided you don't object, Miss Hall?"

"I shall be pleased to accept," said Cecily. But she thought, 'How can I say anything else? Oh, I do wish we had come up with Hasty.'

"You're stubborn as two mules," grunted Broderick, adjusting Toreador's saddle and tightening the cinch-strap. "You're in no condition to ride all that way. Have some sense for once and let me go."

"Someone must be here to care for my brother," argued Hastings, abandoning the effort to ease his right glove on. "You'll stay by him, till Paige brings the Runners and a doctor, and see that he is carried home, Toby?"

"Of course I will, you dolt! But you're the logical choice to take care of him—not me. And only look at you! Can't even get your glove on! Your hand's likely as broke as our traitor's jaw, and his boot didn't do your head any good! You'll fall out of the saddle before you're half-way—"

"You've only been to my uncle's house once or twice. You'd never find it after dark and in this fog."

"The fog's lifting, if you haven't noticed."

"Thank heaven for that," Adair muttered fretfully. "God knows I want to stay with Nigel, but—Oh, give over, Toby! I *must* get down there! My grandfather and—and Cecily . . ."

Broderick straightened and peered at him anxiously. "What did you say?"

"I must get there before Harrington, don't you understand? The man is obsessed with his zeal for Bonaparte. He'll destroy anything or anyone who stands in his way! You've seen that!"

"Yes. So I'll ride with you. York can—"

"York is guarding Droitwich and Harrington's louts, and I need you to tell the Runners what has gone on—if Paige ever gets them here!"

His awkward climb into the saddle drew an explosion of curses from Broderick. Seizing the bridle, he looked up at his friend's sagging figure and exclaimed, "Hasty! For Lord's sake! You can't—"

"I'll—be all right." Dragging his head up, Adair argued in a thread of a voice, "A touch pulled, is all. This cold air will—will soon wake me up. You and Paige—come when—when you can, will you?"

Broderick's profane response followed him as he guided Toreador into the lane. He checked the big horse when Billy New ran out from the shadows.

"Want me to go with yer, Guv'nor? Won't cost yer nuthink. I'm a good fighter, I am."

"Yes, I'm sure you are. Go and help Lieutenant Broderick and Mr. York. You can—you can tell them you work for me now."

The boy let out an eldritch screech of excitement and leapt three times into the air before making his exuberant way back to the ugly red brick house.

Adair rode on, groping his way towards the river. For a while he thought that Broderick's remark about the fog lifting had been overly optimistic. London's streets were silent and ghostly. The vapours drifted and swirled about him and created misty haloes around the occasional lanterns and flambeaux that materialized eerily through the murk. But soon he realized that a strong breeze really was dispersing the fog—or perhaps much of the fog had been inside his confused mind. His head throbbed so brutally that it was hard to collect his thoughts, and when he instinctively attempted to use his right hand he was reminded most unpleasantly that he had hit Talbot Droitwich very hard. Not that he had the least regret on that score. And gradually, as he had hoped, the damp air and the bitter cold restored him so that he felt steadier.

As the moments ticked away, his anxieties for Cecily and his family increased to the point that he could think of little else. He urged Toreador to greater speed. Briefly, the mighty river gleamed below him; occasional coaches loomed up and were gone; great wains trundled past en route to London's markets; a Watchman wandered wraith-like through the dark with his lantern and his bell, calling the hour while the City slept.

Was Cecily sleeping? Was she—heaven forbid—passing the night at Blackbird Terrace? Was Nigel still alive? It was taking

274

too long . . . Did he dare attempt to cut across country in the dark? If he became lost—

A mail coach burst from the mists and thundered straight at him. He reined Toreador aside desperately, and the dapple-grey bounded into the ditch and almost went down. Adair managed to hold him together and to keep his seat while directing a flow of barracks-room language at the fast-disappearing coach. The profane response of the reckless coachman drifted back to him as he urged Toreador onto the road again. He peered about for familiar landmarks that were so hard to find in the darkness, and was then perversely horrified by the awareness that it was getting lighter. Was it dawn? Had he been such a fool as to fall asleep in the saddle? He peered upward and saw a lamp above him; a celestial lamp. The breeze had strengthened to a wind that had bustled away the fog so that the moon could shine down. "Thank God!" he muttered, able to breathe again. With the aid of that silvery light the way became easier to follow. Ignoring the unending throbbing in his head, he pressed on, determined to make up for lost time.

Soon he was in open country, racing past quiet hamlets and lonely farms; past inns, dark for the most part, but with an occasional lighted window that spoke of some wakeful guest; clattering over cobbled streets or slowing on unpaved muddy lanes. And always before his mind's eye Cecily's lovely face alternated with Nigel's closed eyes and terrifying pallor. Mile after weary mile. An eternity of effort, accompanied by the pound of hooves, the creak of saddle leather, the voice in his head that commanded, 'Keep on! Keep on! Faster! Faster!' Until it dawned on him at length that he was pushing too hard; his splendid dapple-grey was losing his stride, the jaws gaped wide, the proud neck was lowered and splashed with foam, the sturdy barrel laboured painfully.

Remorseful, Adair drew to a halt and dismounted to caress the big horse fondly and murmur his apologies. He bent to pull up some grass from the verge beside the lane, and learned at once that a fellow with a broken head did not bend down. He had to clutch at the saddle to keep from falling on his face, but when the world stopped dancing he tried again, keeping his head up this time. He managed to gather enough grass to give Toreador a hurried rub-down. When the big animal was breathing more easily, Adair walked beside him for a while, chafing at the delay even as he reproached himself for not having stopped before this. As soon as he dared, he mounted up again, an ordeal that made him swear and caused Toreador to sidle about uneasily. But they were off once more and minutes later he was surprised to find they had passed Hampton Court. Small wonder his gallant dapple-grey had been near exhaustion. But there was still at least an hour's ride before them. Another hour . . .

Tormented by such feverish imaginings and by the constant pounding in his head, he failed to notice that Toreador had slowed to a walk. He roused to that awareness only when his face touched the horse's mane. He was bowed forward over the pommel! Dragging himself upright he touched his spurs to sides that seldom felt them. Toreador was startled. More startled when a stray dog suddenly rushed from the hedgerow to bark frenziedly and nip at his hooves. Toreador shied. Adair, reeling in the saddle, was unhorsed and hurtled into the ditch. He didn't feel the shock of landing, and in fact felt nothing at all until Toreador snorted into his face and woke him.

For a minute he blinked up at the dimly seen dapple-grey in bewilderment. With the return of full consciousness came anguish and remorse. Toby had warned that he'd fall out of the saddle and he'd been so stupid as to do just that! Staggering to his feet he gripped the stirrup. Toreador loomed up; enormous, unreachable . . . For how long had he sprawled in that damned ditch? And now he couldn't muster the strength to mount up . . . He *must* get onto the back of this monstrous animal . . . for Cecily's dear sake . . . And somehow, he was up and the reins were in his hands. Thank God Toreador had stayed close!

Urging the horse on, he was scourged by the terror that he would be too late. He prayed that his love was safely home in London, or the General had decided to overnight at some inn

... But even so, Uncle Willoughby and Aunt Hilda and Minerva and the servants would be sleeping in the house ... and if that devil Harrington made good his threat ... The Terrace was largely constructed of wood and centuries old. It would go up like kindling. He must get there in time to warn them! He *must!* Surely, Harrington couldn't be there already? The devil was in it that he had no way of knowing for how long he'd been unconscious after Droitwich had kicked him. How much time had elapsed between Harrington's leaving Appletree Place and Droitwich shooting Nigel? How long after that had Toby helped him into the saddle? How much time had been lost while he'd lounged in the ditch?

Time ... so relentless, so damnably unalterable ... He groaned aloud as a church clock somewhere struck the hour. Eleven! Then he couldn't possibly reach Blackbird Terrace before midnight!

"Lord—help them. Please help them!"

He bowed over Toreador's neck, stroking him, talking to him. "Faster, old fellow! Forgive me for asking it, but—faster!"

"I think everyone in the kitchen must be deaf." Minerva Chatteris walked across the Blackbird Terrace drawing room and tugged again on the bell-pull. "Whatever has happened to our other pot of tea?"

Cecily said that one cup was quite enough for her. "You gave us such a wonderful dinner, I doubt I've room for any more."

"I'm so glad you enjoyed it. Mama was sure it would be a disaster with a kitchen maid and footman unable to work." Minerva gave the bell-pull another tug and frowned at it. "I'm sure you would like another cup, Grandpapa, and I imagine you and my uncle will want to stay up and chat till all hours."

Willoughby, who had no least desire to "chat till all hours," smiled politely, and the General, who was more than ready for his bed, said evasively, "I thought that was a new man who carried in the tea-tray. Had a siege of illness here, have you?"

Cecily was so drowsy she could scarcely keep her eyes open, but she had noticed that the "new man" seemed rather too large for his garments and that he had very dirty fingernails. "If that is the case," she said, "we should not have accepted your invitation, Miss Chatteris. Your poor mama must have her hands full."

"No, no. Our difficulty is solved now, and we are so very glad you came." Minerva returned to her chair. "Actually, it all seems to have been a mistake. You see, our kitchen maid's home is north of Woking. Her mother sent a note advising that her father had been taken ill and was calling for her. My mama gave her leave, of course, but our coach was at the wheelwright, so the footman drove Millie in the gig. En route, a wheel split and the gig went into the ditch."

"How dreadful," said Cecily. "Were your servants much hurt?"

"The footman's arm was—er, broke," said Willoughby. "And the maid twisted her knee so badly she cannot walk."

Minerva said, "It could have been worse, I suppose, but it was so needless. We learned this morning that the girl's father is hale and hearty and had not summoned his daughter. Some idiot's notion of a joke!"

The General gave an exasperated snort.

"How very odd," murmured Cecily thoughtfully.

"Where did you find your new fellow?" asked the General.

Sure that his choice was about to be criticized, Willoughby drew on an unimpeachable source. "That was a lucky chance. An old—er, friend of mine is now the Mother Superior of a nunnery. She had sent a man to me with a letter recommending him highly and asking that—that I consider him if I knew of a place for a reliable servant."

"It seemed providential," put in Minerva. "And when he told us his wife was an experienced maid—"

"You snapped 'em up, eh?"

"I did, Papa." Willoughby lowered his voice. "Though I must admit they're not quite the type I'd have thought—" He broke

278

off as the new footman carried in another tea-tray. "Oh, there you are, Gillis."

"I am most awful sorry, sir," said the footman, affecting what he evidently believed to be a cultured accent. "Your maid what was injured was raising of such a dust that Mrs. Chatteris and your lady cook they had to go up and see to her. My missus, as is by name of Dolly Gillis, made the tea. Mrs. Chatteris asked as how you doesn't wait for her."

Very aware of his father's beetling eyebrows in the wake of this unorthodox performance, Willoughby dismissed the man hurriedly, and Minerva poured the tea, wondering whatever that charming Mother Superior could have been thinking of, and chattering brightly about her dogs.

Cecily was too tired to pay much attention and, refusing more tea, soon excused herself. Minerva summoned Gillis and told him to desire Randall to light Miss Hall to her bedchamber. Gillis bowed so low that his thinning black hair came near to dusting the floor, and with a sweeping wave of his arm ushered Cecily from the room. The stately butler did not conduct her up the stairs, however; her candle was lit and she was escorted to her room by the wife of the new footman. Dolly Gillis was a stony-faced woman whose manner bordered on the insolent. Cecily refused the cup of tea that was then set on the bedside table. She also refused an offer to be of assistance while she changed into her night-rail. Mrs. Gillis bobbed a sketch of a curtsy, advised that the tea was good and hot and would help Miss sleep, and left her. But just before the door closed it seemed to Cecily that those hard bright eyes glittered as if with sly laughter.

She was quite accustomed to dance the night away, and even allowing for the long and tiresome journey it was unlike her to be so terribly sleepy. The bed looked inviting and she lay down for a minute before getting undressed. There were several things she meant to discuss with the General in the morning. Several things that were ... really ... most odd ...

The scream woke her. The candle on the chest of drawers was guttering and she blinked stupidly around the unfamiliar room. Where on earth was she? And why was she sleeping while fully dressed? She could not seem to think, and when another scream echoed along the corridor it was with a great effort that she managed to stand. The bedchamber tilted. She fought the dizziness. Someone was in trouble. She must go and help. If only her silly feet would move . . .

The door was a long way off and seemed to retreat from her outstretched hand, but she reached it at last, and flung it wide. A cloud of smoke billowed in. Coughing, she thought, 'My heavens! The house is afire!' At once, her mind cleared. The air felt hot. She made her way to the top of the stairs and peered down.

Through the billowing smoke she saw Willoughby Chatteris staggering along the lower corridor. He seemed only half aware, and was clinging to one of the servants and screaming, "Are all— the women—out?"

The footman, or whoever he was, shouted, "Everyone's safely out, sir! Don't worry!"

The man was sadly mistaken, thought Cecily. There was no sign of the lady who had uttered that piercing shriek, and she herself wasn't "safely out." She attempted to call to them, but the acrid smoke was burning her eyes and making it hard to breathe. She must have made some sound, however, for the footman turned and looked up at her.

It wasn't a footman. It was Minerva's fiancé, Mr. Julius Harrington.

Smoke billowed upward then, hiding him from her view. If he really loved Minerva he might indeed have helped her outside. But what of the General and Mrs. Hilda and the servants?

With an eye to propriety, Willoughby Chatteris had positioned the female bedchambers on the east side of the house while gentlemen occupied rooms in the west wing. To try to reach the General through this dreadful smoke and heat would be folly. But Cecily determined at least to try to make sure that the women were safe.

Coughing, she tottered back along the corridor and managed to shout a hoarse "Minerva . . . ? Mrs. Hilda . . . ?"

There was no response. The smoke was thickening. Men were shouting somewhere, and behind their voices she could hear a terrifying crackling roar. She thought, 'I must get out!' But even as she turned, snatching for the stair railing, her bare toes caught against something on the floor. She bent lower, her smarting eyes peering. Minerva Chatteris lay in a huddled heap at her feet.

"Oh . . . good heavens!" Cecily dropped to her knees and tugged at the girl's shoulders. "Miss Chatteris! Wake up! We—we must get out!"

Minerva's eyes opened. She blinked but seemed unable to focus. "Can't . . ." she muttered. "Too . . . tired . . . Much . . . too . . ." Her eyelids drifted shut again.

Cecily shook her without effect. In desperation, she slapped the girl's face, then slapped it again, hard.

Minerva roused and frowned at her. "What . . . on earth?" Comprehension dawned. "Oh! The house . . . is afire! My mama . . ."

"We must help her," panted Cecily. "Can you get up? Put your arm around me—so. That's—that's good. Now—hurry! Hurry!"

Clinging to each other, coughing, they struggled towards the stairs, trying to see through the ever thickening smoke and to ignore the appalling voice of the fire.

18

Long before Blackbird Terrace came into view, Adair could see the red glow that lit soaring clouds of smoke. The dark premonition that had haunted his frantic ride was realized when Toreador carried him up the drivepath. The east wing of the old house was ablaze, flames licking from several ground-floor and basement windows.

Toreador lurched to a halt some distance from the house and stood, head down with exhaustion. Flinging himself from the saddle, praying he hadn't ridden his gallant horse to death, Adair staggered across the lawn. The smell of the fire hung heavily on the damp air. House servants, grooms and gardeners were milling about, carrying water buckets from the pump, passing articles from the house, shouting and gesticulating. The glow from the flames lit their features eerily; some still wore their night-rail, others were half-dressed, and they all looked frightened and dishevelled. As he came up, Adair searched for a glimpse of Cecily or his grandfather, and finding neither dared to hope they hadn't passed the night here.

Grimed with smoke and barely recognizable in shirt and breeches, the butler ran to grasp his arm. "Colonel!" he shouted.

"Thank heaven you came! There's been some—" He interrupted himself as Adair flinched away. "Oh, Lord! You're hurt, sir! You'd best—"

"Is everyone out?"

"Mrs. Chatteris is safe and caring for those who were burned. Mr. Willoughby was out but I believe he ran back in again, and the General—"

"The General?" His heart plummeting, Adair gasped hoarsely, "Do—do you say he stayed here? And—Miss Hall?"

Randall nodded.

"Are they out?"

"Oh, God, I wish I knew, sir! I've not seen Miss Hall. She may be upstairs still, with Miss Minerva. General Chatteris went back inside to help a maid who was injured in an accident. It's been so hard to wake people. I suppose they're overcome by the smoke, but—Sir! Don't! You can't get through that way!"

Adair was already running up the front steps and onto the terrace. The smoke that poured through the open doors was acrid and blinding. Plunging into the house was like running into an oven. Flames were licking at the lower stairs but he wrapped his cloak about his arm, held it across his face and started forward.

The burly man who was his uncle's head groom/coachman and Burslem's beloved Henry caught at his arm and howled, "It's no use, sir! We can't reach them! We can try the back, but—"

"Like hell!" snarled Adair and wrenched away.

Heat seared him as he took the stairs two at a time. Half-blinded by the smoke, he peered through the clouds and stumbled along the corridor, calling, praying for a beloved voice to answer, refusing to admit defeat when no answer came. His cloak began to smoulder but his heart leapt to the sound of a faint cry. It had come, he thought, from his aunt's bedchamber. He groped his way to an open door, and blinking through drifting smoke saw Cecily on her knees by the window, trying to pull Minerva to her feet.

Tears of relief washed some of the soot from Adair's eyes.

He ran to take her in his arms. "My love! My dearest love!" And, dishevelled, scorched, her beautiful face grimed with soot, she clung to him croaking, "Hasty! Thank . . . God!"

There came a thunderous roar, and the floor lurched under them. He pulled Minerva to her feet, but she sank down again. Leaning to Cecily's ear he howled, "We must go out through the window. Is she hurt?"

"No. It's just—we're all so very tired. Dearest . . . Harrington is here!"

For an instant Adair stood motionless, staring at her.

The doorway brightened to a red glow. He lifted Cecily and sat her on the window-sill. "Take my hands. Now—out you go! I'll lower you as far as I can, then you'll have to jump."

She obeyed at once.

Pain lanced savagely up his arm as he took her weight, but it was something he could not heed now. Lord above, but it was hot! Leaning perilously far over the window-sill, he gulped in a few breaths of clearer air. Cecily screamed something. He heard a male voice yell. God send there was someone down there to help her . . . He relaxed his grip and she vanished into the smoke.

Minerva was trying to get up. She croaked, "Hasty! I don't—I don't know why . . . so tired . . ."

Coughing rackingly, he picked her up and gasped out his instructions. To his relief she seemed to comprehend and did as he said. She was heavier than Cecily and he swore in anguish as she clung to his hands.

From the impenetrable and crimson-tinted murk below, someone shouted, "Jump, Miss! Jump!"

Minerva shrieked a frightened "Hasty, I—I can't see! I daren't jump!"

"You must!" he howled, "Or I can't come!"

At that her hands relaxed their frantic grip.

Adair half-collapsed across the window-sill, suddenly drained and lacking the strength to get up.

Through the smoke and heat came the echo of Cecily's voice. "Harrington is here . . ."

He pulled himself together and turned to the door. It was rimmed with flame. Peering from the window again, he tried to wave away the smoke and saw flames shoot out below him. His eyes were streaming. It was increasingly hard to see—or to breathe.

Harrington . . . Harrington had done this. He had almost killed Cecily and Minerva. Heaven only knew if everyone was safe. If the General had perished—and Uncle Willoughby . . . ! God forbid! That murderous traitor mustn't be allowed to get away! He had come for the Lists, of course. Probably desperate to make sure that Willoughby didn't recover them. Hastings wrapped the cloak around his arm again and sprang through the doorway, trying to shield his eyes, praying there was still a corridor on the other side.

Mercifully, there was, but the cloak burst into flames and he had to throw it off. To his left the main staircase was ablaze, but wiping a hand across his streaming eyes, he could detect no flames to the right. There was a chance that he could reach the back stairs.

He stumbled along, dizzied and coughing, his tortured lungs fighting for breath, until he came at last to his knees. He was done. He couldn't keep on . . . His overwhelming desire was just to lie and rest . . . He sighed wearily, but a corner of his mind screamed that to rest was death. If Harrington was here, he'd be after the Lists . . . Must help poor Willoughby. Must. And so he crawled on doggedly, driven by the need to find Harrington, to stop him from hurting Willoughby, and to drag the lying weasel back to Town and retribution.

He reached the door opening onto the rear stairs at last but the heat had caused it to warp and he had to drag himself to his feet and kick it open. At once he was greeted by a breath of cooler air. He reeled to the stairs and barely avoided tumbling down them.

It was easier to breathe now and his head cleared. There was a great deal of noise from outside; shouts and crashings, the splintering of glass and the squealing of frightened horses. Through the kitchen windows he caught a glimpse of lanterns and of dim figures rushing about. The neighbours must have seen the flames and had come to help, as people did come in such a disaster; a bucket brigade was probably being organized, though it didn't seem likely that they'd be able to save much of the house.

Rounding the end of the rear corridor, he was confronted by a wall of red-tinged smoke. He threw up an arm against the heat. The fire had not yet reached Uncle Willoughby's study, but it was obvious that in a few minutes this area would be engulfed. He plunged forward, only to stop abruptly.

Julius Harrington ran from the study, a familiar cardboard box under his arm. He was looking back into the room, a triumphant grin on his face that faded into consternation as he turned and saw the man who was rushing at him.

"You . . ." he gasped, disbelievingly.

All the misery of these past terrible weeks, the heartbreak and tragedy this man had carelessly inflicted on many others beside himself condensed into a boiling rage that wiped away Adair's exhaustion and civilized instincts and left only a primitive lust for vengeance.

"Yes, it's me, you murdering bastard!" He drove a fist at that loathed face, and Harrington was hurled backward. Adair pounced after him, dragged him to his feet, and shoved him towards the study. "Get . . . in there, foulness," he wheezed.

Despite the eddying smoke Harrington saw death in the features that were so contorted as to be almost unrecognizable. No coward, he struggled and fought for his life desperately.

Adair had struck Harrington with his right hand, but in the heat of his fury he scarcely felt the pain, and the blows rained at him were as nothing. Inexorable, relentless, he forced the traitor back into the study. As he'd feared, Willoughby Chatteris lay in a crumpled heap by the desk. "Pick him up!" he snarled.

"Madman!" cried Harrington. "Look behind you! For the love of God, look! Another minute—and—and we'll be trapped!"

"You were going to leave him! You filthy sneaking swine, you were going to leave him to die—as you planned we all would die! *Pick ... him ... up!*"

The bright glow of the fire was creeping into the room now and Harrington's control broke. Panic-stricken, he snatched up the box of Lists, slammed it at Adair and sprinted for the door.

Adair launched himself at his legs and brought him down.

Harrington screamed as an ear-splitting crash shook the room. "This whole curst place is—is collapsing! Do you *want* to—to die? God! Why did I come back ... ? You need a confession! I can't confess, if—if I'm dead!"

Adair wheezed a laugh. "We've got Droitwich. And you've an enormous debt to pay, my *dear friend*"

"I'll confess! I promise you! I'll clear your name! I *swear* it! Only let me—"

"You'll confess, all right," gritted Adair. "Now ... *pick ... him ... up!*"

Sobbing with fear, Harrington dragged Willoughby up and over his shoulder. Adair gestured to the hall door. The roar of the flames was a terrifying sound and the heat and smoke made it all too clear that they had very little time.

Harrington staggered and went to his knees.

Adair bent to seize his uncle's lax form.

With a strength born of desperation, Harrington grabbed a footstool, hurled it at Adair and, standing again, sprinted into the corridor. "Burn, damn you!" he shrieked. *"Vive l'Empereur!"* Laughing hysterically, he raced for the back door.

Adair started after him.

There came a deafening creak, then a section of the corridor ceiling came down with a thunderous roar, bringing with it what seemed a solid wall of heat and flame.

Scorched and gasping, Adair reeled back. He must get his uncle out of this. He spun around and caught sight of Willoughby on his hands and knees gathering Lists.

"Never mind about . . . that now, sir! We've got to—"

Willoughby pushed him away and went on gathering frenziedly. "No! My Lists!"

It went against the grain, but their time was gone. Adair aimed for the jaw and struck once, but the rage that had sustained him was also gone. He was trying to lift Willoughby when the windows burst inward and glass showered the room.

"Here they are!" howled Toby Broderick.

Strong hands were taking Willoughby, who moaned faintly, "My . . . Lists!"

Adair tried to tell them that Harrington had escaped, but they didn't seem to hear him.

Cecily's voice, frantic, cried, "Hasty? Is Hasty in there?"

Someone—Grandpapa, he thought—roared, "It's going to cave in! Get the hell clear! Get clear!"

Scrambling through the shattered window, Hastings learned what "by the skin of your teeth" really meant.

<hr />

By sunrise Blackbird Terrace was a charred and smoking ruin, but to Willoughby's enormous relief nobody had been killed. They had not escaped unscathed, however. General Chatteris had a nasty burn, sustained when part of a blazing beam had fallen across his shoulder while he'd been carrying the injured maid from the house. Mrs. Hilda Chatteris and several of the servants had suffered minor burns and abrasions; Coachman Henry had two cracked ribs to show for his valour in having caught Minerva when she fell from Adair's grasp at the upper window. Cecily's lustrous curls were scorched on one side of her head, and her skirts had caught fire as she'd fallen past the ground floor, so that although Manderville and the cook had at once beaten out the flames, her ankles had been slightly burned.

Thanks to their combined efforts, quite a surprising amount of furniture, Mrs. Hilda's jewel-case, most of the silver and the more valuable paintings had been salvaged. At the General's suggestion everything had been conveyed to the long-unused dower house. The aunt who had left the property to Willoughby had occupied the old house in her declining years, finding it easier to maintain than the mansion, and much of the furniture had been protected by holland covers. It became a haven now. Willing hands had swept away dust, dispossessed spiders and lit lamps and fires. Bedding had been donated, and although some people had to sleep on the floor, no one had any complaints.

In the morning, neighbours returned with food baskets so that an ample breakfast was served.

They'd decided on a conference after they ate, but had first made their halting way to view the heart-breaking sight that a family home presents when it has been destroyed by fire. Minerva and Mrs. Chatteris had wept quietly, and Willoughby had been tearful. They had made an effort to converse sensibly, enquiring about the injured, and discussing the merits of either enlarging and refurbishing the dower house or rebuilding the manor. Anything but the topics that were uppermost in everyone's mind.

Paige, who had burned his hands while beating the flames from Cecily's gown, accompanied a very shaken Minerva to the kennels, and the rest returned to the dower house, where Mrs. Hilda, Randall and the cook went off to make their own lists of necessities to be purchased in Woking.

The conference was held in the drawing room, cleaned and tidied now, but with the smell of smoke still lingering on the air. Looking around at his grandfather, Uncle Willoughby, and Toby Broderick, and with his love very close beside him, Adair knew each one of them was in some degree of pain today, but he could only marvel that there had not been more casualties.

Broderick, who had been slightly burned on one arm and cut by flying glass, said with his dauntless grin, "Well, Colonel, sir?"

"Very well that you and Paige came, and saved my bacon once more, Toby. I don't know what we'd have done without you, but—Gad, you've paid the price! You'd best not visit your mama until your good looks are restored; if she set eyes on you this morning, the poor lady would be frightened to death!"

Broderick laughed and called him an ingrate.

The General said, "Have you looked at yourself this morning, Hastings? Egad! I wondered who that scarecrow was!"

Much of Adair's hair and both eyebrows had fallen victim to heat and flame, and his forehead was cut and blistered; the apothecary, who had spent a busy night, had declared that he'd very likely suffered a concussion, and there was a bone broken in his right wrist which was now splinted and carried in a sling.

He said ruefully, "The pot calling the kettle black, is that the case? I can only hope my lady won't abandon me."

Cecily said with a fond smile, "Small chance of that, sir."

"But if she should," said Broderick, sobering, "no one could blame her after she endured such a frightful ordeal."

There was a brief pause. Adair found that he could recall only cameo-like episodes after they'd climbed through the window of Uncle Willoughby's study barely in time to escape the collapse of the ceiling. He remembered Toby telling him that Nigel's wound was not as severe as they'd at first feared and that the boy had been carried home to Adair Hall. He remembered leaving the fire as soon as everyone was safely outside, and making his way to Toreador; he remembered his relief to find the big dapple-grey standing, ready to greet him, and being pampered by an admiring young neighbour lad. He remembered a small, scorched and dirty hand slipping into his own, and Cecily murmuring her sympathy for Mr. Chatteris and his family, who had lost so much; and he remembered the lump that had come into his throat and the tears that had filled his eyes at the thought of how nearly his exquisite lady had been taken from him. He remembered the apothecary's painful ministrations, but he couldn't recall having gone to bed, nor anything else until Paige had shaken him gently and said, "I may have the wrong fella, but if you're Colonel the Honourable Hastings Adair, you'd better get up before all the food is gone!"

General Chatteris broke the silence by clearing his throat

and declaring in his official voice, "Very well. Now things must be dealt with. I never knew a fire to spread so fast. Does anyone know where it started?"

Broderick said, "In several places at once, I'd guess, sir."

The General stared at him. "Eh? What's that?"

"It was deliberately set, Grandfather," said Adair, and before the old gentleman could recover from that revelation, he asked, "Did anyone see where he went?"

Broderick frowned. "Where—who went?"

"Harrington, of course. I had the varmint, but—"

"Harrington?" boomed the General, his whiskers vibrating. "That damnable villain was *here* last night? Were you aware, Will?"

"To my sorrow," said Willoughby. "He—er, he tried to kill me, and if Hastings hadn't come, would have succeeded. As it is," he added sadly, "he destroyed my Lists. The labour of years . . ."

"We saved some of them, sir," said Broderick encouragingly. "Perhaps there are enough for you to put the rest together again."

Willoughby sighed. "I suppose they were really only—er, valuable to me."

"They were more than valuable to me, sir," said Adair. "It was those Lists of yours that enabled me to see what treachery I had to deal with. And they were certainly of major importance to Harrington. I think he had no intention of returning here save to make sure the Lists were destroyed, but curiosity drove him to try and discover what you actually had learned about him."

Broderick said, "Hoist by his own petard, you might say, since his bravos set the fire."

"What?" roared the General, leaping to his feet. "Why was nothing said of it till now? Where is the filthy bounder? We'll get the Runners after him! Why the deuce did you allow him to escape, Hastings?"

"He's slippery as an eel, sir. But actually, I had no choice.

There was barely enough time for Uncle Willoughby and me to get out. We went through the window, thanks to Toby and Randall. Harrington escaped through the rear door."

"Devil he did," argued the General. "I'd gone back there myself, thinking that was the way you would come. If he'd opened that door before the passage ceiling fell, I'd have seen him. I didn't go round to the side till there was no hope of anyone getting out that way."

"By George," muttered Broderick. "D'you suppose . . . ?"

Cecily said falteringly, "Hasty—might he have been caught by that collapsing ceiling?"

"It certainly sounds like it." Adair frowned, and muttered, "In which case, Harrington is spared a traitor's death, and I've lost my witness and am properly against the ropes again. Unless . . . If Alice is a widow already, she could testify—"

Cecily shrieked, "*Alice*? What are you saying?"

"You curst trickster," exclaimed the General. "You found Miss Alice and you wait until now to tell us?"

Adair groaned, "Cecily, forgive me. I meant to tell you first thing this morning, but—No—don't cry love, please! I'm a sorry fool, but your cousin is alive, and—"

"And safe," interposed Broderick loftily.

Adair turned around to face him. "You—*found* her?"

"She's a *widow*?" cried Cecily.

"Harrington was the scoundrel who kidnapped and held her prisoner, then forced her into marriage," explained Adair.

"Why, that—that unspeakable *filth*!" roared the General.

Cecily's lips trembled. She asked, "Where is she, Toby? Oh, the poor darling! I must go to her at once!"

"There was a coach standing near the crossroads when Paige and I arrived last night," explained Broderick. "I thought it suspicious, so I glanced inside, and recognized the lady from—from her portrait, y'know."

"So?" barked General Chatteris. "So?"

"So we—rather—er, collected her, sir."

Wide-eyed, Cecily said, "You did?"

"I'll not believe he dared leave her unguarded," said Adair.

"Well, that's true." Broderick looked at their eager faces and said diffidently, "The fact is, we, er—persuaded the guards to go away. Well, one, anyway. The other sort of—fell down. And then I took Miss Alice to a place where I'm sure she'll be quite safe. Which is why I was a trifle late getting here, Hasty. But I think you're quite right, Miss Hall. We should go to her. She will like to know she's no longer wed to that slug."

Cecily said, "I can scarce believe it—that between you wonderful men my—my dear cousin is found at last."

"Where did you take her, Toby?" asked Adair.

"To the Blessed Spirit Nunnery. A good place, wouldn't you say?"

Adair glanced at his uncle's sagging jaw and smiled. "A very good place, old fellow. Well done!"

"And now," snorted General Chatteris, hiding the fact that he was enormously impressed by these exploits, "will some sane person kindly tell me why this was kept a close secret all these hours?"

Adair answered, "Well, you see, sir—Well, the thing is—She was here and—well, I just couldn't find the words to tell her."

Cecily said tenderly, "My very dear! As if I could be anything but overjoyed."

"Not you, love. Minna."

"Oh—Lord!" muttered the General. "She thinks she's betrothed to the scum! Well, she's better off out of it!"

Adair said, "Except—she loves him, sir."

"She won't, when she hears what an evil creature he was. But someone must tell the girl." The General glanced to Willoughby's chair, but it was empty.

Cravenly, Willoughby Chatteris had slunk away.

The General marched off at once to track down his cowardly son; Broderick went off to escort Cecily to a reunion with her beloved cousin at the Nunnery of the Blessed Spirit; and Adair walked with slow reluctance across to the kennels, dreading the fact that it was left to him to break the heart of his gentle cousin.

His fears proved to have been unnecessary. He found Minerva seated on a bench outside the dog runs, weeping on Paige Manderville's shoulder. Knowing how fond she'd been of the old house, Adair came up and said, "I think Uncle Willoughby means to rebuild, Minna."

Paige looked up at him and made no attempt to remove the arm that was around the girl. "I told her about Harrington," he said, adding a defiant "Well, somebody had to!"

Adair stepped closer and under cover of Minerva's sobs murmured, "With suitable omissions, one trusts?"

"For the time, at least, Colonel, sir."

The kennelman appeared and all the dogs began to bark.

Manderville added sardonically, "But it will be interesting to see how Whitehall's exalted blockheads will deal with this case of crabs!"

"I can only hope"—Tobias Broderick cast a cautious glance around the quiet waiting room in the Nunnery of the Blessed Spirit—"I can only hope that falling ceiling did write *finis* to Minister Harrington! If ever there was a heartless swine! That poor little soul may very well go into a decline thanks to his slithery schemes!"

Adair, feeling somewhat more like himself this afternoon, asked, "Is Cecily still with her?"

Broderick nodded. "Thank heaven. They're devoted, all right, and I fancy your lovely lady can help her more than anyone." He frowned worriedly. "What's to be done, Hasty? Will Miss Alice be ostracized because of this horrid train of events?"

Adair thought that very probable, but noting the anxiety in his friend's honest eyes, he said, "I'm sure many people will be compassionate, but she may be wise to keep out of Society for a year."

"Have to, if she's to be a widow, old fellow."

"Yes. After that—well, such things are soon forgotten, and if she should re-marry and change her name—"

"Not much doubt of that." His face becoming very red, Broderick looked Adair steadily in the eye and gave a little nervous cough. "Matter of fact, I'd—I'd be dashed proud to offer for her myself."

Adair thought of Nigel and of another possibility, but he said, "I rather thought you might, but—"

He paused and both men stood as the Mother Superior came to join them. Miss Prior was asleep, she told them, but Miss Hall would stay with her until she was well enough to be conveyed to her home. "Her family must be notified of what has happened. Could one of you . . . perhaps . . . ?"

"I'll leave at once," said Broderick. "They'll be overjoyed to hear she is safe." He looked at the nun searchingly. "Won't they, ma'am?"

"If they are not, they must be a most strange family," she answered with her serene smile. "You will also perhaps be so kind as to arrange that Miss Hall's maid will come and bring with her a change of clothing and those things necessary to a lady's comfort."

Broderick nodded and hurried out.

The Nun said thoughtfully, "He is a good man, that one. And has, I think, a *tendre* in the little widow's direction?"

"He has. My brother has a similar *tendre*. I doubt the lady will want for offers, ma'am."

Her beautiful eyes turned to him. "I hope not. Though—it is possible, you know, that whoever weds Miss—Mrs. Harrington, may have *un petit paquet* to care for. Have you considered that, Colonel?"

"I have, Reverend Mother." He wondered if Toby had, but said staunchly, "Knowing both men, I'd think it would not constitute a major problem."

She smiled. "You have give me the answer I prayed for. Now you will please to tell me what is troubling you, *mon colonel.*"

Despite everything Harrington had done, they had once been friends and had shared many light-hearted moments.

Memories of those times and the manner of his dying had haunted Adair.

He hesitated, then said, "Just before the fire at Blackbird Terrace, my aunt took on two servants to replace two of her own people who were ill. They were a married couple named Gillis. They claimed to have come from you. Had they worked here very long?"

He knew what her answer would be before she spoke, and why the people at Blackbird Terrace had been so difficult to waken on the night of the fire.

"I have never known anyone by that name," said the Mother Superior. "There is, perhaps, the mistake?"

He assured her it was of no importance. But there had, he knew, been no mistake, and he felt a shadow lift from him. The late Julius Harrington had set his traps without mercy.

19

There was no sign of the sun on this cold morning. March had been ushered in on gale-force winds that whipped the smoke from London's countless chimney-pots, rattled windows, and sent many a roof tile tumbling down.

Inside the Horse Guards the outer uproar was no more than a background to the excitement that permeated offices, corridors and meeting rooms. Spurs jingled, military boots stamped briskly, rumours flew, and everywhere was a buzz of excited speculation. An hour earlier, business had been proceeding as usual, and then that rogue and former Lieutenant-Colonel, Hastings Adair, had been brought in under heavy escort and taken to the very room in which, only last month, he had been sentenced to death. Within minutes everyone in the building, from the lowliest private to the highest-ranking officer, had heard the news. Nobody seemed to know why Adair had been arrested again, but a sentry stood as if carven from stone outside the door, which would indicate that the dastardly young libertine was not here voluntarily. Soon, distinguished senior officers began to arrive and one by one went inside, leaving behind another flurry of comment.

As the door closed behind the sixth newcomer, a bright-eyed ensign announced importantly that these were the same gentlemen who had formed the Court Martial Board that had originally tried Adair, and another burst of excitement sent voices rising. Was it possible that the missing lady had been found at last? Was the villainous Colonel to be tried for murder this time? Adair, known for his good looks, had presented a haggard and worn appearance, one arm was carried in a sling, and he had obviously been subjected to some very rough handling. Perhaps the silly fellow had resisted arrest, though someone who'd had a close look at him suggested that his hair looked to have been singed; perhaps he'd been caught in a fire.

A ringing shout of "Atten-*shun!*" stilled the increasingly lurid theories.

A retired General Officer stalked along the corridor, eyebrows bristling, his eagle glance raking the now silent and respectful assemblage. "One gathers," he barked, "that none of you young fellows has anything better to do with his time than to hang about, gossiping!"

The ensign flung open the door to the Hearing Room, and the fierce old gentleman stamped inside.

"Phew!" said the ensign, closing the door. "That was General Sir Gower Chatteris. He's a regular Tartar!"

"He's also Adair's grandfather," offered a sour-looking captain who wore rifle-green.

"Likely trying to wangle another hearing," said a Lieutenant of Dragoon Guards.

The captain snorted derisively. "Much chance he has! Adair was caught red-handed. Guilty as sin! No getting—" He yelped as a boot came down hard on his toe.

"I say! I do beg pardon, sir," drawled Paige Manderville.

"Well, it ain't granted," rasped the captain. "Take yourself off, Lieutenant."

Coming up behind Manderville, Broderick said, "We'd be glad to, sir. Only it seems we're wanted—inside."

The captain gawked and a brief hush fell as the sentry admitted the two men.

"Did you notice, sir?" asked the ensign softly. "Those two fellas also looked as if they'd been in a fire."

"By George, you're right," said the Lieutenant of Dragoon Guards. "There's a story there, I warrant."

"Of one thing you may be sure," observed the sour-looking captain. "It's going to be damned hot in that room for Hastings Adair—grandfather or no!"

Half an hour later, facing the six officers who were conducting this hearing, Adair was hot indeed; with anger. The General and his friends had testified and been ushered outside. No other witnesses had been called. Aside from the fact that he was seated and there was no ominous sword on the table, he found the atmosphere in the room not much different from that of his court martial. In a voice edged with steel, he said, "Perhaps I do not understand you, Colonel Fuller. You have heard my testimony and that of General Chatteris and Lieutenants Manderville and Broderick. If you still do not believe us—"

The grey-haired colonel who had been President of the Court Martial Board smiled and interrupted with a faintly chiding air, "Now did I say that, Adair?"

Major Wandsworth, a youngish man with pale icy eyes, put in curtly, "You have presented us with an extraordinary tale that impugns the reputation of a highly respected member of the Cabinet. The details must be verified beyond any possibility of doubt before we can arrive at any decision."

"Verified?" Seething, Adair said, "I understood that the Intelligence people had questioned Talbot Droitwich and that he'd made a full confession."

The officers facing him exchanged swift glances.

Colonel Fuller said hurriedly, "Oh, yes. Quite true. And don't think we fail to appreciate the splendid work you've done, Adair. You and your friends have been of inestimable assistance. But—"

Too angry to bow to military etiquette, Adair snapped, "But you don't believe that, Cabinet Minister or not, Julius Harrington was a murderer many times over, besides being a filthy traitor!"

Through a tense pause they all looked anywhere but at Adair.

Choosing his words carefully and unaware of how much he sounded like Willoughby Chatteris, Colonel Fuller said, "You must realize that this is—that there are—er, many . . . ramifications."

"For instance," said Lieutenant-Colonel Thurston, a thin, tired-looking man, "it is regrettable that the Intelligence people were quite unable to identify the—er, human remains in the area where you claim Mr. Harrington met his end."

"I *claim*?" Adair stared at him. "Do you say that he was never really there? Or that he escaped?"

"We don't dispute his presence," said Colonel Fuller, smiling reassuringly. "From what we hear the heat was intense, and has left us only three of—these." He leaned forward and handed Adair a small, twisted and blackened object on which was the faintest impression of an anchor.

Adair stared down at it and could all but feel the heat of the flames once more. He caught his breath and gave it back with a hand that trembled slightly. "I believe this came from Harrington's coat, sir."

His reaction had not gone unnoticed. The officers glanced at each other, and Major Wandsworth murmured something to the lieutenant-colonel seated next to him.

Colonel Fuller said, "Most probably. But the absence of an identifiable corpse could make things difficult for Mrs. Harrington. Or—does her father mean to have the marriage annulled?"

Adair answered with slow reluctance, "I'm sure Mr. Prior would be glad to do so. Unfortunately, the lady was—well, as you know, Harrington held her prisoner in that ghastly house for some time. For her sake, the marriage will have to be acknowledged."

Colonel Fuller nodded. "Poor girl. Poor girl. But what I do

not understand is why at the start she agreed to the plot to stage her 'abduction.' She did, after all, write the note asking that you escort her home."

"That's true, sir," said Adair. "As I understand it, she was deeply in love with a—er, young gentleman—"

Major Wandsworth held up one hand and said impatiently, "No need to wrap it up in clean linen, Adair. We know of the secret attachment between the lady and your younger brother."

Colonel Thurston asked, "How is the poor fellow? Going to pull through, I trust?"

Adair had visited Nigel directly he'd reached Town, and found him in a good deal of pain, and frantic with anxiety about his beloved. "Thank you, yes," he answered. "Our doctor expects he will make a full recovery."

"Pretty well, for a man who is shot in the chest," observed Colonel Thurston.

Adair nodded. "Luckily, Nigel wore a locket that deflected the bullet to an extent, else we'd be mourning him today."

"Then it was actually Mr. Nigel Adair whom Miss Prior summoned to escort her home that evening?" asked Major Wandsworth.

"No, sir. Apparently, a lady named Mrs. Vanderhorn had struck up a friendship with Miss Prior, claiming to be the aunt of a girl who had been at her seminary. She introduced Miss Prior to Harrington and the pair of 'em very cunningly avoided Miss Hall and acted as a sort of *deus ex machina* in arranging trysts between my brother and the young lady. They both knew they were misbehaving, and Miss Prior was deeply troubled. On the night of the ball, unknown to Nigel, Miss Prior intended to beg my escort home and during the journey confide in me and try to win my support."

"Instead of which," put in Colonel Fuller, "after she'd written the note the young lady was drugged, and as you entered her coach you were struck down from behind."

Adair frowned and muttered, "But—how, sir? The doctors could find no marks of violence."

Major Wandsworth said pithily, "A charming new weapon coming out of the East. A small bag filled with sand. Efficient, seldom fatal, and leaving no evidence."

"And before you regained consciousness, you also were drugged," explained Colonel Thurston.

Adair looked from one to the other searchingly. "If you knew all this, why was I—"

Colonel Fuller said hurriedly, "Acquit us of that, Adair. We did not know of it until Mr. Talbot Droitwich very kindly—er, volunteered the information."

"Did he also explain how Miss Prior was spirited away from her father's country estate?" asked Adair.

Major Wandsworth answered, "Droitwich said one of Harrington's lady loves, the Vanderhorn woman, no doubt, crept into Singletree late that night and lured Miss Prior from the house saying that your brother had been taken ill and that Harrington had kindly brought his coach to take her to him."

"The girl should not have agreed to go without informing her sire, of course," said Colonel Fuller, looking grave.

"Which is yet another reason," Major Wandsworth said, "why we should not start hurling accusations about. For a while, at least."

'They're throwing sand in my eyes,' thought Adair. He asked, "Is the public then to go on believing me guilty?"

There were shocked exclamations. As if Colonel Adair and his family had not suffered enough! As if they would be subjected to more humiliation!

"Certainly not, my dear fellow," said Fuller with remarkable joviality. "You have had a very nasty time of it. We know that, believe me, we do. Your name will be cleared, you will be commended, and your rank restored. I can promise you that much, eh, gentlemen?"

His promise was echoed by the other officers. Enthusiastically. Only Major Wandsworth's eyes remaining as cold and unsympathetic as ever.

"And you are to be awarded a month's leave of absence,"

purred the colonel. "We hear that you are—enamoured of a certain very lovely and much sought-after young lady. That will set all London by its ears, eh?"

Hearty laughter.

"Thank you, sir," said Adair, and thought, 'Look out, Hasty! Here come the big guns . . .'

"There are just—one or two points . . ." murmured Colonel Fuller.

"Humbug!" Seated in the drawing room at Adair Hall, Lady Abigail Prior tossed *The Times* from her with loathing and snatched *The Gazette*, which Hudson Adair chanced to be reading.

"It's the same thing, in all of them, ma'am," said Hudson, politely relinquishing the newspaper.

Looking up from the *Morning Chronicle*, Toby Broderick gave a snort of revulsion. "They report what they've been told. Listen to this gem of wisdom: ' . . . and having bravely rescued the unfortunate lady from the villainous T——D——, now rumoured to be a French spy, the late Minister Harrington—' "

"*What?*" shrieked Lady Abigail. "That little wart didn't rescue my poor granddaughter! He's the monster who *kidnapped* the child!"

Broderick nodded, and read on: ". . . late Minister Harrington made her his bride. They were, in fact, setting forth on their honeymoon when they saw the fire at Blackbird Terrace. Mr. Harrington, being well acquainted with the owner of the estate, immediately turned aside and raced to the mansion to render any assistance he might—"

Lady Abigail cried furiously, "Are they all gone daft, or what? Hastings?" Her scan of the room revealing only the three of them, she demanded, "Where is the dratted boy gone to? And Cecily with him, I don't doubt!"

Hudson coughed and said gently that he believed they had gone for a stroll in the gardens.

Glaring at the windows, Lady Abigail snarled, "It is a bitter day, with a wind from the east fit to freeze the blood, and they go for a stroll in the gardens! A sorry pair of loobies! And not officially betrothed as yet! You may wipe off that grin, Tobias Broderick! Don't imagine I'm blind to the fact that you've called on my poor Alice three times since she came home! Your behaviour, sir, is just as improper as that of Colonel Adair!"

Scarlet-faced, Broderick stammered, "No—really, ma'am, I—" Rallying, he said desperately, "You may be aware, my lady, that there is an ancient superstition, originating with the Turks, I believe, that says when the March wind blows from the east it carries with it some of the spices and romance long associated with the nomadic tribes who followed the trade routes across Asia. Furthermore . . ." He went on at length.

<hr/>

"If ever—if *ever* I heard such a sorry collection of rubbish," declared Cecily, removing her hand from Adair's arm and waving it to emphasize her indignation. "You know what it is, Hasty!"

"Yes, love," he said, reclaiming her hand and tucking it under his arm once more. "It is too cold for you out here, and—"

"Cold! I am liable to boil over like Vesuvius! You may think yourself all the crack now that you are wearing that dashing hussar uniform again, but—"

He chuckled. "The important thing is—do *you* think I'm all the crack, dearest girl?"

She thought him so handsome that it was all she could do to be cross, but she struggled to persevere and said, "Do not try to change the subject, sir! The thing is, and you know it, that those Whitehall slow-tops are ashamed to have it known they appointed a traitor and murderer to the almighty Cabinet!"

"Very probable," he admitted, preventing her from walking into an unoccupied flower bed. "Toby and I reached the same conclusion. But I am shocked to hear you use cant, my dearest. I brought you out here so that we could—"

"And sooner than admit their colossal folly," she swept on,

"you—who deserve at least a dozen medals and promotion to general—"

He laughed, "Now, really, my darling girl—"

"—are to be thrown to the wolves. Again!" Her eyes glittered with rage. "It is so—*wrong*, Hasty!"

"My name has been cleared, and my rank restored, so—"

"Pish! If you do not mean to stand up to them, I shall take General Chatteris to the Horse Guards with me, and we will—"

"Whoa!" He drew her to a halt and looked down at her lovingly. "You will do nothing of the sort. I fight my own battles, Miss Cecily Hall!"

"Your method of fighting this rank injustice smacks more of—of surrender than fight!"

The smile left his eyes. He said quietly, "If you wed an army officer, my love, you'll have to learn that a lieutenant-colonel does not defy the Horse Guards on a matter involving the security of Britain. Nor does he fight his commanding general."

"Perhaps not. But from what I know of Lord Wellington, he likes the ladies, which could be—"

"No!" His response was sharp and immediate.

Her chin lifted.

She looked magnificent when she was angry, he thought.

She said stormily, "I do not care to be told what to do, Hastings."

"And I want always to hear your opinions, darling Cecily. But I allow no one to interfere in military matters. Not even my wife."

"Then perhaps you should find yourself a more biddable wife, sir! A lady who will never fly into a temper and is possessed of a more gentle nature than I."

"Someone like—your cousin, for instance?"

Adair spoke lightly, and with a smile in his eyes, but to the overwrought girl he might as well have dashed cold water in her face. So he found Alice gentle, and herself—what? A fiery shrew, perhaps? If his sympathy for her cousin had deepened into the more tender emotion, then by all means he should not be hampered by promises made to a—a bad-tempered termagant in a moment of danger. Stepping away from him, Cecily said haughtily, "Exactly so."

"I rather think Toby—and my brother Nigel, for that matter, would call me out if I dared make the attempt."

"Really? Another instance of not wanting to fight for what you—desire, Colonel?"

"Don't say such foolish things." He reached for her hand, but she stepped back, averting her face and struggling against the absurd notion that she was drowning in tears.

"Cecily, this is ridiculous," said Adair firmly. "We're arguing about something over which we have no control. Besides . . . I suspect that as time goes on—well, too many people know the true facts. Sooner or later it will all leak out, I fancy."

"An obliging fancy, sir, presenting you with the opportunity to take the line of least resistance."

Adair had been gazing at the wind-tossed trees, and seeing instead the officers in the Hearing Room at Whitehall, but at this his eyes flashed to meet her own, a look in them that made her turn away and say hurriedly, "You're right, it is too cold for me out here. I'll deprive you of my—tempestuous presence, sir."

She took one short step, was seized by hands of steel, whirled around and swept into a crushing embrace. "How dare you!" she exclaimed. "I do not like to be mauled, Colonel! We are not formally betrothed, and I think—"

"No, you don't. Now—be still, woman, and stop talking such fustian. I brought you out here to give you something."

"I want nothing from you, Hastings Chatteris Adair," she declared, made angrier by the knowledge that she was telling the most dreadful untruths and that her voice trembled. Pushing at his chest, she felt something in his pocket and curiosity got the better of pride. "What is this? Let me see!"

"No! Let be! Oh, wretched girl! It's not that, but—"

Her seeking fingers had found the object in his pocket and

she stared down at it. "My blue flower," she murmured softly. "I was wearing it the night you told me you loved me." And in a feeble attempt to regain anger, she added, "As if you meant it. I did not give this to you, and I shall take it back, if—if you don't mind."

"I do mind." He whisked the flower from her grasp. "And you know perfectly well I meant what I said—then."

Then . . . ? An arrow seemed to pierce her heart. She looked up at him, never dreaming how pathetic were the tear-drops that beaded her lashes.

Adair said huskily, "And I shall mean it to the day I die, most desirable and beautiful of women."

"Oh . . . H-Hasty . . ."

"It's—it's no use looking at me like that. I am *not* going to kiss you. It wouldn't be proper until—"

Between tears and laughter, she said, "Oh—would it not, you horrid, horrid creature . . . Then how is it that just now—"

"Never mind about that. I am trying to tell you—in spite of constant interruptions—that I have called upon your uncle, and—"

"Uncle—Alfred?" Her eyes opened very wide. "When? Why was I not told? Whatever did he—"

"Be quiet! This is my story and by your leave I'll finish it."

"Yes, Hasty," she said meekly.

"I don't think he considers me quite up to snuff, but—" He put his hand quickly over her parting lips. "But your grandmama spoke up for me, and he says he is grateful because I found Miss Alice, so—well, he has given me permission to try and fix my interest with you. Are you listening, Miss Hall? If I take my hand away, will you promise to stop interrupting?"

"Yes, dear Hasty," she mumbled.

He removed his hand and glanced around, then swore under his breath.

A small figure was galloping across the lawns towards them. A young boy with a fresh, clean face, softly curling fair hair, a neatly tailored habit, and an expression that was pure mischief. "I got it, Guv," he panted, and with a sidelong glance at Miss Hall said in a stage whisper, "Did yer—"

"Never mind," said Adair, taking the small packet that was offered. "Where the deuce have you been? You were supposed to fetch this half an hour ago."

" 'S truth," said Billy New. "But the old 'un, she wanted ter see it, so I had ter—"

"See—what?" asked Cecily, peering at the packet that Adair promptly swung behind his back.

"Never mind. And that'll be all, Billy."

"Yussir," said the boy, and turning to gallop off, stopped and called, "Ain't yer gonna give her a—"

"Go! Revolting brat!" roared Adair.

Billy laughed, and went.

Looking after him, Cecily murmured, "What are you going to do with that child?"

"Train him to be my batman someday. Or a groom, perhaps. He's had a rotten life, poor little devil, but he's bright as a penny and always cheerful. He'll do well in life, I think."

"Thanks to you," she said, her eyes very soft.

He met that look and stepped closer, then pulled back and said gruffly, "Yes. Well, never mind about that. I didn't drag you out here to talk about that young savage."

He led her to a fallen tree trunk on which he spread his handkerchief and, having motioned to her to sit down, dropped to one knee beside her.

Her eyes alight with laughter, she said, "No, really, you don't have to—"

"I shall only do this once in my life, Miss Hall," he advised austerely. "So I mean to do it properly. Ahem. You know that you have had my heart since first we met—"

"Although I tried to shoot you."

"I knew you wouldn't keep your promise not to interrupt! I have rehearsed this, madam, but if you make me forget the words—No, why must you giggle? I am trying to be romantical, Miss Hall."

"Yes, Colonel Adair."

"Sssh! Where was I?"

"You said I wasn't to inter——"

"Ah, yes. And the time has come when . . ." He faltered to a stop, and seizing her hand, pressed it to his lips. "Oh, the deuce! Cecily—I adore you. Will you do me the very great honour of—"

She leaned to him, her eyes like stars. "How you do talk, Colonel Adair."

"Yes—but . . ." He got up and sat beside her. "That's no answer, ma'am, and I can't give you this until—"

"What? What?" With a squeal of excitement she opened the small box he held out. "Ooh . . . Hasty! What beautiful diamonds—and such a lovely setting! Put it on for me!"

"Are you sure? You mustn't sell yourself for a pretty bauble, sweet girl."

"Wretch! Only see how it sparkles!"

"Yes. I thought it was rather nice. But I've told you my expectations and you've lots of admirers who are wealthier than I shall ever be. If you cannot really care for me—"

Cecily interrupted him again.

Oddly enough, Colonel the Honourable Hastings Chatteris Adair did not protest as he was kissed into silence.